THE SOUND OF A SECOND

A.R. BEARCLUFF

Printed in the United States of America.
First Edition Printing, 2019.

Print ISBN   978-1-7331574-0-7
E-book ISBN   978-1-7331574-1-4

*Dedicated with love and thanks
to Derek, Lily, Leia, Mom and Dad.*

Chapter One

Sound and Vision

Gunnar Ahlgren wanted to bury the importance of the statement he was about to make, so he took a bite of fish and chips and said bluntly through chews, "That's why I'm blind."

"Oh, I'm so sorry" responded his date, whose name Gunnar had already forgotten. Her reaction was typical of all his blind dates—feigned understanding touched with sympathy and discomfort.

Knowing this point of the evening from experience, Gunnar offered the woman an easy way out of substantial conversation. "So, how do you like the fish? It's world famous here." Gunnar heard crunching and knew his date was disguising nothing to say with a mouth full of food.

The remainder of the evening was boring, consisting of small talk, requests for condiments, and mentions of the weather. The highlight was the playful bashing of the mutual acquaintance that set them up. Gunnar's sister, Astrid, was perpetually matchmaking him with every single woman she encountered. He had told her repeatedly to stop and let fate handle his love life, but whenever he complained, she would retort with the same jest. "What better way for a blind man to find love than on a blind date?"

When the check came, his date muttered, "Dinner's on me. I insist." One didn't need the enhanced hearing of a blind person to pick up the subtext. What the woman really said was, "I can't take advantage of a disabled person by letting him pay." This unnecessary act of compassion proved to Gunnar that this woman was not "the one." No, the girl meant for him would treat him the same as any other man and expect him to get the check.

The end of dinner wasn't the end of the date. It never was. As if following a script used by every single woman he'd been set-up with, the lady walked him to his door, robotically started to kiss him, and said, "It must have been such a long time since you've had sex. I can remedy that for you." Being a bloke, he never turned down a thrill, but he hated that women believed they were being altruistic by taking him to bed. Nevertheless, he did the deed and was not a bit surprised when his date had to leave right afterwards due to her "big meeting in the morning."

As the warm August Friday rolled into a muggy Saturday, Gunnar woke up alone on crumpled sheets. He arose, walked to his bathroom as if sighted, and splashed water on his face. He didn't even need to count steps anymore. He had lived in his flat in Sheen, London, Borough of Richmond-Upon-Thames for about three years now and getting around it without visual cues had become second nature. After the quick refresher, Gunnar put on some clean tracksuit bottoms and walked to the kitchen to make breakfast. As soon as he pulled the eggs from the fridge, the phone rang. "Astrid," said the automaton voice of his cell phone.

Preparing for the interrogation, Gunnar answered his speaker-enabled cell phone. "Hello, Astrid."

"You act like you were expecting my call," stated his sister in her posh English voice.

"You always call the morning after you match me up with someone."

She chuckled. "Can I help it if I'm dying to learn whether or not my big brother found true love?"

"Astrid," Gunnar replied, his brow furrowed. "I really wish you'd listen this time and not set me up with anyone else. It's never going to work out this way."

His sister's joviality disappeared. "It doesn't sound like it went well. I'm surprised really. Kimberly is a veterinarian, so I thought for sure she'd be able to handle a medical problem."

Gunnar shook his head. "You know, for being the learned professor you are, and in fact a woman, you don't seem to grasp the simple concepts of what females look for in a mate. Women generally want a clever chap, not one who makes stupid decisions that renders them blind."

"Gunnar!" Astrid cried in her chiding, parental tone. The same old tirade was about to charge through the phone. He hadn't seen Astrid since she was fifteen, so he didn't know what she looked like now, but he could just imagine a more grown up, harried version of the blonde- haired, blue-eyed waif he remembered yelling at him. "It wasn't your fault!"

"Technically, it was," he interrupted.

"Even if that was true, you were a child. You're thirty-nine now. Women understand that men grow up and become more responsible with age. You know, this isn't even about your blindness or why you're blind. You just don't want a relationship. You're afraid to share your life with someone. You're going to turn forty soon, and you'll be doing it alone if you don't give someone a chance!"

There was no point in arguing with Astrid, as she never backed down from this position. There was only appeasing. "Yes, Astrid."

His little sister was regaining composure. "It's just that, well, I'm thirty-five, you're thirty-nine, and I'm the one about to have a baby. You were supposed to do all of this first. It's the natural order of things."

He would never admit to his sister that he was jealous of her personal successes, so he put on the nonchalant act. "Sister dear, I really am okay with you having a baby first. I really am happy for you that you've found a man you love. And I'm really very okay and very happy being single for now. As for forty, that's still young in the grand scheme of things. Why don't you give me the next ten years to find someone on my own, and if I don't, you can berate me on my fiftieth birthday about growing old alone."

He heard her sigh deeply. "Fine. No more matchmaking. But please, do try to be open to love."

"I'll be on the lookout," he said, following his pun with the sound of a comedic snare drum.

He had hoped to end the call there, but before he could say goodbye, Astrid changed the subject. "How are things at work? No problems?"

Gunnar often wondered if Astrid detected the irony of her own actions. She protected him, accepted him, fought the world to prove that her blind brother was normal and not in need of help or special treatment, yet she continuously worried that he couldn't do things on his own.

"I'm a sound engineer, not in charge of watching the radiation levels at a nuclear reactor. Everything's fine, just like it's been fine for the past ten years."

"Well, you know, with upgrades in equipment, I just don't want your superiors to think you can't handle it."

"I'm pretty much my own boss, Astrid. You do know that rock stars seek me out, right? That I get paid more to work on one album or attend one concert than you make for an entire quarter teaching? I'm not in any danger of getting sacked."

"I know you think I'm a nag, but Mum is gone and Dad would never say anything. I'm the only one looking out for you."

He exhaled loudly to stifle his frustration. "I know. You are, as always, a wonderful sister. Now, I was just about to have breakfast when you called and I'm famished, so I'm going to let you go."

"Okay. Just one last thing and then I'll hang up. You are coming to Beaconsfield on the 22nd for Brian's birthday, right? I'm going to cook dinner."

"Yes, I'll be there. When should I arrive?"

"I think 5-ish will be fine."

"There's not going to be a strange woman there to make a party of four, right?"

"No! I promise."

Gunnar smiled. Astrid really was a good sister, and Gunnar loved her. As much as she griped, he couldn't imagine his world without her attentions since she was the only person that kept him from feeling completely isolated. After all, his mother was dead and his father was dead inside.

Their mother, Agneta, had died the year before Gunnar went blind. She was a young victim of cancer and wasn't even diagnosed until she was so sick, she couldn't move from bed. She was old stock from Norway and didn't believe in going to doctors. Her last days spent with her children were clouded by pain, speaking through hallucinations that made absolutely no sense.

After their mother passed, Gunnar and Astrid's father, Nils, got a second job. His excuse was that he needed the extra money to support the family, but the kids knew that story was rubbish. Agneta had never worked, brought in no income, and the four of them had lived on Nils' solo carpenter's salary quite comfortably. Gunnar suspected his father's seclusion occurred because he couldn't stand to look at his kids anymore, as he and his sister were painful look-alike reminders of his beloved dead wife. It was easier for Nils to busy himself then to deal with the anguish of his loss through the eyes of his children.

"Gunnar?" Astrid interrupted.

"Yes, I'm here," he said, snapping to the present. "I'm going now. I'll see you in a fortnight."

"Perfect. Love you."

"Tah." He hung up as Astrid did and realized he was no longer in the mood for boiled eggs. He put them back in the refrigerator and sat down on a nearby stool.

Though Nils would never win a "Father of the Year" award, Gunnar still thought of his dad fondly because he truly had loved their mother. Both native Scandinavians, the couple met at the Vemdalsskalet ski resort in Vemdalen, Sweden. The way his mother told the story, Nils was a carpenter's apprentice whose job was to repair damaged wood at the resort. Agneta came to the resort on a ski holiday with some girlfriends. She was a bookworm who had never been on the slopes before. She wasn't used to the bulk and length of the skis, nor did she understand the proper etiquette of removing her skis prior to entering the lodge. Agneta plopped through the lobby with her giant feet and clumsily fell into a pile of wood that a nearby carpenter was working with. A hand stretched out of grubby work clothes to help her up, she looked into Nils' crystal blue eyes, and fell in love.

At first, Nils tried to ignore Agneta. Nils was a poor Swedish carpenter; Agneta came from a wealthy Norwegian family. He was hardly suitable for her and he knew it. But she wouldn't leave him alone her entire vacation, and after three days of constant flirtation, Nils resigned to do what felt right and returned her affections.

Agneta went back to Norway when her girlfriends did, but within a month, she got a job at Vemdalsskalet. Agneta didn't need to work, but she loved Nils so much, she hid her social class to work in the ski shop. He vowed to get a stable job when his apprenticeship ended, give her a ring worthy of her, marry her in a ceremony befitting her status, and take care of her so she would never have to work again. He kept his promise. A year later, Nils started his own business, took on some corporate clients, and made a name for himself in nearby Sundsvall. As soon as he could afford a diamond, he proposed and they married a month later in July of 1974.

Three years later, in September of 1977, Nils, a member of a trade union and a loyal Social Democrat, became quite vocal in the movement against the right-wing coalition seeking control of Sweden. After the ousting of the Social Democrats from government, Nils became fed up with the state of his country and decided to leave. Nils offered to move to Norway for Agneta, but she declined. After she married beneath her status, her parents had barely spoken to her. Instead, Agneta suggested they start somewhere new—somewhere they'd never been before. They settled on Great Britain, even though it would be a challenge to assimilate to a new language and restart Nils' business from scratch. Succeeding in both endeavors after only a few years in London, they decided to start a family. Gunnar was born in October of 1979 and Astrid in March of 1983. They were a well-liked family that truly loved each other. Up until Agneta got cancer, it was a picture-perfect existence.

Everything changed though the month after Gunnar finished his GCSE. It was an unusually hot July day when Agneta told Nils she was too sick to get out of bed. The whole family assumed it was the flu. But after a week, Agneta still couldn't move and now she couldn't eat either. Nils demanded Agneta see a doctor, but Agneta insisted she'd be fine. After another week, their mother's skin started to turn pale and clang to her bones. She would often throw up in bed. Nils switched from asking to begging his wife to see a doctor. Even in the horrible state she was in, Agneta still refused. Nils loved her too much to go against her wishes.

Finally, Astrid, the headstrong teen who had inherited her mother's stubbornness, called a doctor regardless of what her mother wanted. The doctor made the house call, took one look at Agneta, and called the ambulance. Within a few hours of arriving at the hospital, the doctors dropped the bomb. Agneta had Stage 4 breast cancer that had metastasized. No amount of operations, chemotherapy, or radiation could turn back the clock on the tumors, which had entered her lungs and brain. Agneta had just a few days to live.

She lasted eight days from the time she entered the hospital, and they were, at the time, the worst eight days of Gunnar's life. His mum, on heavy doses of pain medication, offered simple phrases of advice and encouragement. "Find true love like I did. Don't settle." "Take care of your father and sister, they need you." "Enjoy your life; only do what you love." This was the pleasant chatter. It was her other speeches that haunted him.

"Gunnar, I can see the future," she said once after a dose of morphine. "I can see you'll have to go through some bad times when I'm gone, but they are necessary to mold you into the man you need to become."

Once after waking briefly, she said, "When you hear the hum, listen closely."

And the day before she died, she muttered, "Listen to yourself when you speak to you."

As the nonsense poured from her lips, Gunnar felt ravaged with guilt that he'd spent so much time dallying with girls and enjoying scrums instead of spending time with his mother. Though he knew he should soak up every moment with her he could, he avoided being in the same room with her. He was afraid of her hallucinations, and he was ashamed that he wanted her to stop rambling when he knew it wasn't her fault she was going senile. When at last she passed away, Gunnar felt simultaneous sorrow and relief.

But the next day, when the grief sunk in, the only feeling he had was overwhelming anger. He was so furious—at the world, at God, at himself, at his father. There had to be somebody he could blame for taking his mother away. While Nils and Astrid were with the mortician, Gunnar isolated himself in his room and played the loudest, angriest music he owned. He tore his rugby shirts to pieces, ripped his posters off the wall, and decimated a whole bottle of his father's akvavit, which only barely calmed his rage.

After the funeral, Nils became a workaholic, Astrid threw herself into her studies, and he turned into an entirely different person. Before his mum died, the birds universally adored him, as he was tall, blonde, and inherited his father's striking blue eyes. His male peers admired him, since he was outgoing and great at sports. He was on his school's rugby team and was the star of the program. He had tons of friends and loved it when people hung on his every word. But after his mum died, he was so bitter—so full of hatred and angst. He shunned popularity, wanting nothing to do with his "cool" image. He was done with dating, quit rugby, opted not to continue to A Levels, and shaved his head. His clothing changed from khakis and polo shirts to ripped jeans and flannels. And he started to drink more than one bottle of akvavit.

He found a new crowd who shared his fondness for spirits. In retrospect, Mick and Rob were actually poser punks, but at the time, Gunnar believed them to be his nonconformist saviors. They provided liquor in exchange for him bringing girls to parties at Mick's place. This tradition started out at once a week, but by the time Agneta had been gone a year, it was a nightly occurrence. Nils was never home long enough to see what Gunnar was doing to himself, and while Astrid noticed, she ignored it as she aced her own GCSE. Gunnar was self-destructing, but as a stupid teen, he believed he was invincible. That he was frying his brain, destroying his liver, and ruining any chance of having a normal future were not even thoughts in his mind.

The grumbling of his middle-aged stomach brought him back to the present. Gunnar smiled to himself, as he so often did whenever he pondered his situation. He always found it ironic that a terrible tragedy was actually the best thing that ever happened to him. While taking his sight, his blindness spared him from winding up a drunk dead in the road.

Bangers and mash from the local pub started to sound good. Gunnar went to his closet, grabbed a shirt and a light jacket, and threw them on casually. He ran his hands through his short-cropped hair and checked the length of his razor stubble with his fingertips. "Good enough," he thought. "Highly doubt I'll run into my soulmate on the way to the pub."

Gunnar had been memorizing Sheen ever since he moved there. It was 1,876 steps from his front door to the Kew Gardens tube station. It was 212 steps from his front door to the bus stop. It was 194 steps to his dry cleaners, eleven steps less than that to the sushi bar, and about twenty steps less than the sushi place to the pub. Counting steps to the blind is instinctive. After you do it half-a-dozen times, the counting is almost subconscious.

Ever-concerned Astrid had pleaded with him to get a seeing-eye dog, but he wasn't sure he wanted the responsibility of a pet when it was off duty. Besides, he was capable of getting to the only places he really needed to go all by himself. He knew the route to the tube station, he could hear the loudspeaker announce the oncoming District Line train, the tube told him when to get off at Hammersmith for the Piccadilly, and told him again when to get off at Holborn to catch the Central Line. Once he got off at Bethnal Green, it was easy for him to walk the 984 steps to the recording studio where he usually worked. He took taxis to see Astrid and their father and to go on his horrible blind dates. If there was anywhere new he wanted to go, he simply called Astrid for directions, GPS'd his route, and pulled out his white-tipped cane. There was no need for any help. His other senses more than made up for the missing one.

After he lost his vision, Gunnar was surprised that the old saying was true—blind people do compensate for their lack of sight by sharpening their other senses. He could no longer see a flower, but all of a sudden, a bouquet across the room smelled as sweet as though the perfume was on his collar. He could no longer see an apple, but as soon as he took a bite, a wave of intense fruit flavor enveloped his mouth.

Yet, despite his improved taste buds and olfactory glands, what astounded him most was the increased sharpness of his hearing. At seventeen, after his release from the doctor's care, he walked outside to a barrage of noise. At first, it clamored in his ears and gave him a headache. But as the days went by, the noises separated into distinct sounds. The cacophony of traffic to other people was to him the whirring of engines, the screeching of brakes, the varying tonality of horns, and the roar of various speeds on pavement. A crowded street was not just a place of overlapped conversation, but a space where he could pick out the children, the teenagers, the elderly, who was married, who was happy, and who was annoyed. And music! The sound of music was a revelation to him. Other people heard the lyrics they liked or the guitar solo that accompanied, but he heard each individual instrument. He could sense the harmonics, the rhythm, and the beat as surely as if they were visual in his mind. Though he wasn't much of a singer, Gunnar soon found musicians praising him for his unusual gift of perfect pitch—a gift he did not seemingly develop until after the blindness.

It was this ability to see notes and keys, as well as a profound love of music, that led him to choose the career path of a sound engineer. Not an easy gig, especially not for a disabled person, but it seemed that fate had this very destiny chosen for him.

When he was nineteen, Gunnar won tickets to see Aerosmith in concert. His win also allowed him backstage passes and early entry to Wembley Stadium. Astrid insisted on being his "tickets for two" second so she could guide him through the crowds. The pair entered the arena during sound-check, thrilled beyond belief that they were going to get to meet the band. But as soon as the duo entered the concert hall, Gunnar's ears began to catch fire and not in a good way. Technicians were performing the sound check and the harmonics were way off. It almost hurt to listen. The pitch was wrong for the acoustics of the space, and it would have made the music dissonant with a grinding tinny sound.

He approached the soundman and politely suggested, "Hey mate, you really should fix that. I don't know how you'd do it, but can you adjust down the reverb on the speakers to the left of the stage?"

"Ain't nothin' wrong with the sound, boy." Gunnar's observation clearly insulted the American soundman.

"Look, just try it. I'll leave you be if you do and if I'm wrong you can take it back up."

To get the boy to sod off, the soundman agreed. The man, who introduced himself as Vic after recovering from the embarrassment of being schooled by a novice, remarked how Gunnar's suggestion sharpened the sound quality and calmed the reverberation. Feeling brave, Gunnar continued by mentioning that the bass could also be adjusted. Vic moved a knob until Gunnar said "stop!" and the instruments sounded better than crisp. Vic was so impressed, he let Gunnar stay awhile. When Vic asked Gunnar to look on stage and tell him which finger the guitar tech was holding up, Gunnar explained that he couldn't do that and why. Astrid later recounted that Vic's jaw dropped and he took a step back realizing the boy was blind. Vic let his guard down, chatted with the lad, and invited him and Astrid to sit in the booth during the entire show so he could explain the audio console. Gunnar continued to offer suggestions throughout the concert, and when it was over, Vic applauded Gunnar, saying that the sound quality had never been better. The band agreed when Vic introduced his new protégé.

Gunnar had always liked listening to music, but on that night, he also fell in love with musicians. He knew he wanted to work with them, to help make their musical creations sound amazing. Luckily, Vic was covetous of his find and insisted that, just as soon as the tour was over, Gunnar come to work with him in New York City.

A month before Gunnar turned twenty, despite his worried sister and pessimistic father, he headed for the Big Apple to be Vic's apprentice. Initially, he thought New York wasn't that much different from London, since both had millions of people swarming everywhere, terrible traffic, and strange smells coming from a mix of ethnic neighborhoods. After almost being run over by cars on several occasions while crossing the street, Gunnar soon discovered that Londoners and New Yorkers were not the same at all. In polite England, his white-tipped cane ensured his complete safety. In fast-paced New York, it made him a target for horn blasts and colorful adjectives.

Upon learning why Gunnar was showing up to work whiter than a ghost most days, Vic assumed Astrid's role of protector, barely leaving him alone to sleep. Though Gunnar was grouchy about it and continuously reminded Vic he was fine, he let the man coddle him since he was receiving such valuable career training in return.

For two years, Gunnar hung on Vic's every word. He got comfortable with both recording studio equipment and live sound tools and memorized every single knob and lever on all kids of soundboards. His ears heard and his mind saw the exact placement of each knob to elicit exquisite levels and timbres. He memorized the sounds of equalization as he attenuated bass, midrange, and treble frequencies. He mastered the twenty-four and thirty-two channel consoles and digital and analog recording. He was a virtuoso of tuning graphic equalizers and stabilizing crossovers. While it may have taken some time for Gunnar to soak up the technical knowledge, it took nothing more than being blind to make him a virtuoso of his art.

Vic spread the word of Gunnar's skills. Pretty soon, musicians were becoming interested in the "blind sound man." While most of them probably came to him to see if the rumors of his abilities were true, most of them stayed because they realized his talent was a fact. Gunnar worked with a host of major artists and rising stars, making their records sound better than ever. He crossed the U.S. several times, touring huge arenas. 2004 to 2006 was, to date, the most fun and adventurous time of Gunnar's life.

But as 2007 approached, Gunnar decided it was time to return to London. When asked why, his answer varied depending on the questioner, though all his answers were true. To his colleagues, he gave the respected answer that the London Symphony Orchestra wanted him to do their sound for a long-term film score project. To Nils and Astrid, his reason for coming home was the desire to see his family, whom he truly missed. While he had been gone, he received e-mails and phone calls from Astrid recounting her accomplishments. She had excelled in her A Levels and was accepted to Oxford. She was taking honors classes and found a particular love of ancient history and literature. Astrid had big goals of becoming a renowned writer and professor teaching others the fascinating world of antiquities. Gunnar felt like he was missing out seeing his kid sister blossom into an intelligent young woman.

When alone and reflecting on the decision, he admitted internally a truth he would never tell anyone else. He just couldn't handle the New York party scene anymore. Gunnar was daily in contact with some of the most famous people in the world, and these people had unlimited access to any club, bar, or soiree they wanted. These people could go to a church or a library and create a party. Being a prop that musicians loved to show off, they always expected him to tag along. At first, it was easy to resist the temptations that came along with these parties. He wasn't particularly interested in the groupies or the drugs, as neither were his style. But, when his host or hostess dropped $130 on a bottle of Dom Perignon or ordered a round of drinks for the house, it took an immense amount of willpower to pass.

He lived under the weight of knowing that a drinking binge led to the worst decision he ever made. After his discharge from the hospital at age seventeen, Gunnar vowed he would only ever drink alcohol on extraordinarily special occasions. So far, he had kept that promise, planning a glass of wine for his wedding or a pint of Guinness for the birth of his children. But in New York, every celebrity bash started to seem like a special occasion.

Gunnar moved his hand from his chin to his stomach, which made an obnoxiously loud rumble. "Enough of the past," he thought to himself as he walked by his clock and pushed the button for an audio reading of the time. "10:37" announced the robotic voice. Gunnar didn't really need his cane, but since it was a weekend and more people would be out and about, he put it in his pocket just in case and walked out the door.

Chapter Two

Someone to Watch Over Me

*****

"Watch out, you bloody wanker!" Mick, scrawny for a teenager, tacked seventeen-year old Gunnar's left arm with a sloppy punch that barely made contact.

"You're the one running into me!" Gunnar yelled back through a snotty cackle.

Gunnar was wasted, as usual. So were Mick and Rob, as usual. Gunnar loved being hosed. He didn't have to think about his mum that way.

"Where's the vodka? Come to me, Stoli!" Gunnar stumbled his way to Rob's car, parked haphazardly near the tent they had set up in an empty field upon which they were trespassing. The boys had been camping since yesterday, though camping was just an excuse to get sloshed. Rob had a banged-up Saab. The paint was chipping off, there was rust by the boot, and the interior reeked of Rob's filterless Camels. Gunnar couldn't have cared less about the mode of transport. His only concern was what was in the back.

Rob was older than Mick and Gunnar, who were both still teens. Though biologically twenty-three, Rob was less mature than both the other boys. Truth be told, Gunnar didn't really like Rob as a person. He was smelly, intolerant, and banal. But he could buy liquor legally, so Gunnar spent most of his time in Rob's company. Rob was a mean drunk, slinging insults and profanity when alcohol passed his lips. Mick was much more pleasant to be around, though he was a bit of a gorm. He tried so hard to dress punk way after punk was dead. He listened to Elvis Costello, pretending to get it. He had the social skills of a leper when it came to chatting up girls. Gunnar, though, at least liked him, since Mick was a quiet drunk who often got lost in the sky after imbibing. Gunnar was a fun drunk, but also a way-too-trusting drunk. He didn't have the wherewithal to realize when he was in danger and constantly got into situations that he was surprised to survive.

He opened the boot of the car, which was twisted from a crash and tied together with a frayed piece of rope. Inside were a couple of bottles of Stoli, but there were empty. "Bloody hell!" yelled Gunnar.

"What are you on about?" screamed an incoherent Rob, his greasy brown hair waving in the slightly cool wind.

"We're out!" Gunnar's face was red with ire and poor liver function.

Mick laughed and belched simultaneously. "Shite!"

"What am I supposed to drink now? I don't want to lose my buzz!"

"Stop whining like a bitch," Rob said like it was no big deal.

Gunnar walked back toward the other campers in a sour mood. "This camping trip is going to get real lame in a few hours."

"Shut your hole, wanker!" commanded Rob, trying to joke while being dead serious.

Gunnar wasn't about to take the abuse lying down. "How'd you like never to get laid again, you idiot! If you're going to be nasty to me, I'm not introducing you to anymore birds."

Rob smirked mischievously. "All right, all right. Calm down. No need to get your knickers in a twist. I happen to have one more bevy in the car glove compartment. I'll go get it."

"Cheers," Gunnar exclaimed through blurred vision, watching Rob stumbling over to the car.

Gunnar rested his yes just for a second, but nearly fell asleep. Someone kicking his boot awoke him.

"Here," said Rob, handing Gunnar a plastic cup.

Gunnar smiled and put the cup to his mouth. Before he could drink it, he recoiled at the strong smell.

"What is this?" asked Gunnar. "It ain't vodka."

"It's alcohol, mate," responded Rob. "Either drink it or don't, but don't blame me if you sober up."

Gunnar thought, 'what the hell," and he put the cup to his mouth and took a huge gulp. God, it tasted manky! He waited a minute, testing whether the unfamiliar liquid would make him gag, but nothing happened. He took another swig just to be sure. No bad side effects other than the hideous taste. He tried two more sips before deciding that alcohol in the cup tasted too awful to consume. He threw rest of the cup to the ground and looked around. When he saw Rob, he had this overwhelming urge to beat him to death.

For no reason at all, Gunnar rushed at Rob and grabbed him at his waist, forcing him to the ground. Caught off guard, Rob fell like a sack of flour. "Have I ever told you how much I despise you?" Gunnar screamed mere inches from Rob's face, his spittle wetting Rob's cheeks.

"Get off me!" Rob snarled back, unable to move. He was far too wasted to put up a physical fight. For that matter, so was Gunnar. It had taken all of Gunnar's energy to throw Rob to the ground. He could have fallen asleep right there on top of Rob.

"We're not really friends, you know," Gunnar confessed as he slid off Rob to his side. Both boys lied there in the dirt next to each other.

"You guys are so bladdered!" Mick said, staggering toward his mates.

"I really do think I'm going to pass out right here," said Gunnar looking up at the stars. "What time is it anyway?"

"Night," laughed Mick.

"Time to sleep it off," gurgled Rob, who was still lying in the exact position he'd landed after being tackled.

"Good idea." Gunnar was done. He couldn't move, his brain was swimming, and his stomach ached. His eyes fluttered open and closed as he fought off sleep. He thought about getting a sleeping bag, but his body wouldn't respond to his mental urge to rise. "I'm knackered!" he said with a tear, not caring about anything as he passed out uncovered in the dirt.

An intense pain in his stomach woke Gunnar suddenly. Confused and with no idea where he was, he curled into a fetal position for comfort, but then shot his leg out straight forward to massage away an agonizing Charlie horse. He was dizzy and sweating and angry inside. When he looked at the sky, the moon was blurry. He couldn't tell if it was his eyes or his brain that was fuzzy. This was undoubtedly the worst he had ever felt after drinking. Looking around, Mick was nowhere to be seen. Rob was exactly where Gunnar had left him, still fully clothed and drooling on the ground through loud snores. He tried to wake Rob, but found his mouth so dry, he couldn't speak. All he could do was try to sleep off these odd symptoms.

He awoke again, not knowing if minutes or hours had passed. Gunnar heard movement around him and opened his glazed eyes. Mick was holding his head and Rob was panicking. Gunnar didn't know what was happening, but his abdominal muscles seared as if on fire. There was foamy spit dripping from his mouth and his sight was going in and out.

"What the hell do we do?" asked Rob, clearly shaken.

"Gunnar, mate, what's happening to you?" begged Mick.

Gunnar couldn't answer. His body involuntary crunched.

"We have to take him to the ED," cried Mick.

"No! I can't take him! He's a kid and I bought the liquor. I'm not getting arrested because he can't hold his alcohol."

"You really are a wanker!" Mick exclaimed. "He holds his liquor better than we do. What did you give him in that cup?"

Rob huffed. "Camping stove alcohol."

"What?" yelled Mick. "Isn't that poison?"

"I don't know," screamed Rob. "The bottle said alcohol and I thought it would just taste like shit. Serves him right for threatening me!"

"You better hope you haven't poisoned him," warned Mick.

"I didn't mean it if I did. It was a joke!"

"A bad fucking joke," retorted Mick. "Look, he has got to go to a hospital in case you did poison him. Just drive us there and drop us off. I'll take care of it."

For a moment, Gunnar's vision stabilized and his body relaxed. He looked at Rob's eye-rolling, shirking any responsibility. Some friend he was!

"Rob, look at him! His lips and fingers are blue! That's not normal. He may not be your friend, but he is mine, and I'm not going to let him die out here in a field. Are you?"

Still barely able to move, Gunnar looked down to his fingers. Just as Mick said, they were blue. What the hell was going on? He felt anxiety race through him.

Rob huffed. "You get his arms; I'll get his legs. Put him in the back."

Gunnar remembered being moved, a car trip, and drifting in and out of consciousness. He also recalled Rob being absent and Mick's worried face hovering above him, as figures in white lab coats lifted him onto a gurney. That's all Gunnar remembered until he heard Astrid's voice.

"Dad, he's awake!" Astrid must have been talking to Nils, though Gunnar couldn't see because his eyes were still closed.

He felt two different hands grasp each of his—one, large and callused and the other, dainty with long nails that scratched into his flesh. Again, he could not open his eyes, though he was sure he was awake. Gunnar ripped his hand away from Nils and put his fingers to his eyelids. His eyes were open. He could sense the lashes hitting just below his brow. But everything was blurred and dark. It was like looking at a dark gray television image from a blocked channel. What was happening?

"Son, don't touch your eyes," said Nils sternly with a slight Swedish accent, as he physically took Gunnar's hand back into his.

"What's going on with my eyes?" Gunnar was in a frenzy, and he started to thrash around. For the first time, he felt his legs were bare, covered by just a thin sheet.

"Calm down, Gunnar! You've been in a coma for a week," said Nils.

A coma? It wasn't possible. What did a coma feel like anyway? You'd think if it were true, he would remember it. "What?"

"If you settle down, I will explain everything," said his father.

Involuntarily, the sound of Nils' voice soothed him and he released the tension in his back.

"Something happened to you," explained Nils. "We are not quite sure what. We've not been able to find your friends to piece this together. You left for your camping trip on Friday night, and we got the call from the hospital Sunday morning. It's now the following Sunday morning."

Gunnar slung his words fast in agitation. "Why don't I know it's morning? Why can't I see the light?"

Nils took a deep breath. Gunnar sensed bad news coming. "Son, the doctors think you have lost your sight. Your pupils were not reacting when you were in the coma. They were curious to see what would happen after you woke, but I think it is safe to say, you are still without vision."

"What?" Gunnar was in disbelief. "No way, that's bollocks!" He tried to get up again from what he guessed was a hospital bed.

"I'm going to get the doctor, Dad," Astrid said with concern.

He heard Astrid walk out of the room. Heard. Gunnar couldn't ever remember a time when he heard footsteps so loud, and yet so soft. Astrid wasn't wearing the clanking high heels that tapped when they made contact. She was wearing something with a soft sole, perhaps trainers. Yet, bristling in his ear canal was the squishing sound of rubber.

"The doctor is coming in right now," said Nils. "Let him answer your questions."

Just then, a harder tapping sound accompanied Astrid's squishy walk. It was not high heel tapping. It was a broader tapping, like a man's dress shoe.

"Good morning, Gunnar. I'm Dr. Lynch. May I check you for a moment?"

Gunnar heard the whirring and beeping of machines as a light finger pushed buttons. He felt a cold stethoscope chill his chest. Then, large hands started manipulating his eyelids. After about thirty seconds of the doctor examining each eye, Gunnar couldn't help but pull his head away. "What's going on?" Gunnar could hear the sheepish tremble in his own voice.

"I'm afraid your sight has not returned. We were hopeful that once your brain was reactive, your pupils might once again react, but they still aren't. Now, this could be a temporary condition, or permanent, but we need to get some answers from you to diagnose correctly. Gunnar, we conducted blood tests on you shortly after your arrival. They revealed you had methanol poisoning. Do you know what that is?" A pen snapped on the wood of a clipboard and papers blew in the wind.

"No."

"Methanol poisoning occurs when a person ingests a substance containing methanol. Methanol is a kind of alcohol. Not a liquor or cordial, but an alcohol used for industrial purposes. Have you been exposed to any type of industrial chemical?"

"I don't think so."

"How about antifreeze? Do you work on cars at all?" More papers rustled and the slow glide of a pen on parchment stimulated his ears.

"No."

"It's also in paint thinner and varnish. Do you do any crafts?"

"No!" Gunnar was getting upset and inpatient.

"I heard you were camping when this happened according to the boy who dropped you off. Perhaps, some sort of denatured alcohol for a camping stove was used?"

All of a sudden, Gunnar remembered in vivid detail the events of Friday night, which was unusual because he normally blacked out after drinking as much as he had. He was conflicted. He had tried to hide his drinking from his family and telling the doctor the real story in front of them would reveal the extent of his recent self-destruction. "Yes."

Gunnar sensed the doctor was waiting for more. "And, did you wash your hands after using it? Did you spill any of it?"

There was no way around it; Gunnar had to confess. "Mick, Rob and I were drinking that night. Vodka. We had a few pints out in the field. At some point, Rob gave me a cup of something to drink. I didn't know what it was, but I drank about half of it before I realized it was too disgusting to drink. I passed out after that, but when I came around, I heard Rob saying he had slipped me some camping stove alcohol as a joke."

He could hear Nils sigh and Astrid gasp. "That explains it," said the doctor after a brief silence. "Methanol doesn't poison instantly. It takes 12 to 24 hours for symptoms to present and once they do, the damage is done and treatment doesn't help. When you first got here, your CBC showed a pH of 7. That's not good. People who present with that pH level often die, and in the case of methanol poisoning, can also lose their vision. We immediately administered sodium bicarbonate to get your pH under control, but even then, you went into a coma and had a few seizures before we could stabilize you. Quite frankly, you're lucky your friend's joke didn't cost you your life."

Gunnar could hear tears now. Low sobs. Two sets. He hated making his family feel this way.

"Look," he said emphatically. "I know I shouldn't have just drunk whatever was given to me when I didn't know what it was. But let's talk about getting my sight back. When will it return?"

He sensed hesitation in the doctor's voice. "Gunnar, it might not ever come back. With severe methanol poisoning, total loss of sight is not uncommon. Now that we know we're dealing with the ingestion of a large quantity of methanol, all the ophthalmologic tests in the world aren't going to tell you any more than what time will. I think it would be wise for you to prepare yourself for a permanent life change."

It was now Gunnar's turn to cry. A small female body came close to him. Though he did not reach for her, she grabbed him and held him tight. She worked herself into a position to hug him properly, and he let loose his anger and clung to his sister like a frightened baby.

"I'm going to leave you for a bit," said the doctor. "You can talk to your family some more, but then I want you to try to get some sleep. I'm going to have someone from adult social services come and speak with you tomorrow about assistance you might be entitled to as you learn to deal with your new disability." Gunnar heard Dr. Lynch's breaths get shallower and shallower as he walked out of the room.

He was still attached to Astrid when he felt his father's broad arms separate them. For the first time since their mother died, Nils wrapped his arms around his son. "Gunnar, I am so thankful you did not die. I do not think I could have taken the loss of you and your mother. It would have destroyed me." Unaccustomed to a show of emotion from Nils, Gunnar was hesitant to reciprocate. There was no need, for soon after, Nils let go and sat next to Gunnar on his hospital bed.

"You're right, son. You should not have been drinking at all," he continued, with a new fury in his voice. "But it wasn't your fault. Damn that friend of yours! He needs to be accountable. And you are never to see him again!" His father drew in a breath, trying to calm down. "We will worry about punishing the one that did this to you later. For now, I want you to know that I will help you with the blindness if I can, and Astrid will look out for you as well. On that, we are agreed, right Astrid?"

"Yes, Father," said his sister in a tone that reminded him so much of this mother. "Gunnar, from now on, I'm going to watch out for you. I promise."

*****

"Stop! Stop right where you are. Don't move!"

Curiosity made him comply. Gunnar was lost in thought during his walk to the pub, reflecting on his old friends Mick and Rob and the night that blind trust blinded him. The warning jarred him. He turned in the direction of the command. At the same time, he had to stick his finger in his ear to clear out a strange, low-pitched buzzing sound. "Are you talking to me?"

"Yes," said a voice.

"May I ask why you're telling me to stop?"

"There's danger ahead.   Just wait ten seconds before you take another step," the voice stated.

He listened intently. No rushing gusts of wind to blow him into the street. No cars careening down the sidewalk. Some machinery indicated construction nearby, but no plows or trucks in his immediate vicinity. "Are you quite sure there's danger?"

"Trust me. You won't hear this." That voice, it sounded so familiar.

And how did the stranger know he was limited in his senses to "hearing" something? His white-tipped cane was still in his pocket. "How did you know I was listening?"

"Just wait a few seconds more."

Gunnar was about to speak when his brain clicked on a specific sound. "Wait, can you say that again?"

There was silence. Yet Gunnar still felt a physical presence close to him. "Look, I know you're there. If you don't say something, I'm walking."

"Just don't."

Those two words were enough to confirm that he had indeed not been hallucinating about what he heard. "Who are you? What is this?"

"Just someone trying to help you."

"But you sound exactly like *me*."

Was the similarity between his own voice and the voice of the stranger a coincidence? Had the flashback to his stupid teenage decision altered his otherwise impeccable hearing?

The stranger spoke again. "That would be impossible, wouldn't it?"

Gunnar heard his own sarcasm resonating back at him. "What's going on? I know I'm not crazy. I know this conversation isn't in my head. Who are you?"

"I'm someone who is trying to speed up the process and save you from a six month setback."

"What process? What are you talking about?"

"Nothing," said the voice curtly. "Let's just say I know something bad is about to happen and I can stop it."

"Stop what?"

"That," the voice said with ominous inflection.

CRASH!!! Gunnar jumped backwards with intense fright when he heard the boom. Something fell, something big. It wasn't too far from where he was standing. The clamor of bystanders grew louder and people swarmed him. He listened for clues from the crowd.

"Oh my God, are you okay?" asked a female voice.

"It's a good thing you stopped when you did," said a kid.

"What happened?" demanded Gunnar.

"Didn't you see?" asked an old man.

Gunnar pulled out his cane. "No, I didn't see. Can someone please tell me?"

The female responded. "One of those big metal advertisements just fell from the top of this building."

The man clarified. "The cable holding the sign must have broken and the sign dropped about ten feet in front of you."

"Blimey!" Gunnar was stunned. The stranger with his voice saved him from a lot of pain, if not saving his life.

"Hello, who's the person that told me to stop?" There was no reply.

"Mister," said the boy. "It's only us three here. None of us warned you."

The other two onlookers agreed that they had not been his savior, and the old man said, "I'm sorry, but we don't know who you're talking about."

Gunnar's confusion made him stutter. "But, but . . . no, I . . . just talked to someone about a minute ago. He saw the sign and warned me to stop."

"Well," said the man. "Whoever it was must have run off because there is no one here now but us."

He was so preoccupied with the identity of his mystery guardian, he hadn't been paying attention to his own body.

"Oh dear, you're shaking like a leaf," said the lady in a motherly tone. "Would you like me to call for some help or take you somewhere?"

He took a deep breath and realized he had completely lost count of his steps. He had absolutely no idea where he was. "Um, actually, if you see a cab, could you hail it for me?"

"Of course, let me." The man whistled and Gunnar could hear the sloppy sound of tires on wet road coming closer.

"Let us help you." Gunnar didn't refuse. Two sets of hands were on him, a strong pair on his back and left shoulder and a smaller pair holding up the opposite bicep and elbow.

"Duck your head," the lady instructed, and Gunnar complied as he got into a cab that smelled of window cleaner, shoe polish, and spicy food.

"Thank you," Gunnar said to the good Samaritans. The door closed and Gunnar realized he didn't know where to go. He could ask to go home, but what if home was only a hundred steps behind him. That wouldn't justify the expense of a cab fare. He couldn't go to Astrid's, since she spent her Saturdays at the shops. He could go see his father, but would hate to get there and find Nils not home. There was only one place where he knew other people would be—the studio. Sure, it was his day off, but he could always do some experimental mixing. Plus, rock bands worked whenever the mood suited them and not just nine to five on weekdays. There was always something going on at the studio. Taking his mind of his near-death experience was precisely what he needed.

"E8 please, London Lane."

Chapter Three

Help!

*****

Agneta stretched out her prematurely wrinkled hand to her son. "Gunnar, my precious boy, come sit by me."

Gunnar sighed deeply. Being close to his mother's dying body made him feel uneasy. He didn't want to leave her side, yet he got chills when he sat too close. "I'm coming, Mum," he said, obeying despite his reluctance.

"I know you are scared for me, my darling. But you do not need to be. This is just the way things work."

He didn't want to fight with her, but he was angry. "Not for someone who isn't even fifty yet."

She smiled through the pain. "You are very special, son. You have no idea how special. And I do not just mean special to me or special as a son. Gunnar, there are things I never told you. Things you need to know before I'm gone. You and I, we are the same. We can both do things, just different things. I can see the future, but you will be able to see everything."

He braced for another hallucination. Gunnar hated this—his once brilliant mother reduced to incoherence. "Mum, you need to rest."

"There is plenty of time to rest soon. Right now, I need to do the last thing I am meant to do. I need to prepare you for your destiny."

He opted to humor her since to fight her would only depress him. "Okay, Mum. What's my destiny then?"

"To learn about yourself and to use what you learn for the benefit of all. To lead your friends, and even your enemies, to defeat the one who would do away with this world."

He was tuning out her insanity as best as he could without seeming disinterested. "Uh huh, okay, I'm going to save the world."

"Oh, I wish you would not miss me so much, I don't want you to be bitter and disbelieving. But I know you must. You have to make the choices born of your sadness. You must lose some things to gain others. I am truly sorry for that, my son."

He nodded though he had no idea what his cancer stricken mother was talking about.

"And I don't want you to worry too much about the things you lose. The loss will be an adjustment in the beginning, but you will get used to it."

Agneta was beginning to tire. Her words started to slow and her voice became shaky and quiet. "It won't be long now. It will be later tonight. Will you make sure that you and your father and sister are all here in three hours?"

Gunnar refused to believe Agneta was correct in the prognostication of her time of death. He could feel tears streaming down his cheeks, and with each word, saliva stretched from the top of his tongue to the roof of his mouth. "Mum, stop talking like this. You're not going to die tonight. You have lots of time left."

"Gunnar, please?"

"No! You're wrong. How can you possibly know that you're going to die tonight?"

"I told you. I see the future."

Gunnar rose from next to Agneta's hospital bed. He started to pace, confused and unhappy with his mother's hallucinations. His gut wrenched from the pity he felt, and his heart nearly collapsed when he looked deep in his mind and visualized his mother dying that very night.

He couldn't help by weep. "Mum, you can't leave me. You, you're supposed to critique my girlfriends so I know who to marry. You're supposed to be there when I have babies because I won't know what to do with them. At the very least, you need to see me graduate from University."

"Gunnar, I've already seen your life. I'm already so very proud. But I can't help you on your journey. I couldn't even if I were to go on living. I must do nothing to alter your destiny. I don't want to say even one word that might influence your choices and lead you down a path different than the one you need to follow. But, I will give you a hint about your future wife without giving away too much, so you know who will be the one I approve of. Peaches and butterscotch, that's all I am going to say," Agneta said, mustering the biggest smile she could through the pain.

Peaches and butterscotch? She was so out of it, so mentally gone. Gunnar finally accepted it— she was dying. And with her, his dreams and his childhood. He would trade everything—his looks, his popularity, his intellect—for his mother to make it through the night and return to her senses.

Agneta was starting to fade out. Her eyes fluttered, her head fell sharply to her chest then jerked back up, and she spoke in a whisper. "Promise me. Three hours."

"I promise, Mum. Sleep now. You're tired. No more talking to yourself, okay?"

As her eyes closed, she whispered a sentence of gibberish. "One more thing, Gunnar. In the future, don't be afraid of the vardoger."

Agneta had been right. Three hours later, the family gathered as she requested, she said goodbye, and passed away.

*****

Sitting in the taxi, Gunnar dragged both of his hands from his forehead, over his closed eyelids, and down his cheeks. What was with him today? It seemed every bad memory he had was surfacing in his current consciousness.

The stress of remembering was starting to get to him. Stress caused him migraines and migraines always started with a pain in his neck. He had that pain now as he started to smell the familiar odors of Bethnal Green from outside the rolled down cab windows. He needed a minute to compose himself before going into the studio. He had to clear his mind before he would be able to concentrate on his hearing.

"Excuse me sir, have we passed the tube station yet?"

"Not yet, it's right up the street."

"Can I ask you to drop me off there instead?"

The taxi pulled over and Gunnar paid the driver by feeling the creases in his money. He knew the walk from the station to the studio would give him the extra time he needed to focus. He would be fine as long as he paid attention to step-counting and stopped reminiscing.

Gunnar focused on his numbers for about a hundred steps when he lost track. He heard that brief buzz in his ear, followed by, "Sorry about leaving you so abruptly this morning, but I didn't want the other people around to see me and ask questions."

It was . . . himself again. His voice at any rate, since it obviously wasn't him. Was he starting to hallucinate like his mother? His frustration and curiosity made him loud. "Who are you? I want some answers."

"I haven't got time to answer you now. There is a girl we need to help and we don't have much time."

"Excuse me?"

"You need to walk forward eighty-four steps, and then walk left another twenty. Do it now, or I won't explain anything."

His "twin" sounded serious. What did he have to lose? This stranger obviously didn't mean him harm. If he had, the stranger wouldn't have saved his life earlier. Gunnar rolled his limp eyes and followed the voice's directive.

After 102 steps, Gunnar was about to confront the voice when he heard a hushed commotion.

"Leave me alone," a girl said assertively. She was American, no mistaking that.

"Come on, love," said a man with a Brummie accent, slime oozing from his voice. "You've got that slag look about ya. Let's have a go."

Gunnar heard two sets of heavy footsteps come close to each other. Two men were nearing the girl.

The girl retorted, "Absolutely not." He couldn't tell where in America she was from, he just knew it wasn't New York.

A second man, another Brummie with a darker voice and thicker vowel usage, snapped, "You're wasting your time, mate. Just grab her money and her jewelry and look for a passport and go."

The other man cackled. "No way, she's too tantalizing. I'm fuckin' this bitch!" Gunnar didn't know any party to this conversation, and yet he started to despise his boorish countrymen and feel sorry for the victimized American.

The high-pitched Brummie howled. His footsteps got closer to the girl. He was trapping her! "If you know what's good for you, you'll go down on me right here. And you'll do it voluntarily, and you won't make a peep!"

A third set of footsteps, dainty but determined to move, tried to make an escape. But the patter lasted only a second. "Not a chance," responded the girl. Gunnar was in awe of her defiance.

He found himself starting to get mad on her behalf, but he held back. However, his whole world changed with the dialogue that followed. "You'll do it, or I'm gonna run a knife through your gullet," said the high-pitched Brummie sickly.

"If you're really gonna stick her, we need to kill her anyway" said the darker one, laughing callously. "Americans always complain to the coppers. I'm not going to prison as an accessory to your cock."

The girl continued to shock Gunnar. She was not giving in. "Fine. You want to stab me? Stab me! I'd have rather you try to kill me than rape me!"

Gunnar could feel the heat in his face and fluids rushing like tidal waves through his skin as the Brummies laughed off her bravery. He was afraid they were going to take the girl up on her offer.

"Get involved! That's why you're here!" his twin said. The voice wanted him to intervene. "Trust me, she's worth the risk."

"How? I can't see them?" Gunnar was trying to reason with the stranger, hoping his companion could answer how a blind man was supposed to take on two obviously dangerous men.

His voice assured him. "They have reeking breath. Smell it out. We're good at that. When they're in breathing distance, make a fist and punch with the rage we've bottled up since we went blind. Beat them with all the fury you would have if Astrid were the one that was about to be raped."

His hesitation ended when he heard the situation become dire. "Oww! Oww!" cried the girl in pain.

"That was a warning slice," said the evil, higher voiced Brummie. "Now, are you gonna cooperate and take down your kickers, or am I gonna plunge this knife into your stomach?"

The Brummies barely had time to laugh again before Gunnar erupted like a volcano. It took him less than five seconds to make up the twenty-pace difference between himself and the Brummies. He launched his first punch towards the foul beer breath in front of him. An incredible strength Gunnar never knew exploded from his fist as it made contact with a man's eye socket.

"Hey, hey, hey man!" He had apparently hit the higher pitched Brummie with the knife, as the low voiced one was now talking to him from a standing position. "You knocked him out cold! We're just having a bit of fun with a friend of ours."

Gunnar ignored the lie. As though he were an action movie hero, he reached for the stink in front of him and picked the second Brummie up in two arms as easy as if he were lifting a dumbbell. Throwing him against something that made a metal crashing sound, Gunnar heard a snapping sound reminiscent of when pulling apart the wishbone of a turkey. The weasel moaned and screamed and there was no sound at all from the high voice.

Gunnar screamed at the only one he was sure was awake, "If you know what's good for you, you'll tell everyone you were hit by a bus. Or I will tell everyone, including the police what you did to this poor girl. I heard everything! Rapists in prison don't have much fun!"

"Let's go," he said to the girl, taking her hand. She probably hadn't noticed yet that he was sightless, so he just ran with her in tow until the sounds of traffic were so loud he knew they were safely in a public place.

Finally stopping, he asked while catching his breath, "Are you okay?"

"I am now," said the girl in a low voice. He heard gratefulness in her tone. She then unexpectedly let go of his hand, bombarding him with a surprisingly tight hug around his neck. As she hugged him, he smelled something sweet and fruity.

"Thank you," she fawned. "You really didn't have to do that. I would have been fine. But, thanks nonetheless."

"From the "oww" sounds, it didn't sound like you were fine," Gunnar argued politely.

"Well, it did hurt, but they wouldn't have killed me or anything."

Since there was no getting her to see the danger she was in, he shifted his attention to her injury. "How bad is the wound? Do we need to get you to a hospital?"

"It's really not as bad as it looks," she said as her body shifted away from him.

"That doesn't really help me. Do you need to go to the hospital, or not?" said Gunnar with slight impatience.

There was hesitation in her reply. "No. I'll be fine. Do you . . . not see where he cut me?"

"No. I'm blind," said Gunnar succinctly.

"Oh." It was a different sounding "oh" then he was used to from women. It wasn't condescending or sympathetic, but stated matter-of-factly. For all the care she gave to his statement, he might as well have just told her he preferred pens to pencils. "Well, for a blind man, you throw a hell of a punch." He heard a slight chuckle. It was a sweet and genuine. Just the sound of it made his skin tingle and goose bumps appear.

"What can I say? I just heard myself, I mean, said to myself, I have to help her, and then adrenaline took over."

"You have to let me repay you somehow," she said earnestly. "A 'thanks' seems inadequate for you risking yourself on my account."

"I do have one small favor. Do you see the tube station from where we're standing?"

"Yes."

"About how far would you say it is?"

"Three minutes, maybe?" she said with uncertainty.

"Could I possibly bother you to walk me to the station? I was counting my steps when I heard the commotion. I'm afraid I've lost count, and I don't know exactly where I'm at. I need to start over."

"How about I just walk you to where you're going. There's no sense in walking backwards and starting over. Where are you headed?"

"London Lane. I work at a recording studio there."

"Well then, allow me to escort you to London Lane." Gunnar felt her tiny arm slip through his own. It felt strangely comfortable.

"So, what are you doing in London?" asked Gunnar. "I can hear that you're American."

"I'm here on a study-abroad. I'm getting my Masters in architecture and you've got some great buildings over here."

Gunnar found himself being uncharacteristically open. "Interesting. You're smart, but not so smart that you wouldn't challenge strange blokes with a knife trying to kill you."

She tried to be blasé. "It sounded worse than it was."

Gunnar corrected her. "I may not have sight, but my hearing is impeccable. Those guys meant business, even if you were brave."

Their walk slowed down as she sighed and stated, "I can't believe I'm telling this to a complete stranger, but you seem, different. Like I don't have to worry about telling you. See, I'm very . . . physically capable. Strong, if you will."

Her confidence captivated Gunnar. "Are you a body builder or bionic or something?"

He heard a lone chuckle as the pace quickened and the subject changed. "No," she said. Quickly changing the subject, she continued, "Hey, I've been talking to you for five minutes and I haven't even asked your name."

"It's Gunnar. Gunnar Ahlgren. And yours?"

"I'm Roxanne."

"Were your parents fans of Cyrano de Bergerac?"

She laughed again. He was starting to become addicted to her laugh. "No, as in The Police and 'you don't have to turn off the red light.' Yes, I am named after a prostitute. Thanks Dad!"

He joined her laughter. "I've worked with Sting, several times. He would absolutely love that your name is Roxanne."

"Really? The real Sting? How did you work with him?"

"I told you I work at a recording studio, right? Well, I'm a sound engineer. I work with producers and we make records for musicians. He's just one of the many I've made records with."

"That's awesome! What a cool job. But if you don't mind me asking, how do you know what you're doing being blind?"

"I've memorized the board. That's the easy part. What's really important is the sound quality, and there's nothing wrong with my ears. In fact, I've mastered the engineering side so well, I've been dabbling in producing."

A sudden gust of wind blew by them and Gunnar felt incredibly soft flat hair wisp past his cheek. It was his first clue as to how this girl would look—she had long straight hair. Again, he savored the aroma of flowery fruit. It must have been her shampoo. But what about the rest of her? He was almost obsessed with the idea of putting an image to the laugh.

Before she could ask another question, Gunnar stopped their walk. "I hope this doesn't sound too forward, but I'm quite curious as to what you look like. I just want to be able to put a face to the voice is all. May I touch your face?"

As if it were the most natural thing to ask, she said, "Sure, go ahead."

Given her permission, Gunnar put both hands out in front of him. The direction of her voice drifted up, so he knew she would be shorter than him. He put his hands directly out in front of him and gently lowered them until about five inches down, when his palms rested on that soft hair.

Curious about the length, he grasped a lock of strands between his thumb and forefinger and slowly pulled down. It was straight, as he thought, and ended just below her shoulders. Slowly, he brought his fingers up to her fringe, which swept to the right side with a slight cowlick to the left.

"Your hair is so soft." He hadn't intended on telling her this; it just slipped out. "May I ask what colour it is?"

She paused for a moment. "Do you know what colors are?"

He smiled. "Oh, I haven't always been blind. It didn't happen until I was seventeen, so I have a frame of reference for pretty much everything. I can picture things in my mind as clearly as if I was seeing them."

"It's brown."

"Oh, come on," Gunnar said playfully. "Surely you can do better than that. What colour of brown? Is it like milk chocolate or dark chocolate? Is it the color of desert sand? Or perhaps the brown of autumn leaves?"

"Hmmm." He felt her hand go to her own head. She must have been examining. "I would say it's the color of a fudge brownie. Pretty close to black, but not quite. Do you know that color?"

In his mind, he saw a silky dark chocolate waterfall. "Yes," was all could say. He continued his exploration down from her hairline. Her forehead wasn't too long and not at all craggy. The skin was extraordinarily smooth and relatively free of bumps and blemishes. She was young. Her brows were fairly thick, with a hint of a pluck that she had not kept up completely. Her face was full at the cheeks, with plump apples directly south of the ocular bone. The jaw extended down and then squared off with the slightest indentation. Her nose was straight and thin with a small bulb at the end. Her lips were full, but not overly so, with the top lip being just a bit thinner than the bottom lip.

As he traced her lips, he felt her take a deeper breath. The exhale sent chills up his spine and stirred his core. God, he wanted to kiss those lips. But she must be a child compared to him, probably about twenty, and here he was, thirty-five. Not to mention, the poor girl had almost been a rape victim this very day. There was no way she would be interested in an old geezer like him, if she was interested in men at all right now.

He quickly retracted his hands as a reminder that he couldn't let himself think this way. "Uh, thanks. I'm glad to know the face of the American girl who has now become my friend."

There was a silence, and he wondered if her reticence meant that she didn't want to be friends. But then, her arm slipped through his again, this time more assertively. She gently pulled him forward back into their walk.

"You know, I can't stop thinking how lucky it was that you were there in that alley," she said. "But how did you know to go there? I mean, that's not something you would have memorized? And it took you off your counting path. What made you get close enough to be able to hear what was going on?"

For some unfathomable reason, he knew he could trust her with the truth, but he couldn't bring himself to speak it for fear she would think him insane. "I honestly can't recall," he offered instead. "Perhaps it was luck."

"Or maybe, fate," Roxanne said. Gunnar remembered what it was like to be the object of flirtation from his youth, but he had guarded himself for so long in the romance department, he wasn't sure anymore if what she was conveying was interest.

"Perhaps," he said shyly.

They fell silent for a bit as they walked. Roxanne's grip on his forearm was slowly tightening and releasing, almost as though she were massaging. Gunnar started to breathe deeply and could feel himself inching a bit closer to her. Soon, he was close enough to smell her hair and that distinctive shampoo. He finally recognized the aroma. It was peaches he smelled. The sweetness made him inadvertently lick his lips.

Gunnar couldn't see it to confirm, but his sixth sense was sure Roxanne was looking him over. He hadn't seen himself in a mirror in almost eighteen years, and while he would feel his face practically every day for changes, he wasn't at all sure of whether he still had a look that a lady would like. Gunnar felt brave enough to ask. "Roxanne, how do I look to you?"

Oh God, that laugh again. If she didn't stop laughing, he was going to lose his mind. "Um, well, honestly, I think you're quite handsome," she said with a giggle.

His head inflated instantly. "Really?" Now he laughed, slightly embarrassed. "This may sound odd, but since I can't see myself, could you tell me what you think I look like?"

Something happened next he did not expect. Roxanne stopped their promenade and placed her small hands on his face, as though she were the blind one. He felt her trace his features as she spoke. "Well, I'm not as good at this as you are, but . . . let's see. Your face is mostly oval. You've got a strong linear chin. Your nose is like, small for a guy, and it kind of pinches where the nostrils come together at the top. You're pretty pale—compared to me, you look like a ghost." She went from tracing to almost poking. "You've got tons of freckles." Poking then became caressing. "Your lips are thin, but very soft. Your eyebrows are so light colored, that from far away, you might not even think you had any." The caressing moved into a scalp massage that made Gunnar weak. "And your hair is this messy, short mop of really light reddish-blonde."

She stopped, drawing Gunnar reluctantly back to reality. "Well, thanks for that. It's a first, someone reading me. You did quite well actually."

"Hey, I'm not done!" Her voice had a cute faux pout to it. "I get to describe your eyes now."

Mocking their earlier repartee, he joked, "They're blue if I remember correctly."

"I can do better. Your eyes are the color of the Caribbean Sea on a calm summer day. A girl could swim in those eyes. And I feel like I've swam there before."

Gunnar was smiling from ear to ear and his jaw was aching. 'Please let this be a come on!' he repeated to himself in an inner monologue. "Wow! I'm speechless. And flattered of course."

Once again, she took his arm and they walked. As they strolled, he replayed the earlier conversation with the man who sounded like him.

The voice had said this girl was worth saving. Was it because she was "the one?" Confused, he wondered if his attraction for Roxanne was genuine or the result of suggestion. Now more than ever, the stranger perplexed him.

"Hey, are you okay?" He heard concern in her voice and realized his thoughts must have manifested on his face. He didn't want his sound-alike to interrupt what he was feeling. Clearing his head, he focused on her.

"Fine. Just thinking about something. You said I was pale compared to you. What does your skin look like?"

"Well, my mom is a full-blood Brazilian, even though she was born in America. My dad is half-Delaware Indian and half-Russian. I'm sort of a mutt, but a very tan mutt." Before Gunnar could say anything, she laughed again. "Oops. I mean I am a mutt the color of, maybe, butterscotch?"

The beautiful picture of what her skin must look like bathed in the Brazilian sun was cut short with a deep breath of memory. Peaches and butterscotch. It was one of his mother's final incoherent thoughts meant to guide him to love. No way. This had to be a coincidence. How could his mum have predicted Roxanne? She was hallucinating and not really a soothsayer. Right?

"Gunnar, are you okay?"

He felt dizzy with doubt. "Uh, I just need to sit down for a minute. I think I'm crashing from the adrenaline rush of giving those tossers a good thumping."

"If you can make it about thirty more steps, we're right by my flat. We can get you inside and get you some water."

The stimulating thought of entering Roxanne's flat was all the motivation he needed to make it the rest of the way. "If it wouldn't be a burden on you."

"Are you kidding? Gunnar, you risked life and limb for me. There is nothing you could request of me that would be a burden."

The pair walked another twenty-six steps before Roxanne guided them left. "Ok, there are five steps here."

It was as though she had always known exactly how to handle his disability and was accepting him as-is. He heard her pull keys from her pocket and fumble with the lock. The door creaked, the two entered into a slight breeze, and the door shut behind him. "Now, we're going to an elevator. I'm on the seventh floor."

Gunnar felt a swooping feeling in his stomach as the elevator rose swiftly, though he wasn't entirely sure if it was from the motion or the fact that Roxanne never let go of his hand. The car dinged six times and then stopped with a jerk. "This is me. I'm the second door down on the right."

After the sound of more keys clinking together and the mechanical sound of a lock opening, he was led into a mildly warm room. He counted the steps from the front door to where Roxanne led him, on the off chance he would be at her apartment again someday. In eight steps, she said, "Okay, here's the sofa. Sit down, catch your breath, and I'll get you a bottle of water."

He heard her walk away, followed by the crisp sound of a refrigerator door opening. As Gunnar waited on the sofa, he noticed its cushions and pillows smelled just like her, covered with the sweet fragrance of peaches. Drinking it in, he heard her returning. The cushion of the sofa gave a little with her weight. She was so close to him, her body heat electrified him. She reached for his hand and opened it, placing a cold plastic bottle in his grasp.

"Thanks." He opened the bottle and took a drink. He was quite parched, and the cool water rushing down his throat relieved him.

"My pleasure." It was the way she said "pleasure" that made his temperature rise.   He was terrified of making her feel uncomfortable, but God, he was so attracted to her. He had no idea what to do. He hadn't felt this way around a female for almost two decades.

He was embarrassed. She had to be able to see he was becoming aroused. He found himself reaching for a pillow and pulling it to his lap.

"So," Gunnar said, with an uncharacteristically nervous rasp to his voice. "It's been a crazy day, huh?"

A second later, he felt a soft kiss on his lips. It wasn't a forced wet kiss, but a sweet peck charged with current. He was swept away, though he didn't make the motion back. As soon as it started, the kiss ended.

"I'm sorry," said Roxanne shyly. "I hope I haven't overstepped."

What? He had wanted to kiss her since she first laughed. He was just too stunned to kiss back. He wasn't going to let her be mistaken. He couldn't see her, but he didn't need to. His lips were instinctively drawn to their target. Gunnar reached over to Roxanne and pulled her to him. It was the most passionate kiss he had ever given.

The energy between them seemed to last for hours though the kiss lasted only a few seconds. It was only when Gunnar couldn't breathe anymore that he let her go. Yet, even though he needed air, he didn't want to be too far from her. He rested his forehead on hers. "Roxanne, I . . . I didn't kiss you back at first because I thought you wouldn't like it. I mean, what those guys did to you earlier, I thought you might be scared if I showed interest, and I don't want you to be scared."

Her hand tightened around his. "Gunnar, I don't know what kind of impression you're getting of me, but I can only imagine it must be confusing. You're probably thinking that, after having gone through what I went through with those jerks, any good American feminist would never invite anyone up to her apartment and would reject all men for a while. But, and I don't know how to say this without sounding callous or hardened or putting you off completely, being threatened by those assholes wasn't the worst thing I've ever endured. Given my strange life, it's just one small challenge in a string of challenges. So, I carry on, being myself and doing what I need to do. And from the moment we met, I knew you were different. It's cliché, but I feel like I've known you for years. I want to trust you, and for some reason I implicitly do. I wanted to kiss you, and so I did."

Gunnar shook off disbelief. He had no idea why he let it happen, but he let truths spoken way too early exit his lips. "My soul flew like a bird every time you laughed today. I feel like my whole life is about to change, and all I want to do for the rest of it is hear that laugh."

She leaned over and kissed him again, before pulling away when the intensity heightened. "I don't know what I'm doing. I feel like I'm on a roller coaster," she confessed. "I'm hitting highs too fast. I'm feeling emotions I shouldn't feel so quickly. We've formed a bond in less than an hour and I don't know how or why."

He commiserated. "I know. It's impossible."

"No, it's not," assured Roxanne. "I know people it's happened to. But it's not supposed to happen to me. We cannot possibly form a real bond until you know everything about me, it wouldn't be fair. But I also can't let you know me yet. Man, this is confusing."

Gunnar knew the exact place Roxanne was at. He felt a little odd too about how quickly he'd grown fond of her. And while attraction was certainly at play, he couldn't deny his heart was laying a claim too. He decided to be the cautious one. "Look, I think we both know that this is to be more than a passing acquaintance. And we both also seem to know that there is something between us that goes beyond simple chemistry. I don't want or need to suppress my feelings, but I won't force them on you either. If we become the best of friends, great. If we fall for each other quickly, so be it. Fast is okay if that's our destiny. But going slow is fine too."

He heard her laugh faintly. "And that's why I'm upset. I want to go fast. But we can't. And it's not even for the reason you would think. I just, can't have sex with you."

Gunnar put a finger to her mouth. "Sex? Oh goodness, that wasn't even on my mind!" It was a slight lie, thought Gunnar to himself, realizing that while being with Roxanne would likely be the best sex he'd ever have, he really was wanting to savor the relationship-building. "Look, we've just met, literally. I would never expect sex from a woman before she's ready, which I fully recognize is typically longer than an hour. I want to know you. I want to see if this can be something real. If you can tolerate being with someone blind and eventually learn to forget that I am blind. If you can learn to live with me and my limitations, I sure as heck can be patient with any requests you have."

Her arms wrapped tightly around his back. "Thank you so much."

They kissed again, this time softly, lingering. He dropped his plan of going to the studio. All he wanted to do this day and for the rest of his life was get to know this amazing girl.

CHAPTER FOUR

Rock Superstar

*****

Aaron walked back over to his dresser and picked up the fuchsia flyer he had casually tossed on a pile of homework he would never complete.

*"COLLEGE NIGHT!
COME MEET COLLEGE RECRUITERS FROM OVER 50 OF THE NATION'S INSTITUTIONS OF HIGHER LEARNING. THURSDAY NIGHT, OCTOBER 22, 2002, 7:00 PM, ROSEVILLE HIGH SCHOOL GYM."*

He flung it back on the dresser. He didn't even want to go to college. It was a waste of time. But he had made a promise to his mom to try college for at least a year and didn't want to disappoint her, so he begrudgingly tucked in his shirt and meandered out the door.

Aaron had resolved that wherever he went, he would major in something useless and easy and spend the rest of his time playing music at local coffee houses. Academia was not what he wanted, having dreams too big to be contained in a classroom. Aaron wanted to be a star. Singing and playing piano for adoring fans was his deepest desire. He had the talent, but he had to get out of Michigan to cultivate it. His goal was to get close to either Los Angeles or New York, places where he knew he could get his big break.

When he got to the College Fair, he intentionally avoided any school that started with Mich-, Minn- or Wes-. Unfortunately, those schools made up the brunt of attendees. The only coastal schools seemed to be Ivy League, and he had a zero percent chance of getting into one of those. He was just about to head out when he noticed a school with a map of Boston on its bulletin board. He was intrigued by the name of the school—

Berklee College of Music. A music school on the coast not too far from New York! What could be better? Then his eyes shifted from the banner to the person standing behind the booth, and he knew what could be better.

She was incredible looking. She was right out of a movie—a living Jessica Rabbit. Her red hair was curled ever so slightly to frame her face. Her skin was amazingly flawless, as if airbrushed. Her eyes were greener than emeralds and accented by smoldering purple eye makeup. And to complete the masterpiece, her lips were perfectly plump, perfectly round, and perfectly pink. She wore white leather boots hidden under slim fitting white jeans and a fluffy white sweater that reminded him of a cloud.

Aaron took two cautious steps towards the beauty, unsure if he should get that close to perfection. He had temporarily forgotten why he was there; any thoughts of college obscured by his hormones. He was mesmerized by her, but also wary of the rejection that would surely come if he admitted interest to this woman who had to be at least five years older than him. He took two tentative steps forward and nearly lost his footing when she eyed him, smiled, and waved him over. Aaron swallowed nervously, took a deep breath, and approached the table.

"Hello," she said in a voice that sounded as sweet as the honey flower perfume she was wearing. "I'm Alexis. Are you interested in music?"

Aaron was still hypnotized, but he tried to speak as though nothing in the world bothered him. "I am."

"What's your name," she asked while slowly rolling a lock of hair between her fingers.

He wiped away the perspiration forming in the dimple of his upper lip. "Aaron."

"So, what are your goals in life, Aaron?" Alexis queried with a smile.

With an audible exhale, he answered, "I want to sing. I play piano and keyboards, but I see myself more as a front man, like Billy Joel or Elton John."

"Ah," Alexis said slyly. "You want to be famous?"

Of course he did, but he didn't want to appear shallow. "Who doesn't? But it's not all about that. I want to create, to inspire. I want to entertain the world."

"Wow," she said with a nod. "Then I think Berklee may be the place for you!" Alexis started selling her campus, filling a paper bag with brochures. Captivated by the movement of her lips, Aaron lost track of what she was saying. She snickered. "Aaron, I'm actually done with my spiel. Do you want these brochures or not?"

God, he was so embarrassed. She must have thought him a huge dork. "Uh, sorry. Yes, please. Thanks."

She giggled softly, then smiled. His heart skipped a beat as he swore she licked her lips lightly. "You know, I like you, Aaron. I'm going to do something I don't normally do." She then took one of the interest cards and wrote her name on the back. "If you get to Berklee, look me up."

More than ten years had passed from that fateful night, and here Aaron sat, propped up on his chin, resting his head on a toilet bowl in a recording studio bathroom. He pulled his hand towards his mouth to wipe away the residual vomit. 'Why does my life suck so bad?' he thought for what must have been the twentieth time since opening a bottle of Crown an hour before.

A snort popped some saliva bubbles in his mouth. He knew why. He knew exactly how he went from that bright-eyed, infatuated high school kid to a prematurely aging drunk, who was still, unfortunately, infatuated with the same bombshell. "That bitch!" he screamed, laughing, crying, and slobbering all at the same time.

He had two women on his mind, and he couldn't shake either of them. Alexis, and oddly enough, Virginia Woolf. Ever since reading *To the Lighthouse* in English class at Berklee, Aaron found a sort of kinship with Virginia Woolf. When he learned that she'd committed suicide in the most clever and painful way—by filling her pockets with heavy stones, walking into a river, and drowning herself—he was saddened. But he also admired the bravery it must have taken to walk the last few inches for her head to submerge. As macabre as it was, he studied her suicide note, memorized it, and recalled a few sentences sitting there on the bathroom floor.

> "You have given me the greatest possible happiness. You have been in every way all that anyone could be. I don't think two people could have been happier 'til this terrible disease came. I can't fight any longer. I know that I am spoiling your life, that without me you could work. If anybody could have saved me it would have been you. Everything has gone from me but the certainty of your goodness. I can't go on spoiling your life any longer. I don't think two people could have been happier than we have been."

What an amazing love she had for her husband—so intense, so passionate, and so devout that it would be the only thing that could save a person.

God, why didn't Alexis love him like that? He loved her that much. He would quit music for her, kill for her, die for her. But no, she just wouldn't love him back, not anymore, if she ever really did.

His hazy memory flashed back to freshman year at Berklee. He was accepted, got a scholarship and a job, and ran to Boston. He registered for classes and then went by the administration office to see if he could find Alexis. Hiding his desperation in the guise of seeking financial aid, he asked practically everyone if they knew where to find her. Eventually, he caught a glimpse of that incredible red hair and irresistible face.

He nervously entered her office and watched her uncross her ankles to stand on her shapely legs and five-inch heels. He didn't know how he managed to speak to this creature, but somehow, he muttered, "You said I should come see you if I got here."

She smiled, leaned in close, and whispered in his ear. "I love that you do what you're told."

From that moment, he was lost. He fell painfully in love and spent every minute doing things to make her love him. He completely changed who he was hoping she would be more attracted to him. Where once he had been a fairly simple dreamer from America's heartland, now he had maxed out his credit cards on gym memberships, hair bleaching, and Armani. Where once he had just wanted to sing and tickle the ivories, now he was schmoozing and playing the music business game. All because of her. And as if that weren't enough, after sophomore year, she talked him into dropping out so he could devote his energy to her and making it big.

It had been heaven for the first two years, purgatory since he cut his debut record, and hell since he went double platinum. Those first years at Berklee, she built up his ego, got him connected, and inspired many a hit love song. There was no denying that he got his foot in the door of stardom because of her. Perhaps that's why he put up with what came after the record deal. As soon as the money started coming in, she quit her job at the school and started spending his growing fortune. She demanded to go on tour with him, but then she'd get him pass-out drunk after the shows and disappear nightly to sleep with other men. She wanted him to marry her in a wedding that would make the covers of the all rags, and yet after he spent more than the gross national product of a small country on their "commitment," she had her tubes tied without his knowledge so they could never have a family.

All that, he told himself, was forgivable, because he loved her so damn much. She was his wife, his bliss, his cross to bear. Only now in retrospect, sitting in front of a toilet, did he realize he only forgave her many transgressions because he had drunk himself into a forgiving stupor and dulled the knowledge of her cheating with Hydrocodone and Xanax.

Six weeks ago, his fourth album debuted at number one. His manager threw an amazing party to commemorate the sales. He got so wasted, his liver stopped functioning and he ended up in emergency with alcohol poisoning. His 'wife' never once came and saw him at the hospital when he was dying. She didn't even call. He had no idea where she was the entire week he spent in recovery.

Five weeks ago, after being discharged, he returned home to find Alexis naked and asleep between some random man's legs. That was it! He'd had enough and told Alexis it was the end. She yelled that she didn't want to be married to a drunk anyway and that she wanted someone better looking and better in bed. With that, his beautiful and spiteful red-headed girl packed her bags and left him, but not before swearing he'd pay dearly if he tried to divorce her.

Damn that woman! The only reason he even drank was to deal with her bullshit! The only reason he had aged twenty years in ten was because she walked all over him. The only reason their sex life sucked was because she screwed anything that moved and he was afraid of the diseases his own wife was exposing him to. This was all her fault, and she had the unmitigated gall to leave him?

He hated her—hated her with all his might! And he loved her—loved her so much he wanted to scream! She was terrible for him, but he longed for her more than he longed for his pills. Aaron put his face in his hands and cried like a three-year old.

He would do anything for that woman, quit for her, kill for her, die for her.

Since she left, all he had done was drink like a fish and increase his dosage of pills. But the drinking wasn't working and they didn't make enough painkillers to erase her from his mind. He had secretly hoped for weeks now that his liver would fail again and that this time it would be over. But his body kept pushing on. If he wanted to die for her, he would have to take more proactive steps.

So what if it would be weird to commit suicide at the studio where he was recording his fifth album? It's not like anyone was going to bother him. He was a rock star, a huge one, and he could order people like food. If he wanted privacy, he could sit his ass wherever he wanted, tell people to leave him alone, and his word was law. It was a just a matter of how? What could he do to himself that would make that awful woman realize what she had done to him? How could he leave her with all the pain she had left with him?

Blood was required. She needed to see him bleed for her. Pain was required. She needed to know the extent of his agony. And publicity was required, so the world would know how the whore treated him and so his fans would brand her the pariah she should be.

It had to be a gunshot that ended it all. His bodyguards had guns and they were over in the studio waiting for him. He could sneak in, grab one of the pistols, sneak back out to the lounge, put the steel in his mouth and pull the trigger. His brain would splatter, she would be called, and his dripping crimson gray matter on the green paint would finally make her see how terribly she'd treated him.

He got up off the cold tile floor, flushed, wiped at his mouth with his shirt sleeve, and went out to the studio. He passed one of his bodyguard's holsters that draped over the sofa and slyly took a gun, pushing it into his pocket. Finally, he went to the control room and got a piece of paper and a pen.

Others would think he was going to the lounge to write a song. Instead, he put pen to paper and began to write his suicide note.

*****

"You need to go to the studio."

Gunnar snapped to attention as he heard the voice through a low buzz. He had almost fallen asleep sitting on Roxanne's sofa, waiting while she used the restroom.

"Roxanne, did you say something?" Gunnar raised his voice so Roxanne could hear him.

"No, I didn't say anything."

Gunnar relaxed back on the sofa cushions and slipped back into his adrenalin crash.

"Now, Gunnar! You have to go now!"

It was the person that sounded like him again. "Who are you? How did you get in here, in a private flat?"

"No time. You have a friend to save. Go to the studio now. Go to the lounge. A.J. Rhodes needs you."

"A.J. Rhodes? The rock star?"

"You only have about thirty minutes. Hurry!"

"Wait. Why does A.J. Rhodes need me? I've never worked with him—I don't even know him. He's not my friend."

"Just go!" The voice pressed with increased urgency.

He was about to speak to the stranger again when he heard Roxanne's dainty footsteps. She eased back into the cushion next to him. "I don't know about you, but I'm hungry. Want to grab something to eat?" she asked.

"I've got to make an appearance at work for a bit," Gunnar whispered in a bit of a daze.

Her tone was deflated. "I thought you said you weren't going in?"

"I wasn't going to, but I've just remembered I have a meeting. It should only be a few minutes.

Why don't you come with me? We can eat after that."

She perked up. "I'd love to go with you. I've never been inside a recording studio before."

"Great!" He rose from the sofa and held out his hand toward the sound of her voice. "I'm in a bit of a rush, so we'll need to get a taxi if the walk is longer than twenty minutes."

"I'd say it's cutting it close, so let's get a cab."

As if they'd been together for years instead of hours, her hand met his and she helped him to his feet. He almost lost himself in her touch when he remembered he was on a mission. He didn't know why he kept listening to the voice. But the stranger had been right in every prediction so far and only a fool would intentionally disregard good advice.

Within fifteen minutes, Roxanne was guiding him by the hand again, this time to help him out of the cab. They had arrived at the studio and Roxanne was giddy with excitement. Her tug on him was soft yet aggressive, and her grasp tightened the closer to the door they got.

Entering the breezeway, the familiar smell of the studio infiltrated his lungs. There was the permanent smell of cigarette smoke that no cleaner in the world could remove. Layered over that was a faint citrus furniture polish scent used on the wood in the lobby.

"Hey, Gunnar me man. What're you doin' 'ere? Ain't it yer day off?" Rick, the security man, stood up and approached him with the same secret handshake they exchanged every day.

"Hey there, Rick. This is Roxanne. She is a very good friend of mine and I thought I'd show her around the studio."

"Oh? I didn't know you 'ad a girlfriend. Does she know yet that ya' can't see?"

Gunnar smiled. "You'll have to forgive Rick. He's Irish. Not much for manners."

In a melodramatic farcical way, Rick feigned distress. "Shite, mate. That 'urt! But I'd be lyin' if I said ya' were wrong. Very lovely to meet ya'."

"It's nice to meet you too." Roxanne was being polite, but Gunnar could sense a hesitation in her voice that betrayed she wasn't quite sure how to take Rick.

Before Rick could say anything else to make Roxanne uncomfortable, Gunnar interrupted the flow of conversation. "Is there anyone good here today?"

"Got some studio work goin' on, some background vocals, but the big deal is A.J. Rhodes."

Roxanne's shyness evaporated. "Oh my God! I love him. 'With You Now,' is so amazing!" Her excitement sent shivers of contentment through Gunnar.

"Yah, e's good. But rumor 'as it e's piss drunk and 'as been sittin' on his arse all day wastin' everyone's time. He's in Studio 4, but I don't know if I'd bother takin' 'er there. Don't know if you'll get to see much."

"I guess we'll avoid that, then," Gunnar joked. "Well, I'm going to take her for the grand tour. I'll see you later."

"Good luck. And, it was nice to meet ya, gargeous!"

He didn't hear Roxanne respond, but knew she was looking back at Rick by the contortion of her body. Now that he was no longer protecting Roxanne from Rick's likely lecherous eye, he remembered why he was there. He had to find A.J. Rhodes. He had to get to Studio 4.

"Roxanne, I've got to go to that meeting now. I'm going to drop you in one of the empty studios for a moment. There's no one here today, so you can look around until I get back. Will that be all right?"

"Of course."

He expertly led her around the corridors he had memorized and opened the door to the room where she would wait. He was delightfully surprised when her lips kissed his in a quick peck.

Walking to the lounge, Gunnar reflected on the day's events. This was the strangest, most wonderful day of his life. He had survived a potentially fatal accident and met the woman who seemed to be his soulmate. No offense to a big-time rock star, but meeting A.J. Rhodes was going to be the low point of this monumental day.

The buzz sounded again. "He's not in Studio 4. He's in the green room lounge," said his vocal doppelganger.

"You again? asked Gunnar. "First, you get into Roxanne's flat and now you breached Rick's security? How are you doing this? When are you going to tell me what's going on?"

"After you go to the lounge," responded the voice firmly. The buzz and the voice disappeared and Gunnar knew he was alone again.

He found the door to the lounge and entered.

"What the hell? Get out of here!" Gunnar guessed the brash American voice yelling at him must be A.J. Rhodes.

"Sorry, mate. Um, is everything okay?"

"What?"

Walking closer to the other man in the room, Gunnar was repelled by the smell of alcohol. It reeked from every pore of the body before him.

"Are you A.J. Rhodes?"

"What does it look like?" asked the angry drunk.

"Dreadfully sorry, but I'm blind and can't actually see you."

A.J.'s outburst subsided, which was everyone's reaction. Now, the drunk star was just ambivalent. "Yeah, I'm A.J. Rhodes, for now."

That was an odd caveat. "For now? You planning on being someone else soon?" Gunnar hoped to hear a laugh at his jest, but instead heard a sniffle.

"I was going to be dead before you walked in."

At last, Gunnar knew the reason the stranger sent him there. "I hope you don't think it intrusive to ask, but what do you mean?" Gunnar queried.

The anger was back. "I mean exactly what I said," stammered the rock star. "You can't see it, but I've got a gun in my hand, and if I could figure out how to use it, I'd be gone and everything would be better." Anger turned to frustration. "But I can't get it to work. Why can't I get this stupid gun to work?"

Gunnar quickly improvised. "Well, I do know a bit about guns. Perhaps I can take a look and see what's wrong with it."

"But you're blind. How can you see what's wrong with it?"

"I can feel what's wrong with it. I don't need to see it." Gunnar held out his palm without reaching for the weapon. He wanted this to seem like a nonchalant exchange, but he was sweating buckets. Moments later, he felt a cold steel lump in his hand.

Gunnar knew nothing about guns from personal experience. He had heard true crime audio books and knew a few fancy gun terms, but that was the extent of his knowledge. He hoped his ruse would work. As he ran his hands slowly over the steel, he exclaimed authoritatively, "I'm afraid this gun is broken. It appears as though the hammer won't cock. Could be a loose pin in the safety. I'm afraid you won't be firing this gun today."

He wondered whether the rock star would try to take the pistol back, but when the sobbing began, Gunnar knew he could put the gun out of reach. He moved over to the lounge sink and placed the pistol inside a dish cabinet.

He was not used to comforting men and felt a little odd doing it, but he sat close to the source of the sobs.

"Why can't I kill myself? Why can't I just die?" cried A.J. Gunnar knew every human emotion by its sound and knew instantly this one was misery.

"You're gutted. I can hear it. Do you want to tell me why? Maybe it will help."

"My wife left me, that's all," said the rock star, trying to minimize his turmoil.

"It's not that simple, is it? What I hear is gut-wrenching heartache. It must have been one hell of a break-up."

A.J. laughed through a sob. "You're good, man." There was a pause before the lyricist continued. "I'm in love with a woman who has knocked me down and spit on my soul. I wanted her to be my light, but instead she's my darkness. She's the reason I am what I am, good and bad. I can't live without her or stand to be near her."

Gunnar had never felt like this about a woman, but he knew a similar feeling. It was the way he felt when his mother died. The pain of losing your beacon can be unbearable.

"And you can't stand the agony, so you drink yourself into oblivion?" Gunnar was merely rehashing his own past, but the rock star responded.

"You know what it's like then?"

Gunnar had told the story on a hundred blind dates; why not rehash it for a good cause?

"I lost someone close to me, and I went off the deep end. I drank and drank and drank until there was no pain. It was like I was in a permanent night, but with no stars to guide me. God, did I want to die too! I couldn't make the overt gesture to end it all, but boy, did I want to. Instead, I did the stupidest crap imaginable. Culminating in me blinding myself by drinking something I shouldn't have. Oh yeah, mate, I've been there."

"Drinking caused your blindness?"

"That and being too trusting of someone who didn't have my best interest at heart. Kind of like you. Look, I'm not going to tell you what to do, but killing yourself is not the solution. If you did that, you'd miss out on meeting a truly wonderful woman, a person who would never do the things to you that your wife has done. I've got some personal experience with that feeling too."

"But I'm so tired. I can't deal with her lingering. I mean, she's gone. I haven't spoken to her in weeks, but every conversation in my head is with her on the other side. Everywhere I go, she's there. I just want her out of my head."

Gunnar sighed in empathy. "It sounds like she's put you through the ringer. But I can tell you from personal experience that it's not just her that's destroying you; it's also the drinking. You doing anything else besides the alcohol?"

"Whatever my doctor will prescribe to numb me."

Gunnar nodded. "You may think the pain is lessened by the drugs and the drink, but it's not. Don't end up like me, doing something amazingly moronic before you realize that. Something perhaps like putting a bullet in your brain?"

A.J.'s sobs slowly stopped and turned to a mucus-laden conversation. "I just want her to regret me, you know? Like I regret her."

"I think you have to possess a heart in order to regret something, and from the sounds of it, she's pretty heartless."

A.J. snorted a cackle. "You pegged that."

"So, killing yourself isn't going to have the desired effect then, is it?"

A.J. blew his nose. "No. She probably wouldn't care at all."

"And I'm betting you haven't done anything to change your will or get divorced. Which means, if you blow your head off, she gets everything you built."

Gunnar finally heard the sound of acceptance. "Oh my God, you're right. I can't believe I almost made that tramp a multi-millionaire."

"Well done for realizing that without permanent damage."

Gunnar felt a new hand take his, and it was a good feeling. "Man, I don't know you. But you saved me today. My head is clear for the first time since I was seventeen. I know what I need to do. I've gotta put this album on hold. I'm gonna do that one last charity show they're organizing and then I'm taking some time off. And I've got to quit drinking. I don't think I could stand to be blind, no offense."

Gunnar smiled. "None taken. And I think quitting the sauce is a bang-up choice. Just don't tell anyone that I had anything to do with you putting your album on hold. I think I'd be sacked."

A.J. laughed a little. "What is it you do here?"

"I am a sound engineer. Right now I'm working with the Royal Philharmonic down the hall."

"Really? How do you do that blind?" The rock star sounded amazed.

"Old hat. I try not to let this disability limit me."

"What's your name?" asked the star.

"Gunnar. And yours is A.J. Rhodes."

"No, man. My name is Aaron. A.J. was her creation."

"Well Aaron, the best of luck to you on getting clean. When you do, and when you least expect it, the right girl who accepts you no matter what will find you. It happened to me." Gunnar smiled even in the dreary moment.

"Thanks, man. And I promise, we'll be seeing each other again. I don't have any real friends, but now I consider you one. Probably my only one."

With that, A.J. rose from the sofa, Gunnar settling down further into his spot as the other side of the cushion inflated. Gunnar heard the lounge door open and close and felt an amazing sense of purpose.

He had truly saved a life. This wasn't an almost-accident, as it was with himself earlier, or a could-have-turned-ugly, as with Roxanne later. This was an actual death he prevented. And it, like the entire day, was all thanks to the mysterious imposter. An imposter who knew he was saving someone who was going to be his friend.

Gunnar was certain the man with his own voice would return again. The next time though, he would refuse to take any instruction until the imposter revealed himself. Gunnar needed to know who to be angry at, and who to thank profusely.

CHAPTER FIVE

Tell the Truth

*****

Astrid was beaming. "Gunnar, I met the most brilliant guy last night. I think, I really think I'm going to marry him."

Gunnar smiled, but mentally rolled his eyes, as he heard his sister gush with glee. Sitting in the living room of their childhood home, as they often both did on lonely Friday nights, Gunnar recalled that easily infatuated Astrid had often decided that her current paramour was "the one."

"So, what's this one's name then?"

"Brian. Brian Apfel." Even the way she said his name dripped with reverence.

"And what makes him so special?"

Astrid swooned just talking about him. "I can't explain it. I just feel it. When we talk, it's like we've always known each other. The conversation is so easy. And we're already ourselves around each other. No pretenses. It's just, comfortable. Being with him feels like being home."

Gunnar's dismissiveness began to change to jealousy. He had always longed for the relationship she described but had never been lucky enough to find it. Worse, due to his blindness, he probably never would. Still, he feigned interest. "What does Mr. Perfect do?"

"He's a petroleum geologist. He describes it as him watching and listening to the earth and having the earth tell him where to find fuel."

Perhaps this was something serious. Astrid had always been a genius and a priss when it came to her impeccable grades, yet she typically managed to date losers. She sampled an aspiring guitar player, a vapid male model, and a wannabe Formula

One driver. She had yet to date her intellectual equal, until now.

"How did you meet a geologist?"

"That's a funny story, actually. But you can't repeat it because it'll make us both look stupid. We both saw rather nondescript fliers up at the campus advertising a meeting on fossils. I thought it was for archeological relics, he thought it was for fossil fuels. We ended up seated next to one another and were both baffled when a trendy promoter started trying to sell the crowd watches and handbags. We left at the same time and once outside, we both commented on how daft we'd been not paying more attention to the details on the flier. Then we started talking about our identical love of history, though from different perspectives. Gunnar, he is so clever. I know you're going to love him."

Gunnar tried to be supportive despite his envy. "I'm ecstatic for you."

"Thanks. I can't wait for you to meet him." Gunnar didn't need to see his sister to know that her skin was aglow and her smile was wide.

"And before we meet, you have told this Brian about your blind brother and he's okay with that?"

"Of course! You're the first person I talked about. He's dying to meet you."

"Yeah, you've mentioned this meeting a few times now. When is this meeting supposed to happen?"

"In about twenty minutes. I've asked him to meet us here at your apartment. I figured, at home, comfortable in your own surroundings, it would be easier to meet a stranger."

Gunnar tensed up. He didn't mind visitors, but he hated surprises. "Astrid!"

"Sorry, but it's really important that you meet him soon."

"Why so important?"

She hesitated. "I haven't told him yet. About the female issues. I mean, how do I even broach that subject? I figured you'd know what to do, to get it out in the open."

He breathed deeply. "For me personally, I prefer the direct approach with my dates. I like to start conversations with 'Hi, I'm Gunnar. My alleged friend blinded me when I was shit-faced pissed by having me drink the equivalent of lighter fluid. And how are you?' Just take a cue from me. Say, 'Hi, I'm Astrid, I can't have children.'"

"You might be able to do that Gunnar, but I can't put it out there like that."

Gunnar whispered to soften the blow of his words. "In all seriousness, before a guy starts to fall for you, you need to tell him that he can't have a family if he chooses you. It's really the only fair thing, for both of you, so there's less chance of getting in too deep and getting hurt feelings if he can't get beyond that."

"I know. There's no point in letting myself fall even more in love with him if he's going to reject me for someone fertile. Which is why I wanted you to meet him. I was hoping you would tell him for me." Astrid's tone seemed desperate.

"What?" Gunnar was stunned.

"We can all just be talking around the table after dinner, having conversations about whatever, and you can bring up your blindness and Mum's cancer, and then segue into other family illnesses, like my infertility. Then I can laugh it off and see how he reacts."

Gunnar didn't want to be a part of this. "I thought you said you had great conversations with this guy and you communicate well. Don't you think you should be able to talk to him about this without the charade? I bet he'll think that."

"It's not an easy conversation to have, Gunnar. I mean, it's easy enough to say I can't get pregnant, but then, there's the inevitable why? How do I answer that? How do I have the courage to tell someone new that I once had an out-of-wedlock teenage ectopic pregnancy that destroyed a fallopian tube and a subsequent botched surgery that scarred my uterus? You know men—they hate talking about lady bits. And then you have to deal with the question of who got you pregnant, which opens the can of worms on ex-boyfriends and how many men I've slept with. All dreaded topics in a new relationship."

She was right. Men do not enjoy wondering how many other blokes have been with their girl before them and enjoy even less words like ovary and cervix. He heard sadness in her voice. "Please, Gunnar. This is the first person besides my family I'll have ever told. Please?"

Astrid didn't have to plead any longer. "Okay, Astrid. I'm just afraid if he reacts poorly, I'll go into big brother mode and toss him out on his ear."

She laughed. "Thanks. This is best, Gunnar. You were right. Brian is the one for me, but I need to make sure I'm the one for him. After tonight, I'll know."

Gunnar excused himself to the loo to prepare for the intrigue he was about to start. He rehearsed his part aloud several times in several ways. "It's nice to know there's someone out there for Astrid who doesn't want children either." No, not that. "There are so many babies out there that need to be adopted. I think it's wonderful that you and Astrid are on the same page about adopting due to her infertility." Too presumptuous. "How long has it been since that surgery on your uterus, Astrid?" Ugh, definitely not.

Any way he said it, he was sure he'd want to hide after starting this conversation. His body was getting overheated from anxiousness. He needed to calm down. He took four deep breaths, exhaled rhythmically, and focused on relaxing. Cold, he thought. Snow, he thought. Ice, he thought.

Wafting into his bathroom, he smelled the distinct smell of Drakkar cologne, a scent he memorized as a teen. Astrid's man must have arrived. Putting on his polite English smile, he exited the lavatory and entered the living room.

"Hello, I'm Gunnar. Pleased to meet you."

"Gunnar," Astrid interrupted. "Who are you talking to?"

He was befuddled. "Um, your friend, of course."

"He's not here yet," said a confused Astrid.

"Really? That's odd. I swear I caught a whiff of Drakkar and figured another man must be in my apartment. Oh well, it must have been a memory of someone else."

"But Gunnar, Brian does wear Drakkar. How could you possibly know that?"

*****

Gunnar couldn't believe he'd only known Roxanne for a fortnight. Ever since the day he met her, they had spent all their free time together. Her flat was more convenient to the studio than his own, so it made sense to spend his nights there. And Roxanne joked that she felt safer with the bionic blind man around.

That first night, he tucked her in and promised to watch over her. After she fell asleep, Gunnar moved to the lounge and listened to the telly. He memorized the smells and sounds of her flat, from the constant creak of her hardwood floors to the peach shampoo and strawberry body wash that floated from her shower. The ambience felt so peaceful, he fell asleep on her sofa with BBC 4 in the background.

The next night, Roxanne told Gunnar that while she wasn't ready to "sleep" with him, she did want to sleep in the same bed with him. So they lay together all night, falling in and out of sleep, stirring every now and again at each other's touch.

By the beginning of the new week, sleeping in the same bed and huddling close seemed like a well-worn routine, and while there was no intimacy beyond kissing, he was content with that.

While intertwining toes under the covers was fun, he was finding even greater joy getting to know her. They talked music, and he was thrilled that Roxanne had knowledge of everything from ABBA to Arcade Fire. They talked of food and drink and their mutual love of upscale dining and spicy foods. They both loved snow and couldn't wait for winter's chill. They found so much pleasure discovering commonalities. But, as with all burgeoning relationships, the taxing topics of family and the past were casually avoided.

Still, Gunnar felt so connected to Roxanne, so easy with her, that it was only right he invite her to his brother-in-law's birthday party. He just hoped he wasn't moving too fast for her.

He broached the subject over breakfast that Friday morning. "You know, it's my brother-in-law Brian's birthday today. My sister is throwing him a dinner party tonight. Nothing fancy—just him, my sister, and I. I know typically it would be a little early in the relationship for you to meet my family, but I would love for you to be there."

"No, it's not too early. I'd love to meet them," she said.

"I have to go back to my place to grab Brian's gift. Do you want to come with, or do you want to meet me at their house?"

"I need to get ready. I have to look presentable if I'm going to meet the most important people in your life for the first time. I'll meet you there. When is it?"

"I told her I'd pop around about 5 o'clock," he stated.

"Where is it?"

"It's in Beaconsfield. It's 420 Amersham Road, Beaconsfield, HP9." Gunnar heard her scribble as he spoke.

"I'll be there with bells on!" she exclaimed with a cute American colloquialism. Like ripping off a bandage, he hurried out not much longer afterwards to get his separation anxiety over with.

He hated being away from her, even for a few hours, and was antsy awaiting her arrival once he got to his sister's house. The only thing that kept him preoccupied was his sister's excitement.

"I have to describe this to you, Gunnar!" He heard the giddy footsteps of his sister skip towards him. She put the ultrasound photo paper on the table in front of him and moved his fingers to trace the image as she spoke. "Here's his head, and this is his arm, and this is his . . . well, that's how we know he's a boy."

In part jest and part instinct, Gunnar pulled his hand way. "I'm not touching my nephew's willie, am I?"

Astrid chuckled as she took the ultrasound photo from him. "I hope that won't be your reaction when you help me change nappies."

"Don't even think I'm changing that kid. I can just see it now, putting my hand right in . . ." He shuddered.

"Okay, that is disgusting!" she admitted. They both laughed for a minute as Gunnar tried to shake the image from his head.

A break in the conversation provided Gunnar the opportunity to ask again, "What time is it?"

Put out, Astrid said, "A quarter after. Will you stop worrying? I'm sure your date will arrive soon. Remember, we live out in the middle of nowhere and this is her first time coming out. She's probably lost. Now, calm down and wait here. I'm going to start the dessert." He listened as his sister stepped lightly across the wooden floor toward her kitchen.

Within minutes of being left alone, he heard the familiar buzz again and knew what was coming next.

"No time to think of Roxanne now. You've got to save Astrid and your nephew."

Gunnar perked up. "Who are you? Why do you keep following me? And why do you sound like me? How are you getting into places where I am?"

"No time for questions. Go save her."

Gunnar remembered his promise to himself. "I'm not moving from this spot until I get answers."

"Are you willing to let your sister and the baby she thought she'd never have die?"

Gunnar shifted uneasily. "You're bluffing."

"Jesus, you're a stubborn bastard. Look, I promise to tell you everything I can after you save them. I haven't been wrong yet, have I? Every person you've saved was on the verge of tragedy. I'm telling you one last time. Astrid's baby is about to die and with it, Astrid's faith. You need to save them. Go to Astrid's right side, now!"

The voice was right. It hadn't been wrong yet. Astrid was in trouble. Instinct took over and Gunnar rushed to the kitchen.

"Astrid?"

"What?"

Okay, she was still fine. But her voice sounded far away.

"Where are you?"

"I'm trying to get down this jar of molasses. I need it for the cookies."

"Are you up high?"

"Well, it's above the refrigerator."

"Are you on a ladder or something?"

"Nah, I just need this chair. If it could just tilt a little more to the left."

He needed to get closer to her and pinpoint her location. He had to keep her talking.

"What kind of cookies are you making. Describe the recipe."

"Sugar cookies basically. Flour, sugar, butter . . . "

He found his way to her immediate right as she continued talking.

"Vanilla, eggs, AHHHHHH!"

Instinctively, he held out his arms in front of him. Astrid fell into them, but he wasn't prepared for the heft of it and his elbows buckled. He collapsed on his back and his head smacked the floor, causing an instant headache. The brunt of Astrid's weight impacted him square in the stomach, knocking the wind from his lungs.

"Oh Christ!" yelled Gunnar, coughing from the pain.

"Oww," Gunnar heard Astrid cry. Just then, he remembered why he was hurt.

"Astrid, are you all right?"

"Yes, I'm fine. You broke my fall. The question is, are you okay?"

He couldn't move. "I'll let you know in a few minutes."

Astrid gasped. "I know you can't see this, but had you not been here, I would have hit my head on the granite countertop on the way down. I probably would've landed on my stomach." He felt Astrid get off of him, removing the pressure from his lungs. "Gunnar, thank God you were here. You saved me and the baby."

"Nah, you'd have been fine," he said modestly to make her feel better, but knowing the voice had diverted disaster again. Still lying on the floor, he began to twitch his limbs. "I think I'm going need some paracetamol or something."

"Of course." He heard the rustling of her clothes as she got to her feet. Her heels tapped lightly on the linoleum floor.

"Really, are you going to be okay?" she inquired with concern.

He held his arms up and waved his fingers one at a time. "I'm resilient. What about you? Any contractions or anything? Baby still kicking?"

He felt her gentle hand on his palm, cupping it and bringing it to her stomach. It stretched with a third-trimester kick. "The baby is fine. No problems. It was like falling onto a pillow." She placed the medicine in his grasp.

Groaning as he sat up, Gunnar made light of the serious situation. "Is that your way of saying that I'm porky?"

"Of course not, tubby!" Astrid needled. "Let me get you some water so you can take those pills."

He heard the faucet running and her footsteps again. "Here."

Gunnar popped the capsules in his mouth, put his lips to the glass, and relished the coolness of the water that pushed the medicine down his throat. She took the glass and started lifting him.

"No, no. I got it. Don't strain yourself, Astrid."

Gunnar rose slowly, working out a few muscle kinks as he reached his full height.

"Well, at least let me sit you back on the sofa," she pleaded.

He didn't protest. His sister took his hand and led him to her couch.

"Okay, just rest. I'm going to finish cooking."

"You're not going to keep looking for the molasses, are you? No more heights, please," Gunnar pleaded.

"No. We'll just have ice cream. From now on, I'll keep my feet on the ground."

He listened as she walked away. He had just settled his neck onto a cushion when his privacy was disrupted.

"It's a good thing you listened to me."

Gunnar turned sharply in the direction of the voice, causing a twinge in his stiff shoulders. Pain forced him to settle down. "You owe me some answers. Who are you? And how do you know everything that's going to happen before it does?"

"Look, it's not that I'm trying to hide anything or don't want to explain. It's just that my ability to speak to you is time limited. I only have a few minutes to get out the necessary information you need to know before my window to converse closes, so don't have time to chat."

"Then use your remaining time to tell me who you are," demanded Gunnar.

"I'm can't, yet. You won't understand who I am really until several more pieces fall into place. For now, vardoger will suffice," said the voice. Before Gunnar could ask further questions, the voice continued. "Roxanne will be here soon and I've got to go. Ask Astrid about the vardoger. It will get you started on the road to understanding."

Gunnar's keen hearing picked up on a car pulling up to the outside of the house.

"When can we speak again?" asked Gunnar hurriedly.

I'll talk to you again when you go to Roxanne's house," responded his double. Then the buzz faded.

"Hello?" asked Gunnar. The voice no longer answered back.

"Were you calling me?" Astrid's voice grew closer. She had come back from the kitchen.

"Astrid, this is going to sound like a crazy question, but do you see anyone besides me in the room?"

She huffed. "No." She hesitated. "Are you sure you're okay? You did hit your head pretty hard."

"I'm fine, I think. I'm just anxious for Roxanne to get here."

His sister bought the ploy. "That explains it. The distraction of infatuation."

The doorbell rang and Gunnar's curiosity faded, replaced by his anticipation of being with Roxanne again.

"That must be your girl. Stay on the couch Gunnar, I'll get it." He heard Astrid's steps tap quickly past him, the click of a lock, the creak of the door hinge, and then the most happy sound. "Hi! You must be Astrid. I'm Roxanne."

"Hello, Roxanne. It's lovely to meet you. Please come in."

A refreshing breeze blew through the tiny airs on his arms as the door shut. He could smell Roxanne's familiar peach shampoo in the air that grew more intoxicating the further inside the house she walked. He sensed a little trepidation in her voice and thought it endearing that she was nervous to meet his sister.

"Thank you very much," Roxanne responded.

As her scent grew stronger, he knew they were in the same room. He smiled and tried to get up, but a pain in his back kept him glued to the cushions of the sofa.

Astrid's concern was audible. "I'm afraid Gunnar and I had a small accident before you got here, Roxanne. He was standing behind me in the kitchen when I lost my balance and fell right on top of him. I think me and his nephew in here may have given him a good bruising."

Almost as soon as Astrid finished her sentence, he could feel Roxanne sitting next to him. She took his hand. "Are you okay?"

"Ahh, don't worry about me. A few laughs and some good food and I'll be right as rain."

"Well, it's going to be a good half hour before dinner's done, and we're still waiting on Brian to get back from the store with some of the stuff I forgot to buy. So no food quite yet. But that's fine, because it will give me a chance to get to you know your . . . friend."

Gunnar hadn't really told Astrid much about Roxanne or his depth of feeling for her. How could he? It would be impulsive to announce his intent to spend the rest of his life with a girl after knowing her only two weeks. When he told Astrid he was bringing a date to the party, he simply described her as a "friend," not wanting to get into a deep discussion with his sister.

Apparently, Roxanne didn't care about approval. "I think you mean girlfriend, right Gunnar?" Roxanne's tone was playful with a bit of possessiveness thrown in for good measure. He found what others might perceive to be clingy as exhilarating. He didn't know why he let it slip out, but he took it one step further. "Friend, girlfriend, future wife."

Roxanne's grasp on his hand tightened and he detected approval in her touch. With his right ear that faced his sister, he heard a stifled gasp.

"Um, how long have you two known each other?" Astrid queried with sisterly concern.

There was concession in Roxanne's voice. "Two weeks. Believe me, feelings this strong this fast would concern me if I were in your shoes too. But when you know that it's right, you don't fight it. You embrace it. You know what I mean, Astrid?"

"Actually," interrupted Gunnar, "she does know. A few years ago, my sappy little sister here came rushing to me to tell me how she had fallen in love with Brian Apfel, and how she knew after only a few dates, and before they'd even had any really important conversations, that he was the one. Now, they're married with a baby on the way. Remember that, Astrid?"

He heard Astrid settle back into the love seat, indicating her rigid backbone had gone soft. "Of course, I remember," she conceded. "And you're right, when you know, you know. Well, it looks like congratulations are in order then. I'm thrilled my big brother has finally given a woman the chance to get close to him. He's had a wall up since he was seventeen. Kudos to you, Roxanne, for breaking through it."

Just then, a loud jovial voice bellowed from the back door. "I come bearing gifts from the cheese gods!" cried Brian.

By the time the salad was served, both his sister and easy-going brother-in-law accepted the idea that Roxanne was family and started treating her as such. With no-holds-barred jokes, tasteless ribbing at her expense, and no pretenses of trying to put on a good show, it was exactly the right amount of frivolity to introduce Roxanne into his life permanently.

After dinner, Astrid remembered the ice cream in lieu of cookies, and the foursome were licking cold spoons. Everyone was at ease, especially his usually tense sister. It was time for Gunnar to test Astrid about the imposter's strange word.

"Hey, Sis. Have you ever heard of the vardoger?"

"Of course," she said, as though he had just asked her the color of the sky.

"Well, for those of us that are not university professors, can you tell us what it is?"

"It always amazes me how little knowledge you have of your own culture. It's a figure from Norwegian folktales. It's like, a person's double." She paused while recollecting. "Actually, it's more than that. Our ancestors believed that every person has a double of themselves, and sometimes, that double exists in time and space before we do. For instance, let's say someone swears they see you on the street and then ten minutes later, you arrive to that same spot on the street. What the person saw earlier was your double, or your vardoger."

Gunnar sat quietly, more so than he had all night. Both Astrid and Roxanne noticed his sudden change of mood. "Is everything okay?" asked Roxanne.

"You're very pale," added Astrid.

He was trying to comprehend what he heard. The mystery man did know everything that was going to happen a short time before it did. Was it true? Was there a Gunnar existing in time and space before he himself experienced time and space?

"Uh, yeah." Gunnar didn't want to alert the ladies, but he did want more information. "So how far in advance do these things exist before you do?"

Astrid laughed snottily. "They don't really exist. It's just a myth."

Sensing tension, Brian tried to diffuse the situation with a question. "Why do you ask, Gunnar?"

He wasn't ready to discuss his recent experiences. He wanted to understand them better first before responding that he himself may have had an encounter with a vardoger. It was then he remembered the last conversation he had with his mother before she died, and it offered him the perfect excuse. "It's one of the last words Mum ever said to me. I always thought she was having end of life hallucinations, but what if . . . what if there really is such a thing as a vardoger?"

With that, the joy dissipated from the dining room. Astrid was no longer mad, her tone now filled with sadness. "It's been ages since you've mentioned Mum. What made you think of that?"

"I don't know," he lied.

"I haven't researched vardogers much, but I'm happy to do so if it will ease your curiosity. Tell you what. I know tomorrow is a Saturday, and I don't typically like to work on the weekend, but I'll make an exception. Come with me to the university tomorrow and we'll see what we can find out. I'll even call on a colleague who knows more about this stuff than I do and see if he's free to join us. Okay?"

He perked up. "Cheers, Astrid. Thanks!" He was thrilled he wouldn't have to wait long for more clues to the mystery.

"Right then," said Astrid. "We'll go tomorrow morning. Why don't the two of you stay here tonight? We have the guest bedroom. It's closer to work than your flat."

"Oh, would it be okay if we stayed here?" begged Roxanne of Gunnar. "I'm not in the mood to have to deal with other people on the tube."

He couldn't help but oblige her. "Of course, we can stay."

With plans set for a sleepover, the four found themselves in the kitchen at about midnight still having a grand time. Sober Gunnar and his pregnant sister were gobbling down sugar, while Roxanne and Brian guzzled down lager. Gunnar couldn't remember when he had been so happy. Finding Roxanne completed a puzzle, the solution to which had long plagued him.

When the entire tub of ice cream was devoured and the bottles of beer empty, Brian and Astrid excused themselves to their bedroom to change. Alone now with Roxanne, he noticed her playfulness had changed to perceptiveness.

Wrapping her fingers through his, she asked, "So, what's really the sudden interest in the vardoger?"

He tried to play it off. He knew she felt strongly for him but was afraid insanity would be a deal breaker. "Like I said, it was just something my mum said."

"Yeah, that's what you told your sister. But you went white as a sheet when she told you what it was. I have a feeling there's more to this story."

He didn't want to come off as cross, but didn't want to tell the truth either. "It's not important," he remarked.

He felt her pull away and heard her walk to the other side of the room. She got very serious. "If this were just any other date, I would drop the matter. But I thought we had something more special than just dating, based on what you said to your sister earlier. If you truly think of marrying me someday, shouldn't you want to be honest?"

Panic flushed through his body as he pictured in his head all the fallback he could get from coming clean. He felt sick imagining her leaving him because he sounded like a nutter. He made one last ditch effort to avoid the topic. "I'm afraid of telling you too much, too soon. I don't want to say anything that would drive you away."

Roxanne's train of thought had not been derailed. "You can't be afraid that what you say might cause me to leave. It won't, because I would want you to stay if I told you something crazy. Besides, what could possibly be so bad about a myth that you're scared to tell me?"

His fear dissipated into a sigh. He didn't want secrets between them. "It's not bad exactly, it's just . . . it's going to sound mad. I can't imagine you'd want to stick around with an insane person."

A new tone entered her voice. He didn't recognize it, but it was a kind of understanding acceptance. "Gunnar, believe me when I tell you that I have experience with crazy. You aren't it. And even if you tell me the most outlandish thing in the world, I'm positive it can't rival some of things I've seen and heard."

Gunnar heard rustling from the back bedroom and knew his sister and her husband were done changing. "Astrid's coming back. I promise I'll tell you after they go to bed."

Roxanne sat back down and grabbed his hand. "Deal."

Gunnar relaxed a little as he prepared for more merriment. But in the back of his mind, he couldn't help but wonder what experiences she had which qualified her as an expert in the bizarre. Clearly, there were secrets she hadn't told him yet either.

CHAPTER SIX

Girl, You'll Be a Woman Soon

*****

Yum. The air smelled of café au lait and beignets, as it always did this time of morning when she walked by the Café Du Monde. Too bad she was dieting. What fool would limit their calories in New Orleans? Only a native who'd grown up smelling the sweet aromas of the Mississippi since she was a kid. Of course, since Katrina hit three years ago, the perfume odor of cinnamon and jambalaya was masked by the faint stench of dry rot and mildew. While reconstruction occurred slowly but surely, old boards and water soaked paper still littered the streets here and there. Truly, the smells and sights

151

of post-hurricane New Orleans actually made dieting easier.

Ugh, she was sick of dieting. She only did it because she didn't want to be labeled "the fat cheerleader." Recently though, she'd decided she was sick of being a cheerleader anyway. Sure, it was a passkey to high school popularity and everyone knew who she, Roxanne McCabe, was. But as she spent time with her sisters in spandex, she couldn't help but notice she was much smarter than most of them. She had goals and aspirations outside of the pyramid and had even been thinking lately about taking her art talent to the next level and going to art school after graduation in two years.

That small reminder that she wanted to be more than just a pom-pom pusher made her give in to her craving. One beignet wasn't going to hurt. And now that tourists were still scant after the hurricane, she wouldn't have to wait in line that long.

Or so she thought. There was an unusually long line today and she was getting inpatient to buy her pastries. She was just about to leave the line when she finally paid attention to her surroundings and realized the reason for the backup. It appeared as if some sort of field trip was going on, an outing for those with special needs. She was sad watching the Down Syndrome kids, people using sign language back and forth, and teens her own age confined to wheelchairs.   Seeing handicapped people always made her feel guilty and petty. They were seated all around her, and she was compelled by morbid curiosity to watch as their caretakers ordered in front of her.

After ordering, she sat down and continued to watch, through trying to appear discreet. "Excuse me." She had been examining a teenager with a slightly misshapen head in front of her when a young man's voice grabbed her attention from behind. "I'm sorry to bother you, but I think I've dropped some money somewhere around us. I was facing your perfume when I dropped it, and I heard the quarters hit the ground, but I can't see them to pick them up. Could you look around our feet and tell me if you see fifty cents?"

The boy was her age and objectively not bad looking, though he stared ahead with a dead glance. He must have been a blind kid, here with the rest of the special needs bunch.

"Oh, sure." She looked around the floor and sure enough found two quarters lying close to each other near the boy's feet. Picking up the coins from the sticky cement, she handed the boy his money. As she did, their hands brushed lightly against each other. She no longer felt sorry for him, she felt . . . attraction. "Here you go," she said coyly, as though she was flirting with any other handsome guy.

"Thanks."

Afraid the boy would turn and ignore her, she swiftly interjected, "My name's Roxanne. What's yours?"

"Um, I'm Austin."

"Hi, Austin." She was bizarrely unabashed. "So, are you blind?"

Her question surprised him. "Yeah."

"Are you here on like a field trip with your special ed class or something?"

"No." He was curt and she was afraid she'd offended him.

"I didn't mean to be rude, I was just curious."

"This isn't *my* class I'm here with. I'm a volunteer, helping this class. If you must know, even though I'm handicapped, I can and do volunteer my time to help other handicapped people. Just because I can't see doesn't mean I can't give."

She was uncomfortable around someone so magnanimous. "Wow. That's awesome. I mean, I would volunteer more, but . . . " She really had no good excuse for being lame and selfish.

"It conflicts with your important social schedule?" asked the boy snidely. Man, did she ever feel horrible. The guilt of being in the presence of those less physically capable than herself was bad enough, but heaped on that was the knowledge that even someone disabled did more to help her fellow man than she did.

"I'm not *that* social," was all she could muster.

"Maybe you should volunteer with me then," offering a pleasant olive branch.

And that's how her volunteer work started—with a challenge. Though she never ended up dating Austin, he inspired her to commit to making a difference. She grew to embrace the differences in people and genuinely care about human beings she previously ignored after a guilty glance. No more did she harbor the embarrassment or shame that other "normal" people did when around those with different abilities, as she had grown so comfortable around the disabled teens she volunteered with that she counted many of them as her good friends.

Soon after graduation and starting a part-time job with the Deaf Action Center, Roxanne became best friends with a deaf girl named Bridget. Like herself, Bridget was eighteen going on thirty. Both cared probably too much about fashion, makeup, and boys and both had an unhealthy obsession with *The O.C.* Though Roxanne had become near fluent in sign language over the last two years, the pair communicated almost exclusively though notes when in public so no other deaf persons in the vicinity would be privy to their gossip.

Their relationship was just like any two BFF's, at least until one hot August Saturday night in 2008. Before that, Roxanne had opened her mind to the new experience of living around those whom nature had made different. After that, she had to open up her mind to the new experience of living around things that were not of nature at all.

Roxanne had a friend from high school who joined a fraternity invite her to a back-to-school kegger at Loyola. Roxanne and Bridget had glammed up and were on their way to the frat house via the St. Charles streetcar. They had just passed Jefferson heading for their stop at Broadway when Roxanne got a tingly feeling inside. She loved flirting with boys and couldn't wait to find a guy to make out with at the party. Just as she crossed her legs to stifle the anticipation, her silent friend grabbed her arm. Roxanne turned to see Bridget shaking. The scrunched pout on Bridget's face said without words that her friend was in discomfort, but it wasn't pain. Instead, she just pointed to Roxanne's ears with a quizzical look. Bridget was trying to see if Roxanne heard something.

On her notepad, Roxanne scribbled, "*I don't hear anything.*"

Bridget's face remained contorted. "*Don't you feel it?*"

"*What?*"

"*VIBRATION,*" Bridget wrote.

"*It's probably just the streetcar.*"

"*No, it's not. Didn't feel it til just now. It's freaky.*"

"We're about to get off. See if it goes away once we're not on the tracks."

At Broadway, the girls filed off the St. Charles line with the rest of students. Roxanne pulled Bridget to a nearby bench and waited until the streetcar was just the size of a pinhead in their view. Then she wrote to her friend. *"Feel better?"*

"I still feel it. It doesn't hurt. It's like I'm standing right next to a huge speaker. It's pulsing through my body. I can't hear the sound wave, but I can DEFINITELY feel it!"

"Do you want help? Should I take you back to Metarie?"

"No. Like I said it doesn't hurt. Let's walk around and see if it goes away."

Walking now and no longer capable of written communication, Roxanne examined her friend's face every few minutes to see if she still looked uncomfortable. When they got close to campus, Bridget tugged on Roxanne's shoulder and gestured with both shoulders upward. The sensation had gone.

Had this been the last experience with the sound wave, it would never have held a place in Roxanne's memory. But throughout the night, Bridget would get a frustrated look on her face and make the sign language gesture for "again". After the first few times, it started to annoy Roxanne because the occurrences of the sound seemed perfectly synched with whenever a cute guy would hit on her. After eight or nine times and many notes back and forth, Bridget admitted her fright. Not having any fun, the pair left the party, agreeing that if the vibrations continued into the next hour, they would make a trip to the hospital. But before they made it home, the sensation was gone and Bridget's nerves were calmed.

160

The next morning, both girls went to the Deaf Action Center. There, Bridget described the previous night's events to one of the teachers. The astute woman found her story interesting, but puzzling. How could two people in very close proximity not be subject to the same sound wave? Roxanne should have been able to hear whatever Bridget was able to feel.

Bridget was agitated and desperate to understand.

"*Would you do me a favor? Can you make the exact same trek that we did yesterday and take the trolley to Loyola and see if you hear it? I'm afraid to go with you though, so do you mind if I stay here?* " her friend scribbled in her notebook.

Roxanne wasn't thrilled with the monotony of the idea, but appeasing her friend was paramount to her boredom, so Roxanne agreed. Just as she did the day before, Roxanne took the train at the exact same time and crossed the exact same streets. She approached the stop where her friend had started squirming the day before and again heard nothing. She was just about to scrap the adventure as futile when a total hottie got on the street car. He looked just like Jared Leto. She was about to explode from the intensity of her insta-crush when a high-pitched noise caused her shoulders to rise to her ears.

The screech, as best it could be described, lasted a fraction of a second then was replaced by a long, dull hum. Thinking it must be the same sound from last night, she exited the tram to investigate. Noting she was at the Jefferson stop, Roxanne watched the trolley chug far down the tracks. As it left, she realized that the grinding of the gears had been muffling the annoying pitch. With nothing but the occasional car whizzing by to drown the din in her ears, she felt like a bee was buzzing inside her head. She turned in a full circle to see if she could determine the direction of the sound. The buzzing grew more intense to the southwest.

Walking towards the river on Jefferson, then making a right on Perrier, Roxanne practically ran into the sunset. The hum remained steady. At first, she thought she might be going the wrong way, but when she made a sudden turn to go back the other direction, the consistency of the hum started to fade. Roxanne turned back to the park. She continued on in whatever direction created an increased tone.

Not wanting to be cut off at the golf course, she headed south again to Magazine Street. Right when she hit the park, the sound beckoned from due south. The buzz got the loudest it had been when she reached a large round plot of earth covered with mosaic stones. She didn't really know its purpose, but she knew this must be the labyrinth. When she reached the center of the stones, the noise suddenly stopped completely, almost like it had swallowed itself. Looking around for a reason why, Roxanne was surprised to see someone else approaching the labyrinth, apparently looking for the source of the sound too. The new companion, a pretty black women in her late 40's or early 50's dressed in bohemian rags, had a finger in her ear, as though clearing it out. She looked as dumbfounded as Roxanne felt.

Both women instantly realized they were at the park for the same reason.

"Did ya hear dat too?" The black lady was not wary of strangers and was easy to speak. Her accent was tainted with a strong Cajun drawl.

"Yeah," Roxanne replied.

"Huh. Strange, in't it? Dat we two are da only people in N'awlins who chased down da sound?"

"Yeah, but surely others heard it too."

"Did ya hear it yestaday too? I heard it den, but couldn't chase it 'cuz I had to tend to my son."

"No, I didn't hear it yesterday. But my friend did, kind of, when we were over at Loyola."

"Ya'll were out here yestaday, by Audobon Park, in da evenin' time?"

"Yeah."

"You out here a lot?" she asked.

"Uh, no," admitted Roxanne. "I live in Metarie. I've only been here, like, twice, and both in the last two days."

There was nothing left to talk about, but the older woman continued. "Name's Jeanette, but everyone calls me Mama."

"Oh, uh, I'm Roxanne." They shook hands and the woman held on to her for an unusually long time. When she finally let go, the woman grinned and looked overly happy.

"I'm tinkin' dat I know why da sound called to me. But do you know why da sound called to you?"

"I'm not sure what you mean."

"Well, I bein' a voodoo mambo, I'm used to dealin' with da unexplained world. But you, do you know yo' gifts?"

Roxanne snickered. "Uh, I got a computer for Christmas." The woman was not amused by Roxanne's dismissive jest.

"Woman-chile', t'isnt funny."

The woman's lack of humor rattled Roxanne. "Um, I'm sorry. I didn't mean any disrespect. It's just, I personally don't believe in supernatural stuff."

The woman wrinkled her chin and nose. "Maybe not. Yet. But da power is in ya anyway. Udderwise, ya wouldn't be standin' here."

Roxanne remained politely incredulous. "No see, if that were true, I would have heard it yesterday and I didn't. Only my friend did. I mean, sort of. Well, she's deaf, and she actually felt a sound wave."

"How old are ya, girl?"

Roxanne had no idea why she answered the stranger's question truthfully. Maybe she was under a voodoo spell. "Eighteen."

"Still growin' den. No wonder t'aint constant yet."

"I'm not sure what you're talking about," peeped Roxanne hesitantly.

"Darlin', you are blessed with da gifts," exclaimed the woman.

She tried hard not to sound judgmental. "What gifts?"

"Some like mine. You got da gift of da spirit and da gift of da foreknowin'. But you got sometings I ain't got. You got da gift of healin', and of travelin'."

Lacking restraint, Roxanne made the inadvertent chuckle noise again.

The black lady's volume raised with seriousness. "Where we stand right now, do ya know da purpose of da labyrinth?"

"Um, no."

"Da labyrinth is a place of meditation. Learned folks walk its trail slowly and pray and tink as dey do. 'Tis a place for mystics. 'Tis precisely da type of place dat might call to da gifted."

Roxanne looked to the stones to avoid making eye contact with the woman.

"I heard da hum yestaday and today, and as long as yo' around, I'm bettin' I could hear da hum every day. See, I only hear it when you around it. It must be sometin' to do wit da travelin'."

A hum was actually a very good way to describe what Roxanne heard once the noise crystalized. But despite the woman's knowledge, Roxanne was uncomfortable. Her dad was super spooked by voodoo, and a bit of that fear had passed on to her. She wanted to get away from Mama but couldn't think of a good way to extricate herself from this conversation.

"Look, I'm not what you think. I'm just a plain old ordinary girl."

"Plain? Ah, couyon! Chile, you 'bout as plain as my daughta, who also has da gifts, but can't see tru' her stubbornness long enough to accept it. But dat's anutta story. Da only reason ya tink ya don't have the gifts is cause you ain't been a woman til naw. See, the powers of youngins have to be awakened by their hormones. While ya still growin' and yo' hormones are goin' tru ups and downs, da gifts ain't constant or controllable. If yo' like my son, da gifts come when ya feel excited by da sex. I'm guessin' dat yestaday and today, when da sound came, you was feelin' lust. Am I right?"

Roxanne was taken aback by the woman's audacious question and wasn't about to provide such personal information. Yet, she couldn't help but ponder that the hum did seem to correspond to seeing cute boys and being hit on by college guys.

Jeannette accepted the girl's silence as an admission. "Figured so. But don't worry. When yo' insides are all caught up wit yo' outsides, and you a full woman, you'll see I'm right and yo' mind will be open ta everyting. And maybe den, you come look for me. Look for Mama Gadreau. In da meantime, I'm gonna find a door for us to travel tru. I'm one with the loa and my gros-bon-ange is great, so I can find a door."

All Roxanne could do was smile and nod. Her lack of life experience rendered her incapable of handling the conversation gracefully, so she mentally rolled her eyes at all the "gift" mumbo jumbo.

"Naw, when I said you had da gift of being open-minded, woman-chile, I meant it. But as wit all gifts, da recipient must accept them. T'aint no mumbo jumbo."

What? Did that woman just read her mind? "How did you know what I was thinking?"

"Ah," said the mystical woman. "Now, you startin' to believe, ain't ya? One of my gifts is to read a person's mind like I'm readin' a book. And sometimes, I catch little glimpses of da futua. I'll prove it one mo' time. Ya got a way with da blind folk. Dey like ya and ya like dem and ya know how to treat dem so dey feel normal. Which is goin' to come in handy for yo love life latah." Roxanne must have looked as faint as she felt. The woman tried to be motherly towards her and her voice calmed.

"Look, beb, da reason da ancestors wanted us to meet today is so dat ya would learn to believe. Ya must accept da gifts and be open-minded fo' all time. One day, dere will come a moment when ya must be open to da world beyon' in order to be part of a very important journey. Da five udder folks ya gonna journey wit will need yo' gifts in order to fulfill a divine purpose. And wait, what's this?"

Jeanette stared into space for a moment, at first startled, and then resolved. "Looks like me and my kin gonna need you too. Well, ain't dat interestin'."

Roxanne could never label the feeling that possessed her just then, but all cares melted away as she began to believe that she did have a unique purpose in life.

"Naw," said the woman. "Ya be lookin' like ya got da mal au couer. I suggest ya get on home. And don't be scared of yo' gifts, Roxanne. Dey are a blessin'." With that, Mama Gadreau winked and walked away.

There wasn't a day that followed that Roxanne didn't think about the voodoo woman's prognostications. They made her feel a mix of excitement and shame. Where before, she had been the "normal" one among the different, now, she was more different than any of them. That's why, to Bridget, Roxanne reported that she heard nothing on her St. Charles trolley trip.

*****

"What time is it?" Gunnar asked Roxanne as he slid off his jeans. The minor headache starting to brew from lack of sleep and overindulgence in sugar told him it was past time for bed.

"2:20 in the morning," Roxanne said as her voice trailed off into a yawn. Gunnar could hear her slipping off her jeans too.

With Astrid and Brian asleep on the other side of the house, Gunnar reached for the comforter on the guestroom bed. Falling onto the mattress and clumsily pulling the cover to his neck, he was mere seconds from passing out. But there was unfinished business.

"Now that we're alone, what were you going to tell me about the vardoger?" Roxanne prodded.

He exhaled with reluctance, having hoped she would have been too tired to talk. She must not have had as much to drink as he hoped. "You promise you won't think I'm crazy?" Gunnar asked warily.

"Try me," she replied.

"Well, it all started the day we met. That morning, I was walking in the street when someone told me to stop dead in my tracks. I did, and I somehow managed to avoid getting killed by a falling billboard. Then, later in the day, someone told me to go to an ally and save a girl, which turned out to be you. Now today, that same person warned me that my pregnant sister was about to fall off a ladder and that I needed to block the fall with my own body to prevent the loss of the baby. All of these things were told to me in advance of them actually happening. And all of them were told to me by a person that sounds exactly like me who says he is me."

He expected a big dramatic scene as she called him daft and broke it off. His expectations were unmet. Roxanne was silent for a few minutes. Finally, she commented. "Huh. Do you think it was you that's been warning you?"

Her matter-of-fact attitude surprised him but also put him at ease. "At first, I didn't know. I wondered if I had a twin brother out there somewhere, which is complete nonsense. But now that Astrid has explained what a vardoger is, I mean, if it's real, it makes sense that the person warning me actually could be me from the future."

"So, you were really asking about the vardoger for your own sake and not your mother's?"

"Truly, yes. But the word "vardoger" did come out my mum's mouth shortly before she died, so now I'm anxious to know more about it for both reasons."

"Well, if we're going to find out more about the vardoger tomorrow, we better get some sleep," she said with a peck to his cheek. She snuggled her head into him, intertwining her legs with his. All was silent again and a prime environment for passing out, but it was now Gunnar who couldn't let something go.

"Roxanne, I just have to know. Why are you so casual about this? I mean, you're completely cool with something that makes no sense. What I told you isn't even a natural possibility. What is it about

174

your past that makes you capable of dealing with this so well?"

She breathed heavy and her voice was barely a whisper. She was clearly falling asleep, but had enough breath to say, "Nothing is stranger than me."

He would have pressed further, but a slight snore escaped Roxanne's lips at the tail end of that sentence. Gunnar relaxed into the smell of Roxanne's smooth hair and he remembered nothing thereafter.

The next morning, the sound of a distant honking horn roused him. His nose was still firmly planted into the peach shampoo that had led him to comfort the night before. Hesitant to pull away from this wonderful moment, his arms snuggled tighter around Roxanne's stomach. The movement woke her.

"It's bright in here," she said sleepily.

That was one thing Gunnar didn't have to worry about, as bright light wasn't going to make a difference to him one way or the other. "Hangover, love?"

She exhaled and the scent of last night's toothpaste covering last night's beer wafted past his nose. "No, I feel fine. I was just noticing the sun's up high, so it must be late morning."

"What time is it?"

She moved to her left. "It's 1:30 in the afternoon! What happened to Astrid waking us up to go to Oxford?"

They dressed quickly, and Gunnar opened the bedroom door to call for Astrid. "Wait, there's a note on the door," said Roxanne. Gunnar felt along the door towards the sound of flapping paper and pulled it from the tape. He handed it Roxanne, as Astrid had obviously expected her to read it.

"Her colleague couldn't come until after lunch, so she decided not to wake us. She went in early to grade papers. She says to come whenever we wake up if it's not too late in the afternoon."

"It was nice of her to let us sleep, but getting there is going to be a pain now," Gunnar complained. "It's going to take a while, so we'd better get going."

In the whirlwind of tardiness, Gunnar forgot to ask Roxanne about her cryptic last sentiment of the night before.

While Astrid's home in Beaconsfield was closer in proximity to Oxford then Sheen, the only practical way to get there was by car, as Astrid did. Gunnar had wanted to appear fresh when he met Astrid's colleague, as looking frazzled coupled with his story was going to make him seem all the more crazy. Thus, they opted for an Uber instead of the train trek.

The smell of Astrid's office was familiar to Gunnar. A coffee odor lingered from her morning cup. This barely covered a dingy damp paper smell that came from old books stacked here and there on crowded shelves, mixed with the slight scent of her flowery perfume. Making his way to the sofa that faced his sister's voice, he felt the worn yarn quilt he had sat on many times.

"Sorry we're so late," said Gunnar as he melted into the unsupportive cushions of the old sofa. "We only woke up about an hour ago."

"Lucky you." Gunnar heard in Astrid's voice the exasperation of someone who was awake against their will.

"Morning after the night before, old girl?" Gunnar asked playfully.

His sister snapped back, but with good humor. "Shut it, you wanker. Never, ever let me drink that much again. I don't know what could be worse than this hangover." Then, her tone changed quickly to embarrassment. "Oh, I'm sorry, Gunnar. That was insensitive."

"Well, I'll forgive you if you tell me what you found out about the vardoger."

Astrid exhaled deeply. "I did a bit of research in some of these books and only came up with a passage that pretty much reiterates what I told you last night."

Gunnar was disappointed. "I was rather hoping for a more in-depth explanation."

"Gunnar, why all this fascination now with something Mum said ages ago?" Astrid queried. "She's been dead a long time, and if her final words were going to cause you curiosity, you'd think you would've done some research before now."

He was hesitant to let his sister in on his secret, but figured that since Roxanne took it so well, perhaps his little sister would be as receptive. "Yesterday, before you fell off the ladder, a voice told me to move to the very position where you landed. It wasn't just a voice. It was me. I told myself to move there. I think I had an encounter with my vardoger."

He had placed too much faith in his sister. She snickered. "Don't be silly! That's impossible."

Defensively, he scolded Astrid's narrow mind. "I thought you were a Liberal Arts academic and not some stuffy scientist. Aren't you supposed to give credence to the possibilities of myths?"

"Just because I teach history and not science doesn't mean I'm prone to flights of fancy. There still needs to be some empirical evidence that something exists for me to believe it."

Carelessly inserting herself into a sibling spat, Roxanne interrupted. "If you can't tell us more about the vardoger, what about your friend?"

"My friend?" said Astrid. "Oh, you mean Arthur. Dr. Arthur Snow. I wouldn't really call him a friend, he's more of a professional acquaintance. Anyway, he's an expert in pretty much everything, including all things weird. Aside from just his academic interest in myths, he is also known to be a connoisseur of the paranormal."

"Great," said Roxanne. "When can we meet him?"

Astrid made a quick call, then said, "He's ready for us. He's right down the hall. Before we get there though, just a heads up that he's a bit, socially inept."

"What does he look like?" Gunnar always liked to get a picture in his head of any voice he was about to hear.

His sister thought for a moment. "Way shorter than you, probably my height, maybe 5'5-ish? He's got brownish-black hair, with lots of gray, and it's kind of curly. I think he's around 50 or 55. He's got a beard and mustache, but short and not very well grown in, also dark brown with lots of gray in it. His eyes look gray to me. And, I really don't know a better way to put this without sounding offensive, so thankfully, he's not here, but he kind of looks, and acts, like a middle-aged Christmas elf. Can you picture that?"

"Yes, I see it," Gunnar responded. "He must be a character."

He heard Astrid exhale with a chirp. "He is. But be prepared for this to be a long conversation, because the man, while brilliant, rambles and talks in circles sometimes."

Soon enough, the trio was in a different office fifty-two steps straight down the hall, and new sounds filled his ears. In the background was a small fan set on low whose turning blades flickered in time to white noise rhythms of a computer monitor. He could also hear the crinkling of a thick tweed-like fabric as it rose from a creaky wooden chair.

"Astrid, good to see you! And this must be your brother Gunnar and his friend Roxanne?" The voice was a little high pitched for a man and quintessentially the Queen's proper English.

Gunnar extended his hand not knowing which way to direct the handshake, and a slightly effeminate grip took his own with a small jerk. After their hands parted, he heard Roxanne shake hands with the man too and imagined even her dainty grasp could hurt Dr. Snow's fragile fingers. Meanwhile, as Dr. Snow focused on Roxanne, Gunnar took in the smells. This office had a very strong and distinct odor, though Gunnar could not place it quite yet.

With a posh but wispy voice, the academic said, "So, your sister tells me you are interested in the vardoger. I'm just curious of course, but why would you be interested in that? I mean, it's such an obscure piece of mythology, you might be the only person aside from my doctoral students who has ever heard of the phenomenon."

Having just been rebuffed by his sister, Gunnar was about to fib to Dr. Snow when Astrid beat him to the punch with the truth draped in sarcasm. "My brother here thinks he met his vardoger last night when he was told by an unseen presence to save me from a fall."

Gunnar did not appreciate the snicker coming from the learned gentlemen. "Oh, I really doubt that."

"Why?" Gunnar queried.

"Well, you'd be dead right now, wouldn't you?"

Gunnar was confused and Roxanne must have been too, as she was the one that asked for clarification.

"Why would he be dead?" she asked on his behalf.

The strange man fluttered on. "The vardoger is a staple of Den Gamle Tro, as your ancestors would say. The old beliefs. Many

Scandinavians claim to have *heard* their loved ones coming through the door before they do, or speaking to them before they've walked into the room. Yes, hearing them is quite common. Seeing them though—that's where you get into a bit of controversy among scholars. Some paranormalists believe that a vardoger is a completely neutral spirit and seeing or hearing it has no impact. Others though regard the vardoger as an omen of impending death, like the doppelganger. See, the Vikings encountered vardogers before there was a German word "doppelganger," so they may be one in the same being, and they could both be announcements of doom. I'm tempted to agree with the latter theory. I believe the two words are just culturally specific synonyms for the same being. So I wager if one were to see their vardoger, or doppelganger, one would suffer death in quick haste. Of course, I could always be wrong. Many paranormal researchers conversely feel the vardoger is just a mechanism of bilocation. And we could all, in fact, be incorrect if hard science is right,

184

as neurologists think it's all just left temporoparietal junction stimulation. So, there you go." The man let out a wheezing chuckle as he caught his breath.

Rambling was an understatement. Still though, Gunnar caught just enough of the speech to understand. "So, the vardoger might not be in my head? It's possibly a real being?"

Seemingly embarrassed, Astrid tried to cut short the conversation. "Well, thanks Dr. Snow. Forgive my brother, he's . . . "

"He's simply intriguing!" said Dr. Snow with admiration.

"Come on, Arthur," challenged Astrid. "Please don't tell me you give any credence to myths like this."

"The birthplace of myth is the truth, Astrid. You know that."

His sister silenced, Gunnar asked, "Do you think it's possible I did visit with my vardoger yesterday, even though it didn't kill me?"

Dr. Snow's proper speech seemed to whistle from between his teeth. "I need to know more to render an opinion. Tell me everything."

Dr. Snow's sincere curiosity put Gunnar at ease. Roxanne already knew the whole story, and he felt safe with her in the room. But Astrid's presence made him hesitate. He just couldn't say what he came there to say in front of his judgmental sister.

"Um, Astrid. Is there any tea around? I'd love a cup and it's pretty much tea time."

"You don't want tea, you want to get rid of me!" Astrid's tone was shrill and accusatory.

"No, it's not that . . . "

His sister was audibly upset. "There is no tea, not in this office, not in this building, not at this University, not in the whole bloody United Kingdom right now."

Dr. Snow interrupted. "You know, if you're thirsty, I do have orange juice. I simply love oranges. I've got a whole bucket full and I keep it right here in my office. Right along with a juicer. Nothing like a fresh squeezed juice!"

Yes, that was the smell Gunnar couldn't place. Incredible amounts of citrus, with a slightly acrid overtone of perhaps orange rinds rotting away in the rubbish bin.

Astrid calmed down a bit during the divergence into oranges, but had not forgotten the conversation. "You apparently have something to say that you think I can't hear, and that hurts me. Gunnar, I always want to be someone you can be honest with."

"You don't make that easy when you're criticizing me."

Dr. Snow's wheezy, whistling, androgynous voice interrupted. "Um, I really don't like conflict and the back and forth berating is like acid to my nervous system. Either bicker somewhere else and let me get back to reading and drinking my lovely orange juice, or tell me about your encounter."

There was a tense moment of silence as the siblings silently buried the hatchet. It was now or never to get the answers he hoped for, and Gunnar was just going to have to deal with Astrid after the fact. He recounted for Dr. Snow every detail since the moment he saved himself from the falling sign. He hoped Roxanne didn't mind him sharing the details of their unfortunate meeting, but she made no moves to stop him.

At the end of his story, the elfish man let out a happy squeal and spoke again in a few longwinded breaths. "So very interesting. Yours is a unique story in all of vardoger or doppelganger lore. As I said, authority is split on the vardoger being evil or benign. But no one has ever supposed it could be benevolent. Any recountings of supposed conversations with vardogers describe a few passing words of no consequence, but never lengthy dialogues where the spirit being and natural being are aware of each other's presence. And then of course, there is the mythos of imminent death if you see your spirit double, which you may have busted." Gunnar heard a few seconds of finger pad tapping on wood, then a sudden loud outburst of, "Riddle solved!" The professor sounded delighted. "In agreement with my original hypothesis, one only experiences death upon *seeing* the vardoger, not *hearing* the vardoger or *talking* with it. Since you cannot see, you may actually be being protected by your blindness."

Gunnar heard a dismissive sign from Astrid. For her sake, Gunnar interrupted. "To be fair Dr. Snow, is it possible that this whole thing is just temporo-whatever brain stimulation?"

"There's only one way to find that out, isn't there. Evidence. I suggest you carry a recorder of some kind with you and if you speak with your vardoger again, record it. Or maybe have someone else verify the vardoger's existence by watching you around the clock to see if the vardoger returns."

Astrid interjected. "But this thing supposedly only happens when he or someone else is in danger."

Another whistly chuckle revealed that Dr. Snow thought the answer was obvious. "Okay. Put yourself in danger and see what happens."

"That's enough," exclaimed Astrid. "Arthur, thank you for your time. It's getting late and I'm sure you have plans tonight, so we'll let you get back to doing whatever it was you were doing."

"Well, yes, I do have some plants at home that need watering," said Dr. Snow lightly. "But please, I'm simply fascinated. Kindly let me know if you have any more encounters. I do adore all things supernatural."

All three arose, took their leave with respectful goodbyes, and retired back down the hall to Astrid's office. "I've got to drop something off in the main hall," said Astrid. "I'll be right back and then we can go."

Astrid's no-nonsense voice directed, "Roxanne, would you mind keeping an eye on my brother for a little bit?"

"My eyes are always on him," Roxanne said flirtatiously.

Gunnar heard papers rustle then the door shut. He felt the sofa cushions melting between Roxanne and himself as she scooted closer to him.

"I don't think your sister likes the idea of you being in harm's way," she said.

"Really? Whatever gave you that idea?" he asked playfully.

"Are you thinking of putting yourself in danger to meet your vardoger again? If I have a vote, I say you don't. Let me do it instead. The vardoger came before when I was in danger. I'm sure it will come again. And that way, you'll be safe."

He was incensed by her suggestion. "Absolutely not! There is no way I'd chance you getting hurt."

She grabbed his hand in hers. "Gunnar, I promise you that no harm would come to me. I'll escape any danger just fine."

"Like you could have escaped those wankers that were going to kill you? No one is invincible, no matter how strong they think they are."

She was silent for a moment, probably pondering whether or not to forgive his callousness. Shockingly, she didn't seem too upset with him when she did speak. "I can't explain it, Gunnar, but I know for a fact that the only damage those guys could have done to me that day would have been emotional. I would have been physically fine. Not that I'm not eternally grateful that you were there to rescue me, but even if you hadn't been, well, I would have lived. And just like I know that I would have been okay then, I know I will be okay now if placed in a situation designed for you to meet your vardoger."

He thwarted her proposal. "Look, neither of us has to go anywhere near danger for me to see the vardoger again. I think all we need to do is go to your flat."

"Why my flat?"

"The last time the voice talked to me, it said I should go home with you and he and I would meet again there."

"Do you want to see if Astrid will drop us off at my apartment then?"

"Yes, let's."

Astrid was a little put out, but drove out of her way to get to Roxanne's flat. Upon entering her small apartment, Gunnar felt uneasy. "I'm not exactly sure when he's supposed to make contact; he didn't say. And I don't know if I have to be alone for him to talk to me. I don't know if you can see him, or if you seeing him will be bad for me or you."

"Tell you what. Why don't we order some food, and I'll go pick it up. That will give you a chance to meet him again if he does exist and I can't be around for it."

Roxanne was kind enough to take the long way to a pizza restaurant, giving him a whole hour to sit there and wait like a fool for nothing. No contact. Gunnar stayed over at Roxanne's that night, and the next night, and the next, with not a peep from his vardoger. By the next weekend, with no word from the voice, Gunnar was about ready to jump in front of traffic to entice the vardoger into action. But a pressing work matter came up before Gunnar could be impulsive.

The pair had finally decided to spend the night at Gunnar's, giving up on the vardoger appearing at Roxanne's apartment, when Gunnar got a call from a record company on Friday. A.J. Rhodes was giving a charity concert in America, in New Orleans, in a week, and he specifically asked that Gunnar do sound for the gig. Walking into his flat to the aroma of Roxanne cooking dinner, he couldn't wait to share the news with his girlfriend.

"That smells fantastic. Garlic?"

"Garlic bread. That and some lasagna."

"Sounds wonderful. How close is it to being done?"

"I'd say about ten minutes."

"Good. That's ten minutes for me to share some news."

"What's going on?"

"You remember A.J. Rhodes?"

"I never did get to meet him, but of course I know who you're talking about."

"Well, he's doing a benefit concert in the States, and he wants me to run sound. I want you to come with me, if you can."

"The new terms doesn't start until mid-September, so of course I can go! That's so cool! Do we get to go backstage?"

"Absolutely! And I will personally introduce you to A.J. this time. Not a bad bloke, that one."

"How exciting! This is awesome. So where in the U.S. is it?"

"New Orleans."

"Oh my God, no way! That is amazing! You'll get to meet my parents. This is perfect."

"Your parents?"

"Yeah. I can't believe in these couple of weeks together, I never told you that I'm from New Orleans. You're gonna be going home with me."

Both of them went from elation to eerie recognition.

"You don't think . . . ?" Roxanne didn't even finish her sentence.

"I do think. Perhaps the vardoger meant he would see me at your home in the States. You know, I wasn't going to have us leave until Wednesday, but maybe we should go earlier. I mean, it may take some time to meet your parents and . . . "

"And maybe talk to the vardoger?"

Gunnar nodded with a small smile. "How quickly can you pack?"

He heard levity in her heavenly voice. "How soon can you get plane tickets?"

By early Sunday morning, the pair was waiting in the lounge at Heathrow. Roxanne had called her folks, who were beyond excited that she was coming home for a visit and bringing a guy. To Gunnar's dismay, Roxanne hadn't informed them that he was a decade older than her or lacking all five senses, relying instead on the fact that her parents were "pretty cool" and would "totally love him." They were set to meet at the New Orleans airport in ten hours, and Gunnar was fighting off nervousness. Meanwhile, Gunnar had talked to A.J.'s manager, who begged him to greet A.J. at the airport and hang out with him every waking minute until the show. Apparently, A.J. told his manager that Gunnar was his only chance to stay sober and he wouldn't leave rehab without Gunnar's support. To entice Gunnar's cooperation, the desperate record company was sparing no expense to make sure Gunnar had anything he wanted.

Gunnar was thankful to have the luxury of first class seating paid for by A.J.'s record company—the fewer steps through a crowded plane the better. It was also more private and conducive to conversation. Just after reaching 10,000 feet and receiving champagne service, Gunnar decided it was time to learn more about the woman he loved. After all, he wanted to be able to pass any quiz given by the parents. "We've know each other a little over three weeks now, and I still feel like I barely know the Roxanne that existed before coming to London. Tell me more about her."

She grabbed his hand. "Well, it all started when Yara met Gerry in 1987. He was a newly minted public defender dissatisfied with his chosen profession. She was, at the time, putting herself through nursing school by translating Portuguese and Spanish for the court system. He needed her services one day to communicate with a client at an arraignment. At some point in the conversation, the client got mad at my dad's advice, but took it out on the person communicating the message. When the client tried to strike my mother, my dad risked his job by pushing the guy away and calling for the bailiff. After court, my mom literally staked out the exit from the courthouse, waiting to thank my dad. She found him, they talked for a bit, he invited her out for lunch, and they got married three months later. So you see, the depth of our affection despite the brevity of our relationship is not going to be a problem for them."

Listening to the courtship of her parents, much of Roxanne's own behavior was explained. Just as her mother had fallen for her rescuer, so too had this girl fallen for the man that saved her. He did not interrupt with his observation.

"Two years later, I was born. According to Mom, who is quite tiny as you will see, the birth was complicated, so I never had any siblings. But that was okay because I always had a ton of friends. I grew up in Algiers in a little neighborhood called Park Timbers, which thankfully withstood Katrina. My parents still live there and that's where we're spending the night."

He could tell from the lofty rises and falls of her tone that she enjoyed recounting her youth. "My dad now owns his own firm and does primarily construction defect law, which he still hates, but at least he's his own boss and the firm is so successful it grew nationally. My mom's been a pediatric ICU nurse forever."

"What did they think of you becoming an architect?" asked Gunnar.

"They were thrilled I chose an actual career. As you know, I'm a little late starting grad school a twenty-eight. That's because I didn't go to college right away. I was prepared to go college right out of high school and decide by the end of my freshman year what I wanted to do with my life, but then, in my junior year of high school, the desire hit that I wanted to help my fellow man, particularly the disabled. All I wanted to do was volunteer and maybe go into social work later on down the line. My folks were awesome about it and told me I could do whatever I wanted and take my time thinking about college. So, I started volunteering at lots of places—the Deaf Action Center, Arc, the Miracle League, the Lighthouse for the Blind, and during the summers I was a counselor at a place called the Louisiana Lions Camp."

"Wait a tick!" His brow furrowed. In three weeks, she had never mentioned her benevolence or the fact that she had significant experience with disability. "Do you mean to say that you've had experience with blindness before me?"

She chuckled the same sweet laugh he first fell in love with. "Tons."

He was strangely offended. "Well, I suppose that explains why you're with me. You have a history of taking pity on the less fortunate."

Her voice became serious. "My experience is why I didn't freak out when you wanted to feel my face the first time we met. It's also why I've been able to adjust so easily to things like you counting steps. But it's precisely my experience that makes it so I don't pity you. I stopped feeling sorry for the disabled or thinking of them as less fortunate long ago. You act like I love you despite your blindness, when it's actually one of the many things I love about you. You know, you put off to the world that you are capable and okay with being blind, but I don't really think you are."

He quietly contemplated for a moment. "It's not that I'm blind that bothers me, it really isn't. It's just that it was preventable and I did it to myself that irks me."

"You need to forgive yourself," she said tenderly. "Mainly because you didn't actually do it to yourself. That guy Rob is the one to blame. There is a reason for everything, including why you made the choice and a reason for the consequence. Who knows, maybe if you had your sight, you'd have married someone else long before we ever got a chance to meet?"

She was right, and his mother had known it. He had to make the choices he made to get to the future that she foresaw. Though he missed seeing the sun, the moon, the trees, and the city, he knew he'd rather have Roxanne than visions of those things. "Roxanne, you are more than I could have ever asked for. To be completely accepted is a blessing."

She squeezed his hand. "I don't ever want to hear you say again that being with you has anything to do with mercy." She stopped and took a deep breath. "Because I don't want you to ever stay with me out of mercy."

Perplexed, his forehead crumpled. "What on earth would I need to be merciful about?"

She was very cautious that no one else could hear her speak and he felt her move very close to him. He felt hot breath in his ear as she whispered. "The reason the vardoger doesn't bother me, and the reason I've feared *you* might decide to leave *me*, is because, well . . . I've got a gift. I can see and hear things that no one else can. Ever since I was eighteen."

He didn't know how to process the information, so he just sat there, calm and quiet. Had this conversation occurred two months ago, he probably would have extricated himself from Roxanne. But how could he possibly assign her a label of crazy now that he had encountered the unexplainable? It would be unfair not to accept her baggage if she was accepting his. He gulped, then sighed. "Admittedly, I am curious. What exactly do you mean?"

She continued, barely audible. "When I was eighteen, I heard a strange sound that brought me to a park in New Orleans. I met a woman who was called by the sound as well. She told me I had supernatural gifts. I didn't believe her at first, but then a few weeks later, I had a nightmare about a ten-car pile-up on the I-10. The next morning, that accident happened. A few more weeks after that, I dreamed about an Air France plane crash the night before it occurred. And after that, I dreamt about Michael Jackson's death, the Fort Hood massacre, and the Haitian earthquake. I saw them all before they happened. Interspersed of course with smaller things, like neighborhood thefts, local businesses going bankrupt, and that sort of thing."

Gunnar was perplexed. "If you can see the future when you sleep, why didn't you just avoid that ally with those two guys the day I met you?"

She exhaled. "Sadly, I've never been able to foretell my own future. I couldn't have predicted those assholes would threaten me any more than I can predict winning lottery numbers."

The average person would certainly disbelieve such wild anecdotes, but he trusted Roxanne so implicitly that the only thing he felt was fascination.

"Of course," she continued, "last week, the night before we met in fact, I dreamed that A.J. Rhodes committed suicide, and that didn't end up happening. So maybe I'm losing my touch."

He smiled. "No, you're not. He was going to commit suicide. The day I took you to the studio and left you for a bit, A.J. had a gun in his hand when I walked into the lounge. I stopped him from doing it."

He heard a whistle come from her lips. "Wow. Spooky."

"Roxanne, this whole thing is bloody spooky. Your abilities, my vardoger. I don't know how we could possibly be a more odd couple."

"You mean, a more perfect suited couple," she corrected sweetly.

CHAPTER SEVEN

Voodoo Chile'

*****

In a beautiful old house on New Orleans' famed St. Charles Avenue, a woman on a mission ordered, "Chill'ins, gadder 'round. Mama's gonna show you how we gonna get rid of dat silly tax man. Acadia, go get the cat. Alphonse, bring me da honey from da kitchen."   The twins did what they were told—Alphonse because he never defied Mama and Acadia because she was as curious as a hungry alligator at an airboat crash.

The ten-year olds watched with fascination as their mother mixed in a glass the jimson weed they weren't allowed to touch with honey and something that smelled like week-old rotten eggs. They watched as Mama's eyes fluttered and she dazedly rubbed the glass along the side of their cat's fur. Then they both eyed each other with disgust as their mother drank the smelly substance.

"Dat oughta do it," said Mama, wiping the residue from her lips. "Naw we can go to bed wit no worries. Ain't no way dat IRS man is comin' to audit me tomorra'."

And sure enough, he didn't.

Mama Gadreau was no Marie Laveau, though she played up the rhyming of their surnames to capitalize on the legendary voodoo queen's reputation. Still, she was powerful enough to be feared and prominent enough to know everybody in New Orleans. And just as she was begrudgingly accepted by the locals, so too were her offspring.

Mama had, back in 1985, desired a wealthy white man. He didn't desire her, partly because he was married and partly because he was racist, but his lack of fancy disappeared with one of Mama's spells and soon he had not only bedded Mama, but impregnated her too. Mama promised a scandal if he refused a generous monthly stipend as hush-hush child support, and shortly after their birth in 1986, the mother and her twin newborns were able to leave their hovel in the bayou and move into a Garden District mansion. Mama never identified their father despite the children's constant pressing, and after decades of questions, both children finally gave up on figuring out who their father was. Nonetheless, the twins never felt stigmatized by their mixed race or mystery background because in New Orleans, voodoo commands respect.

Alphonse and Acadia could not have been any more different, their genders being only one of the things that set them apart. Alphonse was his mother's son, clinging to her words and obeying her every command. Acadia was rebellious and would often test her mother's boundaries. At ten years old, this meant not doing the dishes when she was told or not eating everything on her plate. But as she became a teenager, and then a young adult, Acadia disobeyed in more pronounced ways. While a priestess-in-training was meant to be spiritual, Acadia grew increasingly secular, wanting to be popular and the prom queen. Where voodoo daughters wore plane white dresses, Acadia dressed in the trendiest fashions. She borrowed designer jeans from school friends, spent her allowance on expensive shoes, and straight-permed her naturally kinky black hair. Where voodoo children believed in magic, she believed in what she read in psychology books. By the time she graduated high school, Acadia had rationalized that "magic" was only a manifestation of the fear people had for the occult.

Alphonse, on the other hand, believed in magic strongly. Under Mama's tutelage, he was grooming to become a houngan and thought his twin sister's rejection of her natural role of mambo was a disgrace. The two sparred often, especially when Acadia would sneak home having forgotten to wipe away her lipstick or change out of her mini-shirt. Initially, Mama would break up the spats with praise for her son and a disappointed shaking of the head towards her daughter. Eventually, Mama stopped showing her disapproval, which irritated Alphonse. Mama simply reminded him that one cannot be forced to believe, and that there would come a day when Acadia would come face to face with the supernatural realm whether she wanted to or not and could no longer deny it.

This kept Alphonse quiet, for a while. But the barrage of insults resumed worse than ever after Mama disappeared on a blistering hot August day in 2008. Alphonse and Acadia had not two weeks before celebrated their twenty-second birthdays, Alphonse with a voodoo ritual overseen by Mama and Acadia with an extravaganza at a jazz club on Bourbon Street. Alphonse still lived at their Garden District home under the watchful eye of Mama. Acadia's official address was at the house, but she typically crashed at friend's houses after long nights of partying. The last time that Acadia saw her mother was on a night when she'd elected to sleep in her own bed at home.

It was just after sunset. Acadia was reading in the library that was used mostly as a voodoo supply warehouse. Alphonse, as usual, ignored her and went about his business cooking up something putrid in the kitchen. She heard the front door burst open and her mother cheerfully scream, "Alphonse!" Her reading enjoyment was interrupted as her mother burst into the library, feverishly looking for something on each shelf.

Alphonse came running. "Mama, what is it?"

"Chile', I just had an amazin' esperience. I don't know what t'was dough. It's mystifyin' me."

"What happened?" Alphonse asked. Acadia was clearly excluded from the conversation, but her presence in the room allowed her to hear every word of the discussion.

"I was out and about and I heard dis strange noise. T'was like a screech and den like da emergency sound on da TV. It lasted a real long time, long enough fo' me to track da source. And it took me to da labyrinth in Audubon Park. Den it stopped. And right dere was dis beige girl touched with the gifts."

Acadia was pretty sure her eyes rolled and she tried to escape back into her book, but Alphonse's excitement made it impossible.

"Wow, Mama. Was she a mambo?"

"Nah. T'was different magic den what we know, someting I never seen befoe'. I tell you, this woman-chile' got no idea who she is or what she can do. She's a clairvoyant, like me, but her hormones ain't fully awake yet so she ain't had da visions. She got a healin' touch too, but she don't know it yet. What makes her really special dough is dat she has da power to open doors to udder places. She can find out all the secrets of the universe."

"I wish I would have seen it too," said Alphonse, free of any Cajun accent. While Mama could barely be understood sometimes, Alphonse and Acadia's schooling had taught them proper pronunciation.

By this time, her reading enjoyment stifled, Acadia would do anything to get her family out of the library. "What are you looking for Mama? If you tell us, maybe Alphonse and I can help you find it."

"Somewhere in dis mess, I got me a book about da sounds of da universe. I tink da sound dat brought to me to da labyrinth might be talked about in dere."

The trio feverishly searched for an hour, but could not find the book Mama sought. It was getting late when Mama finally sat in a chaise and put her hands up. "Ah well. Don't matta. I'll just get up tomorra' and go to da spiritual book shop. I'll be goin' to bed den. Night chill'ins."

Mama left for the new age bookstore early the next morning, but never returned from it. Alphonse searched feverishly for his mother for months, casting all kinds of spells and holding nightly rituals asking for sight from the loa. He was never granted the knowledge of Mama's whereabouts.

After months of failure, Alphonse turned on Acadia. At first, he would ignore her and cast

214

fuming looks. But one night, Acadia said something innocuous about Mama and Alphonse lost it. He blamed her immersion into secular culture for Mama's desire to leave her children. He ransacked her room, throwing her clothes out of her window onto the lawn. He demanded she move out and take her ungrateful, unspiritual ways with her. She yelled back, slammed her door, and went to bed. The next morning, she awoke to the smell of sulfur. Upon investigation, she found the yolk of a rotten egg running down her bedroom door with broken shells on the ground with her name written on them. Fearful he would escalate from stupid superstitions to physical violence, she decided to oblige her abusive brother and move out.

Angry and wishing she had been a singleton, she started packing. Thankfully, Alphonse wasn't there, allowing her to leave in peace. As she walked down the stairs and headed for the front door, she spied an envelope with her name on it sitting by a vase at the base of the steps. Opening it, her feelings about her brother became complicated again.

There were one hundred $100 dollar bills, along with a note.

Sister,

After our fight yesterday, I found the book that Mama was talking about that night before she left. I think I know where she is, or at least how to find her. I am leaving to search for her. It's going to take money to travel, so I am cleaning out the bank account. But, I don't wish to leave you completely empty handed. Enclosed is $10,000 to get you by until you find a job. The house is yours until we return. I reversed the go-away spell I cast last night, but you may want to cleanse the house with some black salt. I brought in all of your things I threw out last night- they are piled in the library. My deepest wish is that while we are gone, you will come to embrace the magic ways of our family. And if you won't accept voodoo, at least be open to magic, so that when Mama returns, she can be proud of us both.

Alphonse

She was furious that Alphonse had taken all the family's money and left her with a pittance in comparison, as she didn't like the idea of having to get a job when she had been so spoiled with free luxury up to now. At least he had left her some money, which after last night's feud was surprising. And she had the house, which for the time being was all hers.

It stayed all hers for eight years. Over that time, Acadia had matured. She had worked at a clothing store right after Alphonse left, then moved to Los Angeles for a few months to try her luck at acting. As the $10,000 started to dwindle and Alphonse and Mama had not yet returned, she knew she needed a real job. With the money that was left, she moved back home and put herself through paralegal school. After graduating, she obtained gainful employment with a decent salary, working for a fair and honest attorney who, despite his loathing of his own profession, was a generous boss. She got Christmas bonuses, time off when she needed it, and was even invited to family dinners on occasion. Alphonse's leaving and removing her access to money was probably the best thing that had happened to her. The only thing absent from her life was a person who she could start a new family with. But what kind of man was going to accept an ex-voodoo princess with a crazy brother, a missing mother, and a secret desire to find the magic in herself that allegedly existed?

*****

Roxanne's parents could not have been nicer people. As promised, Gerry and Yara accepted Gunnar with open arms despite his blindness, his age, and his quick affections for their daughter. They were not as skilled as Roxanne at handling his disability, but they made every effort. They let Gunnar feel their faces, though Gerry started laughing. Yara continuously straightened and vacuumed, giving Gunnar no credit for being able to feel around clutter.

When Yara questioned how the two met, they were both ready with a prepared white lie designed to spare Roxanne's parents from worry.

He recounted how he was walking by Roxanne's flat and heard a noise that made him lose count of his steps. He had forgotten his white-tipped cane that day and was in need of help to get him to the tube station, where he could resume count. Luckily, a wonderfully helpful girl saw his predicament and offered assistance. They started talking about where he was going, and since Roxanne loved music, he offered to show her the studio. That turned into lunch, which turned into dinner, which turned into not leaving each other's side since. In turn, Gunnar got to hear the story of how Roxanne's parents met straight from the source, and though he could not see Gerry and Yara, he knew from the sounds of the crunching couch cushions that they were sitting very close together. He could also hear slight coos in their tones and knew they were still in love. Gunnar remembered how his parents were in love like this once.

Other tough questions followed. He had never met a girl's parents before in a dating situation and knew these must be common questions, but he wasn't entirely prepared to answer them.

"So, Gunnar, tells us about your parents," queried Gerry.

"Well," said Gunnar. "My father's name is Nils. He lives in London too. We don't see each other as often as I'd like. My mum, her name was Agneta, she passed away when I was seventeen."

He felt Roxanne's firm reassuring grasp on his hand and he heard a sympathetic "aww" from Yara.

"No, it's okay," he said to reassure Roxanne's mom that she was not dredging up bad memories. "It took a really long time to get over, I won't lie. But I am in a good place about it now."

The calmness in Yara's voice indicated he felt comfortable prodding Gunnar further. "Were you born blind?" she asked.

Gunnar couldn't admit the truth. He had never shied away from it before because he didn't really care if any of his conquests respected him or not. He did, however, care what his future in-laws thought of him. Again, he opted for a half-truth. "I didn't go blind until after my mum died. I had a bad reaction to an environmental toxin."

Gerry was curious. 'So, you mentioned a cane. We haven't seen you with it so far."

"I only need it in unfamiliar places when I'm alone. To and from work, and to places around my flat, I know every step and have mapped it out in my head. When it's time to walk across a street, most of the street signs are audible, and they tell me when it's safe to go. And when I'm with someone, they're usually kind enough to guide me."

Roxanne chuckled. "Yeah, I've been his seeing eye-dog the last few weeks."

He turned his head towards her. "Please don't ever say that. You're not a dog, and I would never treat you as such."

He felt a quick peck on his cheek and then Yara said, 'Well, I've seen all I need to see. It's clear you care for my daughter, and that's good enough for me. I think it's beautiful that you two are in love."

"And I'm very happy, too," Gerry announced. "But if we don't get some food soon, Crabby Gerry is going to battle Happy Gerry and win."

The rest of the night was wonderful but odd, as Gunnar got used to being part of a real family again. He was taken to the French Quarter for what surly was the best tasting meal of his life. "My paralegal recommended this place," Gerry mentioned to Gunnar in-between bites.

"You must thank her for me," Gunnar replied while licking chocolate mousse off his spoon.

Next, his hosts treated him to live jazz performed by street musicians. He could sense the electricity charging from person to person and the sense of history floating in the air. It was too bad there was an underlying stench of old trash, but he supposed it was worse to him than to others due to the sharpness of his sense of smell. Despite the stink, he was having the time of his life.

The next day saw more good food and good company.   Over breakfast, Roxanne's father wrestled Gunnar for details about working in the music industry, especially with Sting. By the last bite of his crepe, Gunnar had promised Gerry backstage passes to any concert where he worked the sound, including the sold-out A.J. Rhodes show. At lunch, Yara wanted to know every last detail about London, as she had never been to England. In a good mood from the most delicious shrimp he'd ever tasted, he also promised Yara a trip to the UK and himself as a personal tour guide. After another decadent and tasty dinner, it was Gunnar's turn to prod. As the four of them relaxed awaiting dessert, Gunnar decided to test the open-mindedness of his future in-laws.

"So, you know that there have long been myths in the music business about how some classic rock songs have hidden supernatural references in them. Are you believers in the supernatural?"

Yara was quick to jump in. "Oh, I am. I swear to you that I can see ghosts. Not all the time though. I can't see them if I want to or try to look for them, but when I least expect it, I'll see a figure out of the corner of my eye. If I look away, even for a just a second, it will be gone."

He heard Gerry's stifled laugh and mocking tone. "Yeah, my wife sees dead people."

"And my husband's a skeptic, which I think is an occupational hazard of being a lawyer," Yara said defensively. "Ever since I was nineteen, I could see them. It's actually quite frightening, but I also believe it's a gift to know that life exists after death. It takes some fear out of dying."

Was it a gift to see his vardoger? Certainly it was, given the fact that the vardoger had saved him, his love, his sister, and his friend. If he could just let go of the fear that he was going mad, maybe he too could embrace the strangeness as Yara did. Gunnar further prodded Roxanne's father. "So Gerry, are you a skeptic? Have you never experienced the paranormal?"

He was hesitant in his reply. "I wouldn't say that. I mean, I'm a native of New Orleans. I grew up here with all kinds of voodoo influence. Heck, my paralegal is the daughter of a voodoo queen. So, I'm sure there's something to it all. I just try to stay on the good side of voodoo and stay blissfully ignorant of anything else."

"What's your opinion of what Roxanne can do?" The instant he said it, Gunnar wished he could swallow the words back down. What if she had never told them about her visions?

"What do you mean?" queried Gerry.

Roxanne interjected quickly. "You know, how I can massage away your aches and pains like magic?"

Gunnar decided to keep quiet since Roxanne obviously hadn't told them about her abilities.

"Ah, yes. Magic fingers McCabe, that's what we call her. Has Roxanne given you a massage yet? I swear, she can make even the worst backache disappear with just the touch of her hands on your shoulders." Gerry's vocal inflection rose as if he were remembering a flashback. "Unfortunately, I always seem to get back rubs right when a case is going to hell and I get ticked off, so the relief doesn't last long and poor Roxanne never gets the credit due to her."

"Um, no, I haven't gotten a massage yet," Gunnar responded.

"Well, if you ever get a headache or backache, have Roxanne rub it out for you."

Her mother chimed in. "I suggested she try nursing to capitalize on her healing talents, but she didn't want to."

He felt nervous being outside of her lies to her parents and stayed silent, not wanting to blow another secret. Just then, a cell ringtone interrupted.

"That's odd," said Gerry. "What time is it?"

"10:30," answered Yara.

"Who'd be calling me this late on a Monday night?" Gunnar heard the rumple of leather as Roxanne's father rose. "Hello?" he said cautiously. Gunnar couldn't make out every word, but he knew that a frantic woman was on the other side of the call.

"Wait, wait. Hold on, now. Calm down." Gerry's voice grew fainter as he moved away from the living room. While the mother and daughter wondered who the caller could be, Gunnar used his super sharp hearing to listen in. Someone was in trouble, and Gerry was offering to come right over and help.

Gerry's voice returned to full volume when he was back in the room.

"Sorry about the interruption, ya'll. That was my paralegal, Acadia. I guess she and her brother had a fight and she's afraid to go back into the house. She left with no money, so she's stranded and walking the streets. I offered to pick her up and let her stay at our house tonight. It'll be a bit crowded, I hope ya'll don't mind."

"Of course she should come stay," said Yara. There wasn't an ounce of jealousy or hesitance in her supportive reply. Gunnar could tell that Acadia must be like a part of the family. "I'll go with you. Roxanne, Gunnar, why don't you stay here and make yourselves comfortable. We'll see you guys in the morning for breakfast."

With the parents gone, Gunnar and Roxanne decided to go to bed after a very long day of flying. As they undressed, Gunnar took the opportunity to apologize. "By the way, I'm sorry about bringing up the supernatural stuff. I wasn't aware that your parents didn't know about your visions."

"Oh, that's okay. You didn't know and I didn't tell you not to bring it up. I never told them because my dad gets a little skittish. He's so superstitious. He won't walk by cemeteries or black cats, and if you spill salt, he has a meltdown."

"He must be okay with it a little if he'll hire the daughter of a voodoo queen." Gunnar felt himself smile and let out a small chuckle as he said the last words in jest. He had always thought voodoo was fiction.

"Don't make fun, Gunnar. Voodoo is real around these parts, especially to my dad."

"So do you know this Acadia person?"

"No, I've never met her. My dad hired her after I went to London. I've seen pictures of her though, like at firm Christmas parties and stuff. I'm kind of glad you're blind so you can't see how pretty she is."

Gunnar jabbed at Roxanne lightly. "There could never be anyone is this world lovelier than you."

They kissed as they fell onto the bed. Kissing became caressing, caressing became stroking, and as usual, that's where it stopped. Roxanne still hadn't given Gunnar the go ahead for sex, and he didn't push it. Uncomfortably aroused, Gunnar stirred restlessly in Roxanne's arms late into the night.

Gunnar awoke at a time when he could sense no warmth from the sun. Nonetheless, the smell of brewing coffee told him someone was up. What really roused him though was a faint droning sound in his ear. It was so faint, no sighted person would have probably heard it. He tried to focus on the placement of the sound, but it seemed to be emanating from all around him. He put his fingers in his ears, trying to clear them, but the sound was still there. Eventually, the noise from Roxanne's dainty snoring and some sort of bug chirping outside the window drowned out the buzzing. Yet when he tried to return to slumber, the sound grew louder again. Since there was no chance of getting back to sleep, he decided to follow the smell of coffee.

In the two days since he had been at the Algiers house, he had memorized the number of steps it took to get from the bed to the kitchen table. He'd also learned the pattern of progress was forward ten steps, left fourteen steps, another left thirty-one steps, and then right four steps. Still, he felt along the wall, just to be safe.

"Oh!" As he drew close to the table, an unfamiliar female voice was surprised by his presence.

"Sorry to disturb. I didn't mean to frighten you."

Releasing a deep breath, the woman whispered, "No, it's okay. I just wasn't expecting anyone to be up this early."

"If you don't mind, could you tell me the time?"

"It's 4:55."

"Brilliant. So much for rest. You must be Acadia. I'm Gunnar."

"Yes, Gerry told me all about you last night when he came to pick me up. Did I wake you up? I was trying to be quiet."

"No, I don't think it was you. I heard this . . . oh well, it's not important. Gerry told me last night that you'd had a fight with your bother. I'm sorry to hear that. Is everything all right now?"

She hesitated. "Well, I'm not at the house with him, so it's already better."

Gunnar naïvely tried to cheer her up. "You know, me and my sister Astrid fight all the time. We have a good row and then it's over, and we're the best of friends again."

"It could never be that simple between me and Alphonse," said Acadia softly.

"I'm an exceptional listener, if you feel like talking about it."

She exhaled again and tapped her nails on the table. "Guess I've got nothing to lose. I know you're not from this country—do you know what voodoo is? It all stops and starts with that."

He cocked his head. "Well, from rock music. And I once saw Live and Let Die when I was a teenager into James Bond."

"I suppose that's basic knowledge, very basic. My mother is a voodoo queen, a woman who everyone knows they can go see if they want magic done. And my brother, he's a houngan. Um, to you it might be the equivalent of a pastor in a church. And I was raised to be this mambo, which is a high priestess, but I never wanted to be. My brother and I always got in fights about it. A few years back, my mother disappeared, presumably on some quest following a girl around trying to sponge off of her powers. My brother went looking for her, so I had the house all to myself. It's been all mine for years with no word from my mother or my brother.

Then all of a sudden, yesterday, out of nowhere, he's back. And he's crazy. He's ranting about how he's been to England and Australia and New Mexico and Indiana and South America, and how he knows Mama is at one of those places, but without the girl, he can't get to her. Then he tells me he was possessed by the loa, uh, kind of like an angel or a messenger I guess, and that the loa told him that I was the key to finding the girl. The beige girl as Mama called her." She exhaled, and her voice started to shake. Gunnar could sense from the breaks in her words that she was stifling a cry. "I told him he'd lost it. He told me that if I would embrace the magic and use it, I could find the beige girl and bring back Mama. As usual, I told him magic was foolish. And then, he pushed me around the house and he threw me to the ground."

Gunnar took the opportunity between quiet tears to comfort her. "I'm dreadfully sorry. You needn't continue to talk about this if it upsets you."

She smirked though her weeping. "That's just it. I'm not upset about the fight or even the violence. It's not unexpected from him. What I'm upset about is what happened next. You see, I was very angry. I couldn't control it. Somehow, and this has never happened before, my emotions caused me to use the very magic I don't, or didn't, believe in. And there I was, having a vision. Just like my Mama used to have. I can't believe I'm actually saying this out loud. You must think I'm crazy."

He couldn't help but smile on the inside, since his whole world had become crazy lately. Rather than criticize or patronize, he asked her a perfectly rational question. "What did you see in your vision?"

Sounding relieved that she wasn't being criticized, Acadia answered honestly. "I saw the beige girl in my mind, as if I was looking at a picture of her in the newspaper. I know exactly what she looks like. And I know she's the key to helping us find our mother."

"Really?" Gunnar was truly intrigued by her story. "Did you tell your brother?"

"No way! If he knew I had power, he'd gloat and try to control me. And God only knows what he would actually do with the beige girl once I did lead him to her. I mean, he was saying all kinds of strange things, like doing whatever it takes to force the beige girl to open the door. No, I lied and said I couldn't help him. He knew though. He got this crooked smile and asked me if I'd had a vision. I told him I didn't see anything. He got even madder and told me that if I didn't have a vision, I was on the verge of having one because I was in a trance. He yelled that my lack of faith stopped what could have led to Mama."

"Wow," said Gunnar. "How did it end?"

Acadia was no longer crying, but there was still hurt in her voice. "He accused me of being selfish and not wanting to find our mother. I tried to get him to explain where he thought Mama was, but he just kept ranting about following a sound that Mama heard in the park and finding the beige girl to open the door. He made no freakin' sense. When I told him I didn't understand and he needed to calm down, he lost control and dragged me by my arm to the front door. He opened it and tossed me out, screaming that his travels were over and the house was his alone until I agreed to cooperate. I was not welcome until I allowed the visions to come."

As she exhaled deeply with her last statement, Gunnar could hear a cup drag across the table, followed by a swallow. He tried to change the subject for her benefit. "So, how's the coffee?"

He could hear a soft "humpf" of amusement. "Fine. Thanks for listening by the way. And not freaking out on me."

"My pleasure. Any friend of Roxanne's family is a friend of mine."

Now it was Acadia's turn to be fascinated. "You know, I've never actually met a blind person before. When I look in your eyes, they look completely normal. Bright blue, no spots, they don't cross or anything. Can you see at all?"

"Not really. I guess what I do see is sort of a dark gray, kind of like staring at a blank television set. Every once in a while, the gray will move, sort of like a very slow wave, which tells me there is movement. But I can't define shapes or see what's moving."

"Huh. Is it true that you feel people's faces to tell what they look like?"

"Yes, but I don't go asking everyone permission to touch their faces. That would be quite off-putting for most people. I try to limit my personal-space intrusion to people I know."

"I wouldn't mind. I'm curious to see how it feels? Do you want to feel what I look like?"

He was always grateful when someone agreed to allow this bizarre ritual. "That would be great."

"Here," she said alongside the movement of the chair. "I'll come to you."

Soon enough, he felt breath on his cheek. He raised his hands towards the heat. Starting with a caress of the outside of the face, he felt a large forehead that hit a kinked and tightly curled widow's peak. The temples sloped to very pronounced cheekbones. The cheeks descended to a somewhat pointed chin, indicating a combination between a heart-shaped and rounded face. She must have been ticklish, for as Gunnar rounded the chin, Acadia smiled tightly. Her smile was very broad— it seemed almost ear to ear. Her lips were broad as well and possessed the fullness usually seen in people of African ancestry. Her nose, however, was not typically African, for it had only a slight pronouncement on either side and the slope was pointy as opposed to flat. Her eyelashes were long and they flittered against the outside of his hand as he moved away from the bridge of the nose.

"Are you mixed race?"

"Yeah! Half white, half black. How did you know that?"

"Part of my guess is based on the stereotype from that James Bond movie. All the voodoo people in it were black. Your full lips and the tightly curled hair that meets your forehead conform to that vision. But I must admit, the nose threw me off a bit. I've never really felt a black face before, though of course I'd seen them before I went blind, and your nose doesn't feel flat. It's rather pointy actually, like northern European."

"I take it then you don't hang out with any black people in England?" she queried.

"Not really. I've worked with some, but have never really socialized with them. In my defense though, I don't socialize with people generally. Until recently, my social circle consisted of myself, my sister, her husband, my father, and the occasional date."

"What about Gerry and his daughter?"

"I only met Roxanne three weeks ago," Gunnar confessed. "I met your employer only two nights back."

"You've only known Roxanne three weeks? Gerry talks about you like you're his son-in-law already."

Gunnar couldn't help but grin. "I like to think that relationship is inevitable. I do love

Roxanne. It's the only natural progression of my feelings, really."

Acadia sounded envious. "I've always wanted that to happen to me. To fall instantly in love with someone and have them see me and just know."

"I never thought it would happen for me," Gunnar confided in his new friend. He felt surprisingly carefree around Acadia and didn't stop to think before speaking. "I thought I'd be fifty and alone, but great things can happen when you give in to the supernatural."

"What are you talking about?" Her tone was curious, with a slight hint of judgment.

He hesitated for a second before continuing. "Since you confided in me, I'll confide in you. But since I didn't judge you, you can't judge me. It was something supernatural that led me to Roxanne."

She was curious. "What happened?"

"About three weeks ago, I heard a voice tell me I should save a woman who was being mugged. The voice that warned me was my own voice. I had experienced an encounter with what I think is my vardoger. I'm assuming you know about as much of Scandinavian mythology as I know about voodoo."

"Less, I'm sure."

"A vardoger is like a doppelganger. To make a long story short, it's kind of like a twin of yourself living in the future and experiencing events before you do. Mine warned me about Roxanne being mugged so I could save her."

"That's crazy. Good crazy, I mean."

"My vardoger has given me all sorts of advice. He saved me from being crushed. He helped me be in the right place at the right time to save my sister from falling. And he helped me stop A.J. Rhodes from shooting himself."

"The singer?"

"Of course!" said Gunnar with disbelief.

"Oh, I know who he is. He's in all the tabloids all the time. But I don't listen to that stuff much. My iPod rotates between Beyoncé, Rihanna, Ella Fitzgerald, and Sarah Vaughan."

Just then, he heard footsteps coming from the direction of the bedroom. He smiled as they approached, knowing it was Roxanne. Soon, his new friend would get to meet the love of his life.

"Ahhh!!" Gunnar let out a sharp scream, as hot dripping liquid scalded his hand and dripped onto his pajama pants. He could smell the coffee and heard the cup Acadia had been sipping from drop and spin across the table. As Gunnar yelped in pain, Acadia gasped.

"It's you." Acadia squeaked with panic. "You're the beige girl!"

Chapter Eight

You've Got a Friend, and Enemy

*****

After the blind stranger talked him out of shooting himself, Aaron felt both relief and regret. There was a part of him, that seventeen-year old inside, who was grateful to have been stopped. But there was another part of him, the thirty-three year old heartbroken alcoholic, who still wished his plan had worked. Overcoming Alexis, pills and booze was going to be a huge struggle and death would have been easier. Just thinking about his new friend though and all his struggles gave him hope.

He tore up the suicide note and scribbled that he had a headache and was going back to the hotel. Instead, he flew home to Michigan incognito and checked himself into a hospital using a fake name. He called his manager after arriving and learned his handlers from the record label were flipping out. According to them, this was not a good time for rehab, as a big charity show had been in the works for months and they would lose millions if he flaked. Aaron had to be in New Orleans in three weeks or it would spell the end of his record deal and likely a lawsuit. After talking with the doctors, Aaron told his manager he would be there, on two conditions: First, he needed two weeks of absolutely no contact with anyone while he flushed the alcohol from his system. He wanted to get the worst part of detox done in private with no outside stress. Second, he wanted his new friend, Gunnar the blind sound guy from London, at the show, working his sound. He knew two weeks wasn't long enough to chase the demon away, but he felt confident he could stay away from alcohol if Gunnar was there to help him. Only if Gunnar picked him up from the airport and stayed with him throughout his time in New Orleans would he consider leaving rehab center.

The following two weeks were the most brutal in Aaron's life. There was no tragic experience he ever had with Alexis that rivaled the physical and emotional agony of withdrawal. Like Virginia Woolf, he couldn't read or write or concentrate with all the dry heaving, drooling and headaches. He shook like he had Parkinson's disease and seemed to fall down all the time, as if his legs had disappeared. He couldn't drink enough water and felt like when he didn't, he was going to have a heart attack. He even started hallucinating Alexis berating him. It was no wonder detoxing fools like him were under tight supervision. Otherwise, they too might put stones in their pockets and look for the nearest river.

Somehow, Aaron survived that terrible time. His body felt better. He had an appetite again and was able to go to the bathroom without foul smelling urine. His head was a little clearer too, though depression still lurked. He even realized he didn't actually love Alexis anymore and hadn't for a long time, confusing obsession with love. Exactly two weeks from the moment of admission, his manager called to ask if the show was still on. Relieved to hear the answer was yes, his manager instructed that a driver would pick him up from the hospital Tuesday morning and take him to DTW, where his ticket to New Orleans would be waiting. Once he landed, the man who'd saved him would be there to greet him.

Apparently, however, his record company didn't trust him. The "driver" that took him to the airport accompanied him to the ticket counter and also picked up a ticket for himself. While insulted at the thought of needing a babysitter, he couldn't blame them for being cautious given his disappearing act. The pair made it through security and into the VIP lounge without being recognized.

It had been two weeks since A.J. Rhodes went missing. Having necessarily grown into a bit of a narcissist as one does in the spotlight, he was curious if the press knew what happened to him and if anyone cared. While waiting for the plane, he glossed over the newspapers and magazines in the lounge. As usual, the tabloids had somehow gotten a tip and the headlines screamed, "A.J. Rhodes Rehab Drama," "A.J. vs. Alcohol," and "Is It the End of the Road for Rhodes?" Of course, they all had to mention his wife and their "separation." As he pictured Alexis, he caught himself rolling his eyes and realized that was a good thing. He wasn't crying or longing or desiring. He just let the thought of her roll away like rain on a slicker. He smiled, realizing she no longer controlled him.

With a little less than two hours before boarding, he decided to make the time count. He told his handler he was going to a private room in the lounge, as he wanted to be alone to write a song. He took his guitar along for effect. His handler agreed only after he pointed out there was no other exit. Alone, Aaron first called the drummer in his band who had just went through a divorce and got the phone number of his divorce lawyer. Aaron grew a pair, called the lawyer, and initiated the divorce process. One of the last things Alexis said to him was that he wouldn't have the balls to divorce her; that she was going to have to do it and she would do it when she was damn good and ready. He wished he could see the look on her face when she got served with the papers.

After a subsequent call to the bank authorizing a wire transfer to his new attorney and the removal of Alexis from all his accounts, the fourth call Aaron made was to People magazine. A year or so ago, a representative from the magazine had called seeking an interview. The record company thought it was a great idea, but his manager knew that A.J. was in no condition for an interview. Drunk as always, his slurred speech would have resulted in negative press. So his manager took the number of the staff writer and told the rep that when A.J. was ready to be interviewed, they would call her. To this day, even though he was passing in and out of consciousness when he overheard the number for the writer, he remembered how to contact her. The writer was shocked to hear from him, but dropped everything to record their twenty-minute conversation. Up front, A.J. told the writer that he wanted to address the rehab rumors, the public drunkenness, Alexis's escapades, and his pending divorce. With every truthful word describing Alexis as she really was, as opposed to the goddess he had elevated her to in his mind, he felt more empowered.

After hanging up, he was bursting with energy. He really could live life without her, and he'd already started his journey. He felt a happy tear roll down his cheek. He thought of Gunnar's intervention and smiled. Free of the obsession that had enslaved him, he could now search for a woman that truly loved Aaron, not A.J. Rhodes. Someone with whom he could share everything, even his deepest secret, the one that not even Alexis knew.

With only a few minutes left before his handler was sure to come check on him, Aaron decided to experiment. He wanted to see if his secret skill still existed. It had been years since he tried to use it, as he was never able to focus long enough when he was drunk, high, or emotionally battered to try it.

He pulled out his guitar and strummed a slow melody. He closed his eyes and concentrated on the reverberation of each note. His thoughts drifted into each chord as he envisioned himself being carried away on a wave of sound.

Drifting out of his own body, Aaron looked down and saw himself in an airline captain's uniform. He was unusually anxious today about flying, a task he had performed a hundred times. But this day, he was awaiting a phone call from his oncologist that would reveal his remission results. He prayed for good news, selfishly of course, but also because he didn't want to see his wife and daughters go through watching him die.

And then he was back strumming the G chord. It was a short connection, but a connection nonetheless. Yes, he still had the ability to inhabit someone else's body along with their consciousness and feel what that other person was feeling. It was a skill that no one knew helped him write his earliest and best songs. Maybe now that he was sober, and apparently capable of calling upon the power again, he could write that well again.

*****

Roxanne rushed to Gunnar's side. "Oh my God! Are you okay?"

Gunnar was dripping wet with scalding hot coffee, but the initial shock of the sudden splash of heat was subsiding.

He was waiting for Acadia to apologize or at least help, but she was completely unresponsive. Standing with Roxanne's aid, he felt a towel wiping along the wet part of his pant leg. "I'll be all right," he said, as the cold air in the home hit the dampness and cooled the burn.

He sensed contained hostility in Roxanne's voice not directed at him. "Um, hello? I could use a little help here!"

Finally, Gunnar heard Acadia's chair move, steps across the tile floor, the pulling and tearing of paper, and more tapping on the tile. Now, there were now two pairs of hands on him, a gentle one fiddling with his pajama bottoms and another clumsily trying to wipe off his hands. Wondering what was wrong with Acadia, Gunnar recalled her recent words and understanding replaced his confusion. "Acadia, when you said she's the beige girl, were you talking about Roxanne?"

Her voice trembled. "Yes."

Roxanne, having not had the benefit of their conversation, was annoyed with her parents' houseguest. "Would someone mind telling me what's going on?" she asked.

Acadia didn't answer, and Gunnar imagined she must be very frightened that her vision had come true. Gunnar eased the tension by making introductions. "Roxanne, this is Acadia. Acadia, this is Roxanne. Now, I know you two have never met, but you definitely have things in common."

Roxanne's tone was still exasperated. "I'm listening."

"Roxanne, Acadia has visions like you do. And apparently, she had a vision of you last night. I think she's just stunned you turned out to be real. She's never had visions before, let alone ones that happened."

Roxanne's demeanor rapidly changed, and she stopped fussing with the wet spots on Gunnar's night clothes. He heard a chair on the other side of him pull away from the table, followed by a soft exhale. "Really? I remember my first visions," Roxanne said with concern. "They freaked me out too. I get it."

Finally, Acadia spoke. "It's so surreal. And that you are my boss' daughter? You've been one step away from me and I never knew it."

Confused, Roxanne inquired. "I'm not sure what you mean?"

Acadia's speech came back full force, and now she barely took breaths between sentences. "Do you remember 2008? Do you remember meeting a woman who said she was a voodoo queen?"

Gunnar could hear Roxanne start to say something, but stop. After a hesitation, she said, "Mama Gadreau?"

Chills went up Gunnar's spine at the coincidence. He was now more fascinated with the supernatural than ever.

Acadia continued. "Yes! That's my mother! After she met you, she came home and started looking for a book. She said something about you opening doors."

Roxanne excitedly jumped in. "I remember that. She said I had the gift of travelling and told me she was going to go look for a door for us to travel though. No offense, but I thought she was off her rocker at the time."

"None taken. I thought she was off her rocker too. And to this day, I have no idea what door she was talking about. Because the day after she met you, she disappeared. I haven't seen her in eight years. I guess I'd always thought she had found you and you guys went travelling together."

Roxanne shook her head. "No, I never saw her again. She told me to come look for her after I grew up, but I never did. I thought about it after my first visions came true, but I wanted to be normal, so I threw myself into volunteer work and suppressed my questions."

"I've just always been curious where she went."

"Now that I'm thinking about it," Roxanne exclaimed in recognition, "I do recall her saying her daughter had gifts like mine but that you didn't know it."

"I guess she was right," conceded Acadia with a heavy sigh. "But if I do have visions, how come I've never had them before? And why have I never had a vision of where she went? As much as we disagreed, I would give anything to know she's okay."

"Did you never have any visions during puberty?" asked Roxanne. "That's when mine hit. That's when your mom said they'd hit. She said they were tied to hormones."

Acadia shook her head. "No, never. If I'm being honest though, much of my puberty was spent drinking and smoking pot, so maybe that affected it. Or maybe it was denying the gifts. Or maybe it was both, I don't know."

"Well, I don't know how your visions are going to work, but I can't see things that personally relate to me. My visions come in dreams when I'm not trying to have them. I can't just sit down and try to see the future. Maybe your power is limited too in some way, and it had nothing to do with puberty, sobriety, or denial."

Acadia huffed. "If only we were at my house. I'm sure we have some book about this."

"Well, let's go to your house and look," offered Roxanne.

"No!" Acadia blurted. "No, what am I thinking? You can never go to that house. And I can't stay here. I'm endangering you. I've got to protect you."

Gunnar's concern was instant. "Protect her?"

"Yes, I told you. From my brother, Alphonse. He's looking for you. He wants to use you to find our mother. He'll use any means necessary to force the beige girl's, your, cooperation."

Awful visions filled Gunnar's head of something horrible happening to Roxanne. He absolutely couldn't bear it and wondered if he should cancel on A.J. and take Roxanne back to London. He needed a moment to purge the images. "Okay, I know there's a lot to discuss, but I really do need to remove these wet clothes. You two continue talking. I'm going to the room to change and think for a bit. I'll be back soon."

He briskly walked the path back to the bedroom and shut the door. Taking deep breaths, he allowed himself to relax and visualize Roxanne as safe. Slowly, the violent images disappeared. Remembering how wet he was, he began to disrobe.

"Hey mate." The gentle buzz and voice of an old friend was almost comforting now. The vardoger had returned.

"Not that I'm complaining that you're here, but you choose now to talk to me?" Gunnar quipped. "Don't you know what's going on out there? I don't want to miss this conversation."

The vardoger was reassuring. "Of course I know what's going on out there. But, you and I need to talk first. Strange things are going to happen today. I can't really be more specific, because they must happen and I don't want to say anything to impact the present, but I just wanted to tell you to go with the flow. Be adventurous. Be bold. And don't worry, even when it appears there is something grave to worry about. No major harm will be done. Oh, and Acadia needs to be with you today, so don't let her go to work. Trust me, by tonight, she's going to be the only reason you get any sleep."

"How do you know about tonight?" Gunnar snapped at himself. "That's more than twelve hours away, and aren't you only supposed to precede me by a few minutes."

"Who told you that?" asked his imposter voice matter-of-factly.

"This professor who knows all about the vardoger, Dr. Snow."

"Dr. Snow, huh?" the vardoger chuckled. "Oh Arthur, wait until he really finds out. I can't believe he thinks I'm a vardoger." The voice's lightheartedness and affectionate choice of a first name to address the professor made current Gunnar curious, but even more so he was struck by the other part of the statement. "Wait, you're not my vardoger?"

"I can see why both he and Mum for that matter thought that, if you are only getting a glimpse of one moment in time, but no, I'm not a vardoger. So to that end, I can precede you by a second or a few minutes or an infinite amount of time. Let's just say ancient Vikings weren't really hip to metaphysics."

"What are you then if you are not a vardoger?"

His twin answered cryptically. "Isn't God called Allah and Yahweh? Is a ghost less of a ghost if you call it an apparition? If a rose by any other name would smell as sweet, does it matter what you call me?"

Gunnar's frustration reared in the form of increased volume. "What are you talking about?"

"You can call me a vardoger if it's easy, and it won't change who I am. But again, can't and won't say much more than that. I can't do anything to change the course."

Gunnar exhaled. Seeing as how the identity question was going nowhere, he shifted his line of questioning.

"Tell me this then. If you can experience events long before me, why do you always wait until the last minute to warn me that something's going to happen?"

"Think about it. If I warned you too far in advance, you'd have time to talk yourself out of reacting. We rationalize too much. If I'd have told you ahead of time about that falling sign, you would have been a stubborn ass and went to check it out anyway."

Gunnar and his vardoger laughed at the same time. "You're probably right about that," said half-naked Gunnar. "Hey, if you saw the sign fall, does that mean you are sighted?"

"I am."

"But if you are me in the future, how is that possible?"

"Because anything is possible."

Gunnar was getting frustrated with his twin. "Are you physically present, here in this room?"

The vardoger paused. "Yes, and no."

Gunnar found his way to the bed and sat on its softness. "I still don't understand."

The vardoger responded. "It's infinitely complicated and full of paradoxes and worm holes that absolutely should not exist according to all scientific reason. But, like a flying hummingbird, it's happening nonetheless."

"Yeah, but what about those paradoxes? Aren't we somehow disrupting time and potentially screwing up the future for everyone? Shouldn't I theoretically have died the day the sign was supposed to fall on me? And shouldn't that have rendered me incapable of assisting Roxanne and A.J.? And if you are me, you would have died before me, so how could you have still been around to warn me?"

"I'm not really the one to ask. Ask Arthur. You're going to end up friends anyway."

"Really," quipped Gunnar. "But he's so odd."

The vardoger snickered. "And this is normal?"

Gunnar shrugged and continued questioning. "If you led me to Roxanne, how did you initially meet her before I did? How did you know that Roxanne was going to be my, our one?"

"Look, I know you have a ton of existential questions and all, but now is not the time to answer them. You have to tend to A.J. Rhodes today, and he is very clingy. You don't want to worry about him and me as well."

"But I need more answers."

"I cannot give them to you at this time. Things will unfold and you will eventually understand. That's all I can say."

Gunnar sighed. "I've been talking to you now for well over five minutes and there haven't been any cosmic tragedies or collapsing planets. So clearly, we can talk without the traditional vardoger death scenario playing out. Next time, can you please try to give me more of a heads up if something serious is coming? More than a few seconds would be great."

"I'll do my best," said the vardoger.

"So let's talk a little more about this ominous day I'm supposed to have today," said Gunnar. "You said no major harm was coming, but that still implies some harm is coming. Can't you give me more than that?"

"Not really, because I don't want to alter the future. Plans are already in motion based on today, and if today doesn't happen in the same order, those plans might never develop. I can give you a hint that will help. Show the gift you get at the restaurant to the stranger when you feel fear."

"That's bloody cryptic. Can't you do better?"

"No, and as a matter of fact, I'm taking off. I've probably said too much and I need to get back anyway."

His spirit twin didn't say goodbye, but when the room felt empty, Gunnar knew the vardoger, or whatever he was if not the vardoger, was gone. Anxious to tell Roxanne about his encounter, he threw on some clothes without bothering to clean up the dried coffee caking his thigh.

As he walked back to the kitchen, he could feel more heat. The sun was coming out. The women were still conversing, more quickly now, as though they'd been friends for ages.

"Hey, babe!" said Roxanne, interrupting the girl talk. "We were just talking about . . ."

"My vardoger just came to me in the bedroom," interrupted Gunnar.

Roxanne grabbed his hand and sat him close. "So you did need to come home with me to New Orleans to see him again!"

"Yes, and boy do I have news for you."

He recounted the tale. After explaining to the girls that his vardoger wasn't really the vardoger, but somehow still knew every point in his future, Acadia interjected. "Isn't it funny how both of you know the future, just by different mechanisms?"

He hadn't thought about it, but she was right.

"I wish I could understand my ability," Acadia interjected sadly.

"Be patient," reassured Roxanne. "You've only had one vision."

"If I could just get a book from my house . . . "

"Well, maybe we can stop by your house sometime today, all of us," Roxanne said. "If we all go together, then your brother will be less likely to get violent, right?"

His new friend's voice trembled. "No, I don't want you there, Roxanne," said Acadia. "And you don't want to get involved either. I'll go by myself after work. He will have had the night and all day to calm down."

Gunnar couldn't believe he was going to say it given his need to protect the woman he loved, but he nonetheless stated to Acadia, "My vardoger told me that you need to spend the whole day with us. I don't know why exactly, but I have to tell you that the vardoger has not been wrong yet. I can't see myself lying to, well myself. Especially not about a friend."

"It's true, Acadia. Gunnar hasn't been wrong. If the vardoger said you need to be with us today, then you need to be with us," Roxanne agreed. "So if you're going to your house, we're going to your house."

"But it could take a while. I have no clothes, no money. Alphonse kicked me out before I could even grab my purse. I had to beg a motel clerk to let me use a phone to call your dad last night. I'm going to have to get all that stuff on top of looking for a book.”

Roxanne's tone was sympathetic and helpful. “Just borrow some of my clothes. They might be a bit short on you since you're taller than me, but they'll cover you. Just grab your purse and the book and we'll be out of there in no time.”

“Do you have clothes suitable for a law office?”

Roxanne scoffed. “My dad won't be expecting you to work today. And if he was, he won't be once I talk with him. You need to take today to just gather your thoughts and start accepting your abilities. And you need to be around friends.”

“Yes,” interjected Gunnar. “If nothing else, it will be one more New Orleans native that can show me around.” He had been so distracted by the vardoger appearing, he almost forgot he had a job to do. “Oh, wait. We have to pick up A.J. from the airport at noon.”

Roxanne interrupted quickly. Turning to Acadia, she said, "You should come with us to do that, of course. It's gonna be so exciting."

"Oh, right—the musician," acknowledged Acadia. "I was telling Gunnar that I don't know much about him. That's fine though. I'll hang out with you guys, so long as it's okay with your father."

The trio's conversation must have been louder than they realized, as not two minutes after Acadia agreed to join them for the day, Gerry and Yara stumble into the kitchen. "What are all of you guys doing awake at 6:30?" Gerry grumbled.

After a short discussion, Gerry instructed Acadia to take the day off. With that decision made, everyone showered, dressed, and ate a quick bite. Around 11:00, Gunnar and his entourage headed for the limo company by the airport to catch the limo that would take them to meet A.J. He hoped A.J. would be okay with the unexpected presence of the two women.

Since none of the three had a car to transport them from Algiers to the airport, Yara offered them a ride in her minivan. Sometimes, it would get Gunnar down that he couldn't see where he was, particularly when he was in a new place that he knew to be historic. Roxanne had described such amazing places, like the St. Louis Cathedral and the above ground cemeteries. He appreciated her descriptions and her educated use of vocabulary, but it still fell short of being able to observe it for himself. Whenever he started feeling sorry for himself this way, he concentrated extra hard on his best sense—his hearing. The sound of the tires as they rolled along the asphalt changed and he knew the surface they were driving on was now concrete. He heard a familiar thumping sound that reminded him of rolling over the expansion joints on the Thames. "Are we on a bridge?"

Yara answered with surprise in her voice. "Yes! It's the Crescent City Connection."

Once the bridge sounds ceased, he heard, "Oh God," come from Acadia in a low tone. "We're passing by the Garden District. My house and my brother aren't far from here."

Roxanne reassured her. "Don't worry. We're almost past the Claiborne exit."

No sooner had Roxanne said this when the sound that had woken him that morning was back, but this time more pronounced. For a second, he worried about his hearing. Was he getting tinnitus? Was it permanent? Would it be fatal to his career? A bit shaken, he hoped he wasn't the only one that heard it.

"Does anyone else hear that? That high pitched whirring sound?"

Everyone in the car was quiet. Then Roxanne said, "I don't hear anything."

"Me neither," said Acadia.

Yara completed the trio of denials. "Sorry, Gunnar. I don't hear anything either." He was about to describe it better when the car veered slightly left and Yara interrupted for directions. "Okay, we just got onto the Airport Highway. Where is the limo company I'm supposed to drop you guys off at?" Before he could give her the directions, the noise stopped as suddenly as it started, and his hearing was once again crystal clear.

Roxanne had never been in a limo before, so it made him smile to hear her giddiness as they entered the car. Of course, he'd been in several limos before, so it meant nothing to him aside from more legroom and mineral water if he felt like it.

Once they stepped in, it would be only a minutes before the limo met A.J. Gunnar had been around many famous people and being star struck had faded long ago. Besides, he had met A.J. before. But the girls didn't have his experience and needed to be prepared for how to handle fangirling. "When A.J. enters the limo, I would appreciate it if both play it cool. No screams of delight, no touching him, no requests for autographs. I'm supposed to be his friend and my job is to make him feel relaxed, so please no fanatical ravings."

"Like I said," Acadia said matter-of-factly, "I don't listen to the guy's music. I don't even think I could pick him out of a line-up. If he's not John Legend, I'm not gonna go psycho on him."

"Roxanne?" goaded Gunnar.

"Well, I love his music and think I have every single one of his songs downloaded, but I promise to be on my best behavior."

Satisfied, Gunnar continued. "I also think it's best if we let him steer the conversation. If he wants to talk music, feel free to discuss his entire discography. If he wants to talk about food, mention all the great places you like to eat in town. I would stay away from the topic of exes or rehab. And I also wouldn't bring up anything the three of us talked about this morning. This is a supernatural free vehicle as long as he's in it. Agreed?"

"Okay," both women said.

Gunnar could feel the wheels slowing and wide turns being made. The whirling sounds of jet engines were foremost in his ears. "We must be coming up to the terminals. Yes?"

"Yep," said Roxanne.

The car slowed, and he heard the muffled sound of an announcer say, "Flight 662 to Cleveland is now boarding at Gate C4." Gunnar was a bit nervous himself, not out of awe, but out of worry. The record company wasn't looking at him as just the sound man, but A.J.'s nanny. Would he have to give A.J. constant attention until the concert to keep an eye on him, at the neglect of Roxanne? Worse, what would happen to his sound job if he couldn't keep A.J. away from the bottle?

The car rolled to a stop. There were no camera flash clicks or panting throngs of fans, which meant A.J. and his record company had managed to keep his travels a secret. Feeling for the door handle, Gunnar opened it and made his way out to the curb using the door frame as a tactile guide. He felt it only right to greet A.J. standing up, man to man. Plus, he wanted to prepare the star for the presence of Roxanne and Acadia.

Just as he closed the car door, he was the object of a bear hug. "Gunnar!" He tried to reciprocate with what part of his arms weren't being crushed, but didn't have any luck.

"Hello A.J. Oops, sorry. Aaron."

The rock star stepped back. As he did, Gunnar felt A.J.'s hair brush along his chin, telling him the rock star was about six inches shorter than he. The hair was also soft, not edged, indicating long hair instead of a short cut. "Thanks so much for doing this, man. I know it must be a pain in the ass, but I really need you. They've put us up at the Roosevelt Suite in the Roosevelt Hotel. I've stayed there before and I know I'll need help staying away from the wet bar."

"Absolutely, mate. We'll have a blast keeping you distracted. But . . ."

"Not a fan of buts," said A.J. warily.

"I do have my girlfriend with me. I hope you don't mind if she tags along."

A.J. took a breath. "Hey, it's one more pair of hands that can be used to pry me away from the Stoli."

"And we've brought another woman with us. It's quite unexpected, but she found herself in a spot of trouble last night, and I'm sort of helping her today."

His new friend chuckled. "What are you doing, running a daycare for screwed-up adults?" Gunnar was glad to hear A.J. make light of the situation. "That's fine. The more the merrier."

"Cheers. So, do you want to go to your hotel first?"

"Not really. My manager and the assholes from my record label will be there to berate me. I'd like to spend as little time there as possible. What I'd really like is for the four of us to just hang out, like normal tourists. I've never been to New Orleans when I was sober and single."

"Don't think you'll be spotted?"

"Nah. Now that the bags are gone from my eyes, the color has returned to my cheeks, and my hair is washed, I don't think anyone will recognize me. And if they do, a few autographs won't kill me."

"That sounds fun. This is my first time really touring New Orleans outside of a stadium. I've been to a few restaurants with my girlfriend's parents, but haven't really gone anywhere else. Hop in, and we can talk to the girls about where to go. They're both natives."

"Here, let me." His new friend opened the door for him, and Gunnar slid back into the comfort of the limo. Feeling around for his seat next to Roxanne, she extended her hand and guided him towards her so that their thighs were touching. Gunnar heard A.J. plop onto a seat to his left. Knowing that Acadia had previously been sitting to his right, he was happy that they were facing each other so the introductions would be easier.

"Aaron, this is my girlfriend Roxanne. And directly facing you is our friend, Acadia."

Gunnar had expected the obligatory small talk and "nice to meet you", but the car was silent. His ears picked up two increasing heartbeats, one belonging to the rock star and the other to the voodoo princess. He could also sense their breathing rhythms change from light and slow to heavy and quick.

It was Roxanne that broke the silence. "Um, A.J? I just wanted to tell you that I am a big fan."

276

The star came around just enough to let a few words escape in an easy listening tone. "Please don't call me A.J. Only the nameless faces in the crowd and my record company call me that. To my friends, I'm Aaron." Gunnar could hear two hands extending in front of him and knew Acadia and Aaron must be shaking hands. But they didn't let go once their hands met, the hand shake lingering. "Acadia. That's a very cool name."

"Thanks." Acadia finally spoke, her voice sweet and slightly trembling. "I was named for a province in Canada where a lot of Cajun immigrants came from. My mother said my father came from a long line of genteel Acadians."

"I think Aaron's from the bible. Not nearly as interesting as your name."

"I like Aaron," said Acadia.

Gunnar smiled, finally realizing that the rock star and the girl who didn't know much about him were stifling infatuation. A.J. had been so low just weeks earlier, Gunnar didn't dare interrupt.

The conversation between Aaron and Acadia was breezy but curt, both parties' voices muted in tension. Aaron seemed too shy for a star, his compliments almost a whisper. "I hope you don't think this is weird, but I can't stop staring at you because you're so beautiful. Your eyes are amazing. I mean, even more beautiful than . . . well, never mind that."

Acadia giggled like a young girl. "Thank you," was all she could muster. "And, I like your hair," she offered shyly, in a tone indicating she wasn't very practiced at the art of flirting.

"So, what do you do for a living?" asked Aaron.

"I work for Roxanne's dad. I'm a paralegal."

"Any ties to the music business?" Aaron grilled politely.

She smirked. "No."

"Good," said Aaron cheerfully. There was silence for a moment and A.J. exhaled. "Do you, I mean, have you been reading about what's going on with me in the tabloids?" This was the first point in the conversation that was uncomfortable. Clearly, A.J. wanted to test whether Acadia had preconceived notions about him based on his addiction.

Acadia was uncomfortable too. "Um, this is probably gonna sound bad, 'cause I know you must be used to everyone knowing who you are and fawning all over you, but I don't really listen to rock music, so I don't know much about you. I think the extent of my knowledge is that you and your wife are separated and that you went to rehab like lots of other celebrities out there."

Gunnar flinched. The dreaded topics of exes and rehab had come up, despite his admonishment. Now was the time to butt in. "We don't need to talk about that stuff if you don't want to."

"No, it's okay," said Aaron. "Not only are we separated, we're getting divorced. So in my mind, I'm as free as a bird, you know, to be open to love elsewhere if it finds me."

"You don't mind that I don't really know who you are?" Acadia said lightly, testing the waves.

"Mind? I think it's perfect," said Aaron happily. "And that whole rehab thing? I admit, I've been weak and have lost myself in drugs and drink, but that's all done with. I hit my rock bottom and I never want to be there again. So, anyone I would date in the future would not have to worry about me being drunk or drugged up all the time." Gunnar could sense he was trying to reassure the object of his affection that he was not a lost cause.

Roxanne interjected. "Uh, I hate to interrupt, but I think we've now circled the airport twice. Does this limo driver know where to take us?"

Gunnar and Aaron had both been so lost in the moment that neither one of them remembered their decision to play tourist. "I wouldn't mind grabbing a bite to eat," Gunnar said, his stomach reminding him he was hungry. "Then we can decide where to go from there."

The rock star agreed. "I'm starving. Acadia, what's your favorite place in town for lunch?"

"Well, for lunch, I know a great soul food place with fantastic peach cobbler."

Roxanne smacked her lips. "Oh yes! Peach cobbler is my favorite!"

Gunnar heard the sound of the automated window separating the party from the driver. A.J. ordered, "Driver, take us to wherever this enchanting lady tells you to go."

"Take this road past the I-10 into Mid-City, and I'll direct you from there," said Acadia.

Roxanne never got her chance to fangirl, as the entire trip, Acadia and A.J. might as well have been the only two people in the car. Instead, she clung to Gunnar's hand and listened to the budding courtship with as much fascination as Gunnar did. Half way to the restaurant, the ringing in his ears started again.

Instinctively, Gunnar removed his hand from Roxanne's and placed both over his ears. The sound was a clear buzz, like he'd just finished working an arena concert, but it was louder.

"Damn! There it is again! And I bet you guys don't hear it, do you?"

"Huh?" Aaron said, outside the loop.

"No," Acadia said.

Roxanne was less terse. "I don't, baby. But, I can't help but notice this is the exact same place where you heard it last time."

"Yeah" joined Acadia. "We had just passed Claiborne when it stopped, and it seems to have ended around Carrolton. We just passed Carrolton."

Gunnar was curious. "I wonder if it will stop then at Claiborne?"

"We won't be finding out," said Acadia. Last time, we were on I-10 and we won't be on it this time."

"So, it's not a noise made by the motorway then," offered Gunnar.

"Tell us when the noise stops," said Roxanne. "We can try to compare it to last time."

Gunnar nodded then waited patiently for the noise to desist. He could barely hear Acadia explaining to A.J. that Gunnar had heard a sound no one else did on the way to the airport.

After about three minutes, Gunnar reported, "It stopped."

"Okay, we just crossed Canal Street on Broad. What is inside the borders of Carrolton, Canal, and Claiborne that could be making this sound?" Acadia queried.

"Is Claiborne really an accurate boundary though, since it curves back toward Carrolton?" Roxanne said to Acadia, both locals spouting off native streets while the Londoner sat clueless.

"No, you're right. Maybe after we eat, we should drive down Claiborne and see if we can pinpoint it?"

Gunnar was beyond curious, and were it not for his hunger, he might have insisted on the hunt now. But between the rattling of his stomach and the loud gurgling of A.J.'s, food was first on the agenda.

The car rolled to a stop soon thereafter, and Gunnar could smell fried spicy goodness come through the metal of the limo. "Luckily, the lunch rush is over. It's 2:30 and they close at 3:00, so there shouldn't be much of a crowd," said Acadia.

"Good," said Aaron as they walked through the door. "Only two tables of four people. That I can handle if I do get recognized."

Just then, Gunnar heard an excitable hostess. "Oh my goodness, it's you! Oh, please, please, come in. We're honored that you and your friends are joining us today. The owner will want to hear about this. Please, seat yourselves at any table you'd like, and I'm gonna go in the back and tell the cook and the manager that you're here."

Gunnar had been around rock stars before and had heard this exact exchange numerous times. He felt a bit bad for Aaron though, as in his recovering condition, anonymity would have been better.

"I have to admit, that was a bit odd for me," said A.J. in a muffled tone.

"Yeah, I know," replied Acadia. "It's because of who my mother is."

284

The blind man was lost, until he sat down and heard four new voices. They were all distinctly black, distinctly Southern, and distinctly thrilled. An older woman said, "Oh Miss Acadia. It's such a pleasure to see ya again. And how is Mama Gadreau?"

Acadia lied. "She's fine." The twins had agreed to keep up the pretense of their busy Mama traveling in an out of New Orleans so that no rival mambos would think they could take her territory.

An older gentleman anxiously said, "Do you want me to make you and yo' friends anythang special today, off the menu?"

"Oh no, please don't go out of your way for us," said Acadia magnanimously. "We'll just order like anyone else."

The voice of the hostess said, "Miss Acadia, I have some school exams comin' up soon, and I'd really like to pass. Can you and Mama and your brotha pray for me?"

Gunnar heard reluctance in Acadia's voice that no one else could, yet she capitulated. "Of course!"

Another man, younger than the first said, "Well, we don't want to take up any mo' of your time Miss Acadia. But just remembah, your money is no good here."

"Oh, Earl, that is very generous of you," said Acadia. "But as usual, I don't want to hear any lip about me leaving a nice big tip."

"Nah, it is you who is good and generous, Miss Acadia." With that, Gunnar heard four sets of feet scamper away.

It was a rather strange irony, probably more so for Aaron than anyone, that the restaurant staff didn't notice the multi-platinum singer who graced the cover of every tabloid and entertainment magazine, but treated a paralegal like a celebrity.

Looking over the menu, Aaron noted, "I love New Orleans. I'm so anonymous here. But not you, apparently."

"All the old school people in this town knew my mother. She was always doing readings and rituals for old N'awlins natives. When my mother left, Alphonse and I agreed to keep up the charade that she was still alive and here in town, just semi-retired. So, whenever I see people who want something, or who still think fondly of Mama, I get fabulous treatment."

Aaron had a true relief in his voice. "You don't know how amazing it is for me to meet someone who knows what it's like to be bombarded by strangers. Who understands the mask you have to put on. And yet, unlike another celebrity, you get to be mostly unknown. I just, I'll think you'll understand me."

Gunnar heard a hand slide along the slick surface of the table, and imagined that Acadia was touching A.J. "I think I do understand you."

Gunnar's stomach grumbled loudly, and he decided to get everyone back on task. "So Acadia, what's good here?"

"The buffet of course!" said Acadia emphatically.

One of the many downsides to blindness is a buffet. Since a blind person can't see what's available in the buffet chaffing dishes, and can't normally find the ladles without occasionally sticking their hands into hot food, it's usually not a good choice. And no one wants to annoy their companion by making them read out every single option. Thus, while three scrumptious buffets were ordered, Gunnar settled for fried chicken and red beans and rice off the menu.

Luckily, he didn't have to wait long for his food after his companions had raided the remains of the buffet. For a few minutes, the new friends feasted in silence, with only "umms" and "ohhs" heard amongst the lot. As their appetites became sated, the conversation resumed.

"So," Aaron said. "I'm a little confused about your family, Acadia. I think I picked up bits and pieces, about a brother and a mother that you pretend is all right. I didn't hear about a dad. And your mother does readings? What's that all about?"

She exhaled. "Well, I don't know if you know who Marie Laveau is, but she was a famous voodoo priestess here in N'Awlins. My mom is kind of like her. She claims to have been a clairvoyant, but she apparently wasn't so good at telling the future that she could tell her own kids she would disappear for a decade. I don't know my dad. My mother never told us his identity. He knows we exist though, because he does, or did, pay child support."

"How many brothers and sisters do you have?"

Still somber, Acadia responded. "Just one brother, Alphonse. We're twins. But we're not close. He's a voodoo priest and I'm not really a believer. Plus he's on some obsessive quest to find a magical door."

Gunnar choked a bit on his fried chicken and all voices turned to him with concern. "Are you okay?" "Need some water?" they chimed in unison.

Composing himself after clearing his throat, Gunnar turned to Acadia and furrowed his brow. She chuckled a bit. "You said not to bring it up in the car, but you didn't say we couldn't talk about it at lunch."

He was only a few years older than Acadia, but felt he was dealing with a petulant child. "By all means then, go on telling him your story," said Gunnar with a forced smile. He placed particular emphasis on "your" as a guide for her to keep the vardoger to herself.

Acadia caught the hint and recounted for Aaron the tale of Mama Gadreau and Alphonse, her voodoo upbringing, and even her vision of Roxanne. Gunnar was sure the craziness would cause the budding fondness the rock star felt for the voodoo princess to vanish. But A.J.'s reaction to Acadia was unexpected. "Wow. Not only are you the most beautiful person I've ever met, but the most interesting as well." Aaron's tone changed from admiration to a resolute surprise that he himself was about to admit something. "Can I, I want to tell you something. Something I've never told anyone, not even my ex-wife."

The table was silent in anticipation as Aaron gathered himself. "I think, well, I've always thought that maybe I have kind of a gift too. It started when I was fourteen. It would only come and go though, it wasn't constant. Sometimes, I would play music on my guitar or keyboards, and the music wouldn't make sense to anyone but me. It was like the instruments were speaking some language that only I could understand. I would hear messages, of things that were happening right then, right now, but to other people. One time, I was practicing my guitar while a football game was being played. I didn't like sports, and I was nowhere near a TV. And yet, my guitar told me that the Patriots beat the Eagles by three points, and for a second, I was the Patriots quarterback, celebrating. And, I know this next thing will sound particularly crazy in light of where I am, and you might think I'm being influenced to lie about it but I'm not. The last week of August 2005, I was lonely because I just started high school and didn't know anyone. I played the piano to cope. Every time I did that week, I knew, not just that Katrina had hit this place, but some of the stories of individual people caught in the storm. I heard a mom freaking out and trying to get her son on a boat. I heard an old lady praying and preparing to take her last breath as the water rose over her. I heard an angry man who had managed to make it across a bridge get turned away by police. It scared me to death."

Gunnar's skin prickled with goose pimples. Just as he knew the vardoger was real, somewhere deep within him, he knew that Aaron was telling the truth. To have music talk to you was something he'd never heard of before, but he couldn't dismiss it.

He didn't get a chance to verbalize his support, as Acadia was the first to talk. "I've had some exposure to this stuff thanks to my mother, and it sounds to me like you're a mix between an auditory psychic and an empath."

Aaron exhaled with relief. "You don't think I'm crazy?"

"No more crazy than me . . . or Roxanne . . . or Gunnar." Acadia said, offering up her friend's truth despite her agreement. "We've all got gifts too." Gunnar rolled his eyes at his inclusion.

Aaron sounded stunned. "You guys too?"

Roxanne spoke first. "I see events of the future, not as they are happening in real-time, like you. Mine come in dreams, where I can usually see major world events a few days before they happen." Roxanne stopped for a minute to think, then resumed. "We've been hypothesizing about Acadia's gifts this morning, and reckon that her gifts never fully matured during puberty because she was partying a bit too hard. Did your gifts fully form through your teen years?"

"No. Between 14 and 18, I was so scared of my ability, I would stop playing and take a break the second I felt out of my own body. Then, by college, I was all wrapped up into the ex. I didn't play music much anymore; I just followed her around like a puppy. And after that, I started drinking and never saw or felt anything else again."

"It sounds like a person needs to be in the right frame of mind to receive and use their gifts," declared Roxanne.

Aaron must have been looking at Acadia, as she timidly stated, "You know, your gifts might come back full steam if you stay clean. It would be amazing to see that."

"That's my plan," said Aaron, both for his own benefit and hers. "I'm done with alcohol and drugs. They stop you from seeing what love is, what it can be, and I really want to see that."

Trying to keep the focus on the four of them and not just the newly acquainted pair, Gunnar divulged information he probably shouldn't have. "Roxanne might have other gifts too."

His girlfriend was casual. "That's just what Acadia's mother told me once. I supposedly have the ability to open the magical doors that Acadia's brother is looking for." She gently ribbed him, causing him to laugh. "But Gunnar's brush with the supernatural is far more unique."

"Really?" The rock star focused on his friend. "What is your gift?" A.J. asked.

Gunnar joked. "Well, obviously, I don't see anything," he said while drumming on the table. "But I do hear something. I hear myself taking to me about the future. I call it my vardoger for lack of a better word, which is like a spirit twin in Norse folklore, but he says that's not what he is. Of course, he won't tell me what he is actually is, so a vardoger he'll remain for now."

Roxanne helped Gunnar explain more quickly, as all the plates were empty and a waiter was sure to come soon. "The Gunnar from the future somehow transports back in time to talk to the Gunnar that is here in the present."

Gunnar continued. "In fact, since we're laying all the cards out on the table, it was my vardoger that told me to go to the studio and save you that day."

"Whoa, what a trip," Aaron said with awe.

"The vardoger sent Gunnar to me, too," said Roxanne. "And, he's the one that insisted Acadia be with us today."

"Well," said Aaron, "I can't thank your vardoger enough then."

Acadia sighed. The flirtation was meandering into sappy.

As lunch wound down, the same four doting Southern voices that greeted them appeared once more. The older lady began. "Miss Acadia, I hope it's okay with ya, but I have some presents for you and yo' friends. See, I dabble in hoodoo a bit. Oh, its nothin' as good as Mama Gadreau would do, but I have some feelings that yo' friends might could use these."

"Oh, that's very nice. Thank you," replied Acadia genuinely.

The elderly woman continued. "For you Miss Acadia, I present a mojo bag for clairvoyance. It will help you use yo' powers." From across the table, Gunnar caught an odor that smelled like spearmint chewing gum and coffee.

"For you," the woman moved to where Aaron was sitting. "This is a mojo bag for musicians. I gotta feelin' that you're a very good piana playa. This will keep you clear minded so you can create yo' best work." Now the coffee smell overpowered, and there was a hint of ginger mixed in.

The old woman's voice came close to Gunnar. It rested just above Roxanne. "For you Miss, this is a mojo bag for dreamin'.'" Gunnar heard Roxanne's arm reach for something and he caught the scent of sweet lavender.

"And for you, my sightless friend, I be seein' that you need some protection. So here you go." The woman placed in his hand what felt like a small leather bag. It was tied at the top. Gunnar gently squeezed and it felt like soft clay in his hand. He put the bag close to his nose and wished he hadn't. Unlike the others, whose bags emitted pleasant smells, his reeked of whisky and tobacco.

"Again, thank you for these treasures. We will wear them happily." Acadia said, not just for the old lady's benefit, but also for the benefit of the baffled at the table.

As promised, no bill was ever brought. Aaron insisted on leaving a hundred-dollar tip, since the restaurant allowed him anonymity. The four friends left the restaurant and filed back into the limo. This time, the sounds of the crumpling leather told Gunnar that A.J. was sitting very close to Acadia.

"You know," started Aaron, "I can't believe how much we all have in common and how we're all sort of intertwined. Like it was destiny for us all to meet."

Everyone was quiet at the thought lingering in the air, and while Gunnar normally dismissed fate, he could not ignore the coincidences of their gifts and seemingly orchestrated acquaintanceship.

"Gunnar, do you still want to try to hunt down that noise?" Roxanne queried.

He had almost forgotten about it, getting so wrapped up in getting to know his new friends and their unique abilities. "Might as well."

He heard the automated window and Roxanne instructing the driver to follow Claiborne under the freeway until he was told to stop. After a short distance, the sound started again, but low. "It's back," Gunnar stated.

"We're at Canal Street again," said Roxanne.

The car was surprisingly silent given that A.J. and Acadia had not stopped talking to each other since the moment they met. He imagined all eyes were on him, wondering about his auditory hallucination. As they travelled on, the hum grew louder. By the fourth stoplight after the motorway, it was as loud as if a baby were crying right next to him. "It's getting louder. Where are we?"

"A street called Napoleon," said Roxanne.

"Is it possible to turn right on the next street? When I turn my ears that direction, it becomes louder."

Roxanne instructed the driver to turn south on Jefferson. Increasingly, the pitch changed from a crying baby to an airplane flying close overhead. "Oh my God!" exclaimed Roxanne as she practically jumped onto Gunnar's lap. "I hear it now too! That low hum. I've heard this exact sound before. It was the sound that took me to the labyrinth in the park!"

Gunnar was relieved that someone else heard something as well, a happy indication that he wasn't developing a hearing problem. But still, her description was odd. "Low? It sounds like my ear is up against a blender."

"Driver," she said with authority. "Go down to Magazine and over to Audubon Park."

"That's where you met my mother, wasn't it?" Acadia asked, confirming a suspicion.

"Yes." There was reluctance in Roxanne's voice.

Aaron piped in. "Acadia, are you sure you feel like going there?"

There was resolve in her voice. "Yes. I want to know what my mother heard that made her want to go away. And since the beige girl, I mean you, Roxanne, will be there, maybe I can finally know."

"I don't mean to rudely interrupt, but this noise is giving me a migraine," said Gunnar, rubbing his forehead. "I know to you it's a dull roar, but to me it's highly annoying."

"Maybe you shouldn't go, Gunnar. What if it only gets louder?" said Acadia protectively.

"I'm not leaving Roxanne," Gunnar practically yelled trying to talk over the sound. "I'll cover my ears until we get there."

Roxanne had the driver park at a church and they quickly walked down Patton Street to get to the Tree of Life. Even with his palms over his lobes, the sound was grating. As the four stepped out of the car, Aaron and Acadia were also taken aback.

"Wow, I hear something too a little bit," said Aaron. "It's like, whenever one of my concerts end, and I can still hear the drums in my ears even though the music is gone."

"I can hear it now as well," added Acadia. "To me, it's still rather quiet, but noticeable. Kind of like a clothes dryer in another room."

"Excuse me," said Roxanne to a woman out walking her dog. "Do you hear a noise?"

"No," said the woman curtly.

More curious now that all four of them could hear what no one else could, they followed the noise. By the time Gunnar felt grass beneath his feet, he was wincing from the pain in his ears.

"Here it is," said Roxanne. The sloshy softness under his stride changed to a hard brick feel. At that same time, the sound mercifully stopped. What was left was like fog in his ears.

"It stopped," said Gunnar. "Did it stop for everyone?"

They all agreed they no longer heard the hum, but none of them could point out any change in the environment that ended it.

Focusing on visualizing where he was, Gunnar asked, "So when you said labyrinth, I pictured a tall wall of trees? Is that where we are?" Gunnar asked.

"It's not that kind of a labyrinth," interjected Acadia. "This is a big red circle of stone on the ground, and then these blue stones in the middle serve the same purpose as tall hedges in what you're thinking. You're supposed to walk inside the blue stones, following the blue pattern, and mediate while you do."

"Is there anything about this flat labyrinth that was causing the sound?" asked Gunnar.

Acadia was disappointed. "I don't see anything. Not even with Roxanne here."

His girlfriend seemed equally deflated. "I don't understand. I know I didn't see anything when I was her as a kid, but I thought for sure I'd see something now that my hormones aren't stifling my gifts. But nothing."

"That's because there isn't anything here for you to see. This is a false door." The words came from the direction they had walked, but the voice was not from one of their party. It was dark and dripping with game show host charm.

"Alphonse!" Acadia was clearly shocked, and Gunnar heard the quick shuffle of Aaron's feet closer to her position.

"Hello, dear Sister. I knew you were lying about the vision. I knew that you knew where to find the beige girl. See, you are a bokor after all."

Gunnar let his hands feel around for Roxanne and found her close by.

"Alphonse, I didn't know where to find her. I am not a bokor."

"What's a bokor?" he heard Aaron try to whisper.

Alphonse had heard him. "A bokor is a sorcerer. Someone born with the gifts that chooses to use them."

Acadia was insistent. "As I said, I'm not a bokor. This is a complete coincidence. She happens to be my boss's daughter."

"Well," Alphonse said smoothly. "That's even better than a vision or magic. That's fate. Surly not even you who rebels against all things spiritual can dishonor Gran Maite's intent to bring the two of you together."

"God has nothing to do with this. And how did you find me anyway? Were you following me?" Acadia asked impatiently.

Gunnar thought Alphonse seemed almost too calm, which was contrary to Acadia's description of him as crazy. "Well I had to, didn't I, seeing as how you weren't being very truthful. Anyway, had I followed you or not, we'd have all ended up here. This is destiny at work."

Acadia was incredulous. "You're not serious."

"I'm very serious. See, I have a made a study of this maze, both in the weeks after Mama left and since I've returned. Every once in a while, it lets out a loud moan. It usually only speaks to me alone though. Today, I see it has called to all of us. What is that if not destiny?"

Aaron spoke up. "Tell you what. You keep your destiny. We'll be on our way and you can have the labyrinth all to yourself."

There was twisted cheerfulness in Alphonse's reply. "I wouldn't hear of it. Stay."

"What do you want, Alphonse?" Acadia asked defiantly.

"To help of course."

"Yeah, sure," she scoffed.

"Really, I do. Each of you has gifts you need to better understand. I can help with that. Of course, I'm hoping that if I scratch your back, you'll scratch mine and help me find my mother. And to attain that goal, I'm willing to tell you everything I know."

Gunnar could sense a dangerous edge to Alphonse and knew negotiating would be better than fighting. "Maybe we'll help you, if you tell us what you know about this place and you promise that absolutely no harm will come to any of us."

With an unsettling smirk, Alphonse said, "What I know is that this place, like many other places with supernatural energy, is an imposter door." Alphonse's volume and inflection moved as he spoke, indicating that Alphonse was twisting and turning through the maze as he explained. "I've been told by one that knows that there exists on our planet doors, or portals, that lead, somewhere else. I believe Mama went looking for these portals, found one, and somehow entered into it. She is wherever those portals lead. I was also told that the portals emit a humming noise whenever they are opened, which is loudest at the point of actual location but which becomes fainter as the portal becomes distant. Anyone, magic or non-magic, can hear the noise when they're in close proximity to the areas where the portals exist, and to them, it sounds like a hum. But those with the gifts can hear the noise even louder than a low-pitch hum at the point of origin. And, they can also her the hum when they are nowhere near an actual portal and instead by a false portal. Any place in this world with spiritual energy is a conduit to the sound because the real doors emit a residual hum in places of spiritual vibration."

"What does Roxanne have to do with any of this?" Gunnar asked.

"Roxanne? Is that the beige girl's name?" Gunnar instantly regretted offering up any personal information about his girlfriend, fearing her name could be used against her. Alphonse continued. "Unfortunately, one of the things I don't know is how to pinpoint the precise location of the actual doors and then open them. As a traveler, she can probably do that."

Acadia smirked and unwittingly offered too much information herself. "That can't be it, Alphonse. Roxanne wasn't even the first person to hear the hum today. And she only knew where to look based on past experience."

"Who was the first to hear it?" Alphonse asked with a hint of surprise.

No one spoke, obviously trying to protect Gunnar. But he wouldn't put his friends at risk and confessed. "I did. I heard it twice today. Once before lunch and once after," he said. "That's why we chased down the sound."

"Hmm . . ." Gunnar did not like the sound of the voodoo man processing the news. "Curious. It doesn't fit the pattern."

"What pattern?" his sister questioned.

"For the last five years, ever since I got the information I needed, I've been to places where strong hums have been reported. Since I'm no traveler, I can hear the hums but can't find their source. I've charted the hums, when they start, when they stop, their patterns. The humming sound never happens twice in the same day and the sound is never strong for longer than about an hour at a time. So what you've reported doesn't make sense. Unless . . . "

"What?" asked Roxanne. Gunnar could hear true interest in her voice.

"Perhaps I've been wrong about precisely what a traveler can do. Perhaps they can only open doors, but can't find them. Maybe it takes a different talent to track the doors. Perhaps, a talent like yours." Though he couldn't see it, Gunnar could feel Alphonse's finger pointing to his chest. His cadence changed to a quick pace. "You both must come with me. I see now that you're the one that can hear the hum from miles away and chase it down. Just as I need her to open the door, I need you to find it."

Though he tried not to let it show, Gunnar was scared. "Look, mate," he said assertively, but politely. "Neither one of us are going with you. You never did answer my question about assuring our safety if we cooperate. Neither of us is going to help you without that assurance."

Alphonse snorted. "I never responded to that request because I don't lie. I won't promise that she'll come out of this alive any more than I promise that you will."

Politeness left the conversation. "Acadia was right. You are insane," scoffed Gunnar in a very non-English like manner.

Just then, Gunnar heard three gasps and a sound like metal on leather.

"Oh my God, he's got a knife!" said Aaron with a trembling voice.

"Alphonse, put that away!" Acadia cried emphatically.

Gunnar braced for pain, believing he was about to get stabbed. But then, he remembered the conversation with his vardoger that very morning. His spirit twin told him that strange things would happen, but there would be no major damage. Gunnar relaxed, knowing he was not going to get punctured. Certainly, if he was actually going to be stabbed, he would have warned himself.

He also remembered the strange direction given to him by the vardoger. Show the gift received at the restaurant to the stranger. Could Alphonse be the stranger?

Anything was worth a shot to get out of this situation, so Gunnar reached into his pocket and pulled out the leather pouch.

There was another gasp, but this time it was coming from Alphonse. "The Gris-Gris," he said with hesitation. "Well Acadia, it looks like you are a believer after all."

Acadia did not tell Alphonse the truth of who had given Gunnar the pouch. "You know you can't harm him with the mojo in his possession," his twin sister said defiantly.

"Maybe not him," Alphonse said eerily. There was a sudden quick movement and the sound of someone approaching fast. Gunnar tried to reach for the sound of the runner, but caught only air in his grasp. He felt a manly figure sprint behind him, as the runner's broad shoulders clipped his own.

Roxanne screamed, "Owwww!" Gunnar turned backwards to clutch his love, just in time to hear the runner make a quick getaway to the other side of the labyrinth. He heard two other sets of steps running towards them, their friends trying to protect Roxanne.

"Ha!" Alphonse shrieked. "I may not have gotten her, but I have her blood. Acadia knows what I can do with this. If you don't cooperate, I will use magic to force you to. And next time, no gris-gris will stop me. There are ways for a houngan to get around that novice magic."

That was the last Gunnar heard of Acadia's depraved twin, as running from the stones turned to running on the grass turned to no noise at all.

"What happened?" he asked, fearful for Roxanne.

"He cut me," she said with pain in her voice, while still eerily relaxed.

"Where?" Gunnar demanded.

"On my left bicep."

Gunnar instinctively reached for the area only to find another pair of male hands applying pressure. "Thanks, mate. I've got it," he said to Aaron. Luckily, it wasn't gushing, though the wetness of the blood covered his palm. "Darling, I'm so sorry I let him get to you."

"Gunnar, it's not your fault," Roxanne said sweetly. "You tried, and you were close, and that's not bad for a blind guy. It was just fast and unexpected. I'll be okay."

"If anyone should apologize, it should be me, for getting you all involved in this mess," Acadia said glumly.

"It's all right, Acadia," Roxanne replied. "Aaron, already said it, but I'll take it a step further. We were all supposed to meet today, and we were all supposed to meet Alphonse today. If there's one thing I know, it's that four people with our abilities don't just randomly bump into each other. There is one more thing that Mama Gadreau predicted that I haven't told you. She said I'd have to be open to taking a journey with a group of people. Five other people to be exact. She said my gifts would be important on this journey and that the six of us would fulfill some divine purpose. At the time, I thought she was out of her mind. But after meeting you three, and after today, I realize her vision of my future was 100% true."

Gunnar was less interested in the past than the present. "We can't just sit here and let you bleed all day. We've got to get you to a hospital."

"I told you, Gunnar, I'll be fine," Roxanne repeated.

Ignoring her bravery, he practically rushed the group back to the limo still protectively holding on to his girlfriend's upper arm.

"The pain is pretty much gone," said Roxanne. "It's probably not bad enough to need stitches."

Acadia interceded. "Let's see if we can wipe away some of the blood and assess it ourselves."

Gunnar felt helpless not being able to be part of the viewing process. Acadia removed

314

Gunnar's dried bloody hand from its resting place. He heard some movement on leather as Acadia scooted over. There was a crisp sound of a refrigerator door opening and cold air escaping, followed by the unscrewing of a bottle. "Can you try to lift up your sleeve?" Acadia instructed.

Gunnar listened to the cleaning intently, anxious to hear the result. "I don't believe it!" said an astounded Acadia.

"How?" Aaron asked, stupefied.

"What? What?" Gunnar was imagining the worst.

"It's almost completely healed. And it's tiny, like the size of a cat scratch. It looks more like a scar, but he just cut you a few minutes ago," Acadia said with awe.

Gunnar was relieved, but confused. "Wait, my hands feel completely soaked with your blood. A scratch wouldn't have bled that much. And I could hear the sound of that knife cut through tissue. Is this . . . is this the healing gift?"

"What?" Aaron asked.

"My mom said Roxanne was supposed to have healing powers, too," explained Acadia.

Gunnar remarked with an accusatory tone directed at Roxanne, "You told me you didn't think it was true."

Roxanne was flustered. "I mean, I haven't, I don't . . . I guess it's possible that I could."

Gunnar huffed. "The last time you were injured, how long did it take to heal?"

She was silent for a long time. "I don't really remember. I never paid much attention. Look, can we just go." Gunnar heard annoyance in Roxanne's voice too.

"Um," Aaron interrupted. "Why don't Acadia and I get in the car? Then you two can have some privacy to talk outside."

Waiting until the others were safely out of earshot, Gunnar had to challenge what sounded to him like Roxanne lying. "You knew! That day in the alley, when you told those blokes to stab you, you knew that if they did, you'd heal. That's why you antagonized them, isn't it? You felt safe doing it!"

She exhaled loudly a few times before admitting, "I knew that I might be able to heal myself, yes."

Gunnar had to stifle his anger. "What about your speech about not keeping secrets from each other? You kept this rather big one from me."

Her frustration turned to resignation. "I know. I'm sorry. I just didn't want to face the two questions I was sure you would ask if I told you."

"What questions are those?" Gunnar asked in angst.

"Can I heal others? Can I heal your sight?"

Gunnar was jarred. He had never even thought about that possibility. Was there a chance that she might be able to help him see again? Surely, the answer had to be no, because wouldn't she already have offered to fix him if she could? "Why wouldn't you want me to ask that?"

"Because I don't know the answer. Maybe I can, but I don't know how. And I didn't want to drive a wedge between us with you thinking I could heal you but was holding back."

All fury was gone. Her reasons for keeping her secret were utterly just. His tone returned to sympathetic. "Well, at least now we know for sure you can fix yourself. I guess I don't have to worry about you so much anymore. I just wish my vardoger was more specific in preparing me for that wanker coming after you today."

He felt two arms hold his waist and a body come in tight for a hug. "You don't have to worry about me physically. But please, never stop worrying about my heart. You have to take good care of that."

He couldn't help but smile. He planted a small kiss on her forehead and then opened the door of the limo so they could join the others.

Acadia spoke the moment they sat. "Everything okay?"

Gunnar exhaled. "Fine. Just a small misunderstanding that's been explained. Nothing for you two to worry about. Come on, let's figure out what we're going to do tonight."

"Let's go to Bourbon Street," said Aaron merrily.

"That sounds fun," said Roxanne, trying to chipper up.

Gunnar remembered his work duties. "Are you sure, mate?" he asked Aaron. "That place can get a bit tempting with all the hurricanes and beer."

Aaron's tone was firm. "I know, but I believe I can resist, and I want to resist. Besides, I want to know I can still have a good time sober."

Resigned, Gunnar agreed. "Then that's where we'll go," said Gunnar. Realizing he felt grimy from dried blood, dried coffee, and a bag inside his pocket that made him smell like a cigar bar, he mentioned, "But before we do, I really could use a shower."

"And you could use some new clothes, Roxanne. Your arm may be fine, but your shirt sleeve looks like you've been shot," said Acadia.

"Yeah," Roxanne replied playfully. "I don't want to scare the tourists. Should we go back to my house?"

Aaron interrupted. "No. We can make a pit stop at my hotel. It's closer. Don't worry about clothes, Roxanne. If you don't mind being unfashionable for a bit, you can wear one of my baggy t-shirts."

"Mind?" Roxanne laughed. "As one of your biggest fans, you'll probably have to pry it off my body if you want it back."

CHAPTER NINE

The Hum

*****

A teenaged girl popped her nose out from a gently used copy of *The Fellowship of the Ring*. "What are you looking at?" she asked the strange boy examining her.

"Uh, oh, nothing. I, I just like what you're reading. Not too many people our age read that type of intricate novel," said a very odd looking, short and slight teen boy.

The girl looked at her admirer curiously, and he sized up the girl now that her face was visible

She had that dewy, sweet look of Karen Carpenter, complete with a mousy brown, out-of-style, sixties hair flip. Her eyewear was current though; giant rose colored glasses resembling goggles swallowed up half her forehead along with her eye sockets.

Her scan of him revealed no threat and she opted to be as friendly as a British child was allowed to be. "Don't you just hate how our generation behaves? Ignorant of art and literature, yet so familiar with taking drugs and placing unnecessary safety pins through their clothes? It's so dreadfully uncivilized."

It was all the boy could do to stop his smile from exploding. Up to this moment, he had assumed he was all alone in the world, a misunderstood outcast destined for loneliness. After all, not many people could identify with genius. "I despise that as well. I don't understand this punk thing at all. Why would someone possibly want to shave a portion of their head here in freezing cold London?"

She smiled and nodded. "Quite right. I say that bucking comfort for the sake of making a

322

fashion statement defeats the purpose of self-preservation. And if punk is supposed to be disestablishmentarian, why do they all follow each other around like sheep, all looking the same, and all listening to the same terrible music?”

Forgetting his normally impeccable manners, he forgot to request permission to sit across from the girl. Sitting in a wobbly chair, he looked near her elbow and also saw *The Tale of Two Cities* and *The Iliad*. His heart skipped beats and he didn’t even know why. “What’s your name?” the boy asked shyly.

“Millie, short for Mildred, which I hate but it is a family name, so never call me that.” He grinned again, this time with his crooked British teeth showing. She even talked like him, quickly in a stream of conscious. “What’s yours?” she asked in return.

“I’m Arthur Snow.”

In 1961, many things happened in the world, including the birth of Arthur Dalton Snow. While no little baby could remember the Berlin Wall being built or the Bay of Pigs Invasion, little Arthur always swore he could. At the very least, he was positive he remembered at age two watching the television when the news announcer told the world that JFK was dead.

In 1964, at the tender age of three, while his mother was becoming obsessed with the Beatles, he was becoming obsessed with beetles. And butterflies, earthworms, and ants. He also liked taking things apart and putting them back together, like 100 piece puzzles and tinker toys. He even found joy in mixing different substances from the kitchen pantry to see what would happen.

In 1967, when he was a boy of six and all of Great Britain was in a flurry about the nationalization of steel, he could name the chemical properties of steel, and neon, and rubidium, and any other element on the periodic table.

Despite all the signs, it wasn't until 1969 that his parents realized he was special. His parents, nice people but not folks that others would describe as especially bright, became fans of a new show on

324

the BBC called Monty Python's Flying Circus. That first hilarious episode was watched by his whole family; he, his mother and father, and sisters, Charlotte and Margaret. Everybody had such a laugh, Arthur wished to extend their happiness beyond the show's end. Right before bed, he reenacted the episode—in its entirety, word for word.

Sure that the eight-year old hadn't missed a beat, his parents tested their theory. Giving him *The Bible*, they asked Arthur to read Genesis. He read it only once and recited it back verbatim. Then they gave him *A Christmas Carol*. Not only did he read it in one day, he then wrote down three entire chapters before bed. In the following weeks, his parents moved from books to scenes. They would put pictures in front of their son, move them quickly away, and ask him to remember what was in the photo. Arthur never missed a single identification.

Unsure of how to handle a child who never missed a thing, his well-meaning parents took him to a psychologist and doctors in an effort to understand what was going on with their son. Testing and observation revealed the opposite of a dire diagnosis. Arthur was just a genius with a 196 IQ and a photographic memory.

Unfortunately, he wasn't permitted to just be a genius in the privacy of his own mind. The doctors reported their observations of him to MI5, who took him from his home and shaped him into a teenager that was barely able to communicate with other people his age. From eight to fourteen, he was a slave to government researchers, who forced him to do calculus and physics almost around the clock. He was presented riddles that stumped adults, solving them in the amount of time required to pick lint from one's navel. He pitted wits with top engineering professors from ETH Zurich and always stumped his elders. He was once even given a code by an American soldier and told to break it, a task that took him four weeks less than American Army intelligence.

In these four years, not only had Arthur become mentally superior to pretty much everyone, he had also gained a level of skepticism unhealthy for a twelve-year old. He was sick of being used, recognized that there was no way he could live a normal life as a government-controlled riddle solver, and sought freedom from his mathematical bondage. So, one day, in the presence of the agents assigned to him, Arthur "fell" from a horse and faked a head injury that stripped his mental capabilities. With 1971's inadequate x-ray technology, none of the experts figured out it was a ruse. His manipulators were devastated and noted that his loss of genius was a great blow to the sovereign's national security, but within six months, no one in power cared about him anymore.

Sadly, the emotional damage from depriving Arthur of a normal childhood could not be undone, and he was socially inept around other teens. He preferred slacks to jeans, considered The Rolling Stones an affront to Rachmaninoff, and couldn't understand why people thought Jaws was so entertaining when the mechanical shark was so obviously fake and could have used some technical improvements. His male counterparts considered him strange and made fun of him, while females ignored him and considered him a square. Arthur did try to speak to girls, but telling them that they were supernovas of positively charged ions wasn't received well as a compliment.

At the tender age of fifteen, he had already contemplated a life alone, believing that no woman in this world was compatible with him. Yet, here he was, having a conversation with someone who, for the first time since his fraudulent brain damage, he did not want to hide his intellect from. Well, not completely.

"So," asked Millie from her seat at the library, "what kind of books do you read?"

He panicked for a moment, not wanting to scare her with the truth that he was at the library to read a paper on subatomic particles. Instead, he reached back to his six-year old experience and grasped at titles he hoped would be of interest to her. "Oh, I love Dickens, of course. *David Copperfield* is my favorite, or maybe it's *Martin*

Chuzzlewit, no, it's *David Copperfield*, but I prefer to read them in the original serialized versions if I can find them. And fantasy is quite entertaining too. I like Tolkien as well, but I think I like CS Lewis more perhaps. I do love the classics most, though. *The Iliad* and *Odyssey* are great of course, but I prefer Greek drama. Huge fan of *Antigone* and *Lysistrata*."

Millie nodded with approval. "I like you Arthur Snow. It's not every day I meet a learned young person. By the way, I'm seventeen, how old are you?"

"Fifteen." Though he knew he should have fibbed and aged himself to eliminate any potential reasons for her to decline his invitation of friendship, he was incapable of lying to her.

"I'm surprised. Those works you've listed are way above the comprehension of a typical fifteen-year old," she stated.

"I'm not typical," he said bluntly.

She nodded. "Well, since I'm not a typical seventeen-year old either, I see no disadvantage in forming a friendship despite the age difference."

Arthur had never heard happier words.

He and Millie were inseparable after meeting at the library that day. When they fell in love over the course of growing up, Arthur finally shared with her the full range of his knowledge. Luckily, she did not find it freakish or intimidating. But she did agree that the world could never know of his genius, since military and government agencies would certainly tear them apart now that Russia had occupied Afghanistan and the SALT II talks had disintegrated. Yet, she didn't want him to waste his gifts either, so he encouraged him go to University but focus his studies on non-science and non-math related pursuits. Finding history interesting, Arthur did just that, taking a particular liking to his classes on myths and legends.

With the ability to take on immense course loads with ease, Arthur plowed through a Bachelor's, a Research Masters, and a Ph.D. in five years. At age 23, Arthur was the youngest Ph.D. recipient Cambridge ever had in its history department. After that came the papers, the lectures, and the teaching, followed by the prizes, the awards, and the accolades. Through all his professional success, Millie stood by Arthur and they lived an enchantingly happy, if very eccentric, life together. While they were occasionally intimate, more so as a mechanism to release energy, theirs was a companionship fostered more on mutual acceptance and caring. Just as she supported Arthur, he supported her as she got her own Bachelor's and Teaching Master's in Literature.

Despite being together since 1976, they never married and never had children. But they loved each other, and Arthur was sad to see her leave his world in 1997 when she was killed in a car accident. Still, both had been so practical and rational and intelligent, that the sadness was easily recognized as his own grief and not sorrow for her, and he was able to surmount it with the scientific and philosophical recognition that death is the inevitable conclusion of every life.

So fancy his surprise when, about two weeks after his companion's funeral, she dropped in for a visit while he was writing a paper.

Frantically typing away, Arthur was initially bothered when the lights went off around him. "Bloody fuse box," he angrily grumbled as he pushed the computer keyboard away. Getting up and heading for the kitchen, he didn't even notice her sitting on the sofa as she had done every night of her life. In fact, if she hadn't spoken, unobservant Arthur would have passed right by her.

"Still working on that project about Aristophanes?" asked the familiar voice.

Stopping in his tracks, he turned and saw Millie sitting there across from him. Unsure of how to react, his logical linear brain took over and he simply answered the question as though she had never died. "Yes. I did a little more research and discovered he may have belonged to a secret society of scribes, but I really must flesh that our more before I publish."

"Same old Arthur. Not even phasing you a bit that I'm a specter, is it?"

He furrowed his brow. "Perhaps a bit."

His companion, now pale and practically see through, but very real, smiled. "Won't you sit with me a bit?"

The genius spoke with unflustered sincerity. "Well, I would, but the longer I speak to you the more I realize the only logical conclusion can be that I am either insane or suffering from hallucinations brought on by carbon monoxide poisoning, though I am quite sure I turned the gas off after dinner."

"I can assure you, you are not insane and this conversation is actually happening. Sit with me."

She had always been the dominant personality in their relationship, so Arthur dutifully complied. He took the seat in the recliner across from the sofa, which had been the same spot he sat in every night of her life. He was unsure how this dialogue would proceed, but thought it only polite to start the talk off positively. "So, how is the afterlife treating you? No complaints?"

She smiled more now in death than she ever did in life and was a lot less persnickety. "Arthur, there is more to death you can imagine. It is nothing like we thought. I mean, yes my flesh is rotting in a box now, but I'm not, as you can plainly see."

"So, agnosticism was the wrong path of thought for us to follow?" asked the near atheist.

"Quite wrong."

"But, you're here, and not in heaven, so is Christianity wrong as well?"

"Arthur, I am not here to discuss the religious implications of death. Quite frankly, what happens when one crosses over is incomprehensible to the living; even to someone as smart you, my love. No scientist, no philosopher, no poet has ever come close to describing the reality that is the post-death experience."

"So, why are you here then? I mean, not that I'm ungrateful for your visit, I'm just curious."

"In the most basic human terms, and please don't even bother asking from whom this directive comes, I've been given special permission to talk to you about your future."

"How do you know the future?" His scientific mind jumped with excitement. 'Ohh, ohh, is heaven in a black hole?"

"Arthur . . ." she said inflecting the last syllable, like she was gently scolding a dog.

"Sorry, but I really can't help it when you talk about things like the future."

"Look, there isn't much time to talk, so you must listen to me very carefully and store this in a place in your memory where you don't obsess over it every day, but where you can quickly remember every detail when the time comes. Can you find that place in your brain to compartmentalize this conversation?"

He nodded. "Of course."

"Here it is then.   The world is not all explainable. Science and math cannot account for all of reality. The myths and legends have a basis in truth. The paranormal researchers we used to scoff at as charlatans are far closer to correct than our counterparts who demand evidence printed in scholarly journals. And you, my darling, must accept this. Open your mind to the world beyond. And someday, that world will come to you and ask you to become part of it, and you must."

He processed her words, but furrowed his brow. "I don't understand why you are getting to tell me this. I mean, why do you get to talk to me and give me advice from beyond the grave when not everyone reports encounters with their deceased loved ones?"

"I love you Arthur, I really do. But you sometimes miss the obvious and the simple because you're wrapped up in complex analysis. It was thought, by someone, that you could miss an important opportunity, even if it stared you right in the face, unless you knew that it was coming and

336

unless you had been previously prepared to be open-minded to it. And that's why I'm visiting, to make sure that you know to be on the lookout for that opportunity.

"Well, what is the opportunity? When will it come to me?" The learned man was frustrated with the lack of clear direction.

"My dearest, you are not ready to know that yet. Let's be honest, you're still trying to analyze my presence here, and until you forego analysis for belief, you cannot possibly assimilate the details of the journey you need to take."

He felt miffed that she would not trust his intellect to be able to translate the inexplicable. "Can't you provide me with one piece of information about this journey? One clue?"

She smiled one more time. "I can only say that you will learn of the journey when you are ready to learn of it. It's kind of like, when you tried to replicate the Fleischmann-Pons cold fusion experiment, and after failing, failing, failing, you finally did it by adding tritium to the deuterium. It wasn't that you weren't smart enough to figure it out all those times. Do you remember what changed?"

"Of course. It was after we talked about our regret at not having had a child. When you proffered that three was stronger than two, and that had there been a third member of our family, we might have been warmer people, instead of standoffish to strangers. I was inspired."

"And it took over ten years of your life to learn all that needed to be learned about cold fusion, so that one day when you felt inspired, you could couple the inspiration and knowledge into a solution."

"So, you're telling me I need to learn all I can about the supernatural?"

"Yes," she said with palpable relief in her smile.

"Can you at least tell me how long I have to learn it?"

"About the same amount of time it took to learn about cold fusion. Now, that's all I can say about this matter, as it's time for me to go."

338

"To where?" he asked inquisitively.

Her brown hair seemed more brilliant now and her brown eyes more soft. "You really are cheeky, Arthur. Trying to squeeze out more information?"

He chuckled his odd, little snorty laugh. "Well, you can't blame me for trying."

Millie rose from her spot on the sofa. "I'll be seeing you, Arthur."

"Um, Millie, before you go. It was kind of sudden you going the way you did, and I didn't actually get to say goodbye or anything. So before you go, I just wanted to make sure you knew, that I love you."

The apparition came within inches of the recliner and reached out. The translucent skin of her hand didn't touch his cheek, but he swore that his cheek grew warm as though a ray of sunlight was on it. "I knew that Arthur. And you must know that I loved you. And still do. And we will see each other again, of that I am sure."

He grinned. "Right, when I'm dead."

She winked. "Or before."

He cocked his head. "I thought you said this was your only visit?"

She was coy. "Arthur, that's not what I said."

And with that, her presence was gone, as was the heat from being close to his spirit visitor.

*****

A.J.'s record company had sent out a press junket to local radio stations advising that A.J. was arriving in town on Thursday, so for the next two days, no one knew the rock star had already arrived. Thus, maneuvering around the exterior of the Roosevelt Hotel was easy, as no photographers or fans were waiting to pounce. The same could not be said for the interior.

From the moment they set foot inside, all Gunnar could hear was a whirlwind of activity.

The first voice he heard said rehearsed words but with the fervor of excitement that always accompanies being in the presence of someone famous. "Greetings, and welcome to the Roosevelt

Hotel, sir. I'm Henry, hotel manager, and will be happy to assist you with whatever you need."

Henry was interrupted by a smooth, fast talking man with an East Coast accent. Gunnar had heard this voice before, when A.J.'s manager called and begged him to watch over A.J. "Hey, my man. Great to see you. And you look fantastic." Aaron grunted in response. The next thing Gunnar knew, his hand was being shaken while another hand had passed around his back to hold his shoulder tight. "Thanks so much, man, you saved this show. Just make sure he stays on the wagon, okay?"

Then a sugary female voice tentatively added to the ovation. "Mr. Rhodes, your room is ready and prepared with all of your rider requirements. I'll be happy to take you up there. Shall I show you first? Then we can have your, friends, join you later?" Gunnar had heard this speech before too. It was the ever-attentive female hotel employee who wanted to get the rock star alone for a few minutes to convince him of her devotion via a quickie.

"No thanks," said Aaron. This was the first time Gunnar had ever heard a star decline the invitation. "My friends and I are gonna hang out together all day, so if you could just show all of us up there, that would be great." Gunnar was impressed with Aaron's willpower, but suspected it had to do with Acadia.

The now silent female employee led the entourage towards the whirring sound of elevators. Just short of where the metal doors clanged together with a "ding," Aaron stopped the procession. "Hey Damon, I just want to be alone with my friends for the rest of the day. Take a day off from managing. You and the record label guys can do whatever you want, but please just let us have my suite to ourselves. And not to be rude, but I really don't want to see any of you guys again until tomorrow."

Gunnar wasn't surprised, but a barely audible "hmm" from Roxanne indicated that she was. She had likely never seen what it's like for a person to be so powerful, they can order others around.

Once in the safety and quiet of a huge penthouse that smelled like window cleaner and flowers, Gunnar was finally able to take a shower. In fact, it was even a fun shower since Roxanne took it with him. In the guise of having to help the blind man since he couldn't see the unfamiliar bathroom, Roxanne offered to clean up her beau. Their shower started with frolicking and playfully flicking water at each other, followed by intimate touching while they made out. This was the first shower they had ever taken together, and while Roxanne and he had been naked before, their bodies had never before touched so closely and so much. It was exhilarating to be this close to her, and yet, lovemaking still did not occur. After very intense kissing, both agreed to get back out to the main room to make sure that Acadia wasn't having trouble keeping Aaron away from the bar.

Emerging from the master bathroom together, Roxanne said, "What's going on?"

"We had a very strange experience when you guys were in the shower, and, well, we both agree that it's connected us."

"What happened?" asked Gunnar inquisitively.

Acadia continued. "As you know, I'm not incredibly familiar with rock music, but I was thinking, maybe I would recognize something of Aaron's if I heard it. So I asked him to play me something. He took his guitar and he started playing the most beautiful melody."

Aaron interrupted with a point he thought was important. "I played her Lover's Symphony off my second CD."

"And about thirty seconds into playing, I had another vision." Acadia sounded excited.

Aaron was excited too. "And at the exact same time, I heard someone's feelings in the music. We had a simultaneous supernatural experience!"

"But what makes it ever more amazing," said Acadia, "is that we compared notes afterward and figured out we were tuning in to the exact same person."

Roxanne moved away from Gunnar's side and skipped toward Acadia's voice. Gunnar followed, stumbling to a chair. Sitting down, he could sense body heat and knew he was close to the conversation. He heard the voice of his girlfriend. "Who was it?"

"We don't know," said Aaron. "Neither of us knew the guy."

"What did you see?" Roxanne queried.

Acadia answered. "An older white man. He was reading. Tons of books everywhere. In a little office, with a sofa facing a desk. He had this crazy mop of salt and pepper hair. Sometimes, for no reason, he would chuckle to himself. That's all I saw. About a minute of just watching him read and laugh."

Aaron picked up the story. "And then I tuned in to the guy's thoughts and feelings. He was so smart. I couldn't keep up with all the things in his head. Math I couldn't even understand, at the same time as the philosophical origins of the universe, at the same time as Shakespeare talk, at the same time as thinking about the Vikings. And I swear Gunnar, I swear I heard the same word going through his head that you said earlier. That 'v' word, you know, yourself from the future?"

"Vardoger?"

"Yeah! His mind said that too. And his thoughts were all British, similar to yours, but more Queen Elizabeth like. And he talked a lot in his head, and it was scattered too, like his thoughts, but funny. It sounded like he was on speed, but his brain was way too coherent to be on drugs."

Roxanne jumped in. "Wow, Aaron. You're not just an empath, I think you're a telepath too. And Acadia, this is your second vision now, and both are of people. That may give us a clue as to your gifts."

Gunnar was focused on the idea that someone else would use the term vardoger and knew that the pair's visions could not be coincidence. "Acadia, is there anything else you can tell us about the man? Not what he looked like because that won't be helpful to me, but any details about the way he smelled? Did he say anything in your vision out loud?"

She sucked in air and her tongue was on the roof of her mouth. "The only thing he said out loud was 'so lovely,' and then he took a sip of something. And he sort of had, not really a lisp, but when he said the word 'so' it sounded like he was whistling."

"Anything unusual or out of the ordinary about the space he occupied?" Gunnar yearned for more information, as if he brain were trying to tell him something.

"Just an office, books, papers. Wait, I guess there was something that seemed out of place. This guy had a washtub full of oranges in the corner of his office," Aaron offered.

"That's it!" said Gunnar. "I know the man you both saw."

Roxanne was intrigued. "Who is it, Gunnar?"

"Roxanne, you were there with me. Don't you remember?   Picture a super intelligent, rambling, whistly voiced lover of orange juice who knows what the vardoger is."

"Dr. Snow!" Roxanne declared.

"Precisely," said Gunnar.

"Who's Dr. Snow?" asked Aaron.

"He's a professor at Oxford. He works with my sister. He's the one that explained the vardoger to me."

"What do you think it means?" queried Acadia. "Why would Aaron and I have a psychic link to someone you both already know?"

There was silence in the room for a minute, until Roxanne spoke. "Acadia, your mother said there would be six total people on this journey. We know it starts with us four, but we still need the other two. What if Dr. Snow is one of them?"

Gunnar chimed in. "That would make sense. He did say he wanted to kept abreast of everything. And my sister says he knows all about the paranormal. Maybe he can better explain all of our gifts, on an academic level.”

“Dude,” said Aaron. “You need to call that guy. Get him here, like yesterday.”

Gunnar wasn’t sure of the practicality of Aaron’s request. “He’s got classes, I’m sure he just can’t drop everything. And how’s he going to pay for an international flight at this late date?”

Aaron was snarky. “Um, A, have you ever heard of substitute teachers? And B, no problem. If I want him here, the record company’s paying for it. And tell him it will be first class, all the way.”

Gunnar capitulated. “Mind if I use your phone, mate?” asked Gunnar.

A cell phone was placed into his hand. “I don’t pay my bills,” said Aaron. “Go right ahead.”

Gunnar had completely forgotten about the time difference when he called Astrid to get Dr. Snow’s phone number, but quickly remembered once her sleepy voice chewed him out for the late night phone call. The call lasted longer than he would have liked, for after being scolded, he had to answer her questions about his well-being while abroad. Finally though, he was able to shirk Astrid and place the important call.

Expecting to get another grumpy, sleepy voice, Gunnar was pleasantly surprised to hear a happy, whistly, wide awake voice on the other end of the line. "Hello, this is Arthur Snow."

"Hi, Dr. Snow? This is Gunnar Ahlgren, Astrid's brother. I'm very sorry to call you so late. I'm in America and there's a time difference."

A very cheery sound came through the wire. "Ahh, yes, dear boy. No worries, no worries at all. I don't sleep much. I'm still in my office actually. I've just finished squeezing a lovely orange juice. You know, while I was juicing, I was pondering you. We must be on the same wavelength."

"I think so," said Gunnar, not wanting to allude over the phone that his companions indeed were. "Listen, I have a rather odd request. See, I've had another encounter with my vardoger and this was much longer and more specific and he told me a lot of things that I think would be of interest to you as a scholar. Would you be willing to meet with me to discuss it?"

The learned man was practically giddy. "Of course!"

"The only thing is, I'm in the States right now, on a job. And I won't be back for at least a week, maybe longer."

Dr. Snow was audibly disappointed. "Oh, what a pity."

"However, if you could come to me, I could get the airfare and your hotel room paid for. It would only be a matter of you being able to find coverage for your classes."

There was reservation in the professor's tone. "Well, cancelling classes isn't the problem, and, in fact, my students would probably enjoy a nice respite. And thank you ever so much for offering to pay, though honestly I could pay my own way since I do practically nothing with my wages. It's just that, well, see, I despise airplanes. If I'm being honest, I would also say I have acute aviophobia, or fear of flying. So, perhaps it's best if I just wait for you to return."

Gunnar needed to make the stakes bigger now that he knew of the professor's fear. "That's a shame. I was going to bring you to New Orleans, Louisiana. It's a very historical city, and I thought for sure a history buff like you would enjoy it here."

The professor was still hesitant. "Oh, New Orleans, how wonderful. Yes, yes, that would be a lovely place to visit. The Spanish and the French influences, what tales that city could tell. But, I already know all the historical data from books. And what about that hurricane they had there a while ago? I bet the place is very dirty still. I'm quite tidy and I don't think I would enjoy stepping in mud and debris at every turn. I'd probably catch a bug."

Gunnar corrected the professor. "Oh no, it's lovely. They've done a fabulous job of cleaning up and rebuilding. Not a speck of dust is out of place. You'll see. As you know, because I'm betting you're a geographer as well, Louisiana is very close to

Florida where the oranges come from. The orange juice here is always freshly squeezed from these giant juicy oranges and it's very inexpensive compared to England. You'd have plenty of Vitamin C to keep away any germs that might linger from the flight."

Dr. Snow was still not convinced. Throwing away propriety, Gunnar decided to pull out the big guns.

"Look, I was trying to be discreet until you got here, but I see it's necessary to tell you the whole truth. There are some other people here with me, people with special paranormal abilities. I know you are interested in this stuff, and I told them about you, and they'd love to meet you. But see, they're American, and they can't come back to Britain with me, so if you don't come here, they might never get to meet you, or you them."

Dr. Snow breathed heavily in the other end for a few seconds. "All right then, I'll come."

"Great. And seriously, let us pay for the ticket. We'll make it first class, and trust me, flying is a lot easier when you have lots of room to breathe. Now, when is the earliest you could come?"

"Well, it's Tuesday. I do have doctoral classes tomorrow and I should like to tell my students that I won't be available for the remainder of the week. I'll also need some time to send out an email to my Thursday students that classes will be cancelled."

"Hold on, please," Gunnar said, covering up the lower portion of the phone out of habit. "Hey Aaron, how quickly can the record company make the arrangements?"

"Yesterday if I tell them to," said the rocker confidently.

"How about a Wednesday night red eye arriving Thursday morning?"

"Doable."

Gunnar released the microphone portion of the cell phone. "Dr. Snow, I can arrange an overnight flight for you leaving tomorrow night and arriving here in New Orleans Wednesday morning.

You'll sleep right through the trip and never even know you were flying."

"So you say," said Dr. Snow with a tone of regret.

"We'll have someone call you with the flight information as soon as it's been booked. We're all very excited to see you." Gunnar wasn't exaggerating.

Gunnar heard a gulp. "Oh well, at least if I die on the plane, I'll still get to experience something new. Cheerio!" said Dr. Snow, followed by a click and a beep.

Handing the cell phone back to Aaron, Gunnar said, "He's coming."

Roxanne spoke. "That makes five. But who is our sixth?"

Acadia joined. "And even after we find our sixth, what is this journey we're supposed to take?"

"I have no idea," said Gunnar. "I'm leaving that one to Dr. Snow. Maybe he'll know when he gets here and meets you all."

"Or maybe your vardoger will tell us," said Acadia.

"Or maybe one of you girls will have a vision," said Aaron.

"So what do we do until then?" asked Gunnar.

"Hang out, talk more, and get to be life-long friends," said the rock star.

"I know this isn't going to be a popular suggestion in light of today's events," said Acadia shyly. "But I've got to go home and get some clothes and some money."

Gunnar furiously replied, still stung by the fact he couldn't stop her psychopathic brother from stabbing Roxanne. "And go to where that lunatic is?"

Aaron jumped in to defend Acadia. "Now Gunnar, I don't like it either, but Acadia is entitled to have her things. Just us two can go. You and Roxanne can stay here."

Gunnar responded. "No way. I can just see it now. Alphonse gets mad at Acadia, you step in to defend her, and you get the knife next. Your record company will kill me if anything happens to you."

Acadia jumped in with some logic. "Look, we'll all go. Let's go to the house and stake it out. We'll wait for my brother to leave, then get my stuff when he's gone."

"Gunnar," said Roxanne gently, grabbing his hand. "It's okay. I'm fine. I will continue to be fine. Remember? I think staking out her place is a good plan. Besides, I don't have any more clothes she can borrow."

He was about to voice opposition when he remembered his encounter with the vardoger. He was told that nothing major was going to happen to them in that 24-hour period, and that he needed to just go with the flow. If it was the will of three of them to get Acadia her things, he was going to have to have faith. "Fine. But I do feel compelled to state the obvious that we are not going to be inconspicuous in our current mode of transportation."

"Don't worry," said Acadia. "We'll just have the driver park inside Lafayette Cemetery and wait for us there. I live on Coliseum, and you can literally see our front door and driveway from the corner of the graveyard. And if we hurry, we might catch him out. It's still light outside and he usually doesn't come home until dark."

By 6:30 p.m., the four were wondering around a place that made Gunnar feel colder than it actually was outside. Roxanne guided him by the hand, but there were more than a few times that he ran straight into a hard cement structure that came about to his chest. "What do I keep hitting?" asked Gunnar.

Roxanne responded with some history. "Graves. The water table in New Orleans is so high that if you were to dig the traditional six feet, you'd run into flooding. So here, they build above ground stone crypts just big enough to hold the casket."

Roxanne abruptly stopped walking as Acadia spoke. "There's the house," she said with a tense tone.

"Do you see any sign of your brother?" asked Aaron.

"No, and his car is gone from the driveway."

"Let's hurry then," said Aaron, and soon enough, Roxanne was guiding Gunnar in a quickened pace. They were going so fast, he could not focus on hearing and relied entirely on Roxanne to keep him safe while crossing the road.

"Seven stairs," Roxanne said, stopping then starting again as Gunnar counted seven steps up. Then they all stood still, and Gunnar could hear heavy breathing coupled with at least one rapid heartbeat. Someone knocked. After thirty seconds with no answer, someone knocked again. Still no answer. Then he heard a door creak while, simultaneously, Acadia called "Hello? Alphonse, are you here?"

With no answer, Gunnar felt himself being moved again, this time into a structure that blocked out the small amount of wind in the atmosphere outside.

"Alphonse!" Acadia belted out, checking for her brother one more time before she allowed herself to relax. The house was quiet, without a single squeak of floorboard.

"Aaron, will you come with me upstairs. I'll show you my room and we can get a suitcase together."

"Of course," said the rock star and two sets of footprints scampered off.

Still holding his hand, Roxanne urged, "Let's go check out the house. Oh Gunnar, I wish you could see it. It's insanely beautiful. Hardwood floors, antiques, marble."

Gunnar added, "But it stinks. There's an old sulfur smell pervading everything."

Room to room, in zigzag patterns, they walked. Gunnar grew frustrated with every "Whoa," and "Ahh," that he couldn't see. Then finally, he heard a different reaction from Roxanne. "What the hell?"

"What is it?"

"It's like a mad scientist's laboratory. There are beakers, Bunsen burners, liquids in jars, and powders all over the bookshelves. And the books, they're everywhere, and so old. Let's take a closer look. Gunnar, take three steps down."

Filing into the sunken room, the sulfur smell started to mix with other smells, but instead of acidic odors like pneumonia or salt, there were many natural, earthy aromas. Much like his gifted mojo bag, the smell of fresh tobacco was pungent. Mints, limes, black pepper and honey could also be detected. And there were even some spices his keen nose couldn't place, though he was sure he'd smelt every spice the culinary world had to offer.

Roxanne was like a kid at a freak show, needing to touch and see everything despite being repulsed by it. Gunnar was getting dizzy from the olfactory overload. "Darling, is there a chair you can plop me in while you look around?" asked Gunnar.

"Uh, yeah. By a desk. I'll take you to it."

Feeling cold wood behind his knees, he bent his body over and sat.

"Wait a minute," said Roxanne, and Gunnar heard some papers flurry about in front of him. "What's this?"

"What?" asked Gunnar.

Roxanne murmured to herself as she always did when she was reading to herself.

At that very moment, footprints trampled back downstairs and Acadia commented, "I see you found this mess of a supposed library."

"Whoa!" said Aaron. "It's like something from a Frankenstein movie."

"Hey guys," said Roxanne. "I've found something. A clue as to what the heck Alphonse was talking about. Look!"

The two others walked briskly towards the desk. Gunnar heard motion as one pair of arms reached out to Roxanne and took something. There was silence for a few minutes.

"For us blind people, can someone please identify what we're looking at," said Gunnar impatiently.

"It's a map of the world, but with little funny circles scribbled all over it," said Aaron.

"And a book, doggy-eared to a chapter called "The Hum." It talks about a whole bunch of places in the world where people hear unexplained hums. Alphonse has circled some of the places. Kokomo, Indiana. Norman, Oklahoma. Hull, Massachusetts. Hueytown, Alabama . . ."

"All of those places are circled on this map," said Aaron.

Gunnar heard pages turning and then Acadia continued. "What about Largs, Scotland; Copenhagen, Denmark; and Vancouver, British Columbia?"

"Yep, all circled on the map," said Aaron.

"I think these are all the places Alphonse has been traveling to all these years. He's been looking for places with the hum, because Mama went chasing after the doors that emit a hum," said Acadia.

"But a few of them are crossed out," said Aaron. "What does that mean?"

Gunnar thought that was obvious. "I'll bet there's a crossed-out circle over New Orleans, isn't there?"

"Yeah," said Aaron. "How'd you know?"

"Remember what Alphonse said today about the labyrinth being a false portal? That the sound emanated from it, but no door actually opened? The crossed off ones must be those he's discounted as false portals."

"Maybe we should take this map with us. Maybe it's important," said Aaron.

"No!" Acadia demanded. "If any of Alphonse's things come up missing when he gets back, he'll know I was here."

"She's right," said Roxanne. "But I still think it's something Dr. Snow should see. I'm gonna take a picture of it."

Gunnar listened as the map was fully unfolded and placed on the desk in front of him. But his attention was diverted to a roaring engine not too far away growing increasingly louder. So loud, in fact, it was coming from the driveway.

"Someone's here!" he said in a whisper, interrupting the photography session.

"Quick, everyone hide!" said Acadia in a panic.

"Just one more second, I've almost got the whole map in the view," pleaded Roxanne.

Gunnar could not rise from the desk as Roxanne was blocking him from above. "Just take what you can and we'll worry about it later." He heard the camera on her cell phone snap, then she grabbed his hand to help him rise.

"Quick, quick!" said Acadia. "Just go into the next room. I'll stall Alphonse. Once I've engaged him in conversation, head away from this room, straight back, and you'll find the kitchen. There's a patio door there. Go out of it, go to the limo, and pull around to right in front of the house. Honk when you get there, and I'll run out of the house if I have to."

"Acadia, I'm not leaving you," said Aaron with dire concern.

Gunnar heard a quick peck of lips to cheek skin. "Everything will be okay, as long as he doesn't know outsiders were here." Now everyone could hear a car door slam. "Go! Now!"

As instructed, the three interlopers scattered into the room directly behind the library. They could still hear everything, and waited with baited breath as keys fumbled and the front door opened. It was only a matter of seconds before Acadia was heard with surprise in her voice. "What are you doing here?"

"I should ask you the same thing." The reply came from another woman. "Alphonse told me that you had been escorted out of this house."

Acadia scoffed. "Escorted? He threw me out. If he wants me gone, that's fine, but I need my clothes and my purse. That's why I'm here, to get my stuff. And you can tell him that, Delphine. He at least owes me my own things. And if he were here right now, I'd say that to his face. Speaking of which, why are you here?"

This was the point in time when the friends should have headed for the kitchen. But since Alphonse was not the intruder, they all remained glued to the conversation.

The other woman spoke melodically, her voice slightly lower in pitch than Acadia's and gravelly sounding. Gunnar could hear her pacing the foyer as she spoke. "Your brother came to me right from the park and told me all about your afternoon. Told me all about the white boys and the beige girl and you at the labyrinth. Where are your friends now, Acadia? Where is the beige girl?"

"Wouldn't you like to know, so you can run and tell my brother?"

"Heavens, no. Just call it curiosity. I've never met someone with so many powers before."

"Well, after being stabbed earlier, she left the city. What did Alphonse expect, for her to stick around and get hurt again?" Acadia managed to muster up contempt strong enough to bolster her lie.

"Hmmm. Perhaps she did, perhaps she didn't. The way Alphonse made it seem, you all were like four peas in pod. So I suspect you'll be seein' her again, wherever she is."

Acadia sounded annoyed. "You didn't answer my question. Why are you here?"

"Alphonse left New Orleans shortly after your encounter with him this afternoon. Made a little trip to Indiana. Said he wanted to test somethin'. But he'll be back in a few days I expect. I think he's wrong about the blood, you see?"

"Blood?" asked Acadia.

The other woman had malevolence in her voice. "Alphonse believes that in the absence of the physical presence of the beige girl, a wanga doll with her blood might suffice. And while normally, you know I give credence to the power of the doll, in this instance, I think only the traveler in person can help him through the door."

Acadia's tone changed from intimidation to interrogation. "So, he's told you about all this stuff then?"

"Of course. He calls me from every place he goes where the hum has been reported. Then I mark it on a map for him."

Acadia tried to innocently pump the woman for information. "Oh yeah, that map on the desk. I saw that, but I didn't know what all the circles and Xs meant."

"Circles are the marks I made where Alphonse confirms hearin' the hum. Xs are the marks he makes when your brother has ruled out a place as a true portal."

Acadia played up her confusion. "I still don't get it. What's with all the portal stuff?"

"Your brother believes, based on a lot of research and readin', that there are four portals from this world that lead to four other worlds. He believes that there's a strong current of energy at each of these holes that acts as a door, keeping the two worlds separate. This energy always emits a hummin' noise. Near a true portal, everyone can hear the noise. Near a false portal, only magical folk can."

"Yeah, that part I got. And he also told me that my friend was a traveler who could open the doors. But what I don't get is how Alphonse can rule out any of those places on the map as a false door if he doesn't have the ability to open them? I mean, how can he ever know, for instance, if New Orleans is or is not a real portal?"

The other woman laughed. "Your brother made that mark just today, just after your meetin' in the park. He ruled it out for sure because a traveler was there, your little beige friend, and nothin' opened."

"But he's crossed out other ones too. Places where Roxanne, my friend, wasn't at. How did he know which others to cross out?"

"Your friend isn't the only traveler, you know. There are others. Come here," said the woman. Gunnar heard slow steps on the hardwood going away from the library entrance back to the center of the room where the desk was. He then heard the crinkling of paper. "See this crossed out one—Kokomo, Indiana? About six months ago,

Alphonse searched this area until he came as close as he could to where the sound was the loudest. Naturally, there was nothin' there, except a little diner. He went in, weary and needin' some refreshment. He got talkin' to a loose lipped waitress there who told him that all kinds of people had been through the area seekin' the source of the hum and that she discounted them all as crazy, except one. This waitress had met a pretty blonde woman there who was different. She wasn't tryin' to prove a theory, or tryin' to find aliens. She merely told the waitress that it didn't open for her. The waitress said that this woman also had a map, kinda like this one here. And the waitress peeped at it, and memorized that the woman had crossed off Kokomo; Ontario, Canada; some forest in Belarus; and the main island of Hawaii. Alphonse knew in his bones that the other woman was a traveler too, so he crossed off everythin' she'd crossed off.

But now, Alphonse is back to dead ends without another traveler to lead the way. That's why he wants to ... borrow ... your friend and her beau. Alphonse tells me the hum calls to him louder than the loa calls to us. He don't want to separate them. They are more than welcome to travel together. And if they join Alphonse, no harm would come to them."

"Delphine, we specifically asked him today if he could guarantee Roxanne's safety if she helped him, and he wouldn't do it."

"Well how can he? He don't know what's on the other side of the portals. He'd be a liar if he made such a promise. You'd be doing your brother, not to mention your Mama, a great service if you talked your friends into helpin' out."

Acadia exhaled. "Like I said, she's gone. They're gone. They're probably half way to Miami by now."

"Yes, you did say that. Oh well, you know your brother. Things go a lot more smoothly for people when they see things his way."

"I understand," said Acadia. The implicit threat was not lost on Gunnar as he listened intently through the wall.

"Well," said Delphine curtly. "The reason I came was to get this here map for your brother. He was in such a rush this afternoon, he forgot it and can't remember exactly where he needs to be goin'." The crinkling paper sound turned to a folding paper sound. "Now that I have it, I better go. Tell you what, your brother ain't gonna be back tonight, and I'm sure he won't be mindin' you spendin' one last night here and gettin' all your stuff together. But do be mindful to take only your stuff."

"Of course," said Acadia gruffly.

"And do consider callin' your friend in, Miami was it? And tellin' her it would be a lot easier on her and her man if she cooperated."

"I'll tell her, Delphine."

"By the way, Alphonse will want a forwardin' address, to send you mail and stuff like that. Should I tell him you'll be stayin' with your white boyfriend?"

"What?" Acadia questioned.

"Alphonse said today that he could sense you were in love, and that one of the white boys you were with was in love with you too. I assumed you'd be livin' with him now that you've got no home."

"Uh," Acadia tumbled over her words. She was clearly terrified of giving away that the subject of this conversation was in the next room. Gunnar could only imagine, based on his misgivings after falling in love with Roxanne in a day, that the truth of her socially unacceptable feelings was causing great embarrassment right now. "I'm just going to stay at a hotel for a few days, until I figure out some long terms plans."

"You must know your brother don't approve of a mixed match, and he definitely don't approve of you finding a mate outside of the Societe. But, I'm willin' to bet he would overlook it and welcome your beau into the family, if your Mama were around, since he's famous and all and would bring more notoriety to the family."

Acadia was speechless, and again, the manipulation was easily heard.

"Well, goodbye Acadia," said the woman. "I'm sure I'll see you again." With that, Gunnar heard steps out of the library and down the hall. The knob turned, the front door creaked open and slammed shut, and footsteps were heard on the pavement. Aaron, who had been shoulder to shoulder with Gunnar listening in, made an abrupt move toward the hall, which Gunnar had to stop by grabbing on to the rock star's shirt. "Wait!" Gunnar said in a whisper. "We must wait until the car starts and leaves before we show ourselves. You never know if that woman will come back, or if the whole things was a ruse and Alphonse is waiting to pounce."

Aaron silently complied, though his breathing became heavier with anticipation. Finally, a roaring engine signaled Gunnar it was time to let go of his friend's clothing. Aaron bolted and Roxanne guided Gunnar to hall.

"Who was that?" Aaron asked.

"Delphine. She's sort of my brother's wife. She is the mambo of his Societe. They aren't legally married or anything, but they claim to be spiritually bound and they do sleep together, even though they live in different houses."

"Do you believe her that your brother is away?" asked Gunnar impatiently.

"Yeah. She wouldn't lie to me because, even though I never took the path of being a mambo, it's still my birth right, and I'm still capable of it. So she respects me as her equal."

"Well," said Aaron, exhaling. "That's good. We have time to get more of your stuff if you want."

"There's nothing in the house I really want to be reminded of, and quite frankly, nothing that Alphonse wouldn't feel belongs to him anyway. I've got my clothes. I've got my purse and my wallet. I've got my secret stash of cash from under my floor boards. That's all I need. I just want to get out of here."

"You know," said Aaron hesitantly but sincerely, "You should stay with me, Acadia."

Her voice grew soft and sweet again. "I really do want to. I'm, I'm sorry for that thing she said. I mean, it's crazy, she's crazy, it's . . . "

"Too early?" Aaron agreed, but with a questioning inflection that revealed his own uncertainty.

She stammered. "Of, of course. Yes, I mean, we've known each other less than a day, and I would never tell someone this quickly . . . or I mean, feel this quickly . . . "

"Right, of course." said Aaron, clearly stifling his own feelings.

"Yeah." Acadia gulped.

Hearing that their two friends were terrified of letting go of social convention, Gunnar came to the rescue. "I don't mean to be the chap who's always thinking of food at inappropriate times, but I'm famished again. Why don't we take this conversation to a restaurant?"

The ordeal at Acadia's house had taken longer than expected and it was now peak dinner time. Nonetheless, because it was a Tuesday, they scored a secluded balcony table at one of the restaurants on Bourbon Street without having to play A.J.'s celebrity card. In this tourist area,

Acadia was likewise anonymous, which gave the friends a complete sense of privacy.

After ordering, Gunnar avoided the awkward tiptoeing of Aaron and Acadia around their feelings for one another by bringing up the reason they were likely all together. "So, what do you guys think of Alphonse's theory about the hum and the portals?"

"I wish your professor friend was here already so we could ask him about it," said a perplexed Aaron.

"Agreed, though this isn't going to be easy to recount," said Gunnar.

"Luckily," said Roxanne. "We won't have to. Dr. Snow can hear the theory right from Delphine's mouth. I guess being the kid of a lawyer, I'm all about preserving evidence, so when we went back to the room, I started to record the conversation on my phone. I wanted there to be some tangible proof that Acadia and Alphonse were fighting, in case anything bad happened to Acadia when we left.

Anyway, even though it wasn't Alphonse, I kept recording."

Gunnar laughed and leaned toward the voice of his beloved. "You're bloody brilliant, do you know that?"

She chuckled and he felt a warm kiss on his cheek.

"God, Thursday morning seems like forever away," said Aaron, again referencing Dr. Snow.

"Nope, only a day and a half," said Gunnar to Aaron. "And you need to stop worrying about it. I know for me, when I used to get fidgety, I went right for the bottle."

"I'm not worried," said Aaron with an upbeat tone. "I'm anticipatory. And that other shit? Believe me, you don't have to worry about it."

Acadia joined the conversation. "We're going to be keeping him sober, together."

"Yeah," said Aaron hopefully. "In fact, I want you two to take the bedroom tonight. Get lots of sleep. Acadia and I are gonna stay out in the lounge and talk. She'll watch me."

Gunnar smiled. The vardoger had promised him a good night's sleep if they brought Acadia along with them that day, and sure enough, the vardoger had still not been wrong yet.

Chapter Ten

Have We Met Before?

*****

Arthur sat sweating in his hotel room, catatonically glued to the bed. That had to have been the worst experience of his entire life. He had never flown in an airplane before and certainly never wanted to fly on one again. In fact, though it was completely inconvenient and would take much longer, he was cancelling his flight home and booking passage on a ship. It didn't matter that he knew the inner workings of an airplane from his reading. So what if he had memorized statistics on flying safety and knew his chances of crashing were miniscule? His nerves didn't care about facts. They had not yet recovered from the violent ups and downs his LAX bound jet made as he crossed a storm in the Midwestern United States, or from the fear he would soon be meeting his Millie again.

To add insult to injury, his suitcase had been lost by the airline. After two hours of traipsing back and forth from the terminal to baggage claim in a giant airport with no help, he finally found out from a melancholy baggage attendant that his luggage was inadvertently diverted to Amsterdam. It would take the better part of two days for his luggage to be returned, and the best the airline could muster up was an old travel kit filled with expired personal items and an "I Love LA" t-shirt.

This was supposed to be a fun and exciting journey. He was to give a lecture at UCLA and attend a luncheon in his honor, followed by a guided tour of local museums and libraries. Now, he only wanted to sit, solidly connected to non-moving earth in his day-old soiled clothes.

Sadly, that was not to be. The phone rang, persistently, to the point he felt he'd better answer. "Yes?" he said into the receiver bitterly.

"Dr. Snow, this is Dr. Sweatman from UCLA. I wanted to verify you arrived in one piece?"

"Barely," said Arthur defiantly.

His American colleague mistook truth for sarcasm and laughed. "Yeah, it couldn't have been fun going over those storms in Iowa. Oh well, it will make for an interesting anecdote."

"Yes," said the still cringing professor curtly.

"We've tried to call you several times now. Didn't you get in several hours ago?"

"The airline has lost my luggage, which is currently in Europe. I have no clothing."

"Oh no," said Dr. Sweatman sympathetically.

"I'll still give the lecture tomorrow, but I'm afraid I'll have to do it in dirty trousers and a t-shirt.

"Heavens, no," said Dr. Sweatman. "We take care of our guests. We at UCLA won't let a historian of your caliber suffer. Look, it's 3:30 right now. I'm going to send a car to your hotel to take you to the Beverly Center. I'm personal friends with the manager at Burberry. I'll explain the situation, tell him to expect you, and have everything charged to the school. Burberry will work for you, yes? It should be right up your alley."

Arthur had never worn name brand clothing in his life and didn't even know what Burberry was, but he was grateful for some assistance. "I appreciate that very much."

While Arthur Snow waited patiently to be picked up, Acadia Gadreau was leaving what could only be described as a disastrous audition. She had gone to West Hollywood on an open call for an independent film. The description in the trades requested a young black female with an athletic build who could do "accent work." She could speak with a Cajun accent, a Creole accent, and a French accent, so she thought "accent work" would be easy. Alas, the casting director wanted a German accent, which Acadia botched with something sounding akin to Jamaican. It was just another in a long series of depressing days that made Acadia long for the stability of New Orleans. As she stood there, at the corner of Melrose and Santa Monica, she knew it was time to give up this crazy dream of acting and go home. She made up her mind to head back to her monthly studio rental, pack up what little she had, and trek back to Louisiana first thing the next morning. Until then, she wanted to drown her sorrows in chocolate. The Beverly Center was in walking distance and Godiva was calling her name.

As Acadia craved sweets, A.J. Rhodes looked at his watch for what must have been the twentieth time. It was now 3:45. Alexis was supposed to have met him at Spago for lunch at 2:00 p.m. Like a fool, he had sat there eating bread sticks and drinking scotch for almost two hours. Lately, he couldn't help but notice that Alexis seemed to be changing, pulling away from him. He had repeatedly called her cell phone with no answer, so he was somewhat surprised when his phone rang.

"Hi honey!" came Alexis's sappy sweet voice.

"Where are you? I've been sitting here over an hour and a half!" A.J. couldn't hide his discontent.

"Oh sweetie, I'm sorry. I lost track of time. I'm over shopping at the Beverly Center, and I guess I got carried away somewhere between Gucci and Prada."

His eyes rolled far back in his head. She was spending money again, which always gave him heartburn. Sure, his first few albums did great and they appeared to be rolling in the dough, but so much of it really belonged to the record company. He had wanted to be smart with their money, invest it, maybe buy a house somewhere. But with Alexis's spending habits, Versace would be getting his money instead of Vanguard.

"Well, are you done shopping?" he asked with exasperation.

"I just want to hit Dolce and Gabbana, and maybe Ferragamo's, you know, to see if they have anything for you."

"Fine. But don't leave. I'm coming over there. We'll just have lunch there, okay?"

"Okay. Call me when you get here. Kisses!" She hung up before he could return her affection.

Just as the budding talent threw a hundred-dollar bill on the table and left Spago in a huff, Yara asked her daughter, "What time is it?"

"3:50," said Roxanne McCabe.

"I hope I'm not late," said Yara, trying desperately to find a parking spot in the Beverly Center garage.

"You have ten minutes until your appointment, Mom."

"Are you sure you're going to be okay in the mall by yourself while I get my hair done?"

"Mother, I'm not a kid anymore. I'm sure I can safely occupy my time window shopping."

"It's just that your dad and I are going out somewhere nice for dinner tonight and I want to look special," said Yara with the slightest trace of a Portuguese accent.

"Mom, it's cool."

"I feel so bad leaving you all alone all day," said Yara in a worried motherly tone.

"Mom, you invited me on this trip so I would take a break from volunteering. You're the one that said with as much as I give to others, I need to take a breather and give to myself. Having the whole day at a huge mall is perfect for that. Don't worry, I'll look around, have some frozen yogurt, and then tonight when you and dad are gone, I'll go to the hotel pool and sit in the Jacuzzi. It'll be great."

Her mother smiled and exhaled. "Roxanne, you are the best daughter."

As Roxanne flashed her mother her pearly whites, Gunnar Jensen gnashed on the inside of his mouth as someone in the booth mentioned it was 4:00 p.m. He had been working for nine hours straight, ever since the newest, hottest Latin pop diva arrived at Capitol Studios at 7:00 a.m. to begin recording her crossover single. He'd politely sat though her many fits about not enough lemon in her water, the lack of fresh air in the studio, and her *sin talento* back-up singers. But now, hunger and impatience were taking their toll on his manners.

Thankfully, little miss princessa's boyfriend showed up and within ten minutes from the time he started chewing on this cheeks, the session wrapped. As Gunnar grabbed his jacket and hit the men's room, he was starting to regret taking this job. He only liked to leave London for exceptionally good reasons and working with this tart didn't fit that description. He only took this trip to escape his birthday and Astrid's promised birthday party full of available women. Avoiding that debacle was worth leaving the country for a few weeks.

Hailing a cab outside the studio, Gunnar told the driver, "Take me to the closest place I can get some food."

"There's some pizza places in Beverly Center," said the cabbie.

"Then take me there, please."

Arthur purchased the first thing that fit him at Burberry, not caring to try on clothes or shop one moment more than he had to. Acadia had scarfed down chocolates and was now feeling sick from the sugar rush. A.J. was beyond enraged when he couldn't find Alexis anywhere and she wasn't picking up her phone. Roxanne had just finished her second full walk around the multi-tiered mall, as her mother's hair was still not done. With the help of his nose and his white-tipped cane, Gunnar found the pizza with no problem, gobbled up several pieces too quickly, and now needed a nap.

Yet in spite of shyness, stomach aches, ire, boredom, and sleepiness, each was drawn by a gnawing feeling inside compelling them to the seventh floor. Upon arriving, they each checked their respective time devices to learn that it was 5:00 p.m. on the dot. Suddenly and inexplicably exhausted, they each found a seat in the modern style turquoise and ivory chairs. The only other person there was a woman in her early thirties, with long blonde hair in a sporty ponytail, writing on a map.

Six people sat scattered about, all into themselves and all seemingly ignoring one another. Except for Arthur Snow, whose photographic memory and penchant for noticing detail couldn't help but memorize the innocuous scene. After three minutes of complete silence and passing glances between the strangers, all except for the man with the white cane of course, Arthur finally rose, the spell of his need to be there broken by a phone call received by the young guy with long hair. His yelling at what must have been his girlfriend or wife seemed to irritate the others as well, for all soon dispersed in different directions.

*****

Wednesday went by in a blur, both because of the whirlwind of tourist activities designed to keep them busy and because of the group's anxiousness to greet their fifth member. Exhausted from touring the swamps, the antique shops, and the paddle boats on the Mississippi River, they were all happy to be back at Aaron's suite. Aaron once again allowed Gunnar and Roxanne to take the bedroom, while he and Acadia slept in the front room. After a peaceful rest, Gunnar woke refreshed, but alone. He could already feel the heat from the sun filtering through the edges of the draperies. He heard voices, including Roxanne's, coming from beyond the bedroom door. He must have been the last to wake up.

Gunnar felt his way along the wall until he found the loo. He was just about to use the facilities when he heard that familiar buzz that signaled the presence of his vardoger. "Oy mate," said his double. "I told you Tuesday was going to be crazy, didn't I?"

Present Gunnar replied. "Crazy is an understatement. Why didn't you warn me that Alphonse would have a knife so I could prevent Roxanne from getting stabbed?"

"Because I knew she was going to be okay and because you needed to know about her healing powers. You need to be aware that while she is emotionally fragile, she doesn't need your physical protection. And if you're ever in a situation where the choice is to protect her or protect yourself, you know you can protect yourself without sacrificing her."

Gunnar was still terse with his secret-keeping twin. "What are you here to warn me about today? Does something go wrong with Dr. Snow?"

"No, in fact, it's just the opposite. Once Dr. Snow joins you four, everything will fall into place. You're going to be so entertained when you find out how clever that man is. But I'm not here with a warning. I'm here to say goodbye. You don't need forewarnings from me anymore; you'll have other sources for that."

Gunnar, who had only minutes earlier been mad at his vardoger, was now saddened by the thought of not speaking with him anymore. It was like having a dear friend leave with no clear guarantee that you'll ever see him again. But sadness was overshadowed by an altogether different worry caused by losing contact with his spirit twin.

The vardoger knew what he was thinking and responded before he could voice it. "Hey, me talking to you is not the only thing that makes you special. It's not your only gift. You won't be out of place with the rest of them if I stop making contact."

There were no more words and he was once again alone in the bathroom. Now feeling a little lonely, he wanted to be where the party was and felt his way along the walls towards his friends' voices.

"Hey, baby," he heard Roxanne say, as her dainty feet scampered over to where he was. No longer having to be guided by walls, Roxanne led him to a table. "We have room service coming. I ordered you pancakes."

"Thanks, love," said Gunnar, sitting down at the chair pulled out for him. Just then, he remembered why today was so important. "What time is it?"

"9:30," said Roxanne.

"Oh shite," said Gunnar. "Dr. Snow's plane landed a half hour ago!"

"Don't worry, Aaron sent a limo to pick him up," she continued.

"I feel bad, though," said Gunnar. "He hates to fly and I wanted to be there to cheer him up when he landed."

"I already talked to the driver. He made it just fine. He's in the car now and will be here soon," said Aaron.

"And we took his breakfast order too. By the time he gets here, a nice cheesy omelet and a tall glass of orange juice will be waiting for him."

"Is everyone dressed already?" asked Gunnar.

"They are," said Roxanne. "I'm still wearing my sweats."

"Would you mind accompanying me back to the bedroom so I can change before the professor gets here?"

"Not at all."

Gunnar rose and Roxanne took his arm and led him back to the bedroom. She let go of his arm just as his knee grazed the bed. An increase in heat coupled with the movement of fabric told him she had opened the drapes. He then heard her fiddling with her bag.

While he did the same, he told Roxanne about his short encounter. "Guess who I just talked to?" said Gunnar.

"The vardoger?" she asked curiously.

"Yes."

"What did he say this time?"

"That he's leaving."

She was a little concerned. "Really, why?"

"Something about not needing warnings anymore."

"Too bad. It was great to have all those warnings."

Gunnar reassured her as he finished dressing. "Well, between you and Acadia, I think we have the future covered."

She wasn't so sure. "Maybe."

He confided his fears. "Still, what purpose do I have now in all this? I have no supernatural powers without the vardoger."

She giggled lightly. "Babe, that's completely wrong! You've got super hearing. Not to mention, you are the cutest of us all." Soon, he felt her body rush into his and both fell onto the bed. She had changed from sweats to a dress, as he was easily able to caress her legs while they kissed. The seduction ended when they heard the phone ring, followed by an announcement from Aaron. "Hey guys, he's in the lobby," he yelled. "They're bringing him up."

Roxanne guided Gunnar off the bed with a quick peck before she led him out to the main room. "Sweetheart, can you take me to the lift?" Gunnar requested. "I didn't get to greet him at the airport, so the least I can do is greet him there."

"Sure!" she said opening the front door, and the pair walked hand in hand to the whirring mechanisms of the elevator. The "ding" told Gunnar to put on his smile. The separation of the heavy doors prompted him to say, "Hi Dr. Snow!"

"Ah, Gunnar, dear boy! So good of you to meet me here by the lift," Dr. Snow said as he emerged from the pod and shook Gunnar's hand. "And Roxanne, lovely girl. Nice to see you again as well."

"Same here Dr. Snow. We've all been so excited to see you," she replied.

Gunnar wanted to get the apology out of the way first as they walked down the hall. "Actually,

I'm sorry I didn't meet you at the airport. I'm afraid I slept late, so my friends sent a car around for you."

"About that." Gunnar could hear that happy, whistly tune in the professor's voice. "Who in heaven's name is your friend? The Queen? From the moment I stepped on board that plane, I've been treated like royalty. My every whim was catered to. And then I arrive to a limo and there is an insane amount of newspaper men wondering if I warrant having my photo snapped."

"Well, one of the people who I wanted you to meet is actually a famous musician. I doubt you'd know him though; his records cater to a bit younger audience."

"Gunnar, I can't pretend that I am on trend when it comes to the music I choose to listen to. If it's not Beethoven or Brahms, it's not my cup of tea. But do give me some credit. I do teach the younger generation, and I've managed to pick up on some current popular culture."

Gunnar nodded. "Fair enough. It's A.J. Rhodes."

Dr. Snow stopped the procession. "A.J. Rhodes?" He then started to sing so off pitch, Gunnar had to snap his lips shut to avoid laughing. *"Don't ruin me, just set me free, cause I'll never be, what you want. Your lips kiss with pain, and utter disdain, tears fall like rain, why do you haunt . . . me?"*

"Well, you definitely know one of his songs," quipped Roxanne.

"Yes, I heard that song once at a Wimpy while I was having a hamburger."

"Once? You memorized the lyrics after hearing it only once?" queried Gunnar.

"Of course," Dr. Snow said as though everyone could hear a song once and memorize the lyrics. "Well, at least that explains the five-star treatment."

"How was your flight?" asked Gunnar, still trying to forget the painful singing session.

"You were right. First class makes a world of difference. Much better than my last flight. Did you know the seats fold out into a bed? Completely flat! And hot towels and all the wine I wanted. Let's just say after the third glass, the hydraulics could have gone out and I'd have not cared."

Gunnar laughed. "I'm glad."

Dr. Snow then went off on a tangent Gunnar didn't understand. "And they didn't lose my luggage this time. It's safely tucked in the boot of the car."

"Well," said Roxanne, interrupting. "Here we are."

Gunnar put his hand in front of him and felt around for the doorknob. "I can't wait for you to meet Aaron, er, A.J. And there's another girl named Acadia. She has a gift too."

With that, he opened the door and the three of them walked through. Acadia and A.J. approached and were simultaneously greeting the professor, talking over each other. Gunnar, who had been walking right behind Dr. Snow, lost his balance when the professor suddenly fell backwards into him.

"I need to sit down," said Dr. Snow somberly, and the once jubilant room fell quiet with concern.

Someone else took control of Dr. Snow's body, for he was no longer resting on Gunnar.

"Here," said Aaron. "Sit on the sofa."

"I'll get him some water," said Acadia, as footsteps rushed to turn on a faucet.

"Are you okay? Do you feel faint?" asked Roxanne.

"It's, it's only that . . . I never put it together before when it was just Gunnar and Roxanne. They were mere feet from each other, but all that time in my office, I never realized that we three had met before. But now, seeing the four of you together, well, it's intriguing and certainly more than coincidence."

Gunnar had prepared his friends for Dr. Snow's unusual way of expressing himself. Figuring everyone was as confused as he was, Gunnar remarked, "I don't think we get what you're saying."

"Perhaps we should all sit down. It might come as a shock to you all, since it certainly comes as a shock to me."

Everyone moved toward the same table they had been at when Gunnar awoke. Someone moved some furniture along the tile, and soon, Roxanne guided Gunnar into one of the chairs. Gunnar could tell as each of them spoke that they were all seated in a circle, spaced out like the points of a star.

Dr. Snow continued rambling. "Looking at you all now, I'm sure of it. You are all a bit older, but not so much that you are unrecognizable."

Gunnar interceded. "Professor, I still don't understand."

"A little more than eight years ago, it would have been June 14, 2010 to be exact, we were all in Los Angeles, California, weren't we?"

"Uh, yeah, I lived there," said Acadia.

"I think that's when I was there with my parents for a law conference," said Roxanne.

"I was there working on an album," said Gunnar.

"Uh, I could have been there. I honestly don't remember back that far," said Aaron.

"This is what I recall," said Dr. Snow. "I had just had the most dreadful flight where the airline lost my luggage. I was at a rather large shopping facility called the Beverly Center shopping for a change of clothes, and I remember thinking I had to go to the lavatory. But for some reason, not just any restroom would do. Every toilet I visited wasn't sanitary enough or was too crowded. So, I looked for other lavatories on the same floor as Burberry, and only the one on the opposite end of the floor by the Bloomingdales was satisfactory to me. Afterwards, I remember looking at my watch, noting it was 5:00 p.m., and then having the overwhelming feeling that I needed to sit down at that very moment. So I did, on these funny looking blue chairs that were arranged haphazardly on a blue and white tiled floor. The only person there was a blond woman looking at a map. And then each of you, one by one, joined us in the exact same place."

"Oh my God!" exclaimed Roxanne. "I remember something similar—at the Beverly Center. I remember waiting for my mother, and all of sudden feeling dizzy, like I had to sit down right that second. There were some blue and white chairs not far from the hair salon. I remember looking at the clock on my cell phone and it being exactly 5:00. And I did sit down by a few other people."

"I went to the Beverly Center to get some sugar. I got a stomach ache from eating too much chocolate," interjected Acadia. "Like you, I had to go the restroom, and like you, none of the ones I went to were good enough. I remember feeling physically repulsed by all of them on the bottom level and had to go upstairs. The only one that didn't gross me out was the one by Bloomingdales. When I was done, all I wanted was to sit in the closest possible chair. I plopped down, relaxed, and took the barrette out of my hair. I'll never forget it because I lost the barrette there somewhere, and it was an antique my mother had given me."

"I honestly don't remember the name of the place I went to get pizza, but it was a mall and it did have many floors," said Gunnar. "And I remember being really tired after eating, almost to the point of passing out. I believe I was on the level by a food court. And every chair I sat on just wasn't comfortable enough. I had to go down a level to find a comfortable seat."

Aaron did not speak, so Dr. Snow spoke for him. "We were only there for a few minutes. Then there was a phone call, and you, Mr. Rhodes, starting screaming at someone named Alexis and asking her where she was."

"Holy crap!" said Aaron. "I do remember that now. She was supposed to meet me at Spago and she stood me up. She called me from the Beverly Center and I went over there to find her. The last place she mentioned was Ferragamo's, so that's where I went. I couldn't find her, and I got really pissed off. I walked that whole floor looking for her. When I walked in the direction of Macy's, I got more upset. When I walked in the direction of

Bloomingdale's, I calmed down. By the time I passed Armani, I was completely at peace. All I wanted to do was sit and enjoy a moment of not being angry."

Roxanne spoke excitedly. "I totally remember that phone call! The guy freaked out and started asking the lady where she was and how much she spent, and then practically screamed, '$24,000 dollars?' I remember that because I wondered to myself who could be rich enough to spend that much money at a mall? I looked at you to see what a wealthy person looked like. I remember you! And oh my God, sweetie, I remember you!" Roxanne's volume changed as she spoke in Gunnar's direction. "I . . . thought you were totally hot. And I was hoping you'd look at me and flirt. But you didn't and I was about to write you off as someone who thought I was too young, and then I saw your cane. When I realized you were blind and didn't know I was making eyes at you, I gave up."

Acadia jumped in. "That's right. I remember you too, Gunnar. I was sitting there feeling like my stomach was going to explode and being all sorry for myself, and then I looked at you and thought I had no right to moan about a stomach ache when a blind man was sitting next to me. A blind man with really blonde hair, who didn't wear glasses like a typical blind person. A blind man whose eyes where so clear, I couldn't tell he was blind."

"I don't remember seeing either of the girls," said Aaron. "Probably because I was so upset at one that I was ignoring the female species in general. But come to think of it, I do remember you, Dr. Snow. I was thinking that you looked really out of place in LA, that you had to be foreign because it was the middle of the summer and you looked like you were dressed for rain. And man, I remember seeing a white cane and making a mental note that there was a poor blind guy by me."

Gunnar was a bit miffed. "Lovely that the first thing you all thought of when you saw me was pity."

His sarcasm was ignored. "I can't believe we've all been together before," said Acadia.

"What does it mean?" asked Roxanne.

"Why didn't we pay more attention to each other then?" asked Aaron before the girls' thoughts were responded to. "I mean, I noticed Acadia the second I saw her in the limo. I knew almost right away that . . . well, I mean, I can't imagine being by her then and not feeling the same things I feel now."

"Yeah," said Roxanne. "And this time around, Gunnar's blindness didn't matter at all. Why did it put me off then?"

A knock on the door accompanied by a muffled cry of "room service" interrupted the reunion. "I'll get it," said Acadia.

Gunnar could hear furniture move, feet walk, a door open, and a creaky set of wheels enter the room. Over Acadia's directions to the hotel staff, he heard Aaron in his other ear say, "Hey Doc?

You don't have to be formal and call me Mr. Rhodes. My friends call me Aaron. You're my friend now, so call me Aaron too."

"Oh, all right then!" said Dr. Snow. Gunnar could tell from the surprise in the professor's voice that he was amused at the thought of having a friend.

After breakfast trays were dispersed and the kitchen staff left, the conversation resumed out of mouths that were stuffed with food.

"You know," said Gunnar in between bites. "Something you said, Aaron, struck a chord. You said you felt peaceful when you walked in our direction. Come to think of it, I felt really good too when I was sitting down. I wasn't tired any longer. I felt, really satisfied for some reason. Until everyone left, then I almost felt peevish."

"My stomach ache went away too sitting there and didn't come back until we all dispersed," said Acadia. "And then I felt kind of mad."

"It was the only moment of my trip where I forgot about the terrible flight," added Dr. Snow.

"And those horrible thoughts returned once I got up, accompanied by irritability."

"That's so weird," interrupted Roxanne. "I didn't feel better or worse after sitting there. All I remember is feeling a mix of desire and protectiveness for the blonde guy, hoping that he was being taken care of."

Gunnar was flattered, though also frustrated. Had Roxanne been open to him then, maybe he wouldn't have spent the last eight years lonely and subject to his sister's dating experiments.

Acadia interjected in Roxanne's direction. "You know, if your hormones as a younger person did influence your abilities, maybe your feelings for Gunnar healed us all for a minute."

For a second, Gunnar was intrigued by the possibility, but then the idea started to annoy him. When he first heard about her alleged healing gift, he questioned its truth. After all, if Roxanne really could heal, and if she truly loved him, why was he still blind? He didn't even want to entertain the possibility that his lack of vision necessarily meant that she didn't really love him.

"Roxanne, you have gifts too?" asked Dr. Snow with surprise.

"Yeah," she admitted.

"Why didn't you tell me at Oxford?"

"I hadn't even told Gunnar yet at that point, Dr. Snow."

"Since we are all dispensing with niceties, I insist you all call me Arthur. And since we are all friends, perhaps now would be a good time to share with me the gifts that Gunnar mentioned on the telephone."

Roxanne took charge. "Aaron seems to be a mix between an empath and an auditory psychic. He can feel things other people feel and see things other people see whenever he plays music. Acadia has visions. She's only had two so far and we don't quite know what they mean yet, so we really can't describe her gift. As for me, I supposedly have three powers. I'm supposed to be clairvoyant, a healer, and able to travel through doors. I've had visions of future events that have come to pass, but only when I sleep and they're usually dreams about big world events. I've never had an experience where I knowingly healed another person, except small things like back messages, though there have been several instances of me healing myself. I still don't know what was meant by being a traveler that can open doors, though in the last few days, we've had some clues to what that means."

Gunnar paid attention to only one aspect of Roxanne's description. That she had healed herself *several* times before. Creeping doubt about her honesty was starting to press on his lungs.

"What clues?" asked Dr. Snow.

Acadia felt it was her place to explain. "Well, my crazy bother has this theory about portals into other universes and that Roxanne is capable of traveling through these portals."

Dr. Snow contemplated while sucking air in through his lips. "Interesting. And by the way, Roxanne, your ability to see future events is really more precognitive than clairvoyant. Just to be technically accurate. And you," he said toward Acadia, "what have your two visions been so far?"

She responded. "My first vision was of Roxanne, after my brother told me he needed to find the girl that could help open the portals. My second vision was of you, Arthur."

"You had a vision of me?" The professor seemed pleasantly shocked.

"Yes," Acadia continued. "At the exact same time Aaron connected to you. And Gunnar knew who you were from our description. We thought that was all a little too coincidental, so we thought we should meet you."

"I must confess," interrupted a frustrated Gunnar, "I'm now more confused than ever about my role in all of this. Before this morning, I thought my vardoger's forewarnings were what made me part of this group of gifted souls. But that was before I met my vardoger again just before you arrived. He told me that he didn't plan on any more visits, so I thought I had lost the one special thing about me. Then, you come in here and remind me of our meeting seven years ago, when the vardoger did not come to me at all. So I must belong in this group for some reason. Why?"

"Oh, Gunnar," said Roxanne in a tone that Gunnar took as dismissive. "I told you not even to worry about that. What we should be worrying about is this whole alternative universe thing. I recorded something I think you should hear, Arthur." She then pressed play on Delphine's words. Gunnar sat, fuming but silent.

At the conclusion of the debriefing, Roxanne took hold of Gunnar's hand, but his anger showed in his limp wrist. He heard Dr. Snow scraping his plate and licking his fingers. Finally, the professor proclaimed in a wistfully ecstatic tone, "Riddle solved!" Then he giggled to himself. "I'm sorry about that outburst. Force of habit, I'm afraid. See, long ago, when I was a lad, I was a slave to her Majesty. Though I wasn't being paid for it, I was the United Kingdom's national problem solver. I broke codes using calculus, solved riddles using propositional logical, and figured out the origins of the universe using applied physics. Whenever the doctors or generals would test me, and I would find the answer, I was always supposed to ring a bell and yell out, 'riddle solved!'"

"I didn't know you worked for the government," said Gunnar, distracted from this preoccupation with Roxanne's callousness. "When was that?"

"When I was about 14."

"14?" asked Aaron in awe. "When I was 14, I could barely understand fractions."

"Not to toot my own horn," said the professor, "but I am a genius. My adult IQ exceeds 200."

"Why don't you still do all the math and science? I mean, you teach history. That sounds like fluff compared to calculus and physics," remarked Gunnar.

"My dear boy, being handled by all manner of others, never being your own person, people being fake to you to get what they want from you, and not having the freedom to just walk away, is daunting indeed."

Aaron snorted. "Amen, brother."

Dr. Snow continued. "Had I stayed a scientist, my life would never have been my own. As a historian, no one much cares about me. I prefer the latter way of life."

"Well," said Gunnar. "My vardoger did say that you were incredibly clever."

"Did he also tell you I have a photographic memory?"

Gunnar smirked. "No, but the fact you remembered five strangers from three minutes eight years ago was a clue."

"Which segues nicely into answering our first question. What brought us all together to the exact same spot eight years ago and why did we not meet then? Oh, if Millie could see me now, moving away from a hard line causal determinist to a quasi-compatibilist."

Everyone else at the table had to be as dumbfounded as Gunnar was. "Um, Arthur. For us persons with normal IQs, I don't suppose you could dumb that down a bit? And who is Millie?"

He heard another jolly laugh. "Again, I am sorry. I am just so comfortable surrounded by you all, I've simply forgotten to reign myself in. It's as if we are peers in every regard, so I don't wish to insult you by assuming you don't understand the concepts I know."

Aaron interjected. "Hey, man. Thanks for the vote of confidence and not presuming we're idiots, but I've spent about the last five years killing brain cells by the thousands, so feel free to presume I'm an idiot."

There was a short hearty laugh from everyone around the table.

Dr. Snow continued. "In the most basic terms and subtracting decades of debate amongst physicists and philosophers, causal determinism is the idea that every event in the universe has a cause in this infinite causal chain going back to practically the beginning of our existence, an event called the Prime Mover. In other words, it's the belief that nothing that can happen in this world is uncaused or self-caused. That every event that occurs happens because it must, based on events of the past. I really hope that is sufficiently dumbed down enough for you because I do not know any other way to put it."

"Like fate?" asked Roxanne.

"Well, fatalism is a little different, but I think you get the idea. It assumes we have no control over anything because everything is going to happen the way it's going to happen."

"Okay, I think we're with you on causal determinism," said Roxanne. "What's a compatibilist?"

"Thankfully this concept is easier to explain," said the doctor with a happy breath. "Compatibilism is the idea that human beings have free will, and that our choices do impact the chain of cause and can break the causality of events."

Aaron spoke. "Even I get that."

The professor continued in longwinded refrain. "So here is my hypothesis regarding our prior meeting. Was it causally determined based on prior events that we all were there at the same time? I think yes. For instance, because the airline lost my luggage, I needed sympathy. Because my colleague felt I needed sympathy, he believed new clothes would make me feel better. He probably felt like new clothes would make me feel better because sometime long ago, someone bought him clothes and it made him feel good. And he chose the Beverly Center because there was a Burberry store there and Burberry is a British brand and so it goes back even further to the fact I was born in England and there is a natural psychological presumption that people are more comfortable in their home environments. So you see, my being there was the result of chain of causality.

It's likely the same for each of you, and why you ended up at the Beverly Center. For example, Gunnar, a complete stranger to this land, had to rely entirely on another person to take him to a place with food. It was your cab driver who was actually craving pizza, not you. And it was your driver's desire for pizza and his previous experience thinking the pizza at the Beverly Center was tasty that brought you there. Had he been hungry for sushi at the time, you could have ended up somewhere else entirely. Aaron, it was your wife's desire to shop at specific stores that brought you there, and her desire was built on her experience that shopping at high end retailers made her feel more special or happy than shopping at lower end retailers. Do you see what I mean? This is causal determinism."

Simultaneous sounds of understanding came from around the table.

"But the reason I've changed my mind away from the notion of absolute causal determinism is because if it was really causally determined that we all be there at that exact spot at that exact time, there should have been no reason, at least as contemplated by physics, why we wouldn't have met then."

Gunnar interrupted. "But I'm often in crowds of strangers and I don't actually meet the people next to me."

Dr. Snow explained. "True, but we five were not meant to remain strangers, as is evidenced by this very meeting. Thus, there had to be another factor besides causality which postponed our friendship. Aaron, you weren't ready to have feelings for another woman because you were married. And so, young Acadia here with whom you are clearly now infatuated, was ignored by you based on how much you disliked the woman you were with. Roxanne, you were not mature enough to deal with Gunnar yet, and while you may have thought it had to do with his lack of sight, it likely had more to do with you being too young for a serious adult relationship. Do you see then that free will played a part in stopping us from meeting? But now, the obstacles blocking the two of you, or the two of you, from being open to love are no more. So the meeting that was always supposed to happen is now occurring, but piecemeal as opposed to all at once."

"I get it," said Roxanne.

"Shockingly, so do I," said Aaron.

Gunnar nodded and Dr. Snow continued with complete candor. "As for answering who is Millie, she was my companion for many years. For all intents and purposes my wife, though we were never formally wed. She passed away long ago, but after she died, her spirit visited me. She told me to learn everything I could about the world beyond. This was a request I would have snobbishly laughed off had it come from a living person. However, coming from a deceased person, how could I deny the suggestion? Well, I have done so, learning all about the supernatural realm. I've created my own theories that combine metaphysics, determinism, and the unexplained, which is useful in a discussion regarding the portals detailed on Roxanne's telephone."

Still stinging from before when she brushed aside his legitimate concerns, Gunnar felt twinges of anger when Roxanne's name was mentioned. He crossed his arms, wanting to deflect the discomfort he felt at the attention being paid to her. The betrayal he felt starting to boil to dislike. Yet, he made no move or sound and let Dr. Snow continue. "Allow me to skip over worm holes and black holes and quantum mechanics and the scientific justifications for the possible existence of alternative universes, work under the presumption that they exist, and try to explain them from the supernatural view. Paranormal researchers have always believed in parallel dimensions and it was thought that these other universes were the origin places for things not of this world, like demons or angels or ghosts. But it was assumed that while things can come through those portals to our world, it could not be the other way around. See, our frail physical bodies are supposed to be incapable of withstanding the impact of traveling through a portal.

There have been reports of astral projection, or travel to other dimensions using the mind, to be sure. To this day though, I have never read of an actual occurrence of physical travel to another dimension. Yet, it appears as though this Alphonse believes that physical travel is possible. Only by certain individuals, however, who possess a paranormal ability to do it. Roxanne, he believes for whatever reason that your body can withstand the travel. Assuming that is correct, it may have something to do with your ability to self-heal.

And, this Alphonse believes that the portals can be found by tracking a humming sound. This stands in contrast to what most paranormal researches believe, which is that portals exist at Native American burial grounds or at cites of tragic death, with no real clue of how to find them. But if Alphonse's conjecture is correct, he may be unknowingly referring to the international phenomenon known as 'The Hum.' In different places around the world, some residents claim to hear a low-frequency drone reverberating in their ears. Scientists have yet to fully rationalize it away. Some researchers posit it's simply tinnitus, while others think it's spontaneous otoacoustic emissions, or sounds made in the inner ear. Others deny paranormal reasons for the hum by tying the noise to physical realities, such as industrialization or volcanic activity. Some of the very places mentioned by that Delphine woman as being crossed off on the map are places where science has accounted for the source of the hum."

Roxanne interrupted. "We took a picture of that map. Here!" Gunnar heard Roxanne tapping on her phone. "Ugh, sorry. Some of it got cut off. I was in a hurry. But you can still see most of it.

Gunnar heard the sounds of reaching, followed by Dr. Snow's high pitched "Hmm . . . " "Yes, most of these places have been cited as sources of the hum. A few surprises though. And the concept of a false portal is new to me, though I am not "magic folk" as Delphine described. Gunnar lad, can you tell me exactly what you hear that makes that woman think you can find the noise?"

Gunnar had been lost in his seething and wasn't paying attention to the conversation. He was slightly startled when he was forced to perk up. "Sorry, what?"

"When you hear the noise and you are able to locate the source, what do you hear?"

"Well," said the frustrated blind man. "The further away it is, it's like an annoying buzz, and the closer I get to it, the louder it becomes. Until I'm right there, and then it's painfully loud. Not even putting my hands over my ears can seem to drown it out."

"Goodness," marveled Dr. Snow. "What an amazing gift enhanced hearing must be. I imagine it is tremendous compensation for being blind."

Though the good doctor was not the source of his angst, he was the unfortunate target of the first wave of ire that could no longer be contained. Gunnar rose, yelling "Are you kidding me? Nothing makes up for the fact that I can't see a damn thing that's going on. That I'm in this fantastically historical city and I have to miss everything. I might as well have not even been here because I'm not capable of having a visual memory of it. And stop it with all this gift bullocks. Keen hearing occurs because I have to make up for a lost sense. It's entirely scientifically explainable. I'm just like you, Dr. Snow. I have no gifts, I'm not magic folk. I'm just some crazy lunatic who used to have a vardoger visit him."

The table was silent, which was all right by him because he wasn't in the mood to be placated. He just wanted to be away from everyone, particularly his deceitful girlfriend. In his hurry to escape, he bumped hard into a coffee table trying to find the wall that would guide him back to the bedroom.

Slamming the bedroom door shut behind him, he was half-ready to pack up and call down for the limo to drive him away when he realized he still had a job to do and couldn't leave. He sat there on the bed, upset to the point of tears. How could he have been so wrong about Roxanne? Was he wrong about Roxanne? Was he blowing things way out of proportion? How on earth did his vardoger think that his day was going to be okay and that he wouldn't be needed anymore?

The door opened and gently closed and the smell of peach wafted into the room. It ignited his fury all over again.

"What was all that about?" Roxanne asked gently.

His tone was stinging. "Why don't you go find someone with magical powers like you? I'm even more useless now than when I was just a blind moron."

"That's ridiculous. I love you, Gunnar. I don't care if your vardoger is around or not. And you're not a moron," she said.

"Oh really? Because I sure feel like one when I find out the person I love has lied to me!"

"What?" there was a fear in her voice.

"Your story keeps changing. It goes from I've never healed myself, to I might be able to heal myself, to I've healed myself *several* times before. That means you definitely did know before Alphonse stabbed you what you could do. It wasn't a suspicion that you couldn't have known to warn me about. When Acadia yelled out that you had gotten stabbed, you cannot imagine the pit in my stomach and the fear in my heart. And had I known beforehand that I didn't have to worry, I wouldn't have had to experience the self-loathing that I could not protect you because I could not see you. Then on top of that, you were completely dismissive of my need to get information from Dr. Snow about why I am here when I no longer have a supernatural reason to be."

Her exhale was deeper this time, and followed by a short period of quiet. "Gunnar, please sit down with me. You're right. I need to tell you everything."

At first, his body wanted to refuse. But as much as he didn't like her right now, he still loved her, and his heart felt compelled to acquiesce. He slipped down on the bed until his knee was touching hers.

"Gunnar, I didn't tell you about my ability to heal before because I didn't know how. I was embarrassed and nervous and worried you wouldn't believe me, and not just about the healing. About why we haven't been together yet."

His curiosity settled his nerves even more. "I'm afraid you've lost me?"

Her volume was like a shameful whisper and her words were slow and thoughtful. "I lost my virginity when I was seventeen to a one-night stand who is quite irrelevant at this point. Needless to say, there was the awkward bleeding of the hymen that no one likes to talk about. The next time I had sex, I was eighteen, and it was with a guy who I thought was my boyfriend. I really liked that guy, and I thought he really liked me. Until we did it. Gunnar, I bled, again. And he freaked out, got mad, and broke up with me right then because he said taking my virginity was too much responsibility. After that, I was mad, so I just decided to do it with the first guy I saw, out of revenge. It had only been a week since I'd had sex last, and yet again, my hymen bled as if I were a virgin. I tried sex two more

430

times right after that, mostly as an experiment, and both times, I bled.

I started to worry, so I went to the gynecologist to see why I was bleeding during sex. The doctor thought I was insane because my hymen was perfectly unscathed like it had never been touched. Even the doctor accused me of lying that I'd had sex before. That was my first clue that the voodoo queen may have been right about me. So I decided to cut myself to test the theory. I took a razor blade and ran it clean across my palm. It healed within minutes. That's when I knew for sure I was a healer. But that's also the moment I knew that every time I had sex for the rest of my life, it was going to be the first time. And I would bleed every time, and it would hurt every time, and every guy I was with forever would think he had just taken my virginity.

That's why I didn't tell you about the healing. Because I knew you would ask about it and I knew I couldn't tell the full story of it without also telling you that the real reason I haven't wanted to have sex with you is because, inevitably when we do have sex for the first time and I bled, you would have thought there was something wrong with me being a twenty-nine year old virgin."

Gunnar was stunned silent. She was not wrong. Had she not told him before they had sex for the first time and she bled on their bed after their first act of intercourse, doubt about her would certainly have clouded his mind. What a selfish prick he'd been! With her confession, all of his fury subsided and he put his arm around her. She was shaking, a physical sign that she frantically awaited his reaction. "Darling, I'm sorry for being such an ass. Keeping this from me was your way of considering my feelings, so I apologize for calling you a liar. And as for the healing situation, I can see why you might have thought it best to hide that. But, if this really is forever, we can keep no more secrets, even if we think we are doing the other a favor by doing so. Your words, remember?"

"I promise, no more secrets," she said with relief.

He smiled for the first time since Dr. Snow sat down at the table. "And about your hymen, when we do cross that bridge, I think it's actually kind of romantic that I get to be your first, again."

"And again, and again," she sheepishly joked.

"I promise to always do what I can to make it as least painful as possible for you."

The space between them quickly closed as she threw her arms around his neck and brought him in tightly for a long appreciative kiss. "Thank you so much for understanding," she said. "This is just one more reason why I know I'm meant to be with you. And I'm so sorry that eight years ago I wasn't ready, for whatever reason, and made the stupid choice to ignore you instead of talk to you."

"I wish I'd spent the last eight years with you too, instead of by myself. But I think Dr. Snow's theories make sense. When you combine a causal chain with free will, I think what you get is a cosmic pause button that allows something somewhere to keep us on the path established from the Prime

Mover, but to do it on its own timetable. We six just weren't ready then, but we are now."

"Six?"

"Dr. Snow said there were six of us sitting there, not five. And according to what Acadia's mother told you, six people are supposed to journey together. If it was causally determined for us all to meet that day, but pause was pushed, then the determinism hasn't changed. We should be picking up right from where we left off. Which means . . . "

Roxanne finished his thought. "The blonde lady with the map."

"Who I bet is the same blonde from the diner described by the waitress in Indiana. The other traveler. She's the sixth. Now, we need to find her."

CHAPTER ELEVEN

The Consequences of Falling

*****

Calliope Brown was a normal teenager who gave her parents and teachers little cause for concern. She may have been a bit shy socially—rejecting typical dating rituals and high-school coupling—, but her future was bright and quite planned out to include the picket fence and Stepford family. That was, until she started college.

Soon after settling into her new college dorm in a big college town, she went shopping and saw two women kissing on the street. The first thing that kiss made her realize was that she was very likely a lesbian, as she wanted a kiss like that, and not with a guy. The second thing she realized was definitely not normal, in a way that had nothing to do with her sexuality.

Mere moments after observing that kiss, she strolled into a second-hand clothing store. She picked up one of the gently used sweaters on sale and instantly transported to an unfamiliar room. She watched as a young woman fought with an old woman and listened to a muffled conversation where the rebellious daughter accused her conservative mother of not understanding women's lib. The girl was wearing the very sweater she held in her hand, but it had attached a button with the word 'Nixon' crossed out. The experience was so real, it was as though she was watching television. The moment she put the sweater down, she was once again in the store aisle. The experience was frightening and thankfully, it didn't happen again the rest of the day.

Indeed, it was a few months before she had another episode. Calliope met her first girlfriend, Anne, and lost her "virginity" one casual morning. She was actually surprised when Anne's attentions made her bleed, as she had been under the impression that only the male appendage could do that damage. Nonetheless, the experience was blissful. She rode the high of her arousal all the way to class.

Calliope was a theater major, hoping to become a director, but as all freshmen must, she started out in the prop department. She was in the prop room looking for some candlesticks when she started remembering her girlfriend's hands on her thighs. Then, everything turned into a nightmare. Touching the candlesticks, her mind transported to a dining room where a man and woman were yelling at each other while two small children cried. She was so startled, she dropped the sticks and accidentally backed into an antique wheelchair. She saw visions of a pale and twisted person wearing rags and spitting on himself being wheeled down a dank corridor while mentally ill people yelled from all sides. Quickly running from the wheelchair, she bumped into an old hospital-type bed and was now looking down on a man who just died of something where puss-filled sores were a symptom. Somehow, she managed to get out of that room without hitting anything else and changed her major on the way back to her dorm. There was no way she was ever going back to that prop department again, since apparently her frightening ability to see other people's lives in objects had returned.

She was so upset by what happened, she rushed to Anne's arms for comfort. Comforting turned to kissing, then foreplay, and then an abrupt end. Anne freaked out when, for a second time, sex with Calliope resulted in a bleeding hymen. Anne demanded to know what was wrong with Calliope, and she had no answer. She promised to see a doctor at the university's clinic. Anne, who was majoring in nursing, didn't want to wait for an answer and urged Calliope to go to the ER that evening.

While awaiting a bed after triage, Anne left for a moment to go check out the ward where she was interning. Calliope always thought Anne was so brave to work in the hospice wing. After a while,

Anne returned carrying a small box. She explained that one of her patients with no family had passed away and requested his personal affects go to Anne. The nursing student started looking through the box.

"Aww," said sentimental Anne. "Look at the pictures in this wallet. He must have had family somewhere. Oh, he really must have loved them." Anne practically shoved the wallet into Calliope's palm and she had no choice but to grasp it. She was horrified when the wallet led her to a vision of a man trying to trick a young girl into a van. Calliope practically threw the wallet across the waiting room, apologizing thereafter with a fake story that the wallet smelled bad.

Anne wasn't thrilled by Calliope's odd behavior, but was even more miffed when the doctor examining her girlfriend reported that he could see no tearing or contusion around her hymen that would lead to bleeding. With no answers to the bleeding problem, he suggested it may be mental, as the pressures of college and a newfound sexual orientation were possibly too much for Calliope's mind to process. Anne lost her patience at that point and ended the relationship on the way back to campus.

Adding abandonment to her laundry list of problems, Calliope decided to see the school shrink. Assured by the psychologist that everything they spoke of was confidential, Calliope laid it all on the table—the reappearing hymen, her closeted lesbianism, the sadness of losing her first love, and the fact that she had witchy visions. Expecting dismissiveness, Calliope was pleasantly surprised to learn that the psychologist, who had dabbled a bit in paranormal research, thought she may have been psychometric instead of a witch. The psychologist also wondered if maybe Calliope wasn't a psychic surgeon. As to the matters of love, the psychologist offered only approval of her life choice and told her that true love would find her in a place and time when she least expected it.

Delighted by the fact someone believed her and helped her at her lowest point, Calliope knew that she wanted to so the same thing for others. She declared psychology her new major and was committed to sticking with it. She also learned everything she could about psychometry and psychic healing. Psychometry, the ability to read the past or the future from an object, was a truly fascinating gift. Over the years, with intense study and practice, she learned to control it like a light switch. By the time she graduated with her Psy.D., she could choose when to read an object and when to ignore the visions coming from it. She also learned to deal with the horrors that some objects projected, growing desensitized. In fact, she had grown so comfortable with her ability, it was only natural for her to share it. Thus, she moved to liberal Eugene, Oregon, where her gift might be accepted, and became not only the town's local forensic psychologist, but also its resident psychic crime-solver.

Despite Calliope's confidence in her academics and abilities, Anne had obliterated her self-worth in the relationship department. Calliope hadn't had sex in the nearly nine years between freshman year and the attainment of her doctorate, so she never again tested whether her hymen was still present or whether the psychic surgery theory was valid. But she doubted it. Psychic surgeons have the ability to focus all their energies and project themselves into the human body, and once there, extract tumors or repair torn tissues. While her past experiences ended with repaired wounds, the healing was done without any thought or focus required on her part.

She had all but shrugged off the idea of being a psychic surgeon until 2006, when she met an academy cadet named Lori. At twenty-nine, she never thought she could fall for a twenty-one year-old, but she was instantly smitten by the charm and wit of the funniest person she'd ever met. They were so different from each other—Calliope being an intellectual, feminine, hot-tempered Irish blonde; Lori being a jockish, slightly masculine, fun loving German brunette. Yet they meshed so perfectly, they were inseparable.

Petrified of a repeat occurrence of Anne, Calliope told Lori a little white lie prior to the first time they made love, hoping to buffer what could possibly come. Calliope came up with a story that she had once had a gynecological procedure that left scar tissue on her cervix, and whenever she had an orgasm, she could bleed. Sure enough, the first time they had sex, and every time they had sex, Lori shrugged off the bleeding as medically explainable. Lori's indifferent reaction solidified Calliope's love. For the first time since Anne, she imagined a happy and perfect life where her odd problem would not strip her of a relationship.

Then, Lori was shot during a drug bust. When Calliope first heard that a shooting had occurred, she got a pit in her stomach and knew Lori was somehow involved. She couldn't just call the station and ask. While they weren't closeted per se, they were both very secretive about their orientations and no one at work knew about their relationship. Instead, Calliope went to the nightstand by their bed where Lori usually left her gold "L" necklace while on duty. Touching it and turning on her gift, she grew cold and desperate when her visions depicted her love being shot, once in the side and once smack in the middle of her chest.

Frantic, Calliope rushed to the hospital, only to be told by a bitchy nurse that they could not discuss Lori's condition with her since she wasn't family. The only person medical staff would talk to was Lori's senior officer partner. Already angry at being denied access to her loved one, Calliope lost all sense of reason when she overheard one officer talking to another in the waiting room about how Lori wasn't expected to make it through surgery. Having the most intense emotional experience of her life as she bawled her eyes out in the parking lot, Calliope remembered that some psychic surgeons could heal others too. If she could only make it to Lori, she could try to concentrate and touch her girlfriend's wounds and maybe save her.

Calliope's best shot of getting to Lori was to persuade her partner, Detective Frank Nelson, to let her accompany him on his visit into her recovery room. So as not to tip him off to their relationship, Calliope resorted to lying. Approaching him where he stood with other officers, Calliope flagged him towards her. "Hey, Nelson."

Following the beckoning, Nelson followed her to a quiet corner. "What are you doing here, Doc?" asked the older policeman.

It took every effort for her to appear calm and disinterested. "I heard about your colleague getting shot over the police scanner. What happened?"

"It was dark. We only saw the one guy doing the buy. He ran, so we gave chase. He busted through a door into this dark house. No lights, for sale sign out front, overgrown grass. She must have assumed it was an empty house and only the perp would be inside. I know I did for a second. She was the first in and there was a second person waiting with a gun just inside the door. Whoever it was shot at her, two bullets, close range. Then they ran."

She held back tears. "So, you didn't catch the guys who did it?"

"Nope. Once she fell, I stayed with her until backup arrived."

This afforded her the perfect excuse. "You know, if I could get back to her and read her thoughts, I might be able to see if there's a description of the shooter rattling around in her brain."

"You can do that?" he asked with genuine curiosity. "I thought you could only sense things from objects?"

She tried to play off his astuteness. "Oh, I've read minds before. Not as often or as well as I read objects. But it doesn't hurt to try, does it? I mean, surely you want to leave no stone unturned in finding the guys that shot your partner?"

He exhaled. "That's true. I want to nail those sons of bitches."

"I mean, assuming it's not too late of course. Last thing I heard was that she was in surgery and might not make it." Calliope was dying inside from even thinking this.

"Oh, that's old news. She made it out of surgery alive, but she's in a coma right now in critical condition. Now they're worried about her making it through the night."

"Are we even allowed to see here?" asked Calliope nonchalantly.

"They told me we could go in to take some photos for the investigation, as long as we didn't disturb her. She won't be awake."

"Hmm." Once they were in, she was going to have to touch her body to heal her. She was just going to have to violate doctor's orders. "Well, let's do it then."

"Okay," said Nelson. "The CSA is here. Let me grab him and three of us can go in."

Great, now there were two people to whom she was going to have to try to explain things. But even if there had been a hundred, trampling elephants couldn't have kept her from Lori.

Calliope was mortified when she walked into Lori's recovery room following after the CSA and Nelson. Her beautiful girl was half-covered in bandages and there were tubes protruding from her nose and mouth. She had to capture a gulp of despair that was rising to her throat as a cry. To compensate, she played matter of fact. "Okay, I just have to put my hand on her hand and try to read her mind. Please be quite while I attempt to do this."

"But the doctor's said not to touch her," said Nelson cautiously.

"Don't worry," assured Calliope. "It's just hand to hand. I won't go near any tubes or wires."

Nelson acquiesced. All was white noise and breathing machine pings as Calliope slipped her hand over Lori's. She only hoped the men weren't paying close attention, as it was impossible for Calliope not to caress it.

For the gratification of spectators, she closed her eyes and lightly chanted. But instead of trying to read thoughts, she focused on Lori's anatomy. Pretty soon, it was as though she was looking at Lori from inside out. No longer constrained by skin, Calliope could see vessels, tissues, muscles, and organs. It was actually kind of disgusting to see the sliminess and gumminess of what's inside. But she didn't dwell on repulsion, being driven to save a life.

Making her way to the center of Lori's body, Calliope was able to see the extent of the damage done by both bullets and doctors. There were stitches everywhere in there, but they weren't holding, and at least one organ, the liver, appeared to be leaking. Even a layperson like her knew a leaking organ wasn't a good thing. She knew she needed to repair it, but she didn't know how this psychic surgery thing was supposed to work and didn't really know that much about physiology. She didn't know how to use a scalpel, so she couldn't imagine using one to repair the damage. She didn't know how to sew, so she couldn't see herself doing a better job of stitching than the doctors did. All she could think to do was just imagine, with all her heart, the area going back to what it was this morning.

Her concentration was broken by a cry of, "Oh my God!" coming from Nelson. She opened her eyes to see a very awake Lori staring at her, then looking around in panic at the medical machinations extending from her body. Lori tried to talk, but couldn't through the tracheotomy tube in her mouth. Machines were loudly whizzing and soon, three or four medical types were swarming through the door. Calliope rose as one of the nurses practically ripped her away from Lori and shoved her towards another nurse, who briskly led her and the other two officers out the door. Out of the corner of her eye, she watched as the doctor tried to calm Lori down.

Out in the waiting room again with a squad of officers, Nelson violently moved Calliope back to their quiet corner. "What did you do?"

"What?" she asked, confused by what was happening.

"How did you get her to wake up?"

"Uh, I didn't. She just happened to wake up in the half-hour or so I was trying to read her mind."

"Half-hour? You just barely touched her. We hadn't even gotten the camera out of the bag. No, I saw it all. You touched her hand, there was a weird red light coming from your fingers, and she woke up. I saw it. The CSA saw it. Do you mean to tell me you didn't see it?"

"My eyes were closed. I was trying to concentrate."

Just then, the interrupting doctor came through the doors into the waiting room and made a startling yet happy announcement. "Well everyone, she's definitely out of the woods. She's going to be just fine. You can all leave now if you'd like."

There was a moan of cheers from both male and female team members, a few hugs, and then slowly the crowds started to disperse. Calliope wondered if she should join them, to keep up appearances, but the second she moved, Nelson grabbed her arm and held her in place.

"We're not done," he said gruffly in her ear.

When they were the only two left, the doctor approached them. To the man, he said "You must be her partner." To Calliope, he said, "And you must be, her partner," with an entirely different emphasis on the word. She exhaled and rolled her eyes, as Nelson's opened wide. The cat was definitely out of the bag. "She'd like to see both of you, and quite frankly, so would I. Come on back."

Calliope hesitantly followed the men to ICU. She was excited to see Lori healed, but dreaded the questions sure to come.

When she walked into Lori's room, curious doctors were still trying to examine Lori, though she was trying to shrug them off. All the machines were off, all tubes removed, and even the bandages were gone. The only evidence of trauma at all was the left over sticky gray stuff that stuck to Lori's skin after bandages were removed. Calliope flashed Lori a big smile, expecting to see one in return. There was no such sight.

"What in the hell was that?" asked Lori, looking straight at Calliope.

"What was what?"

"The red lights coming from your fingers?"

Calliope tried to deflect the interest in herself. "I don't know what you're talking about. You must have hallucinated."

"Hallucinating my ass," said Nelson. "You know I saw it too."

"I watched it Calliope!" yelled Lori. "I opened my eyes and looked down and for at least fifteen seconds, your hand produced a red glow that made my hand feel like it was on fire."

"It can't be," said Calliope in denial.

"Young lady," interjected the doctor. "This is the secure wing of the hospital, meaning there are security cameras in every room." The doctor pointed to the corner of the ceiling, where sure enough a black cylinder seemed to focus in on her. "Unfortunately, when we watched the video playback, your body blocked what was going on. But you can see the patient's face. You can see her wake up as if from a nap instead of a coma. You can literally see bruises fading in seconds instead of weeks!"

She took a deep breath. "Honestly, I don't know what's going on. I don't even know what I did. I've never done anything like that before." This was partially true, since while she'd healed herself, she's never healed another person.

"What you did," said the astounded doctor, "is to defy all of medical science. There should be no way someone in her condition is up and around. Her vital signs have completely normalized and her brain activity is utterly normal. And while we haven't x-rayed her internal organs yet, we're pretty sure they're going to be healed. You know why I think so? Because the incisions on her body that I myself made not a few hours ago are gone. Missing. Not there. Not even a scar."

Calliope was stunned by the extent of her ability. "Look, I was only trying to read her mind, to see if I could get a picture of the guys who did this to her."

"You can't read minds," said Lori, practically yelling.

"Well, I thought I would try," replied Calliope, stung by her girlfriend's tone. She had just saved Lori's life and she was being repaid with spite. Since there was no hiding their relationship any longer, Calliope tried to remind Lori of why she shouldn't be mad. "Lori, I love you. I was trying to help."

"Well, I don't love you! Not anymore. You should have let me go, Calliope. Death would have been dignified and those guys could have gone down for murder. Now, there's no evidence they've even committed a crime. And even if we had evidence, the trial would be so sensationalized when we got to the part about where my injuries went, they'd get off on the technicality of not being able to get a fair trial anywhere. And the worst thing of all, is that now, I'm going to be a science experiment. Or a tabloid freak. The incredible healing woman who takes two bullets without a single scar as evidence. There's proof of what happened to me—

CAD logs, hospital records, a dozen police officers. But no one can prove what you did, and no one would believe it anyway. So you get to leave this situation with your anonymity intact, while my life will never be the same."

Calliope was so wounded, the tears could no longer be pent up. "I'm, I'm sorry. I didn't mean . . . I just wanted you to be okay."

"I'll never be okay again, thanks to you!"

Calliope died inside. "Fine, if you don't love me anymore, I'll go."

"And I never want to see you again," screamed Lori. "Pack what I have and I'll send Nelson to get it." The last reminder Calliope would ever have of the second woman she loved was a bitter cold stare of loathing.

"I'll walk you out," said Nelson. In silence, except for Calliope's sobs, the pair walked towards her car.

Just before they got there, Nelson offered a friendly attempt at conversation that only served to add salt to her wounds. "So, how long did you guys

456

date? I guess I always knew she was gay. I mean, she is a little manly. You though, whoa, left field. I never would have guessed it. You're just so . . . lady like."

"A year," was all she could muster, trying to ignore his insensitive, borderline homophobic remarks.

"That sucks," said Nelson. Now at her car, Calliope reached for the door handle, but Nelson blocked her from opening the door. "Hey, I have a favor to ask. It's my dad. He's got Stage 4 colon cancer and he's stupidly choosing not to treat it. Just putting out the welcome mat for death, you know? Anyway, do you think maybe you could, do your red finger thing, on him?"

She was lost in anger and pain after getting her heart broken, but couldn't deny the sadness in his eyes. "Look, I seriously, truly do not know how I did that up there. I'll go to his house with you and I'll try to mimic my exact movements up here, but I can't promise anything since I don't even know how that happened."

He smiled. "I understand. Thanks for at least trying."

Six weeks later, Calliope read Nelson's father's obituary in the local paper. She had went with him and tried to reenact the psychic healing, but it didn't work. Frustrated as to why she could help Lori but not Nelson's dad and unable to escape the pain of Lori's anger still lingering after two months, Calliope decided she needed a fresh start away from Oregon. Hoping to find a bigger pool of psychic kooks to blend in with, she decided to head for San Francisco. She never made it to California.

It was just shy of Medford, right after Grants Pass, in a little town called Gold Hill that she had to make a pit stop for gas. As she filled her tank, a noise filled her ears. It was loud at first, but then settled into a low constant buzz in her ear. It didn't dissipate at all in the minutes it took to fill up. As she went inside to pay, she must have had a strange look on her face.

"You must be hearing it," said the old man behind the register.

"Yeah, what is that? Where's it coming from?"

As though he'd rehearsed an answer to a question he'd heard before, he dutifully replied, "I actually don't hear it myself. Not many people can. But some who pass through do. If there's something strange, it's coming from the House of Mystery at the Vortex. We always send curious folks that way. Go back the way you came on the 99, head up Sardine Creek to Left Fork. Can't miss it. Weird looking crooked shack."

Calliope didn't know why she chose to chase the sound instead of continue south, but she felt oddly compelled. Her resolve only strengthened with each twist and turn into the trees, as the sound grew crisper until it was no longer a buzz, but the ringing one hears just after a bell has clanged. The noise was clearest right in front of the house that seemed to be tilted.

It was about 5:00 by the time she arrived at the house and dusk was approaching. As she exited her car, she heard the sound intensify the closer she walked to it. Noting that the front gate was locked and the backyard was blocked off, she peeped around to see if anyone was looking before she snuck through the gate. Just as she was about to take her first illegal step, another lawbreaker was coming out of the front door.

Startled, Calliope gazed into the eyes of the other woman. Before either could say anything, the pitch of the sound changed, and it started to fade. The other woman put her hand to her ear, and Calliope realized she wasn't the only one tuned into the sound.

"Do you hear that too?" asked Calliope.

"Sho' do," said the woman.

"What is that annoying noise?" Calliope queried with a sneer.

"Still tryin' to figure dat out myself," said the woman in a strange accent Calliope had never heard before.

"Well," said Calliope exhaling. "At least I'm not the only one that can hear it. It makes me feel less crazy."

"Crazy? Nah chile'. Just gifted. Allow me to introduce myself. Name's Jeanette Gadreau, but everyone back home calls me Mama."

*****

Gunnar was anxious to share with the group his conclusions about the blonde woman, so after sincere apologies to Dr. Snow, Aaron, and Acadia for his tantrum, he carefully guided the conversation back to the supernatural.

"So Arthur, I told you the trip would be worth it to meet my talented friends."

His elder whistled a reply. "Oh yes, yes indeed. It's always fascinating to see proof in the flesh of things one reads in books."

Gunnar tried to keep the mood light so no one would fear another outburst from him. "I may not have any special powers with the vardoger gone, but now you have three new subjects to study."

Dr. Snow flashed him a crooked grin. "Gunnar, has it not occurred to you that you possess gifts unrelated to the vardoger? Assuming that Delphine and Alphonse are correct, you'd necessarily have to. It's classic affirmation of the antecedent. If a person hears the hum, then they are magical. You hear the hum, therefore, you are magical."

"You think his super hearing might be a paranormal gift?" asked Roxanne.

"I think it is more than that," said Dr. Snow. "While an average disabled person does sharpen other senses due to the deprivation of one, I am hard pressed to think of any who have honed a sense as keenly as Gunnar has."

Roxanne agreed. "I agree. I've worked with tons of blind people in my life, and I can't recall any of them with as good of hearing as Gunnar."

Aaron butted in. "Yeah, man. When we were at the park, your ears were practically on fire. You were in pain from the volume, dude."

"For all any of us know," interjected the professor, "you may have developed this incredible power to hear even had you not gone blind. Astrid told me you went blind at age 17, right at the cusp of puberty. Your hormones might not have ignited your powers yet, and by the time your hormones did catch up, everyone just assumed your acute hearing was in response to your blindness."

Roxanne took his hand and said, "See? Don't give up on yourself. You're as much a part of this group as any of us."

"Probably even more so than myself," added Dr. Snow. "After all, vast intelligence is not a magical gift."

Acadia spoke as if a teenager pointing out something totally obvious. "Um, hello? You speak to dead people. You told us not more than an hour ago that you talked to your dead wife."

Gunnar heard Dr. Snow's breath sounds change as though he kept wanting to speak, but couldn't. Finally, he mustered slow words uncharacteristic of his typical Christmas elf cheer. "True, but that was only one person, and that person was dear to me. Certainly, it was a fluke."

"So?" rationalized Acadia. "I've only had two visions in my entire life, but no one doubts I possess abilities just because I've barely used them.

Just because you haven't used your gift again doesn't mean it don't exist."

Roxanne chimed in. "She's got a point, Arthur. And, no offense, but you seem a little on the shy side. Maybe you've never had another occurrence because you spend all your time at home or work and don't make friends with people who might come talk to you after they pass away."

Dr. Snow exhaled with resignation. "I cannot deny that I stay to myself on most occasions and therefore seclude myself from scenarios where I might run into the deceased. Nor can I logically say that one is not gifted simply because they experience only one encounter with their gift. I suppose we could test the theory. Perhaps we should go looking for a portal. And if Roxanne opens it and I can hear it, then I too must possess supernatural proclivities."

Of course! Why hadn't Gunnar thought of this before? "That's it! Mama Gadreau predicted that six people, inclusive of Roxanne, would one day go on a magical journey together. Looking for the portals *is* that magical journey."

Gunnar heard a series of agreeing grumblings, but continued to talk without awaiting a response. "We know the destination of our journey and its purpose, but we aren't ready to take it yet. Something's missing. The sixth person. I think our journey did start five years ago in Los Angeles. But because at least two of us weren't quite ready, God or fate or whatever pushed the great pause button in the sky. Now though that we are all ready, the play button has been pushed. It's time to pick up where we left off in that mall, which means we've got to find the blonde with the map who was sitting in the chairs with us. She must be our sixth."

Gunnar heard gasps. He hadn't thought his speech was that prolific, so he wondered the reason for the noises. He didn't need to inquire though once he heard Aaron's concern. "Acadia?"

"She looks like she's seizing," said Roxanne. "Is she epileptic?"

"It doesn't look like epilepsy. She'd be convulsing if it were, but her back is completely arched," observed Dr. Snow.

It seemed perfectly obvious to Gunnar. "Perhaps she's having a vision," said the blind man.

Roxanne quickly interrupted. "Aaron, is this what she looked like earlier when she had a vision?"

"I don't know. I didn't see her. I was already in a trance myself by that time. We just compared notes afterward."

"I think we just need to watch her and let it play out," suggested Dr. Snow.

The next minute was intense. Everyone was breathing hard, every heartbeat fluttered quicker. Finally, the silence was broken. "He's right," Gunnar heard Acadia say in a sleepy tone.

"What?" asked Aaron.

"Gunnar was right about our sixth. I just had a vision of the mall, and the five of us being there again, in the same ivory and blue chairs. But it wasn't a vision of us back then; it was a vision of us now. Roxanne was holding hands with Gunnar, and I was sitting close to Aaron. And there was a sign outside of a store and it said Summer 2018 on it. And I saw her. The blonde lady came up and started talking to us. And in my vision, I looked down at my cell phone, and it said Sunday, August 26th on it."

Dr. Snow spoke. "Well, not only must we go back to the shopping mall in Los Angeles to find the final member of our journey, but we must do so post haste. August 26th is this weekend."

"I wish we could go now," said Aaron, pouting.

Gunnar responded. "Too bad we have that little thing called a sold out concert." He moved his face towards Aaron's voice. "Speaking of which, you and I need to start focusing on work."

The rock star laughed. "Because that's gonna be easy now that I've found out I have psychic abilities and have to go on a spiritual journey."

"Aaron," interrupted Roxanne, "is it safe for you to do this show? I mean, what if you go into a trance on stage and start having visions in front of thousands of people?"

"I have no idea," said Aaron. "But I think I can only do it when I'm focusing and it's quiet. I'm sure the audience will be loud enough that I can't possibly accidentally focus. Besides, if I do, I've got Gunnar here to make a sound miracle to cover it up for a bit."

"I don't mean to be the pragmatist here," interrupted Dr. Snow, "but how are we all going to get to Los Angeles by Sunday if you have a concert tomorrow?"

"I'm afraid you're going to have to fly again, Arthur. But don't worry. We'll all be with you this time."

"My record company owes me big time for doing this show," noted Aaron. "Let me see if I can arrange for us to take one of the company's private jets to L.A." As nonchalantly as if he were ordering takeout, Aaron made a call and a command and all was set for them to leave for Los Angeles Saturday morning.

Roxanne noticed that Dr. Snow was disappointed. "What's the matter, Arthur? Is it the flying?"

The unhappy elf exhaled. "No. It's more so that I had hoped to explore this fine city. It's so historical."

"Well," said Acadia. "We do have the rest of today and tomorrow while the boys get ready for The show. We can certainly squeeze in the Cathedral, the museums and the cemeteries, and take you anywhere else you want to go."

"Yes, Arthur," added Roxanne. "We'll make sure you have a great time. And what better way to tour the city than with two natives?"

Aaron entered the cheer up contest. "You'll be envy of every man, with these two lovely ladies as your guides."

Gunnar heard a whistly laugh. "Very well then. Thank you for indulging an old man's desire for cultural stimulation."

After a whirlwind afternoon visiting St. Louis Cemetery #1, St. Louis Cathedral, The

Cabildo, and The Presbytere, the five were famished. Now that everyone knew Aaron was in town, the likelihood of anonymity was slim, so the group thought it best to have A.J. pull the star card and make reservations some place where they could have privacy. Reserving the Boardroom at Dickie Brennan's, the five settled down to a fabulous dinner. Fueled by steak, Dr. Snow solved even more riddles.

"By the way, I've figure out Acadia's gift," said the professor.

"Really?" asked Acadia. "What is it?"

"Your gift is to have visions of things you need in order to accomplish a task. So far, you've seen Roxanne, myself, the mall, and the other woman. All these things are required to move to the next step of your journey."

Acadia was hesitant in her reply. "I had thought of that, but I discounted it because I never saw Aaron. If my gift is to see things I need, you would think I would have seen the person I was gonna . . . possibly be with."

470

Dr. Snow's social ineptness showed itself. "Ah, but you didn't need him until he became worthy of being needed, and that didn't happen until he met you. Prior to that, he was a drug addled, suicidal drunk. No woman in her right mind wants that for a mate. But upon meeting you, he changed. As of the moment you met, he is the type of man that you could need."

Gunnar felt uncomfortable for both Aaron and Acadia. They hadn't as yet admitted their feelings, at least not openly, and what a chiding, if accurate, characterization of A.J.! As expected, he heard two embarrassed chuckles.

"Well," Aaron fumbled for words. "Let's not presume anything. I mean, it's been like two days. And I'm just barely starting a divorce, so . . . "

"Yeah," continued Acadia, "I mean, look, we know we have an attraction, but we're not putting labels on anything."

The other three mumbled their acquiescence to the pretense, knowing full well that the rock star and the voodoo princess were simply afraid to confront their true feelings about each other so soon.

The next day, Gunnar was busy starting at sunrise, directing the setup of the mixing board, testing the acoustics in the stadium, and making sure pitch and tone were perfect. While normally nameless, faceless roadies tested the sounds of each instrument, the newly sober Aaron wanted to stay busy, so when it came time to test the microphones, he himself surprised his anonymous crew by being the guinea pig.

The girls and Dr. Snow spent the day sightseeing, making it back to the arena an hour before A.J.'s opening act went on. Roxanne, who met her parents at the gig, was in awe of the excitement and muffled masses chanting and clapping. Dr. Snow seemed horribly out of place, yet childishly giddy, parading around with his backstage pass. Acadia seemed to forget that she was intimate friends with Aaron and that she didn't much like rock music, and kept saying fangirl things like, "I can't believe I'm here with A.J. Rhodes" and "this is going to be so awesome." So that Aaron could relax by Acadia's side pre-show, the four of them were the only ones allowed inside A.J.'s dressing room.

When the opening act finished, the crowd went wild. A.J. needed time alone to collect himself, so Gunnar took Acadia, Dr. Snow, Roxanne, and her parents to the sound booth so they could watch him in action. When Gunnar got the cue from back stage that A.J. was taking the stage, he sent everyone to their awesome front-row seats and got himself into concentration mode. He adjusted the knobs back to where they had been before the opening act's sound guy tweaked them into a mess. The crowd started chanting, "A.J., A.J, A.J!" Then the first few bars of one of A.J.'s biggest hits blared forth. A massive acclamation arose in response, and Gunnar knew from the words of other technicians going on in the headset that A.J. had just run out on stage.

Singing clearer and better than he had in years, A.J. gave a top notch performance with two demanded encores.

At around midnight, still high from the concert, the group made the odd decision not to go back to the hotel, but to go to Algiers instead. Aaron felt incredible and knew there was no way he could keep apart from Acadia. To avoid the fans and photographers camped out at the Roosevelt, the party drove to Roxanne's home. That night, they all truly experienced the rock and roll lifestyle. It was 5:00 a.m. before Gunnar and friends could no longer force their eyes open—an experience they might regret in the morning, as they had to meet the record company's private jet at 11:00 a.m. and still needed to go back to the hotel to collect all their things.

Stumbling out of bed the next morning around 9:00, with quick goodbyes and thanks to Gerry and Yara, the five friends barely made it back to the hotel before the limo got there. A.J.'s manager, who had impatiently waited for him all night, wanted to know why they were going to L.A. and wanted to make sure the star had security. A.J. refused both disclosure and bodyguards, simply saying that he needed to, "finish the rehab experience with help from his friends." The company management thanked Gunnar for getting A.J. through the show with a $20,000 "bonus" check. The girls and the professor went upstairs and hurriedly threw everything into suitcases.

By 11:00, they had all boarded a record company jet with a course for LAX. Dr. Snow didn't have the wherewithal to be nervous, as sleep deprivation caused him to pass out before anxiety set in. Gunnar was the next to fall asleep, and he didn't wake up again until Roxanne tapped him on the shoulder and said, "We're here."

Chapter Twelve

Fair Warning

*****

June of 2008 brought throngs of gays and lesbians back to New Orleans for the annual high-spirited Gay Pride weekend. Lori hoped by coming, she could escape her ever-mounting depression. After hitting bar after bar after bar with her friends, she realized intoxication hadn't helped.

In the back of her mind, she was hoping beyond hope to see her ex-girlfriend Calliope there. A chance meeting would make it much easier for her to apologize and hopefully get back into the arms of the only woman she'd ever loved. But she knew this was an unlikely prospect, as Calliope was a private person who didn't go shouting her sexual orientation proudly. Besides, for all Lori knew, her lost love could be anywhere after her cruelty drove Calliope to leave Oregon.

Tired of the crowds, Lori decided to finish her stupor alone at a straight bar all the way at the end of Bourbon Street. There were a few other folks around, but not many, and the music was quiet enough that she wouldn't have to shout her drink order.

"Hey man, can I get a beer? The biggest one you've got on tap."

"Sure thing!" The bartender attentively poured her drink and lingered after serving her, having no other customers to attend to. "So, not out with the rest of 'em?"

She would have been offended if she weren't so somber. There was only a scant amount of anger behind her response. "What do you mean, the rest of them?"

The bartender got that sheepish grin one gets when caught in a faux pas. "Oh, sorry. I just thought you might be in town for the parade, and this isn't a place where parade goers normally come."

"Am I that obvious?"

He smiled a bit and opted for honesty. "I mean, you're not like a total butch where I would mistake you for a guy, but you do kind of have a less feminine way about you."

She took a giant gulp and tried to muster sarcasm. "Gee, thanks. I always wondered, but now that you've confirmed it with your vast knowledge of all that is queer, I can come out of the closet."

His smile faded. "I'm not doing too well here, am I?"

She wanted to loathe the narrow-minded one, but she needed someone to talk to badly. "It's not you," she said with a loud exhale. "I'm just missing an old girlfriend, that's all."

The bartender began to wipe down the bar in front of her while they talked. "That's so funny. I was just thinking the exact same thing about one of my exes."

"Women," Lori tried to scoff with humor.

"So what's the story with yours?" the bartender asked.

The combination of many beers lowered her inhibitions. "My girlfriend, who I loved dearly, saved my life one day. Instead of thanking her, I broke up with her. I have no idea to this day what caused me to go off the deep end, and I've regretted my actions ever since. Especially because my fears never even materialized. I mean, you have no idea who I am, do you?"

The bartender cocked his head. "Should I?"

"Last year, I was shot, twice. I was on the verge of death—in a coma. Somehow, my girlfriend brought me out the coma and I was all better, like I'd never been shot. I was sure I was going to make national news for being freakishly healed and I would never be able to show my face in public again. It made news in Oregon for like a minute, and no one else cared."

The bartender stopped wiping and rubbed his chin. "That's, that's . . . "

"Crazy, I know," Lori answered, taking a gulp.

"No. Coincidental," said the bartender with a twisted pout. "About a year ago, I was seeing this girl and I had this old football injury that was always nagging at my back. I had cracked some vertebrae and I had seen proof of that on x-ray films many times. I kid you not, the first and only time we had sex, my back felt instantly better. But for some reason, I was distraught about feeling good. I broke up with her, literally while I was putting my clothes on. Anyway, I went back to the chiropractor a few days later and got a new set of films. Complete spinal alignment and not a disc out of place or rubbed away. I should have been thanking her instead of breaking up with her. But I couldn't go beg her to take me back. I'd been so mean. When I was dumping her, I called her a liar because she'd told me she'd already lost her virginity and I popped her cherry."

"Don't suppose yours was a feisty blonde?" asked Lori.

"Nah, cute little brunette," the bartender recalled with a smile.

"What's your name?" asked Lori.

"Greg. Yours?"

"Lori. Weird, ain't it Greg? Love healed us, and we went berserk for reasons we can't explain."

"I can explain it," said a black lady that neither one of them had noticed sitting at the end of the bar.

"Oh, hi Delphine," said the bartender nervously. "How long have you been sitting there?"

"Long enough," the woman said cryptically.

The bartender was worried. "I'm sorry I didn't notice you down there. I would have come right away, but . . . "

"Don't worry about it, Greg. It sounded like an interestin' conversation. I'd have been wrapped up in it too," said the pretty, mocha-colored woman with blonde hair extensions. "So, who's your new friend?" asked Delphine, eyeing the stranger.

"Um, this is Lori. Lori, this is Delphine. She's a friend of the owner. She comes by for drinks every so often."

"In exchange for cleansin' the place," added Delphine.

Lori tried to whisper to Greg as though Delphine wasn't there. "Is she a maid?"

Delphine was clearly offended. "I said cleansin', not cleanin'."

Greg whispered back, again as though Lori was the only one in earshot. "She's a voodoo woman. She performs charms on the building to ward off bad sprits."

"He speaks the truth," said the woman. "In fact, I'm here with some red brick dust. Gonna try to keep out the nasty patrons who are buyin' drinks and leavin' without payin' their bills."

Lori was genuinely inquisitive. "What did you mean when you said you could explain why we went off on our loved ones?"

"Sounds like both you were dating magical folks with the healin' gifts. See, there are some people in this world who are blessed with the ability to heal themselves and others. Not just anyone though, for they can only heal those they have strong lovin' feelins for. You two must have been very loved indeed for the healin' magic to have worked on you."

Lori was distraught. "Please don't tell me that."

Greg blew it off. "Yeah, well, it's for the best we broke up anyway. She was a liar after all."

"Was she? I overheard you say she wasn't a virgin accordin' to her, but that you made her bleed when you had sex. If she is a healer, she could have healed her own woman parts, and if she did, she'd have bled every single time."

Lori exhaled and her head dropped. "That's the same thing with Calliope! And here I was thinking it was my finger scraping along scar tissue. Why didn't she tell me?"

"Would you have believed her?" asked the voodoo woman. "Any more than you believe that I can get rid of bad folks with a handful of red sand?"

"Probably not," said Lori honestly.

"Wait, I have a question?" asked the bartender gruffly. "Why didn't she heal my back sooner? We went out for like two months."

"She obviously didn't love you, not completely anyway, until she gave herself to you. Besides, had she healed you sooner, you would have just parted sooner."

"What do you mean?" asked Lori.

"There is a price to be paid whenever a healer performs a miracle. The loa, or even your God, don't allow too much givin' without some takin' in return. Otherwise, the balance of the world would be off center. By givin' to the physical, somethin' is takin' from the emotional. Whenever a healer heals themselves, they feel empty and different and odd, so they stop doin' the things other people enjoy. When they mend the physical of another, they tear the heart of the other. And a torn heart don't manifest as sadness at first. It always starts with anger. That's why you were both so spiteful though you couldn't say why."

"But I'm not angry anymore," said Lori sadly.

"Of course not. Since that healin,' your body has restarted the natural process of agin' and decayin'. You're bein' taken from again, so your heart is bein' given to again."

"God, I would give anything to see Calliope. Tell her I know all about it and its okay," said Lori.

Delphine smiled a sadistic smile. "You can never be with her again. For if the love is true and returns once more, you could never get physically hurt or sick for the rest of your life, which face it, ain't that feasible. If you did, she'd just heal you again, and you'd hate her again, and those terrible pains would start fresh for the both of you. Lovin' a healer is a curse, for the both of you, forever."

*****

In order to keep the press at bay, the five friends opted to travel modestly. Though Aaron could have secured cushy penthouse suites and stretch limos, they opted to drive in an inconspicuous rental to their adjoining rooms at a Holiday Inn.

Acadia's best guess as to the time of the meeting was around noon, as in her vision, the left half of a digital clock was visible and showed the number 12. So, the five of them slept in until jet lag wore off and ate a leisurely breakfast. By eleven, the Beverly Center almost seemed to be calling to them. Each of them reported feelings of serenity the closer they got to the mall. When they parked, they made the decision to go in separately, in case the blonde was already there. They didn't want to scare her off by approaching en masse. By fifteen minutes after noon, they had each found their way back to the seventh floor seating area.

Their sixth wasn't there. Acadia kept time, announcing the passage of minutes in five minute intervals. By 12:30, the blonde hadn't shown up, so Dr. Snow began to question their conclusions. "Perhaps we were wrong. Maybe this woman isn't to be our sixth."

"Who else could it be then?" asked Gunnar.

"Maybe Astrid?" posited Dr. Snow.

"No," said Gunnar. "She's a nonbeliever in the supernatural. Besides, she couldn't possibly accompany us on our journey being so pregnant."

"Maybe your mom or dad, Roxanne," mentioned Acadia. "They're believers.

Roxanne shirked. "Yeah, but they're both scared by the supernatural. They don't embrace it. Whoever is supposed to come along with us can't be afraid of our gifts."

"I'm not afraid of them," said a new voice.

Before anyone else could speak, Acadia blurted out, "It's you! You're dressed exactly how I pictured you."

"Well, we're going on a journey, aren't we? I wanted to be travel ready," said the stranger.

"How did you know about the journey?" asked Aaron.

"Wow! A.J. Rhodes!" said the woman, star struck. "I was so looking forward to seeing you again and actually talking to you this time. I knew who you were then, and was going to ask for an autograph, but you seemed . . . preoccupied."

Roxanne injected herself into the dialogue. "So you do remember us?"

The new person spoke cautiously, her speech slow and specific. "Eight years ago, I was sitting in this very mall, in this very spot, looking at A.J. Rhodes. I knew it was him even back then before your songs were mainstream. I was a huge fan. I had just been in a terrible break-up and 'Heaven's Pain' from your first EP was hugely healing for me.

While I was trying to summon up some guts to talk to you, I looked around at the others sitting by us. I saw the guy with platinum blonde hair and ice blue eyes, then noticed the cane. I saw the silly little small guy who looked like he just stepped out of red London phone booth. I saw a pretty young girl with long brown hair so perfectly straight and smooth, I thought she could be in a shampoo commercial. And then I saw you, the mixed-race girl who looked like she was lost. Yes, I remember all of you."

"You're probably shocked to see us," said Roxanne.

"Not at all," said the blonde bluntly. "I came here expecting to see all of you."

Acadia sounded intrigued. "How did you know you were going to see us?"

The woman looked directly at Acadia and pointed at her. "I've been following *your* movements for the last eight years."

Acadia seemed offended. "Mine?"

"Yes, you. Acadia, isn't it?"

Offense turned to frazzle. "What? How?"

"Eight years ago, I was the last of us to walk away because I had to fold something I was looking at. As I was leaving, I noticed something on your chair. It was a hair clip. I picked it up with the intent to run you down and return it, but then my . . . talent kicked in. I'm a psychometric. I can read objects and tell the past and the present of the owner. I was fascinated by the visions that your hair clip emanated. Your life has been so interesting. I mean, most people don't grow up around voodoo. And I saw wild parties and everyone treating you like a princess and crazy fights with your bother. This is probably going to sound voyeuristic, but I decided to keep the barrette so I could watch your fascinating life. It was almost like a favorite TV show to me."

"That's just weird," said Acadia snappishly.

"After that break-up I mentioned, my life wasn't that interesting and because of these gifts I possess, I can't really get close to people. Don't get me wrong, it's not like I watch you all the time. I check the barrette maybe three or four times a year to see how your life is going. It just so happens I got curious last week. And last week's episode was particularly enthralling. I caught a vicious fight with your brother, and I simply couldn't put the barrette down. Things only got more interesting as other characters were introduced, and characters with powers at that. But it was when you met A.J. that I started watching around the clock. Watching those   heartfelt,   gut-wrenching,   nightly conversations has just been intoxicating."

"You watched us?" Acadia was audibly started. "That's sick. We're not entertainment!"

"Uh, did you see . . . everything?" asked Aaron warily.

The blonde hesitated in her response. "I could have. But a man and woman being intimate does nothing for me, so I put the barrette away whenever things looked like they might go in that direction. And look, I'm sorry for peeping. I know it was supposed to be private. But when I was doing it, I never thought you'd ever know. I mean, how could I possibly have foreseen meeting you? Psychometrics can't read the future. I can only see the present and I had to see you decide to come look for me to know I would see you guys again. When I saw the group make that decision, I swear I stopped looking at the private stuff."

Acadia's temper hadn't cooled with the apology. "I still feel violated."

Leave it to the professor to be the rational one. "Yes, dear girl, but if she hadn't been spying, she wouldn't be here right now and we'd be expending time and energy searching for an unknown person. Realistically, her invasion of your privacy has made it much easier for us to get going on our quest more expeditiously."

Bitingly, Acadia gave the woman the third degree. "How do we even know you're the right person to go with us on our journey? Just because you happen to have gifts doesn't mean you're the one."

Roxanne interjected with a test. "Well, there's one way to be sure. Tell us, have you ever been to Indiana?"

The woman scoffed. "I assume you are referring specifically to Kokomo, Indiana—one of the places in this world from where the hum emits. Yes, I've been there."

"Maybe she only knows about the hum from butting into my thoughts," declared Acadia.

Gunnar heard an exhale and then the stern voice of the woman. "No, Acadia. I heard about the hum from your mother, Jeanette."

Gunnar was surprised and could only imagine everyone else was too. "My mother?" asked Acadia, whose anger instantly turned to curiosity.

The woman sat down, her voice growing quieter. She spoke methodically. "That was another reason I always kept my eye on you. Imagine my surprise the first time I picked up the barrette to see in your mind's eye the very woman that I had met a year before. It was all too coincidental."

"When did you meet her?" Acadia asked with intense interest.

"In 2007. In Oregon. We were both at this vortex, following a sound. She told me she'd heard the sound before, in New Orleans, and had been trying to track down similar sounds. She told me her belief that the sounds came from portals to other universes. At the time, I thought she was insane. But then, without me telling her about

494

myself, she read me and my gifts. She confirmed what I already knew—that I was a healer and a psychometric. But she also told me about a gift I didn't know I had. She called me a traveler who could go from one universe to the other.

Because my heart was broken and I had nothing better to do, I followed your mother to several possible locations of portals. At first, it was a fruitless search. If you have gifts, any gifts at all, you can detect the hum but you can't really track it down. The only way to pinpoint where to look for the portals is by legend, folklore, or word of mouth. And that's how we found the door. We interviewed a crazy old codger who heard from his father, who heard from his father, about a woman that found another world in the forest by a stream. We wandered around the area where this woman allegedly saw the door until, by complete accident, I just happened to step on exactly the right spot for the door of the portal to appear. It was total luck."

From the very low "whoas" and "wows" he heard under his companions' breaths, Gunnar knew he was not alone in feeling astonishment. He had to clarify. "So, you've actually seen one of these portals? It's real? We're not just chasing a fantasy?"

"The portals are very real. I've only found the one though. Through all my travels, I've never been lucky enough to stumble onto another one, despite the local stories."

"Where is it?" asked Dr. Snow with upbeat optimism.

"Taos, New, Mexico," said the woman.

"Well then," said Dr. Snow, "we must get to New Mexico as soon as possible."

"Hold on a minute," said the woman reluctantly. "I realize you all want to go on this journey looking for portals, and may even think that this is some kind of destined idea, but doing so would be a waste of time."

"Why?" asked Aaron.

"First of all, I've opened that portal only once. I was so overwhelmed at the time, I forgot to mark where it was located. I have no idea how to find the exact spot again. It's literally in the middle of nowhere. We could be searching for weeks and not find it again."

Gunnar was now proud of the only thing he could offer the group. "Don't worry about that. I've got that covered. I promise we'll be able to find it again in less than a day."

The woman must have looked more circumspect. "Oh right, I saw that. But even if we find it and do open it, I warn you, none of us should go in."

"Why not?" asked Acadia. "What did you see when you went in?"

"I didn't go in. I have no idea what was in there. I mean, what is it the portal to? Death? Heaven? Hell? I wasn't ready to die then, and I'm not ready to die now. And if death is a possible consequence of entering the portal, I'm not going to take the chance. Maybe Jeanette was brave enough, but not me."

"My mother went inside?" inquired Acadia.

"Jeanette was faithful and didn't believe her god had a plan for her to die, so she went in. I tried to ignore what I saw when she first entered and assume all was well. But I waited for an hour at the same spot, not moving a muscle for fear I would inadvertently close the portal if I so much as flinched. She never returned. Eventually, my foot fell asleep and I was in terrible discomfort, so I had to walk around. The portal closed the minute I moved. After I got rid of the pins and needles, I went back to the same spot, hoping to reopen it. I know it was the same spot because my shoe prints were still imbedded in the ground. But the portal didn't reopen. I don't know why I couldn't open it a second time. Can it only be opened once, ever? Can it only be opened once per traveler? Can it only be opened every certain amount of time? I don't know. And that's yet another reason for you all to abandon this goose chase."

"I'm not abandoning it now that I know where my mother could be," declared Acadia. "And what do you mean, you ignored what happened when she first went in?"

The woman hesitated. "I hate to be the bearer of bad news, but it looked to me like when she went through, that she may have caught on fire. I fear that when she went through, she might have been burned alive."

Acadia gasped and Aaron tried to soothe her. "Shhh. Calm down. I'm sure your mother didn't really burn up. We don't know enough about the portal to say for sure that she died."

Gunnar heard Acadia choke back sobs. "Now, more than I ever, I have to see what my mother saw," she said. "If you say she caught fire, I need to experience that too."

"So you're prepared to go in and look for her?" retorted the blonde. "Acadia, I know all about you. I know you weren't that close to your mom and I know you don't believe in voodoo. Would you really risk your life to go in and look for her, especially now that you've found love? And what about the rest of you? Are you willing to risk dying if death is what lies in the portal? Especially for someone who isn't even related to you?"

Acadia was silent, as was the rest of the group. As for Gunnar, he certainly didn't want to die. He had just found Roxanne and wanted to live a long happy life with her. He wanted to see his nephew born and make up with his dad and experience more of living. If he were faced with the decision to enter the unknown, he doubted he would do it.

Acadia conceded. "I honestly don't know what I'll do when and if the time actually comes to go in. But I want to at least go to the portal, on the remote chance that my mother has been waiting to come back to our world this whole time. Lady, you can come or not. As far as I'm concerned, we don't need you after this meeting since you've told us everything we need to know."

The woman sniggered mockingly. "And just how do you expect to get into a portal without me?"

Acadia huffed back. "At least I know you told the truth about not watching me as much this week. Because if you had, you'd know the answer to that. We have a traveler already. So, you see, we don't need another one," said Acadia firmly.

"One of you is a traveler?" asked the woman with eagerness.

"I am," said Roxanne, as though the novice actually knew for certain.

"That changes things," said the woman cryptically without explaining further. "I'm in."

Dr. Snow interjected. "Here's my suggestion. We try to open the portal, purely for academic purposes. None of us actually has to go in. We can make that decision when we get there, if it comes to it."

Acadia exhaled. "Yes. I agree."

The professor continued. "Such a visit is justified on a purely scientific basis alone. Can you imagine the ramifications to the world of physics if quantifiable proof of another universe exists? There is simply no way I could elect not to go."

Roxanne concurred. "And I'd like to see if this power that I supposedly have actually works."

Gunnar had originally thought to dissent, but after Roxanne spoke, he reconsidered his selfishness. It was important to Roxanne for her to see if everything Mama Gadreau said about her was true. He couldn't deny her wish. Besides, once she found out she could open the door, they weren't obligated to enter. "For you my love, I will go."

"Well," said the woman. "So long as we're all going to be travel buddies, I suppose I should introduce myself. My name is Calliope Brown."

The completed party of six didn't waste any time. They grabbed a quick lunch at the mall food court and then headed to the rental car facility to trade in their car for an SUV. As they prepared to leave, fate played the cruel trick of requiring Gunnar to sit next to Calliope. Aaron and Acadia were both too exhausted to drive, he couldn't drive, and Dr. Snow could only drive a car whose steering wheel was on the passenger side of the vehicle. Whether true or not, Calliope claimed she suffered from highway hypnosis and would fall asleep within a half-hour. Thus, Roxanne had to drive, depriving him of the chance to sit next to her. When he tried to sit next to her up front, Dr. Snow politely begged to sit there instead, so he could get a good view of the rugged American west. Gunnar warily obliged, not wanting anyone to accuse him of wasting a good view.

The hour spent in traffic leaving L.A. gave them all a chance to get to know each other as they shared with Calliope the full range of their gifts. Gunnar had hoped that Calliope's transition into the group would be as natural as the melding of the prior five, but it wasn't working out that way. She was free in describing her gifts, but guarded about her personal life. The most she would reveal was that she was a lesbian with a still-broken heart who could never see herself loving again—end of story. While the others were fired up about their journey, Gunnar heard no passion when Calliope spoke. Her speech patterns revealed a person who was dead inside. Gunnar sighed, knowing it would be a long trip to New Mexico with a misanthrope like Calliope.

To make it less painful, Gunnar suggested breaking the trip into two parts, stopping in Flagstaff, Arizona for the night. That would give them a good seven hours of drive time today and another seven hours drive to Taos in the morning. Surprisingly, Calliope agreed to the rest, but couldn't resist throwing a wrench into the plan, suggesting instead they go an hour out of the way to Sedona, Arizona. She regaled tales of Sedona being a magical place and suggested that some of their abilities might be enhanced there. Though Gunnar wasn't thrilled about the detour, the others were easily swayed by the prospect of intensifying their gifts.

As L.A.'s commerce turned into southern California's desert, Aaron and Acadia lightly snored in the seats behind him. Dr. Snow whistled happy anecdotes about his dead wife to Roxanne from the front passenger seat. He sat quietly while icy coldness emanated from Calliope. After what seemed like an eternity of silence, Calliope finally spoke. "So, what's wrong with your eyes?"

Though he'd told the story many times, he almost resented having to tell his new traveling companion. She had been so rude in closing herself off, it seemed unfair for her to request that he would share. Nonetheless, he answered truthfully. "When I was a kid, I accidentally drank the alcohol you use to light camp fires on a dare. It made me blind."

"And you still can't see? I mean, your vision hasn't improved any recently?"

"No," he answered bitingly.

"Hmmm."

"What?" he asked with a frown.

"Oh, nothing."

He disliked her cryptic interrogation. "If it was nothing, you wouldn't have asked."

He heard a smirk. "True. But the information was purely for my own edification. Don't worry yourself."

He huffed but tried to remain calm. "Since we're playing twenty questions, I've got one for you. Why are you so standoffish? I mean, you wouldn't tell us anything about yourself. How are we all supposed to be friends and trust each other if we know nothing about you?"

"Maybe I don't want to be friends. I'm not tagging along for warm fuzzy feelings," said the ice queen matter-of-factly. "Besides, don't be a hypocrite. You didn't tell me anymore about yourself than I told you about me."

He was about to object when he realized she was right. They pretty much did only talk about their gifts, with minor mentions of relationships, but they didn't all spill the beans about their entire histories. He chuckled. "So then, are you saying you'll tell me about you if I tell you about me?"

He heard a thoughtful exhale. "I don't trust people in general to tell me the truth. But if you let me see the truth, then I'll tell you more."

"See the truth?"

"Yes. Let me read one your belongings. Allow yourself to be my television show."

He was disquieted by the thought of letting her rummage around in his past, but if it would help him melt the tension with her, he was game. "Okay."

"Usually a piece of jewelry works well, but you aren't wearing any."

Gunnar laughed. "What's the point in wearing adornments if you can't see them?"

"What else do you have on you?"

"Not much. My wallet, some clothes."

"How old is your wallet?"

"I got it for Christmas."

"No," said a disappointed Calliope. "That won't work. What is the oldest thing in your possession?"

Gunnar paused to think. "Well, I do have something I got when I was about ten, but it's rather embarrassing to admit having it. Back when Max Headroom was big in England, my mum bought me a button. You know, one of those plastic round things with a safety pin on the back? Anyway, only because she gave it to me and not because I'm still stuck in 1987, I still have it. It's pinned to the inside of my rucksack."

He heard a chirpy laugh. "Okay, cheesy button it is. Where's your bag?"

"Under my feet."

There was movement, followed by a rummaging sound, followed by a zip sound. The commotion caught the attention of the driver.

"What's going on?" Roxanne asked Gunnar.

He didn't get a chance to answer, as Calliope offered, "Your boyfriend is going to let me find out some more about him by reading one of his possessions."

Dr. Snow's attention was caught as well. "Wonderful. I'm anxious to see your gift in action."

Everything in the car was dead silent for a solid three minutes. He wondered what Calliope was seeing about him, if she was really seeing him at all.

Gunnar finally felt a gentle hand take his. At first, it was so tender, he thought it was Roxanne, but that couldn't have been since she was driving. It had to be Calliope's hand, but there was actually warmth in the touch and he was confused.

As she placed the button back in the palm of his hand, the ice queen remarked, "You really loved your mother."

He was taken aback by her words. Of course he did! But it felt strange coming from someone else. "Yes, I did," was all he could muster.

"I never imagined that another person could feel loss like I did when Lori left me. But you have. In fact, your pains are worse than mine ever were."

Gunnar said with a bite of sarcasm, "So, are we BFFs now since misery loves company?"

She ignored him and continued relaying her observations. "The night you went blind, you almost died. The pain was incredible, but you were too drunk to feel the full intensity of it."

"I don't actually recall that."

"I'm not reading your thoughts. I'm watching it like a movie."

"So, you can see what has happened to me even though I couldn't see it?"

"Yes." He wanted to interrupt with a question, but she kept rambling. "Controlled by your sister, ignored by your father, sympathized by everyone. How lonely you were for such a long time." Her insistence at sharing his pain publicly with the whole group vexed him. He was about to interrupt her with a rebuke when she offered, "Until you met, yourself."

Dr. Snow was the one that beat the clock on speaking. "Dear lady, did you see the vardoger? Was it an actual physical being?"

"Yes. At first, I thought it was a twin, but then I realized it must have been the thing you described earlier. You could have reached out and touched it and it would have been as real as you are."

Gunnar was curious. "Did you see how it came and went?"

"I . . . I almost don't believe it, and I'm probably wrong, but I swear, he came and went through a portal. The way the air swirled around a dark opening looked exactly like what I opened in Taos."

"Amazing," said the doctor.

"No," said Gunnar in disbelief. "That can't be right."

"Didn't you hear the hum every time your vardoger met with you? I heard it, every time he visited you. Like a buzzing?"

"Well, yeah I heard a buzz. But it sounded nothing like when we found the false portal."

"Maybe the sound from their world opening to ours is different than the sound of our world opening to theirs?" hypothesized Dr. Snow.

Gunnar was incredulous. "Come on, you think he would have said something if that were true. And how could my vardoger possibly come from another universe if he's me in advance. If it's still me, how can I be in two places at once?"

The professor whistled. "I apologize if some of this is over your heads and I will put this in lay terms as best I can, but in the realm of metaphysics, there exists two polar theories interpreting quantified modal logic. There is the standard Kripkean theory of modal logic versus the counterpart theory. And oh dear, I've done it again.

The confounded looks on your faces tell me I've went too far. Okay, well, both theories suggest there are other possible worlds. Under the Kripkean theory, one person exists as both person X in this world and person X in another world. Under counterpart theory, person X is different from person Y in another world, though they are similar. Do you see what I'm saying at all?"

Roxanne, who had been attentively listening the whole time, said, "I get it. So, if there's another universe, then Gunnar can be Gunnar here and still be Gunnar there under the Kripkean theory, but Gunnar couldn't be Gunnar exactly in two places under the counterpart theory?"

Dr. Snow was excited that someone understood him. "Precisely. Now, if Gunnar's vardoger speaks the truth that he too is Gunnar and not really a vardoger at all, and Calliope's vision is correct that the second Gunnar comes from another universe, then Kripkean theory and not counterpart theory must be correct. If Alphonse too speaks the truth that there are four other universes, though

512

I've yet to figure out the basis for his quantification, then that means there are multiples of each of us. Yet, I still cannot discount counterpart theory, at least not without proof, as it makes more sense. After all, in different worlds, different choices are made. And if different choices are made, then people must necessarily differ between worlds. Good heavens! This is all so fascinating, I cannot wait to go inside the portal and solve the riddle."

Gunnar was anxious to get back to himself. "So, did you get enough of reading my past?" he asked Calliope.

"Yeah," said Calliope, almost audibly letting her guard down. "Thanks, by the way. I haven't felt so connected to someone else in a long time."

After that, the conversation seemed to naturally wane, with everyone lost in their own thoughts. Gunnar guessed Calliope was thinking about her ex, that Dr. Snow was thinking about alternate universes, and that Roxanne was trying to better understand Dr. Snow. He of course was lost in memories of his mum and her dying words. She knew he would have to lose some things to gain others. He had to lose his vision to be able to hone his hearing so he could follow the hum. She said part of his destiny was to hear things no one else could hear. Like the hum. He was supposed to learn things others couldn't and go places others couldn't go. Did she mean through the portals? And something about him was so special it would benefit everyone? No, it couldn't be. He could die going to another world. Further, he was the weakest link in this chain of the gifted, so how could his gifts benefit everyone? Certainly, his superior hearing was of little consequence to the success of the mission when his companions included a clairvoyant, a psychometric, a precognitive, an empath, and the smartest person on the planet. His mum may have had lucky guesses on some stuff, but he maintained that some of her visions were still gibberish.

Shaking off his questions and sadness, Gunnar returned to the present, thinking that he disliked Calliope less now. She had shown genuine heart, though she still owed him her life story before he could be completely at ease with her.

Right around 7:00 p.m., the sextet parked at a Sedona hotel. Checking in separately as two guys, two girls, an old man, and a single lady, they obtained four rooms in the same hallway. Aaron and Acadia, who had slept practically the whole way in each other's arms, both claimed to be sweaty and in need of a shower before dinner. Roxanne, who drove all day, was exhausted and agreed that a shower might be just the thing to wake her up. Dr. Snow wanted a few minutes to call the University and verify coverage for his classes. This left only Calliope and Gunnar. Gunnar, as usual, was hungry, and Calliope claimed to want a stiff drink. So the two told the others they would meet them at the hotel's restaurant.

Gunnar ordered an appetizer of chicken wings while Calliope ordered a chocolate martini. She didn't waste time after their order. "So, I suppose I owe you my story."

He smiled. "That would be the only fair thing."

"My early life was pretty much boring and typical. I mean, I went through typical childhood taunts because I was kind of the smart nerd girl. My mom and dad weren't horrible or abusive; they were just two working parents who couldn't be around that much. My sexual orientation has never really been a problem for anyone, including myself, so there's no major trauma there.

I would say college is when it all got interesting. That's when I had my first girlfriend, Anne. She was freaked out by me I think. It took some time, but I got over her. I mean, it was college. Puppy love in retrospect, really. Then I met Lori. She was my first real adult relationship. With her, I became fun and interesting. I laughed more, I talked more, I was much more at ease around other people. Then, one day, I healed her. I brought her out of a coma after she'd been shot and the minute she woke up, she said she never wanted to see me again."

Gunnar could hear the despair in her voice. "Ouch. That's pretty awful."

"Yeah. And when she left me, I vowed never to love again. And I haven't. Not since then. No dates, no sex, no friends even. It's really safer that way. I'm less likely to lose people then."

At that moment, the waitress interrupted them with Calliope's drink. After hearing footsteps walk away, followed by a deep quaff, Gunnar added, "But people need people, Calliope. You shouldn't give up. There's got to be some woman out there for you. Someone you can love and make love to."

"I hate sex," she said bitterly.

"Even the lesbian kind?" asked Gunnar curiously.

"It's always disgusting with me."

He hated seeking too much information as it wasn't the polite British way, but he needed to know. "You don't by any chance bleed like you're a virgin whenever you have sex, do you?"

She was stunned. "How did you know that?"

"Roxanne is a healer too, and apparently it happens with her as well."

"Apparently? You two haven't had sex yet?"

"No. We've only known each other about a month and, well, she's scared of . . . "

Calliope abruptly cut him off. "Oh my God!" said Calliope, choking up.

He literally could feel Calliope tense up and turn frigid from across the table. Something was happening. "What's wrong?"

"It's her. Lori. She's here, at the bar!"

Thrilled the emergency had nothing to do with him, Roxanne, or the end of the world, he tried to be a good friend. "Maybe, you should go talk to her."

"Or maybe I should gauge out my eyes first," said Calliope with contempt.

He tried to keep it light. "Trust me. You wouldn't like it much without your eyes."

Following a quick grunt, she melted a bit. "I'm sorry Gunnar. That was a terrible thing to say to you. I'm just . . . oh God, she's seen us. She's coming over. Gunnar, no matter what, you are not allowed to leave this table.”

“I don't have my cane with me, so unless you move me around, I won't be going anywhere.”

Gunnar heard Calliope frantically swallow six times in a row while her breathing grew faster and unsteady.

“Calliope?” said the stranger.

“Lori,” said Calliope shortly.

“Oh my God, it's been . . . forever,” said the stranger nervously.

“Eleven years to be precise,” said the icy Calliope.

“Uh, mind if I join you for a minute, just to catch up?”

“No,” said Calliope curtly. “Go right ahead. You can sit by Gunnar. Oh, Lori, this is my friend Gunnar. Gunnar, Lori.”

“Nice to meet you,” said Lori.

She must have stuck her hand out for a shake because Calliope felt obliged to add, “He's blind.”

"Oh," said Lori, in that familiar sympathetic way. "Um, listen. I hope it's not going to inconvenience you, man, but I was kind of hoping to have a moment alone with Calliope."

"No offense Lori, but the last time we had a moment alone, things went badly awry," offered Calliope. "I don't want to take any chances, so Gunnar's staying. Anything you want to say to me, say it front of him. He knows everything about me anyway."

"Oh, okay," said Lori resolvedly. Soon, he felt the leather of the seat next to him cave in slightly and body heat started to warm his arm. "I . . . I told myself if I ever bumped into you again, I was going to apologize for my behavior at the hospital. I know what happened, I know everything now, and, I just wanted to say I'm sorry."

"What does that mean, you know what happened?" There was still sharpness in Calliope's voice.

"I know about your gift. The healing thing."

Now Gunnar was interested in the conversation. "How on earth do you know about that?" Calliope asked.

"I met a woman in New Orleans like a year after we broke up. She was all into magic and voodoo, and when she found out about the healing and the, you know, supposed scar tissue thing, she told me that you have the gift of healing. Why didn't you tell me when we were together?"

Calliope was at a loss for words and stumbled several times. "Um, I didn't, I wasn't sure how you would react."

"Yeah, I guess that would be kind of hard to explain, even to someone you love." Gunnar recalled very similar thoughts when Roxanne finally opened up. "But she also told me why I went off the way I did."

Calliope's need to know was palpable. "I thought you went crazy because you thought I'd turned you into freak. That wasn't it?"

"That's how it manifested, but it's not the reason why. See, according to her, her name was

Delphine I think, when you heal the body, you hurt the heart. Something about cosmic balance and give and take. Anyway, whenever you heal someone, they get angry at you. There's no way to avoid it. And they stay angry until their body is decaying again. Then the anger stops."

Though it was not Gunnar's place at all, he couldn't help but interrupt. "I'm sorry, did you say Delphine?"

"Yeah," said Lori impatiently.

"And did she have a Southern accent?"

"Yeah," said Lori with hesitation.

"That's such a coincidence. I'm fairly certain we know the same Delphine."

Calliope, who had not yet been briefed on Delphine's role in their quest, was out of patience with his interruption. "I don't give a crap about a Delphine. I'm interested in why you skewered my heart."

Gunnar shut up and let the conversation go back to an apology. "I didn't mean to," offered Lori softly. "It wasn't what I intended or wanted. Within six weeks, I was completely back to normal emotionally, and I longed for you and I missed you and I wanted so badly to get back together with you. But I couldn't find you."

"Yeah, well, I had to leave Eugene, didn't I?"

"I can sense that you're still upset about it. And I don't blame you. But, I did want to let you know that I did love you and did care about you, very much, and but for the magic thing we can't control, I never would have treated you like that."

With a deep exhale, Gunnar heard something he had yet to hear in Calliope's voice— peace. She was hopeful when she spoke. "Even knowing about the consequences of healing and that you were required to hate me afterwards, I still don't think I would have done things differently. I'd rather have had you alive and despising me as opposed to dead and loving me. I couldn't even imagine you dead."

He couldn't see it, but he could feel a tension release like a slingshot that had just launched. "I didn't ever thank you for saving my life, but I do thank you," said Lori.

"So, what are you doing here in Sedona?" asked Calliope, trying to lighten the mood.

Gunnar felt a new stone loading onto the slingshot. "I'm on vacation, with my girlfriend."

"Oh," sadness replaced the peace that new-found knowledge afforded.

"And you, what are you doing here?" asked Lori.

Truth disguised as sarcasm returned. "Five friends and I are here for a magical gathering of people with special powers. Gunnar here has super hearing."

Lori smirked softly. "Ah, psychic friends. I guess you're still going the psychic cop thing?"

"Something like that," half-offered Calliope.

"Well, I better be going," said Lori. "I told Sarah I was coming over to see an old friend. I wouldn't dare tell her who, though. She knows how much in love I was with you, and I don't think she'd recover from the jealousy."

"So, do you love Sarah?" asked Calliope.

"In a different way than I loved you. It's stable with her, not passionate. I'd be less than honest if I didn't say that, but for your power, I'd be going to that bar right now and leaving her for you."

Calliope's voice changed. This time it was determined. "Who cares about my power? Don't you think it's too coincidental that we're both here, so far from Oregon at the same time? Maybe we're supposed to get back together."

Lori licked her lips. "No, Calliope. There's something else that Delphine woman told me. If you love me, you'll just keep healing me. Which means every time you do, I'm going to hate you again and break up with you again. I can't put you through that. And I can't put myself through it because when the six weeks pass, all I do is die inside longing for you. Do you really want to go through that every time I get a gash or a bruise? I'm a narc lieutenant now. I get injured at least twice a week. We'd never be able to be in the same room together."

"I can just choose not to heal you, Lori. I can just make the choice not to focus and not to do it," said Calliope desperately.

"I wish it were that simple," said Lori sadly. "But according to Nelson who saw the whole thing, what you think was intense focus took literally a second. And according to Delphine, it's not really a choice. It's automatic whenever you see someone you love hurt. The only way around it is not to love me, or love me but want me in pain. What kind of a life is that?"

Calliope was heartbroken again. "So you're saying that I would have to make the decision that I wanted you to be hurt in order for us to be together?"

"Yeah," said Lori. "And quite frankly, I don't know if you could do it. Let me be hurt, I mean."

Calliope's anger turned to frustration and acceptance. Gunnar could hear the ice queen starting to cry. "You're right, of course. I couldn't just let you be hurt. And I couldn't live with you hating me all the time. So, go back to Sarah. Have a great vacation. Don't worry about running into us again. We're leaving tomorrow. Have a wonderful life, Lori."

The seat next to him was no longer occupied and he heard the voice of the old lover decreasing in volume. "I love you Calliope. I always have and I always will. I always told myself I'd tell you that too, if I ever saw you again."

Timid footsteps followed by muffled sobs told him that Lori had left. Gunnar had never been fantastic at consoling people. He attempted anyway. "At least you know she still loves you. That's gotta make it a little better, right?"

Calliope targeted Gunnar with her rant. "Better? That makes it worse! Knowing you can never be with someone you love despite the way you both feel? There's no greater curse. And welcome to it, my friend, because you are soon to be in the same boat. As soon as Roxanne starts to love you 100% and starts healing your every cut and scrape, you'll be hating her all the time. You won't be able to be with her unless they put you in a plastic bubble."

Gunnar drew in his arms to his chest to shield himself from her diatribe. "That's not going to happen to us. I know, because we're already 100% in love and nothing bad has happened yet."

Her spite had not lessened. "You might be 100% in love with her, but she is not 100% in love with you. The proof is in the lack of pudding. You'd be able to see again if she truly did love you."

Gunnar flinched. He himself had tried to suppress this very thought. He felt his body curl up tighter into itself.

He heard a strong exhale from his bitter companion. "Look," said Calliope, obviously trying to diminish the impact of her truth telling. "Maybe it's fortuitous that she doesn't. At least this way, you can be around her without disliking her. You still get to at least love her."

Gunnar didn't have time to think about Calliope's attempt to soothe him. At that moment, the very person causing him internal strife walked into the room, as he could smell peach shampoo wafting through the air. Soon, he felt the spot previously occupied by Lori taken by someone who snuggled close to him. A kiss to his cheek confirmed it was Roxanne. Gunnar couldn't even muster a greeting, let alone a kiss in return.

The atmosphere was tense. "Well," said Calliope, looking for a way out of the situation that she had created. "I don't think I can stand to be in the same room with Lori for one more minute, so I'm out of here. I'll see you guys in the morning." With that, there was an abrupt screech of a chair followed by furious walking.

"What was that all about?" asked Roxanne.

"She ran into an old girlfriend," said Gunnar with melancholy.

"Sorry I took so long. I confess I conked out for a few minutes before the shower. Those beds are so soft. I can't wait to cuddle with you on one tonight."

When he made no attempt to reply, she must have sensed something wrong. "What's the matter?" she asked innocently.

He was torn in two, half of him angry that she didn't love him and half of him not caring so long as he didn't lose her. "I just found out something not so great," was all he could say.

"What?"

"Calliope's ex came over and chatted with us for a bit. It turns out that when a healer really and truly loves someone with their whole heart, that they can't help but spontaneously heal their partner's every little injury." Gunnar didn't need to finish.

Roxanne spoke as seriously as he'd ever heard her speak. "That can't be true. I mean, I love you, and you're still blind, so that cannot be correct."

"But do you? Really love me?"

She got flustered. "Yes! Of course. I'm almost positive ... " She trailed off once she realized what she'd said.

He exhaled and braced his insides for pain. "Almost?"

She was getting frantic. "That's not what I meant. I mean, I know, like I know there's a sun in the sky, that you are the one I want to spend my life with. And I care about you more than I've ever cared about anyone else. But . . . "

The dreaded 'but.' "But what?" He couldn't hide the string in his voice.

"I'm scared of loving you. And I think that's made me stop just short of letting myself get into this completely."

"Scared? Why? Because of my blindness?" he asked, letting his insecurity show.

"No."

"Then scared of what?" he asked with disbelief.

Her voice slowed and quivered. "Of having sex with you. What's it gonna be like the first time we do it? What if it doesn't feel good or hurts, no matter how much I consent and want it? What if, no matter how hard you try, you can't make me feel physical pleasure? Will you take it personally? Will I feel guilty because you take it personally? Will you leave me because I can't enjoy it? Gunnar, I'd be devastated if you left me. And let's face it—you leaving me is a distinct possibility if I don't sleep with you, and it's just as much a possibility if I do sleep with you. I can't give my whole heart to you because I feel damned if I do and damned if I don't."

He blew out hot air. "Look, I meant it when I said that I'd wait until you were ready. But, if I'm honest, I did contemplate that you'd be ready at some point in time. And I can't answer any of your questions, except to say that I love you enough that I won't leave you regardless of what it's like and I won't expect fireworks. I'll be patient with you if it's difficult. I'll be as gentle as humanly possible if it hurts. If you cry, I'll know it's not me. And if you ask me to stop, I will. I imagine it's going to be somewhat like learning to swim by jumping into the deep end of a pool. You probably won't like it the first time, and it may be all about just treading water, but my hope is that after you get that first

532

time over with, it won't be so bad the next time. And maybe by the third or the fourth time, the shock will be gone and you can learn that it's going to be okay. That people who are in love can make love, and it's different than what you've been through. I'll be there for you, and we'll get through your first time together."

Roxanne grabbed him tightly in her arms. "Gunnar, I don't know what to say. I mean, I want to believe you. I've just, still got to convince myself," she said.

There was nothing else for either to say on the subject. It was what it was. For now, status quo would have to be good enough. In fact, it was an unspoken truth that they both needed to put this whole topic behind them for the good of the group and their journey. Yet Gunnar was still crushed when the other three joined them for dinner. He picked at his food but had little appetite.

By dessert, he was exhausted with putting up pretenses. All he wanted was to go to bed. When Dr. Snow excused himself on the premise of being too old to stay awake with the young people, Gunnar took the opportunity to leave too under the guise of wanting to chat with his fellow Brit.

After a bit of small talk, mostly about Astrid, Gunnar retired to his own room. No sooner had he gotten a chance to use the restroom when there was a knock on the door. Roxanne had a key, so he presumed it must be one of the others. Opening the door, he heard an unexpected voice.

"I watched you come down the hall," said Calliope. "Can I come in?"

"Of course," he moved out of the way and felt the breeze of her movements pass him.

"I wanted to apologize for going off like that in the restaurant. Seeing Lori was just too much for me to process. And who knows? Maybe you and Roxanne will be different because you're both gifted and you know what to expect. Or maybe she does love you and you just haven't healed for some magical reason having to do with your own abilities."

He smirked. "No, actually, you were right. She doesn't quite love me like I love her."

She was silent for a moment and then offered comfort. "You know, we've both had our hearts shaken tonight. I think we could both use a shot of confidence. And luckily, we're in Sedona, so I know just how we can get some."

"What are you talking about?" asked Gunnar.

"You and I need a trip to a vortex. It's a spiritual place where what's inside you awakens and becomes stronger."

Gunnar was tired and not in the mood for an adventure. "What time is it?"

"8:30. But there's one right by the airport and it's not too hilly or rocky. Don't worry, I'll be able to see where we're going."

"Doesn't it close?"

Calliope over enunciated, "It's a geographic energy, it never closes."

"Fine, as long as we aren't gone too long. But please write Roxanne a note telling her where we went so she and the others don't worry."

Gunnar heard footsteps cross to the desk and then a pen scratching on paper. After she finished inking the note, he heard Calliope grab the car keys. Then, he and his new friend exited the hotel into a hot wind.

As the vehicle slowly pulled out of its parking spot, Calliope confessed. "Gunnar, I have to admit that before I ever got to your room, I was planning on taking you to this vortex. It wasn't a spur of the moment decision. See, every once in a while, I'll get a residual flash of someone's life even after I no longer possess the object I was reading. As I was sitting in my room, I saw that silly pin in my head. And it led to another vision. It was a short, scattered one, but it had something to do with a kitchen and you as a teenager. You were scared by something that happened to you in that kitchen. But looking at the rest of your memories, I don't remember seeing anything about that. I think you've either repressed the memory or forgotten it, and I feel like this memory is somehow important. The vortex helps clear your mind and open up channels inside you. I think it might stir up that memory."

He thought intently about the kitchen of his childhood home in England and nothing significant revealed itself. "Don't get your hopes up," he noted. "I'm exhausted and I doubt this vortex will be able to wake me up."

"Well," she offered, "even if you don't remember anything, it's still good that we're going. This particular vortex opens up a person's masculine side. It awakens the part of us that is confident and strong. You need those qualities Gunnar, if you're going to lead us."

Gunnar was taken aback. "Lead you? How can a blind man lead anyone?"

"Don't you realize that you're the reason we're all together? Your vardoger introduced you to A.J. and Roxanne and encouraged you to bring Acadia into the fold. Your need for answers led you to Arthur. And our kindred pain made it possible for me to be open to this group adventure. You're the common denominator."

"But . . . " Gunnar didn't have words to negate the obvious.

Calliope was stern. "Gunnar, I've seen your life. I know you put up a brave front publicly about your blindness and go out of your way to prove it doesn't limit you. But when it's just you in a scary new situation, you let it defeat you. You need to man up and be as determined to lead us as you were determined to have a career or an apartment of your own."

Maybe a shot of self-confidence could help him focus, if indeed this vortex really worked and if indeed he was supposed to lead the six into the portals. He forced himself to get out of car when it parked and allowed Calliope to guide him through a rocky terrain, up hills, and through bushes.

She finally said. "Just a few more feet to the twisted trees."

He was ready to complain about the distance when he heard, "Wow, if you could only see this. Breathe it in, Gunnar. We're here."

He took a deep breath as suggested, but felt no different. "So, is there like a magic chant to get this vortex thing to work?"

"No," Calliope chuckled. "Just relax." He soon felt himself being sat on a large rock. "Think of nothing but the sense of strength you desire."

With eyes closed and the slow warm wind causing the hair on his legs to rise, he was about to fall asleep from the relaxation when he felt an internal strength he had never known. He was driven, decisive, and knew exactly how to lead and be responsible for others. There was a confidence rising that he could take charge of any situation and stand up to any foe, including himself. He opened his eyes with the startling realization that, all along, he had been his own worst enemy. Calliope had been right—despite his brave face and outward determination to overcome his disability in society and with his job, he was still insecure about his lack of sight in the deep recesses of his heart. He wanted to love Roxanne, and even convinced himself that he did, but now he knew that just as she was held back by fear, so was he. There was that nagging part of him that was sure Roxanne would grow weary of him one day, and that part needed to leave him for a sighted partner. The vortex *was* the perfect place for him to recognize and shed those fears.

"I feel oddly powerful," declared Gunnar. "Powerful enough to say that I'm no longer afraid of being blind. Powerful enough to say that blindness makes me no less of a man. I'm a fantastic sound engineer, a wonderful son and brother, and I am worthy of being loved and desired by a special woman. And I am capable of being a leader."

Calliope answered. "And I thought I felt better."

Gunnar laughed lightly. "It's not just my confidence that's intensified. Everything is just so clear. Can you hear nature, Calliope? The scampering claws of some tiny mammal scraping along this gravel road? A bird squawking from somewhere to the southeast?"

"I don't hear anything," said his companion. Then a few seconds later, Calliope gasped when some small animal ran by them and some crow cawed. "Whoa! It's like you knew what was coming."

"And the cool air," said Gunnar. "Even though it's a warm desert night, I feel coldness in the breeze. Just a slight chill on the dew in the wind."

Calliope was thirsty for more insight into Gunnar's feelings. "What else can you sense?"

"A man telling us we shouldn't be at the park this late. God, his aftershave smells awful."

"No one is going to catch us here," Calliope uttered. "I already told you . . . "

"Excuse me, but it's after trail hours. You're not supposed to be here," said a stranger's gruff and perturbed voice.

Calliope hid her gasp as she tried to answer the man. Only a stutter came out.

Gunnar handled the situation with ease. "We know and we really apologize. When we walked up here, it was still light outside. But we're from England and not used to this heat, so we found ourselves dehydrated, exhausted, and tired. We ended up falling asleep and not waking up until a few minutes ago. It's actually fortunate that you arrived, given that I'm blind and my wife would have had to lead me down in the dark."

Playing up the blind foreigner always helped in sticky situations. "Oh," said the park officer as he recognized the situation. "Please, let me guide you down. I have a golf cart we can ride out of here. Hey, I'm sorry if I scared you folks. I thought you guys might have been vandals so I was trying to sneak up on you."

"No worries. I head you coming," said Gunnar.

Calliope said nothing on their trip back to the car, which kept up the pretense that the couple was British. After polite handshakes where Gunnar maintained control of the lie to the end, they both got back into the SUV and Calliope drove away.

"What was that?" she asked.

"What was what?" Gunnar replied.

"You know, I think you may be clairaudient and have clairolfaction," she stated knowingly.

"Well those are some thousand dollar words. What do they mean?"

Calliope explained. "Clairaudient is when you can hear things no one else can hear, and sometimes before the sounds are even made. Clairolfaction is like psychic smelling. You can smell things others cannot and usually before the smell exists. It's all in the mind though. There's not really a smell or a sound, but people like you know they're coming. Tonight, you heard the animals before they made sounds and you knew that ranger was going to stink like too much cologne before he even approached us. You really do have gifts, Gunnar, outside of the vardoger."

"Which must be why I can hear the hum so well," he said assuredly.

"I'd bet anything you have more gifts too. That vision I had of you in your kitchen—when you had that experience, you weren't blind yet. You lost your sight shortly after—maybe even the same day or the next day. What if your other gifts require you to be able to see and you just never had the chance to develop them? Maybe you never used them again because to you, it was just a one-time anomaly not worth remembering. Gunnar, you've got to try to remember what happened to you in the kitchen."

He thought. "I really don't recall. If it was close to the time I went blind, I was probably too drunk to remember."

"Then the only other alternative to see if I'm right is for you to get your sight back."

Gunnar smirked and said sarcastically, "Of course, it's so obvious. Let me run down to the local eye doctor and see if he can correct what two decade's worth of ophthalmologists couldn't fix."

Calliope, who now seemed like a different person, was no longer icy. "Maybe you should try to get Roxanne to heal you."

Sarcasm turned to accusation. "Didn't you just tell me that if Roxanne healed me, we were doomed?"

Calliope had a new optimism. "Maybe you two will be different. Knowledge is power, after all. When I healed Lori, neither of us knew what was coming. If Roxanne heals you, you'll know what to expect. And your friends will be there to remind you that the feeling of hate is only temporary and you will love Roxanne again in a few short weeks."

Gunnar's tone softened as he felt the SUV slow into a parked position. "You forget Calliope that all this is premised on her loving me. I can't make her love me. She's going to have to come to that on her own. And I don't know how long that could take. So, in the meantime, I'll try to recall what happened in that kitchen. I'd put more stock in my memory than in Roxanne's love right now."

Chapter Thirteen

Love Hurts

*****

Gunnar was fuming. It was tea time for God's sake—one of his mother's favorite times of day. The family had always gathered for tea time, but now that his mother was dead, it was like no one else in the family cared about coming together. Every weekday, despite his disenchantment with life and hatred for protocol, he still honored her memory by boiling a kettle and placing the biscuits on the kitchen table. Yet, when he called the others to tea, no one came. This day was no different than the rest of the days had been since she'd died, so as usual, there he sat all by himself

Drinking the tea, he wished it was a good beer. He smiled to himself despite his ire, knowing it was only two more days before he could get piss drunk on the camping trip with his mates. At least they cared about him. At least they would hang out with him and pay attention to him. In the meantime, Gunnar would just have to settle for boring old tea by himself.

Gunnar didn't actually like tea. He only ever drank it to please his mother, who adopted the custom to appear more British. In fact, he could only stand it if it were loaded with honey. Looking on the table for the jar, he realized he'd forgotten it. He looked around the kitchen and saw it sitting on the counter by the toaster. He was already furious with his family, and now he was becoming irrationally angry at the honey for making him get up and walk to it. He didn't feel like he should have to get up and get it any more than he should have to go track down his father and sister. That stupid honey should come to him!

He looked down at the teaspoon sitting next to his teacup. The shininess of the tip caught his attention. He stared at it, and stared at it, and imagined the silver coated in a glistening, sticky amber. The more he stared, the more his mind could see the honey there on the spoon. He could smell the sweetness in his nose. His taste buds started to crave the taste of honey. He was in a trance, concentrating on the nonexistent honey on the spoon.

A power tool starting up in the backyard broke Gunnar's focus. When he looked back down, his jaw dropped. There on the table, next to the spoon, was the jar of honey that only minutes before had been so far away he couldn't bother to walk over to it.

"What the hell?" Gunnar was spooked. Had the honey been there the entire time and he was hallucinating that it was over by the counter? Had he been so lost in thought that he couldn't remember rising from his chair and getting the honey? Those could be the only rational explanations, since the honey didn't, couldn't, actually come to him.

Gunnar looked back over to the toaster. There was still a half a grapefruit sitting there from lunch. Could the same thing happen again? Gunnar stared at the grapefruit on the counter. He pictured the tanginess of the juice going down his throat. He smelled the zesty sweetness. He pictured it on the plate before him. And then, he watched as the grapefruit lifted itself off the counter and floated towards him.

Gunnar shot out of his chair like a bullet. The chair crashed to the ground and the grapefruit fell on the floor midway to the table. Gunnar was shaking. What was happening? Was he actually moving things just by staring at them? No, it couldn't be! It wasn't possible! Forgetting his earlier angst, Gunnar ran for Astrid's room. Busting in without knocking, he alarmed his sister. "Hey!" she exclaimed grumpily.

"Astrid, I. . . I think I'm seeing things. I swear to God the honey and a grapefruit just flew across the kitchen by themselves," he said, frazzled.

She rolled her eyes and frowned. "Gunnar, be serious. I'm trying to write a paper on the French Revolution. I don't have time for your pranks."

"It's not a prank!" he practically yelled.

In an effort to appease him, she put her book down. "Try approaching the matter scientifically. Go downstairs, observe the objects, see if they fly again, and record your data. Once who have a hypothesis we can test, I'll come and look. In the meantime, close my door."

Sometimes he felt like she loved books more than she loved him. He left the room with renewed anger, which only grew more intense as he realized that if Astrid was going to dismiss him, Nils certainly would. Strange and unusual things were so far outside the parameters of Nils' working class mentality, Gunnar was sure his father would rebuff him. Gunnar called the one person he hoped would listen.

"Hey Mick!" he said when his friend answered the phone.

"What's up mate?"

"Something really odd just happened to me and I don't know who else to tell."

"Come on over then," said Mick.

"Twenty minutes," said Gunnar as he hung up the phone.

Arriving at Mick's mother's flat, he was anxious to tell his friend everything that happened. As he walked up the front steps, he swore he could smell Mick's flat before he even walked in. Only this time, he could pick apart the different odors that made up the smell of Mick's house. There was an underlying base of stewed beef and boiled cabbage, covered by the distinct aroma of stout lager. Mix in the sweaty body odor of a father that worked in a factory, a mother who chain-smoked, and three older brothers who all played sports, and Gunnar almost didn't want to go in.

But he shook of the upcoming stench and knocked on the door. Mick answered and Gunnar walked in to the typical sounds of rough housing, *Coronation Street* repeats, and boiling water. Without ado, Mick led Gunnar back to one of the small bedrooms he shared with one of his brothers. Luckily, said brother was not at home so they had the room to themselves.

Gunnar didn't wait for his host to start the conversation. "You will not believe what has happened!"

"Whoa, mate. Slow down. Your hyperactivity is giving me a headache. Can't you see I've already had a few?" said his friend with a slight slur.

Gunnar observed his friend's bloodshot eyes. "Oh yeah. What did you drink? And where did you get it?"

"Rob bought me a big bottle of rum yesterday in exchange for me changing the spark plugs on the Saab. I've drank about half so far. You want to split the rest?"

"Absolutely. I could use a drink."

"Right," said Mick. "Let's get a little toasty first and slow you down. Then you can tell me all about the exciting news."

An empty bottle of rum later, Gunnar and Mick were laughing uncontrollably talking about some trollop that Mick used to date. Their amusement was interrupted by an obnoxious cockney cry of, "Suppa boys!"

"Damn, it's already time to eat. What time is it?" asked Mick.

"I have absolutely no idea," laughed Gunnar.

"My mum will have my head on a plate if I don't go eat her grotty beef stew. Want some?"

"Ugh. After that rum, I'd gag."

"You best be on your way then. Hey, what did you want to tell me anyway?"

"Oh, I like, moved some objects with my mind a little while ago."

There was a dead silence followed by hysterical laughter on both their parts. "Well," Mick offered, "you're either barmy or you've made a huge cock up."

"No, no, I swear it!" said Gunnar, still quite jovial.

"All right then, David Copperfield. Let's see your magical powers in action. Move that ashtray over there."

As he had done with the grapefruit and honey, he stared at the ashtray. But this time, he snorted and crowed hysterically the whole time. The ashtray didn't move an inch.

Both still laughing, Gunnar admitted, "I guess that was a right cock-up, wasn't it?"

"Go on. Get out of here," said Mick. "I'll see you tomorrow night. Rob's going to bring tons of adult bevvies for our camp out. It's going to be so ace!"

*****

Gunnar didn't know how late it was when he and Calliope returned to the hotel, but he felt great and not a bit tired. The vortex had opened up something inside of him. As much as he had always tried to portray being happy and carefree and okay with his disability, he realized tonight he'd lacked self-confidence since the moment he lost his vision. It was only natural for someone who loses something to feel insecurity, but it was time for Gunnar to shed that self-doubt. He really was fine exactly the way he was.

He'd expected Roxanne to be sleeping by the time he got back and was surprised to find her opening the door with haste the moment he started fiddling with the key card slot.

"Gunnar!" she yelled with relief, pulling him in the door and immediately into a hug.

"Well, hello there!"

"I'm so glad you're back," Roxanne said with a sigh and a sniffle. She'd been crying.

"What's the matter?"

"What's the matter?" she repeated. "You left. I wasn't sure if you were coming back."

"We left you a note."

"Yeah," she said impatiently. "That only said 'I'm leaving for a while.' It didn't say where you were going or when you were coming back."

He shook his head with a slight smile. "That Calliope. Not much of a secretary. Darling, I didn't know what she'd written. I assumed she'd say we went for a drive and would be right back. I'm sorry if you were worried."

Roxanne's anxiety declined. She hugged him again, then brought him down to sit on the foot of the bed. "Gunnar, I've spent the last hour regretting every single thing I said at the restaurant. Of course I love you! I love you more than anyone in the whole world. More than I've ever loved anyone. There's no almost about it." The next thing he felt was her kissing his lips tenderly. He loved the taste of her kisses. He opened his mouth wider as the kisses went from tender to sultry. He felt her move closer to him as the kisses become deeper. Then, he felt her hand inching up his thigh.

He stopped the kiss. "Roxanne, stop."

"No, Gunnar. I want this."

He exhaled. "Believe me, I want it to. But not tonight. I will not allow the first time we make love to be clouded by guilt. You don't need to use sex to get me to stay."

"No, really," she pleaded. "When I thought you were gone for good, I realized I was wrong. I am ready to give myself to you completely. I'm not broken. I am a woman capable of having sex with the man I adore and enjoying it. I'm not afraid. I know it's going to be good and happy with you."

"If you truly feel ready, then you'll still be ready tomorrow. But I want you to be absolutely sure because once it's done, we can't take it back. So please, for me, sleep on it. And we'll see how you feel tomorrow."

She held him again and now they just blended into each other's arms. He would have been content to stay there all night, but he had some things to discuss with her. "Roxanne, I want to talk to you about some things I learned tonight."

She pulled out of his chest. "What?"

"I want to tell you where Calliope and I went and what happened there."

"Okay."

"She took me to a vortex. She said it was a spiritual place that had the ability to cleanse your fears and release your demons. While we were there, I realized I wasn't upset about our conversation. That it was okay if you only almost loved me. Because I realized that I too have been holding back from completely loving you."

Her tone contained a bit of hurt, but also support. "Really?"

"Yes. What I've been feeling this whole time is a very strong, very personal connection that I could never imagine severing. I care about you to your core and I'd rather have my head sliced off with a guillotine then to see any ill befall you. But, I couldn't one hundred percent see a future with you. And that's because my best vision of our future included me being dependent on you. Since we've been together, I've become complacent. I've starting letting you guide me places. I've relied on your eyes and your perceptions to make decisions. I rarely challenge you even if I have a different opinion out of fear of being alone again. And that doesn't correlate to the man I want to be. If I'm going to become a unit with you, we both need to be strong parts of that unit. And I can only be strong if I accept that I am worthy and capable, regardless of impairments. I need to go back to what I was like before we met, only better. I need to find my own way and make my own choices, only this time do it with confidence."

They hugged tightly again and she whispered in his ear, "I know. I promise I'll let you try." After that, with sporadic small talk, they went to bed.

When Gunnar awoke, he was alone. He could feel sunlight hitting his skin. The night before, the group had decided to leave by 8:00 a.m. so they could make it to Taos with enough sunlight left to try to find the portal. But the heat coming through the window was strong enough that Gunnar knew it was the late and not the early morning sun he was feeling.

Gunnar reached for his audio watch. "10:49" it said robotically. Where was everybody?

Just then, he was surprised by the sound of the card reader on the outside of the door. He heard dainty running and then felt the bed cave in as the weight of Roxanne's body bounced close to him.

"Oh Gunnar, Calliope took me to the most awesome place this morning!"

He wiped his eyes. "Did she take you to the airport vortex?"

"No, to a different vortex at a place called Cathedral Rock. It's a place for female energy."

"Was it a fruitful trip?" Gunnar asked, his scattered mind clearing.

"Very much so, and for more reasons than you'd think. It gave me and Calliope a chance to become friends. Before we even got there, I found out Calliope and I have a lot in common. We both heal ourselves exactly the same way. When we have sex, we both grow back hymens. I'm not alone! I'm not the only person on the planet that freakishly does that! It's so strangely comforting. And hey, how come you didn't tell me about your new gifts last night? I had to hear from Calliope that you can smell and hear things that aren't there."

"I thought there were more important things to talk about last night than smells and sounds."

Roxanne sighed. "You know, just like you did at the masculine vortex, I learned a lot about myself. As I was sitting there, thinking how ironic it is that I can heal my body but not my own soul, I decided to pray. I prayed to God to take my fear. I don't know if it was God answering, or if the feminine energy of the vortex erased the heartbreak, but somehow, I was able to let go of that fear I have about sex. Now I'm ready. In the dawn, having slept on it, having healed, I'm ready for an adult relationship with you, complete with making love to the most amazing man in the world."

"Then I can't wait until we have some time to be alone," he spoke softly.

She continued while rubbing his fingers. "Unfortunately, that's not right now. Check out time is in ten minutes and we've gotta pack fast and move out. But tonight, Gunnar, tonight in Taos."

He felt a kiss on his lips. It was soft and sweet and full of energy. And for a split second, when he opened his eyes, the ever present dark gray fuzz seemed like tan colored fuzz.

As he zipped his bag, he tried to change the subject. "So, do you think we'll find that portal?"

He heard her smirk. "You know, I have a feeling we will, but I secretly hope we won't. Calliope got me thinking. We might be able to open it, but I honestly don't think I want to go through it. Not without knowing what awaits us on the other side."

"I'm glad to hear you say that actually, because I was thinking the same exact thing. I mean, I'm about to become an uncle. I don't want to give up seeing my nephew for the first time."

"And I would miss my parents way too much," she offered in agreement.

He smiled as he followed her voice towards the door. By the time they got out to the SUV, everyone was waiting on them. "Sleep in?" ribbed Aaron.

"Yeah, sorry about that, mate," offered Gunnar.

He heard a car door open. "That's okay. Acadia and I used the time to check out a few art galleries.   But we better motor," said Aaron assuredly. "As it is now, we won't be seeing any portals tonight. It'll be dark before we get there."

For this stretch of the road trip, he and Roxanne took the back seat while Acadia drove, Dr. Snow sat at her right, and Aaron and Calliope in the row just behind. Listening quietly to their friends' trivial banter, the two of them snuggled, caressing each other's skin. Everything seemed different between them.   He was a more confident, responsible, and ready to take care of her. He sensed that Roxanne was at peace, ready to open up to love without fear of judgment. Every time she would huddle closer or sneak a kiss on the cheek, the tone of the gray in his mind's eye seemed to grow less dim.

The group drove straight through to Taos without stopping for dinner. It had been a peaceful drive, curling along a winding river. Even though the others were talking and the windows were closed in favor of the air conditioner, Gunnar heard the sounds of families frolicking on river rapids.

Finally, a hungry and inpatient Aaron asked where they were.

"A town called Espanola," answered Calliope. "We have about an hour to go."

Acadia ignored her paramour's stomach gurgles. "Why don't we try to find the portal tonight? It won't be that late. We can eat after we find it."

Calliope replied affirmatively. "No. I'm too tired from getting up early and I need to be fresh and completely aware if I'm going to find this place again. Right now, I'm too foggy to remember directions. All I can remember are pictures. We cross the river over a big bridge. We pass this strange business that looks like a green dragon. We pass a neighborhood full of partially underground houses. After that, the roads all meld together in my mind. I think with a little sleep, I should be able to piece these images together and get us close enough for Gunnar to take over."

"What do you remember about the portal itself," asked Acadia, disappointed, but still excited.

"I know there is a hiking trail. I recall having to walk a long way and climb a little, and there were tons of little green bushes that catch your clothes. We had to step in water; I remember my feet were wet and cold. The portal is in a meadow by where two different streams converge."

Gunnar was thankful that Calliope had put an end to talk of finding the portal tonight. A relaxed and awake head is what they all needed if they were going to make a major life decision like whether to potentially kill themselves. Plus, it would give him and Roxanne some time tonight to see where their confirmed love would lead.

When they arrived at a Taos hotel, they all decided to skip a big dinner and just do their own snacks. Gunnar sensed that the other four were feeling nervous, most likely about what they would encounter tomorrow. He wasn't a bit frazzled though, and neither was Roxanne. They both knew their decisions had already been made. They would help open the portal, but they weren't going in.

This left them mentally free to enjoy each other. They ordered sandwiches from room services and ate just enough to sate themselves. Then, they took a shower together to wipe away the day's grime. And that's where it started. The kissing in the stream made it even hotter, the soaped up skin made the rubbing a little more erotic. While still dripping wet, the two ran to the bed and fully released the inhibitions that had been keeping them apart for a month.

Through hot wet kisses, Gunnar whispered. "I love you, Roxanne. I will always do what it takes to make you happy."

In her sincerest voice, she whispered back, "And I trust you to never hurt me."

Gunnar pulled away and was about to say something, but Roxanne wouldn't let Gunnar get in another word, as she wrapped her arms around him and forced her tongue into his lips. She then maneuvered him so that his back was flat on the bed. Resting his head on the pillow, he entered complete bliss as his girlfriend did things to his body that no sympathy quickie had ever done. Just as he was on the verge of the little death, he gently withdrew from her clutches and exchanged the position of their bodies. With a sultry grin, he said, "I don't need vision for this. I can feel my way." He then reciprocated the pleasure until he could feel the rhythm in her hips longing for something more substantial.

With a passionate kiss, he entered her. Sure enough, there was the initial hindrance he was told to expect. He tried not to hurt her as he pierced through, but she reassured him with her body language that she was fine.

Gunnar was lost in a haze of energy with each thrust. He had never felt like this before making love to anyone, ever. He took turns between pulling away so their chests did not touch and coming so close to her that his nose was buried in a bucket of peaches. This was the dance, over and over, and for far longer than Gunnar would have thought himself capable given the month of foreplay between him and Roxanne. It was at the point right before the pressure starts to hurt and a man can think of absolutely nothing else other than release when Roxanne cried out in an orgasmic high. The delightful shriek invited Gunnar to turn his head in the direction of the sound. Just as he ground his hips deep into her with his own release, he looked at her beautiful face and then down at his chest as her red-tipped fingers clawed into him.

Looked . . . at her beautiful face. Looked . . . at the red lights. Saw . . . her straight hair flowing over her right shoulder like melted chocolate. Watched . . . her caramel colored skin glisten with sweat. Gazed . . . at her pink tongue race between her pouty lips. Observed . . . her curvy figure fall onto ivory colored bed linens.

Gunnar couldn't move. His body still surged with waves of pleasure, but his brain was confused and dizzy.

Roxanne finally opened her eyes and she sat up in front of him. They were truly stunning eyes. 'Brown' hardly did them justice. They sparkled like polished lava rocks. But as gorgeous as they were, they belonged to his enemy so he couldn't fully appreciate them. He still hadn't moved and couldn't seem to talk. He was very disoriented. A part of him wanted to tell the person next to him that he could see and jump for joy with her in his arms. But there was another part of him that felt bitter. He didn't know why that part felt mean, but it was a part that didn't think Roxanne deserved to know. There was a battle going on inside him and he didn't know which side should win. He was so distressed, he wanted to throw something. He looked over to the nightstand and saw Roxanne's cell phone. Damn that phone. Why was she always texting on it? What guy was she texting when he wasn't around? If he could only throw that phone at her.

He was taken aback when Roxanne's phone literally jumped off the table and flew right past her, hitting the wall and making a furious smacking sound. Her look of pleasure had turned to sheer terror. What the hell was happening?

In his last moment of clarity, Gunnar ordered Roxanne, "Go get Calliope."

Roxanne didn't even get dressed, merely wrapping a sheet around herself. She went out the door without closing it. Gunnar heard that stupid woman's evil footprints clomping down the hall. Though Calliope's door was five down, he heard the conversation as though it was occurring in their adjoining bathroom.

"Calliope, something's wrong with Gunnar. He told me to come get you."

He then heard two sets of footprints running back towards him. For some reason, he was mad at both women now, since Calliope was obviously siding with that tramp Roxanne.

Calliope came in before the whore. She was way too pretty to be a lesbian, even with no makeup and dressed in raggy gray joggers and an old T-shirt. He couldn't help but remark, if only to make Roxanne jealous, "Wow, Calliope, I must say, you look absolutely gorgeous. Think I could turn you?"

He looked to the brown-haired girl behind the blonde goddess hoping to see tears in her eyes. Damn! All he saw was befuddlement.

"Uh, thanks Gunnar," said Calliope with a sneer. And then her jade green eyes opened wide. "Wait, did you just say, I *look* gorgeous?"

"Yeah, and I don't even care if you're wearing a track suit."

Both women looked at each other in astonishment. Calliope took her card key from a pocket and gave it to Roxanne. "I think you're going to need this for a while." She then turned her attention back to Gunnar. "Am I right in thinking that you can see me?"

"I can see both of you. That whiny little girl and you, a real woman that I just want to bang the hell out of."

The blonde turned to the brunette. "Roxanne, you healed him. You should go to my room, now, before he says anything else that's hurtful."

The brunette looked sad and perplexed as she left the room, and Gunnar reveled in her pain. Now alone with the real woman he wanted, he leaned into her for a kiss.

Calliope pushed him away by his shoulders. "Whoa! Gunnar. I know you think you want me right now, but ask yourself why?"

He was unabashedly honest. "Because it would make Roxanne mad."

"Right. You're mad at Roxanne. But why?"

He had no good answer for this. He didn't really know why. He just went with his feelings. "Because she makes me angry."

"No, Gunnar. You love Roxanne. This is just a temporary reaction. This is me tying you to a tree. Don't you remember any of that?"

"You want to tie me to tree?" He smiled mischievously. "Kinky," he said as he brought his naked body closer to her.

Moving back, Calliope shifted the topic to his good fortune. "Don't you want to talk about the fact that you have your sight back?"

"Nope," he said callously, as he tried to reach in for another kiss. He was startled when the blonde smacked him across the face. The whack hurt; she had a powerful hand. As he raised his hand to massage his cheek, he spontaneously uttered, "Okay, so maybe Roxanne isn't so bad that she deserves me hitting on another woman in front of her."

Gunnar watched as Calliope got a wondering gleam in her eye. "Gunnar, come with me. We're going to see Arthur. But please, put your clothes on first."

After Gunnar zipped up his jeans and put on a t-shirt, the pair went down the hall and knocked on Dr. Snow's door. The man who answered was wide awake and watching PBS on his television set.

"Ah, do come in," he said cheerfully.

"Arthur, this isn't a pleasure visit," said Calliope gruffly, practically throwing Gunnar into the room and slamming the door behind them. "Remember what we talked about tonight after everyone else went their separate ways— the healing I did on my girlfriend and everything I learned about it. Well, Roxanne has inadvertently healed Gunnar's blindness."

With wrinkled eyes, Dr. Snow put his finger to his crooked mouth as if thinking. "And now, he hates her?"

"He did," Calliope said, trailing off.

"I don't hate her," relented Gunnar. "I just don't care for her much. I'm rather indifferent to her actually."

Dr. Snow seemed puzzled. "Curious. His reaction to Roxanne isn't as strong as Lori's reaction to you."

"No, that's what I'm trying to tell you," said Calliope. "It was that strong. He said awful things to her and admitted that he wanted to have sex with me just to make Roxanne mad."

"What changed?" asked Dr. Snow.

"I slapped him. After that, he went from strong hate to moderate dislike."

"Ah. Riddle solved!" he said triumphantly, forgetting to let the others in on it.

"Yes?" Calliope said impatiently.

"Well, Lori said that your heart goes back to normal once the process of aging and bodily decay starts again. Apparently after you heal someone, that process takes about six weeks to resume. By hitting Gunnar, and thereby injuring the capillaries in his face, you sped up the decay process. But only slightly, because you stung him for only a second and it's a nonpermanent injury. I reckon that as soon as the tissues in the cheek recover from the shock, he'll be back to hating her again."

Calliope smartly deduced, "So, if a slap can turn hate to dislike, doesn't it stand to reason that a more significant and long lasting injury could turn dislike back into love? I mean, if we could cause an injury that lasts about six weeks, wouldn't Gunnar's heart return to normal now?"

"You took the thoughts right out of my head," Arthur giggled. "But, while your theory may be correct, it does present practical problems."

"What problems?" Calliope asked.

"Well for one, what if Roxanne heals his new injury? We'd be right back to where we started."

"I can have a talk with her about that. What else?"

"Second," Dr. Snow continued, "how would we cause him an injury of that magnitude, either ethically or realistically? A six-week injury is like a broken bone or an extremely deep gash? Which one of us wants to do that kind of disservice to a friend? And, if we amateurishly cause those injuries ourselves, we could be risking an infection or a poorly healed bone. At minimum, he would require hospital care, which would delay our ability to experiment with the portal tomorrow."

She huffed. "Either way, our trip is compromised. If he's not in his right mind and distrusts a member of this group by tomorrow, it's going to disrupt things."

Dr. Snow nodded. "I suppose that is true."

"And excuse me, but aren't you like an expert in everything, Mr. 200 IQ? You must know human anatomy?"

He smiled. "Like I know the periodic table."

"Well then, couldn't you make the gash in a place that won't be as problematic for mobility?"

"Theoretically, yes. But he'd still need stitches and antibiotics to decrease the risk of infection. And I'm no surgeon. I might know from a book where to cut, but I can't guarantee the steady hand necessary to wield the blade. And where would we even get medical supplies at this late hour?"

Gunnar had been listening this whole time to the back and forth banter about him in silence, feeling confused. He remembered with clarity the journey, their purpose in doing everything they had done to this point, and everybody's powers. He even remembered loving Roxanne at one time. The confounding part was that he hated her now. Yet, he knew that he had to do whatever it took for the journey to go forward.

"So, are you saying then that the only way we can still take the journey tomorrow, and for me not to care if Roxanne is there, is if he cuts me open or breaks a bone?" Gunnar asked, pointing to Dr. Snow.

"That's my best idea," said Calliope.

"Would a broken finger suffice?" queried the still hazy Gunnar.

Calliope looked to the professor. "I don't know, will it?"

The professor nodded. "A broken finger can take anywhere from three to eight weeks to heal, depending on the severity of the break and damage to surrounding tendons and ligaments."

Gunnar continued. "So let's just break my pinkie finger, go to the hospital for an x-ray and a splint, and be done by morning. We can still visit the portal then and I'll allegedly not hate that girl anymore."

"Who's going to break it?" asked Dr. Snow warily.

"None of you will have to. I'll just do it myself," said Gunnar.

"Wait!" said Calliope. "Before you even bother, we have to talk to Roxanne. She's got to be in on the plan."

Gunnar grunted. "Do we have to?"

"He's healed from the slap," said Dr. Snow.

"Gunnar, you're going to have to trust us on this. You love her and she loves you. Now, I'm going to have her come to this room. When she gets here, you have three choices. One, I can slap you a few more times until you're tolerable. Two, I can tie you up and gag you to stop you from spewing any more venom that might permanently damage your girlfriend's feelings. Or three, you can sit here and shut up like an adult and keep your rage bottled up. What will it be?"

Gunnar rolled his eyes. "I'll behave."

Calliope called her room and Roxanne answered. "Stop by your room and get dressed. Then come down to Arthur's room."

Within a minute, a carelessly dressed and unkempt Roxanne entered the room. Her eyes were red from crying. "Roxanne, go sit on that sofa over there. We need to talk," directed Calliope.

Roxanne did as instructed and seated herself directly across from Gunnar and Dr. Snow. Gunnar had promised Calliope he would keep his mouth shut, but he didn't promise to hide his feelings. He could feel his mouth muscles bend into a frown of disgust. Roxanne took one look at him and began to cry again. "What's wrong with him?"

Calliope sat next to the distraught girl and held her with motherly care. "Shhh. Calm down. Everything is going to be okay. We're pretty sure we can fix this. But we need to talk to you first. Now, can you tell us exactly what happened?"

Roxanne exhaled, gathering her composure as she swallowed back sniffles. "We were making love and all of a sudden, when we were done, he was speechless and he wouldn't talk to me. He looked at me with such contempt. Then he told me to get you."

Gunnar couldn't help himself. "Don't forget to tell her about the red lights coming from your fingers, you freak."

Calliope shot Gunnar a dirty look and he bowed his head in defeat. Roxanne was hurt, but also confused. "What red lights?"

"I know what he's talking about," said Calliope. "When you heal someone, red lights come from your fingers."

"I didn't see that."

Calliope continued. "At some point, you had to have wished that Gunnar was healed. Do you remember when that was?"

"I swear I didn't. I told myself right before we started that I like Gunnar blind. I didn't want him healed. I repeated that to myself over and over until . . . "

"Until when?" asked Calliope.

Roxanne was clearly embarrassed talking to strangers about private business. "Until I started to, you know, almost orgasm. Then I couldn't think about anything but that. And I had sort of fantasies about looking at Gunnar and him looking at me with wild intensity and then, you know."

"So you pictured Gunnar looking at you?"

Roxanne was frantic. "Well, yeah, but that's not the same as wishing him healed."

"Apparently, it is," observed Calliope. "It's enough just to picture the end result of the healing, even if we don't picture the act of healing itself."

Roxanne buried her head in her hands. "I didn't know."

"Hey, this isn't your fault," said Calliope with gusto. "It's not his either. It's no one's fault; it's just the way it is with us. I'm amazed he didn't tell you all this before you started having sex. I warned him this could happen."

Roxanne calmed a bit. "He tried, I think. He said he had something very important to tell me, but I didn't let him. I stopped him with a kiss."

Calliope sighed. "I would have told you this morning myself but I didn't want to ruin the energy of the vortex. Damn! Well, at least we think we know how to fix this."

"How?" Roxanne was forlorn.

"We have to injure him."

"What?" Roxanne asked in shock.

Dr. Snow took over. "See, in about six weeks, his body will start to age again and when it does, his heart will mend and he will love you again. But six weeks is an awful long time to wait. So, if we give Gunnar an injury that takes about six weeks to heal, he can start loving you again right away, and that time of healing will naturally dissolve into the aging process. With a new injury, we can make him start loving you and keep him loving you all the while."

"That's it? The only way to do it is to hurt him?" asked Roxanne hesitantly.

"That's all we can think of," said the professor.

"I'd rather take the six weeks!" said Roxanne in defense of the man who despised her right now.

Calliope butted in. "In normal circumstances, I'd agree. But we've got to visit that portal tomorrow. We can't do it if he refuses to be in the same room with you."

"Is that all we care about, the portal?" asked Roxanne sternly. "Well, I care about him and I don't want to see him hurt!"

Calliope was gentle but firm in her reply. "You and I have to make tough choices when it comes to our condition, Roxanne. If we want true love, we have to make sacrifices. In our case, backwards sacrifices that counter logic. We have to let our loved ones suffer physically so that they don't suffer emotionally. Trust me, having had a broken heart and a perfect body for a very long time, I speak from experience when I say that the broken heart is a far worse fate. Let him be happy. Let him love you. Even if it means he's got to live with a bit of pain. And remember, they have prescriptions for pain. There are no prescriptions for lost love."

Roxanne flailed her arms in the air. "Fine. But how am I going to control this from happening again. It's not like I wanted to heal him. It just happened."

"If I may," interrupted Dr. Snow. "I don't believe it's as dire as both of you are assuming. I do not believe a thought or a wish alone will do the trick. I believe you must also be touching your subject in order for the healing to occur. In both of your cases, red light emanating from your fingers appears to have been the source of the healing. If there is no touch, the red lights, whatever their source, cannot do their job."

"Maybe he's right," said Calliope with hope. "Don't worry about your thoughts when you aren't touching Gunnar. And when you do touch, don't even think about his physical injuries at all."

"And what if I do?"

"Slap him, a few times," said Calliope knowingly. "That will at least get him to a state where he doesn't hate you. Then he'll just have to be reinjured again."

Roxanne looked at Gunnar. "I'm so sorry, baby. I'm sorry you ever had to fall in love with me. I'd take it back if I could. You'd be better off if we'd never met."

Gunnar overdramatically rolled his head. "Dear God, shut up! You are so annoying!"

She started to cry again, and Calliope lost her patience. "Gunnar, if you're going to break your finger, do it now!" she yelled.

Gunnar looked around. The professor's closet door was open. Inside the closet on the top shelf was a clothes iron still wrapped by its cord. Rising, Gunnar walked over to the bathroom door adjacent to the closet. He placed his hand on the door frame, wrapping his whole hand around the frame except for his pinkie, which he left straight and exposed. Then he looked at the iron. He stared at it and visualized it as a bullet train rushing from its resting position and hitting the back wall of the bathroom. The trajectory would be precisely along the path occupied by his smallest finger.

"Oh Christ!" screamed Gunnar. "Roxanne!"

As if awakened from a dream, Gunnar looked at his pinkie, half dangling at the second joint, with dark black bruising already appearing as blood pooled under the skin. Some of the fingernail had come off, and there was blood dripping as profusely as if he'd slit his wrist. The pain was excruciating!

Roxanne ran over to him, but did not touch him. "Gunnar, are you okay?"

"Oh my God, this hurts like hell!"

She went to reach for him, but retracted her hands. "Oh Gunnar, I wish I could help you, but I can't!"

He tried to catch his breath through the pain. "I know. I know."

Calliope and Dr. Snow both shook off their shock and went to help Gunnar. "Go back into the bathroom, Gunnar," ordered Dr. Snow. "Calliope, turn on the cold water. Gunnar, the best thing to do this instant while we ready to take you to the hospital is to put your hand under the faucet. Perhaps the cold from the water can numb you a bit. It will help to wash off some of the blood too. Then we'll wrap it in a cold washcloth and be on our way to the A & E."

588

Gunnar did as instructed, and Dr. Snow and Calliope gave him temporary remedy. Roxanne sat in the doorway watching the scene helplessly. Despite his agony, Gunnar had to speak. "Roxanne, I am so sorry for what just happened. It literally was uncontrollable. And I saw everything I was doing and saying to you and chiding myself on the inside, but I could not control it. It was like I was possessed. I love you so much. Thank you for this evening and thank you for my sight. It's killing me that I made you cry."

Relief finally replaced her tears. "It's okay. I'm not upset at you. I know you couldn't do anything about it."

He pleaded with her through his own pain, as the water did little to numb anything. "Please, please, never say it would have been better for me never to have met you. You're my life. I'd be a shell of a person if I'd never met you."

She smiled. "I want to hold you right now, but I'm afraid I'll heal you. I can't stop wishing that your finger didn't hurt so much." She instantly covered her mouth like she was a young girl in trouble.

Gunnar nodded. "Don't worry. Arthur was right. It's the touch with the thought that heals. Words or wishes alone do nothing. Just don't touch me until I get done in the hospital, and then when you do, be glad I have a broken finger because that broken finger will keep us together. You've got to think of it as a good thing, and then you won't wish it better. Can you try to do that for me?"

"Do you know how hard that's going to be?" asked Roxanne, wiping her eyes with her arm.

He was still aching, but things had to be said through painful gasps. "Don't let it be hard. Calliope is right. You're doing me the biggest favor when you maintain our love, not when you maintain my body. I know it's different than the millions of other people out there who want their loved ones to be safe from physical harm. But we're just going to have to be the different couple that we are. I mean, I have super hearing and super smell and you can heal people and see the future. We're not normal, and our love isn't normal. But what we have is far more brilliant than normal could ever be. So please, just be abnormal with me?"

She nodded. "I will," she said. "And besides, what's a pinkie, right?"

"That's the spirit," he nodded, trying to downplay the pain so as not to rile her up into healing mode. "Still, I wouldn't mind getting to that hospital and some drugs."

"Yes, let's go before there's too much damage to repair," said the professor.

"Roxanne, come with me please," said Gunnar. He couldn't touch her, but he needed her present.

"Of course! I'll sit in the front with Calliope. You sit in the back with Arthur."

As the four of them shuffled into the SUV, Gunnar read a clock for the first time in eighteen years. It was a little past midnight. "I'm sorry you guys won't be getting much sleep tonight. I know we all wanted to be rested for tomorrow."

Calliope responded as she turned on the engine. "Sleep? My adrenaline is pumping so hard I doubt I'll be able to sleep for a week."

Roxanne turned on her GPS and directed Calliope to the nearest hospital. As the blonde drove, Dr. Snow interrupted the silence with a question. "So, while we're on our way, and if you're not in too much pain, dear boy, I'd love to know how come you never told me you were telekinetic?"

Chapter Fourteen

Road to Nowhere

*****

It had been over a year since his mother had disappeared, and Alphonse was about to tear his hair out with grief and frustration. He had searched every corner of the country for her, with only the clue that he should be looking for places that emit a humming sound. Every once in a while, he would hear a hum, but could never trace its exact location before it went away. He was starting to run out of money and patience, but he would never give up the search.

Low on funds, he had to go to his bank in New Orleans and convert more of the gold he had hidden from his sister into cash. He also needed a good sexual release, which Delphine would accommodate. And he wanted to attend a voodoo ceremony where he could call upon the petro loa and use the energy of his followers to coax the loa into answering.

Delphine was excited to see him when he walked into her shop that June day. Putting a closed sign in the window and locking the door, she took care of the first of Alphonse's needs before his suitcases had warmed the ground. Afterward, he ordered her to gather the Societe for a ceremony to be held in two days out at the deserted house by the Maurepas Swamp. His intent was to call upon the petro loa and offer up a black chicken sacrifice. He would call upon Maitre Carrefour, the selfish cousin of Papa Legba, and even Baron Samedi himself if it came to it. He was running in circles lacking focus, and would give anything, even to the trickster god messengers, to obtain insight on how to find Mama.

In the meantime, Alphonse was surprised to find his home empty. His sister Acadia wasn't there, and from the looks of it, she hadn't been there in months. It was better this way though. She always irritated him with her secular ways and refusal to become a bokor, and he wanted to be clear minded for the rituals.

Two days after his arrival, in the evening as the sun set, candles burned in the backyard of a torn up and moldy mansion that had been deserted during Hurricane Katrina. He was pleased by the amount of followers that had chosen to come, despite knowing that he was invoking the petro loa instead of the rada loa. It was their choice, and he was inspired that so many of them chose to obey the wishes of their houngan as opposed to worry about their souls. Besides, everyone now and again needs a favor and is willing to make a sacrifice to get it.

Using old tongue Creole, Alphonse urged the petro loa to guide him and offered a sacrifice of blood to tempt the loa. To drive home his devotion and need, he let his own blood flow by dragging a sharp knife along his chest. Repetitively praying for either Maitre Carrefour or Baron Samedi to take a body of one his followers and speak to him, his fevered ecstasy was broken only when one of this followers broke out in seizures, indicating that one of the petro loa was gracing the group with its presence. In their religion, possession was referred to as riding a horse, and Alphonse eagerly anticipated the ride to begin.

Once the possession was complete, Alphonse queried in Creole, "Which great messenger is in our house?"

The possessed follower started to rub his genitals through his clothes. In English, the follower answered, "If I asked you to pour me some rum and bring me some glasses to shield my eyes from the sun, would you know me?"

Alphonse replied in English. "Yes indeed, Baron Samedi. And I have prepared for your arrival. Here is a freshly opened bottle of the finest rum. And from my own head, sunglasses for you. But Baron, why are we not speaking in the native tongue of West Africa?"

The horse put on the glasses and took a swig from the bottle. "You have questions. I have answers. But the concepts I need to explain are complex and do not have equivalent terms in our simple language."

"Of course," said Alphonse reverently in English. "Then you already know what I request?"

"Certainly," affirmed the deity. "But, I shall not tell you what you want to know until you have told me what you are willing to give for the truth?"

"You have only to ask for what you want, Samedi."

"I want you, when you die, to join me," said Samedi, twisting a crooked smile on his horse's mouth. "A powerful bokor and houngan would make a great companion to listen to my jokes for eternity. Do you accept my terms?"

"To spend the afterlife with you would be an honor," replied Alphonse with a mental cross of his fingers.

The horse took another swig and then laughed hysterically. "So, you want to know how to find your mother?"

"Yes."

"This reality is not the only one, houngan. There are four more," revealed Samedi.

"What do you mean, reality?"

"Four versions of Earth exist and you live in but one," explained the jokester.

"There are other versions of Earth?" Alphonse could not grasp the concept.

"Indeed," confirmed the trickster god.

"So my mother is in one of these other Earths then?" asked Alphonse.

"She is."

"Which version?"

"In the only other one where I too exist."

Alphonse bit his tongue to ease his impatience. "You are speaking in riddles."

"No, I'm not. You're just not putting thought into what I said."

Alphonse's frustration with the obscure answers grew, but he still did not dare challenge Samedi now that he had promised to spend the afterlife with him. He swallowed his pride and put up with the evasive answers, resigned to having to figure out the puzzles himself. But, he still needed more pieces to fit together. "How do you get to these other Earths, Baron?"

"Through a door, obviously," said Samedi's horse, laughing and drinking.

"And are the doors? Where are they?"

"Up down and all around. In cities across the globe."

"I don't understand, Samedi." Alphonse was now eating the inside of his cheeks, as it was taking everything in his normally dominant being to submit to the will of this supernatural jester.

The horse laughed again, finishing off about half of the bottle of rum with the next sip. "I'm being so cruel to you, aren't I, houngan? And you, keeping so patient. Admirable, and very smart. Fine, fine, don't let it be said that I don't grant favors when they are requested. It is simply not in my nature to be as forthcoming as you'd like me to be. So, let's ask someone else, shall we? Someone who really knows." The horse looked around and zeroed in on Delphine, who had been attentive to the conversation this whole time. "Is that your woman?" Samedi asked.

"She is mine," said Alphonse.

"Will she give herself over to the spirit?"

Delphine answered. "Yes, Baron. Take this body as you will."

Within a moment, Delphine's brown eyes had clouded over gray, just as the horse's eyes had. Her back was staunchly straight; her facial expression lifeless.

The horse spoke. "I have called upon the dead over whom I have dominion. I have sought one that can answer your question. And she has come forward to provide the answers you seek. Speak woman."

Delphine's southern accent changed to a French accent. "My name is Lucille Redon. I died here in New Orleans in 1882. There was once a time three years earlier when I was traveling in the West with my husband and I heard a hum. I went to the place where the sound was loudest to me, but I could not find the reason for the sound. I was about to head back to town when I accidentally stepped on precisely the right spot. It was like a door opened, and in front of me was a black space with a white light around it. It was set apart from the trees, in an imperfect shape. I did not know what it was. I tied a rope to a nearby tree and secured it around my waist. I figured if I went in, and there was still a part of me that was outside, the door could not close all the way.

What I saw on the other side scared me. It was very different than the place I had left. The sky was different. Things in the sky. Giant loud birds. I did not want to be there. So, I followed the rope backward immediately. I left that place with great haste, never wanting to see what I had seen again. I abandoned the door and went back to New Orleans as quickly as I could, but ailing and in pain from injuries sustained going through the door for even a minute.

There, I met a woman named Marie Laveau. She helped heal me and explained what happened back in the New Mexico Territory. She told me I was a traveler and could open doors to other worlds. She told me the reason I could go inside was because I was one of the few who could survive the impact of the firelight. I invited her to come with me and told her I'd protect her, but she said she could not and would melt like butter in the sun if she touched the door's energy. She supposed though that perhaps an ordinary person could travel through if there were two travelers making a door within a door using their own bodies as a shield. For years, we searched for another traveler in Louisiana, but we never found one. And I never found another door."

Delphine dropped her head and fainted. The spirit of Lucille Redon was instantly gone. Alphonse panicked. "Where exactly were you when you found the door?"

The horse grabbed Alphonse's arm to calm him. "The where is not important yet, as you don't even have the tools needed to travel. But I'll tell you what. Let's make a second deal, shall we? I will, at a later time and in the right moment, provide you with more details to help you on your quest, in exchange for information. You see, there are two Earth planes where I do not exist. I want to know all about those worlds. I want to know why I cannot see or influence those places beyond the doors on this plane that lead to them. Will you agree to share all you find out about those Earths when you return with your mother?"

"Yes, yes of course! Thank you, Baron Samedi," said Alphonse, realizing this was the best he was going to get right now. "Thank you for sharing the dead with me and promising to share more," said Alphonse to the horse. "I will look for places with doors and look for travelers who can help me make the trip. And when I get back, I will tell you everything I see, hear, and learn."

Most of the bottle was gone now as the horse drank again. "Excellent. I should tell you though, when you look for the way in, don't be mystified by false doors." Alphonse shuttered at the curve ball. The horse laughed and continued. "It is not just the four real doors that make the noise. Many places make the noise. You have to figure out which doors are real and which are false."

"Just when I thought you were being helpful, you tell me that my travels might be a waste of time! Why can't you just tell me exactly where to go?" challenged Alphonse, forgetting his place.

The horse lost his laughter and charged Alphonse, taking him down to the ground. Samedi used the body of the horse to press his thumb hard onto Alphonse's nose until the septum was on the verge of snapping. "Do not dare to question my gifts to you. Feel lucky I speak to you at all."

Worried for his afterlife and his nose, Alphonse begged forgiveness. "I'm sorry, Baron. You are the wise one and I am the fool. I am grateful for your presence and your knowledge. I only wish to better understand you."

The horse rose from off Alphonse's chest. Standing while leaving Alphonse in the vulnerable lying position, Samedi wiped the dirt from the horse's clothes. "You are forgiven. And remember," the horse said while stroking his pointer finger back and forth over his lips. "I will give you more information when the time is right."

"Yes, Baron," asked Alphonse.

"Keep in mind, houngan, that the next time you summon me, I will require more than a chicken and a self-inflicted flesh wound as a sacrifice. I'm going to want blood, enough to end a person's life" said the horse.

"Mine?" asked Alphonse, swallowing.

The horse threw the empty rum bottle to the ground. "Let's make it interesting, shall we? If you offer up your own blood and thus your own life, you will die young, but your role in my court will be as my right hand servant, eternally blessed and treasured as a friend. You'll tell me stories, you'll laugh at my jokes, you'll keep me company, and I will reward you with power over the dead.

If you do not wish to die young, you can bring me the life of someone else, and your body will live to be 100 years old and your earthly powers shall triple. And when 100 years is up and you come to serve me, your role will be as my left hand servant. We won't be friends, as you will be my sycophant, but we won't be enemies either, which can only be to your benefit.

If you call upon me, but offer me no life—if you invoke my help with no blood, either by growing a conscience and deciding no one needs to die, or if someone or something else takes your life instead of you giving it to me freely, such a choice leads to neither hand. Which only leaves you as a despised servant at my feet. Do you understand?"

"I understand," said Alphonse.

"And of course, there is a final caveat, which I only throw out there in anticipation of good Samaritans who might interrupt your intent. If you kill yourself, but don't die, we will still be the best of friends, but not in the afterlife. You will agree to lend me your body. Two minds shall inhabit one human shell, with my essence dominating yours. Of course, I'll be looking out for you all the while and lending your body my powers, since we will be so very close."

"I acknowledge my choices, Baron," said Alphonse. "Yet, I am afraid the need to ever make a choice will never come to pass if I can't find the right doors or that right tools."

The horse smirked. "Trying to manipulate me for information, I see. So be it, one more tidbit. Find the beige girl or the blonde lady, and one of them can show you the way. It will be a bokor that you already know who will help you find them." One last time, the horse fondled himself through his pants. "Oh, I do love taking human form. It feels so good. But, I'm out of drink, so I'm out of here. Remember, houngan, do not call upon me again unless you are really, really ready. That said, I might call upon you at any time."

With that, the possessed follower fell to the ground alongside a still passed out Delphine.

The next day, Alphonse set out looking for the beige girl and the blonde lady. He needed at least one of them before he could go to the place of flight where his mother went. With only the clue that a magician he was already acquainted with would be the key to finding them, he set off on a worldwide quest, visiting every bokor he knew and going to every place where people claimed to hear explained noises. While he saw plenty of blonde ladies and beige girls on his travels, he couldn't feel magic in the auras of any other them. Every gifted friend he had was clueless as to the identities of the ones who could help him.

After years of nothing, a desperate Alphonse decided to go back to the only place he had ever gotten the slightest clue, to Kokomo, Indiana. He went to the same diner. He scoured hotels. The blonde lady was nowhere. He heard the hum as before but didn't bother to follow it, knowing that the source of this city's hum had been scientifically explained. It was now 2017, and he was back to the place of despair again that before had prompted him to contact the petro loa. Despite his longing, he wouldn't call on Baron Samedi again, as he wasn't really, really ready to make the required sacrifice.

Alone in his hotel room in Kokomo, flipping mindlessly through channels, Alphonse fell asleep at about 1:00 a.m. with the local news on the television. A little while later, he heard a voice. Pretty sure he was awake and not dreaming, he looked at the television and swore he saw the news still on. Only this time, the chiseled, white, brunette announcer was a black man wearing sunglasses and very tall black hat. As he blinked to clear the sleep from his eyes, he heard the news announcer say, "Poor Alphonse. Didn't give you enough to go on, did I? You've been on such a wild goose chase and you've been so good at resisting the temptation to call on me again. I'm taking pity on you and giving you one more hint. Your sister Acadia is the bokor you seek. She will lead you to the beige girl. If you fly home tomorrow, you can see the beige girl as early as the day after. Forcing the beige girl to accompany you will be your first instinct, but try to suppress it. I know it will be hard for you, houngan, but be patient. If you wait and follow, you could be rewarded with the blonde lady too. And you'll want both. With only one, you can see what you need, but never have it. With two, you can attain your goal."

Alphonse spoke to the television, half-asleep. "Why not make the beige girl cooperate?"

The possessed anchorman tipped his sunglasses to his nose. "I can see you need some help being patient. To keep you preoccupied, I give you this order. For now, take some of the beige girl's blood and smear it on a wanga doll. If that doesn't work, then try it my way and follow her."

Alphonse closed his eyes again as Baron Samedi stopped talking, and upon reopening them, he realized he was actually looking at a blank screen.

*****

Despite being in an immense amount of physical pain, Gunnar was awestruck by the fact he could see again after eighteen years. As his friends waited quietly with him at the hospital, he marveled at his surroundings. Colors were more vivid in real life than in his memory. The bleached-white hotel towel slowly turning red with blood fascinated him. Buttons and beepers and lights flashed green in the triage room, calling his visual attention. The bright yellow light bulbs in nearby lamps looked different than before he went blind, now little squiggles of tubing instead of an oval shape. Places he had only heard about but never seen were now depicted before him on the news playing on a nearby television.

He turned to look at his companions. He had never felt the faces of Dr. Snow and Calliope, so he had never really known what they looked like, but he had to say that they didn't look the way he pictured them. Christmas elf didn't do Arthur justice. Gunnar had pictured pale skin and rosy cheeks and a rotund frame, much like a shorter version of Father Christmas but with dark hair instead of white. A fairy from A Midsummer Night's Dream would have been a far more accurate descriptor. Dr. Snow was slightly built, thin and wiry. His hair was salt and pepper in color, but Astrid had neglected the all too important detail that he wore way too much hair gel, rendering his curls literally sticking up in the air like a frizzy pompadour. His eyes weren't just nondescript gray;

they were blue-gray, the color of storm clouds. And his ears did slightly point and his cheeks were slightly dewy.

Gunnar had still been a somewhat innocent lad in sexually uptight Britain when he went blind and had never seen a lesbian before. Throughout adulthood, he had heard derogatory jokes about dykes and had concluded without being so insensitive as to ask that all lesbians must look like men. Boy, was he wrong! Calliope was quite pretty and most definitely feminine. She had long honey-blonde hair that was slightly wavy curling down to her bosom. Her eyes were vivid emerald green and framed by sculpted light brown eyebrows. Her lips were pouty, full, and pink, still shimmering from lipstick she must have put on earlier in the day. Though you could tell by the small lines framing her lips and eyes that she was close in age to him and a fellow survivor of long term bitterness, her skin was nonetheless still fresh and slightly tanned.

But it was Roxanne who really captivated him. Having had the luxury of feeling her face and body many times, he hadn't been too far off in picturing her. But she was so much more beautiful than he ever conceived. She was athletic and toned with just enough cleavage to keep a man interested without being plastic. Her skin was gorgeous, like a melted ribbon of butterscotch toffee. Her shiny dark hair was long and perfectly straight, with bangs that just touched her brows before becoming longer bangs as it framed her face. What really melted Gunnar though was her smile. Every few minutes, she would leave her thoughts and smile at him with an apologetic look in her eyes. Her teeth gleamed like pearls and there was nary a trace of age or bad habits on them.

Though he was excited by the idea of learning to see again, he was relieved when doctors got him back to a room quickly and gave him a shot to numb the pain. After maneuvering his pinkie back in place and placing a metal splint on it, Gunnar was prescribed pain medication and released. It was 3:00 a.m. by the time the quartet headed back to the hotel.

On the way back, Roxanne sat far away from him. This was because, as he exited the A & E, she cried when she saw the cast. "Oh God, it's worse than I thought. It's all my fault," she said. She was not yet in a place of thinking that the broken finger was a positive thing. Though it was the last thing Gunnar wanted, not having had the opportunity to envelope himself around Roxanne post-coital, Calliope insisted that Roxanne sleep in her extra bed to avoid inadvertently going through this whole ordeal again.

The four of them hadn't bothered to wake Aaron and Acadia to apprize them of the situation and the pair was likely still expecting to stick to the prearranged plan of meeting for breakfast at 8:00 a.m. That wasn't going to happen, not with four of them crawling into bed at 4:00 a.m. Calliope pushed a note under their hotel door before she retired letting them know that there had been an emergency room trip and that the rest of them would be sleeping in as late as possible. Calliope instructed Aaron and Acadia to have breakfast by themselves, and they would all meet out in the lobby at noon to check out.

Not wanting to oversleep, Gunnar only took half of his prescribed Oxycodone. Drifting in and out all night and morning, he finally awoke to a knock on the door at around 11:30. Exhausted and still groggy, he poured himself out of bed and slumped to the door. He hadn't bothered to disrobe when they returned, and he was still in his track suit. Once he was able to focus, the sight behind the door made him smile.

"Hi, baby," said Roxanne. She leaned in and kissed him. He kissed back. Crap! He forgot! He wasn't supposed to touch her. She wasn't supposed to touch him. But wait, he was still in love with her. "How?"

She gently nudged him to sit on the edge of the bed and shut the door. "It's just a broken finger. It's not life threatening. You'll be just fine. Besides, I think you having this broken finger will be a good transition. We're so used to me doing things for the blind you, that to all of a sudden have you completely independent might have been a bit jarring. This way, while you won't need me to help get you around anymore, at least I can still help you text or scratch or be an extra hand."

He pulled her over to him and hugged her waist. She sat down beside him and they kissed on the lips with extreme tenderness. "Now, that's how I wish things would have concluded after we made love," Gunnar sighed.

Playfulness returned to her voice. "You know, Calliope told me that if I ever inadvertently heal you again during sex, I'm supposed to slap you a few times. Our sex life could get pretty interesting. I hope you like it a little rough."

He giggled and kissed her again. "I think I could get used to it," he said and they kissed again, more deeply.

After a full minute, she pulled away, saying, "While I wish we could do this all day, check out is in fifteen minutes and I came here to pack us up."

Just as they had in Sedona, they threw everything carelessly into their bags. Except today,

Gunnar had no idea where they would be spending the next night. "Hey Roxanne, have you thought about what's going to happen after today?"

"Well, I was meaning to talk to you about that," she said, slowing her pace. "I had a dream this morning. One of my visions about world events. I dreamt I was reading the paper from not this Sunday but next Sunday. And one of the headlines said 'Rocker A.J. Rhodes Missing.' I think, based on that, that I know at least part of what's going to happen today. We're going to find the portal. We're going to open it. And at least Aaron is going to go inside of it; I assume because Acadia does. And they aren't going to be coming right back out. I don't know how long they'll be lost or if they'll even be alive once they cross. But I do know that a whole week passes with no word from Aaron."

Gunnar exhaled loudly. "I had a feeling that might happen. And I feel fairly certain that we're going to lose Dr. Snow too. He'll be way too academically curious not to go in. I'm pretty sure that only three of us will leave Taos."

Roxanne smiled. "Calliope told me last night that she doesn't really have a home. Ever since she left Oregon, she travels all over, never wanting to get too comfortable in any one place. Now that she's got some closure on Lori and has seen how it's possible to maintain a romance despite our unique condition, she's ready to settle down again. I suggested, and I hope you don't mind, that she could come stay with us in London for a while. Try things in a completely new country. She said she'd like that. So, maybe once we say goodbye to Arthur, Acadia, and Aaron we can just go home."

"Home. You don't know how good that sounds. Our flats. Our beds. Astrid and my nephew. Real fish and chips."

She laughed. "Don't even mention food. I'm starving! Come on, let's go have lunch. It may be one of the last ones we're ever going to have with three of our friends. We should relish it."

He nodded and they were out the door.

Meeting up at the hotel restaurant after checking out, the presence of Gunnar's cast startled Aaron and Acadia. "Oh my God, man, what happened to you?" asked Aaron.

"It is a very, very long story," said Gunnar, hoping not to have to get into gory details in the restaurant.

"Involving his new found power of telekinesis," offered Dr. Snow.

"You can move things with your mind?" asked Acadia.

"I think that's a discussion we should save for outside a packed restaurant," said Gunnar, looking at Dr. Snow. The jolly man winked and nodded knowingly. Neither Acadia nor Aaron had apparently noticed the even bigger change in him.

They all sat down and started reading menus, as was typical of their group. After a good ten minutes of obliviousness, Acadia finally gasped. "Gunnar! You're looking at that menu!"

"Yes, yes I am."

"But, that's impossible," she marveled.

He smiled. "Not anymore. And by the way, you never told me your eyes were greenish-yellow. I made the faulty assumption that since you were half African-American, your eyes were brown."

Aaron mouth gaped. "You can see?"

"Last night, I was cured."

Aaron shook his head in disbelief. "How on earth?"

Gunnar was uncomfortable with the questions and deflected. "A discussion also best left for after today's portal business. Let's all focus on that instead of me."

"Okay then, well, before I forget," chimed in Acadia. "I had a vision this morning. It was of repetitive numbers. At first, I thought it might be like lottery numbers, but there's not enough and they are too high. So I figured, maybe it's a phone number. Aaron doesn't know it. Is anyone else familiar with the phone number 642-858-7572?"

Everyone shook their head no, except Dr. Snow, who curled his brow. "Dear girl, I do not believe that those numbers represent a telephone number. That time I was in Los Angeles, I got very bored in my hotel room waiting for my luggage, so I memorized the telephone directory. There was a map of all possible area codes used in the United States. 642 was not on there. Those numbers must have an alternative meaning."

Gunnar didn't want to talk about telephone numbers or visions. He wanted to make memories, talking and laughing about fun things. Until he had realized that he was soon to lose Aaron and Acadia, and even Dr. Snow, he hadn't measured their impact on his life. Not since Mick and Rob had he had friends, and never had he had true and good ones. He was going to miss the stories, the trust, and the feeling of being part of a community. Over the next hour and a hamburger, he steered the conversation so that each person reminisced about their favorite childhood experiences. He memorized the sounds and sights of Aaron, Acadia, and Arthur and committed them to his heart.

Shortly after the sun hit its pinnacle in the sky, the group finished lunch and headed out to the SUV. It was the first time Gunnar had seen daylight in 18 years. What an interesting place to be when his vision returned! Taos was sandy brown but with bright swirls of tomato colored clay and deep green brush. Practically every single building was rustic adobe or wood, like it came from a Western movie. The people in the streets were colorful and cheery. But the biggest attention grabber was the bright blue sprawling sky and white sun shining high. He had so missed the sky. He could have stared at his surroundings for hours, reveling in the sight that had returned, if there hadn't been the urgent need to solve a mystery.

Calliope offered to drive so she could test her memory as to how to get to the portal. They asked the front desk clerk about bridges in the area and learned that the Rio Grande Gorge Bridge was located not far to the west. This comported with the location of the sound Gunnar heard the previous day, so west they drove.

"This looks vaguely familiar," Calliope said, crossing the bridge. "I think we keep going north." After a few minutes, she shouted, "Yes, there it is! That unusual green house." Gunnar turned to see a lime green, oblong structure that reminded him of an alligator, carrying a small Taj Mahal on its tail.

As they continued north, Gunnar noted how off the beaten path they were. In fact, there was only one other car on the road, well behind them at over a kilometer. They had just passed a street called Linda Vista when the sound started again. It was the same drone he heard on the motorway in New Orleans. No one else seemed to hear it. He arched his back and pulled away from Roxanne. "I can hear the hum, but it's very faint. When I tilt my head each direction, it seems to grow just a bit more distinct towards the north."

Everyone in the SUV started sharpening their ears. "I don't hear anything," said Calliope.

Roxanne responded. "It was just like this in New Orleans. He heard it way before the rest of us did." As they continued northwest, the sound grew increasingly louder. By the time they were in a neighborhood called Tres Piedras, the sound had changed from the delicate buzzing of a bee to like an air conditioning unit a block away. Continuing north on the 64, Gunnar noticed the sound getting a little fainter. "I think we've passed one of the roads we need to take. The sound is backing off. Didn't we pass a road back there?"

"Yes," said Calliope. "I believe it said 285. Everyone hold on," Calliope said as she made an illegal u-turn. Luckily, that car that had been behind them was still quite a way back and there was no collision.

Gunnar was reassured they were now going the right direction as the noise again grew in volume down the 285 road. That frequency continued for nearly fifteen minutes, annoying Gunnar with every kilometer. Then came a point when the buzz quieted. He tilted his head in all directions and realized it grew louder to the west. "We must have gone too far. We need to be going more west."

"But there are so many roads going west. There's a 118, a 418, an 87, a 576. Which one should I take?" asked Calliope.

"Ah, hah!" yelled Dr. Snow out of nowhere. "Riddle solved!"

Gunnar again had to remind his mentor that no one else could read his mind. "What's the answer and what's the question?"

"The numbers that Acadia thought were a phone number. It is actually the route we are supposed to travel. The numbers she envisioned were 6,4,2,8,5,8,7,5,7, and 2. So far, we took a motorway 64, turned onto a road 285, and now we are presented with the chance to take road 87. It is my hypothesis that 87 will lead us to another road or roads where a 5, 7, and 2 are combinations of the name. It is at the end of those roads that we should find the portal."

"All right, we'll try 87. Here goes!" Calliope said, as she turned left without signaling.

The 87 seemed to wind forever and Calliope got antsy. "I don't remember it taking this long to get there. Maybe this is the wrong road."

Gunnar knew it wasn't. "No, I think Arthur is correct. I'm hearing the hum intensely now. It's like listening to a constant snare drum."

After about another fifteen miles, the sky became shaded by green treetops and the hum started to become slightly painful to Gunnar. A migraine was building. He took that time to tell Aaron and Acadia about the miraculous recovery of his sight, the consequences of Roxanne's gift, and the subsequent need for self-inflicted injury. The story could not have been more perfectly timed, for just as he finished discussing the gruesome details of his stitches, Roxanne said, "Hey look! That sign says FR 572! Arthur was right!"

"Here we go," said Calliope, as she turned right onto another uneven gravel road.

Soon, the road became very rocky and very sandy, but the rented SUV, whose undercarriage they were surly grazing, managed to make it almost two miles until it could go no further. At that point, the group saw a small sign carved into brown painted wood. Calliope pulled up next to it.

"Carson National Forest, Cruces Basin Wilderness. U.S. Department of Agriculture," Dr. Snow read robotically.

"Yes!" yelled Calliope with arms waiving triumphantly. "I remember now. This is it! This is the place. From here, we have to hike for a mile or so."

They parked and slowly started to emerge from the car.

In his new role as leader and protector, Gunnar felt it necessary to bring up the obvious. "Before we set off on a hike, I think we should address the fact that we didn't really pack for an extended trip out in the wilderness. I know I've only got one bottle of water with me and no food. We have no tents or even jackets. Are we sure we're really prepared for this?"

It was the first point in time that people started laying their cards on the table. "I hadn't planned on needing those things," said Acadia. "We're going to be through the portal well before it gets dark and can just get something to eat on the other side."

"Yeah," agreed Aaron. "Hopefully, wherever we end up will have similar weather. If not, we'll swipe some more appropriate clothes and find a place to eat and crash."

The burgeoning couple clearly had faith that they were simply going to another version of the United States when they entered the portal. There wasn't a doubt in their minds that they would survive the trip to the other side. They also seemed to believe that the entire group was joining in their decision.

Not wanting to rock the boat just yet, hoping to stay friends as long as possible, Gunnar just nodded. "Right then. Let's just follow the trail and see where it takes us."

Gunnar led the way, his casted hand swinging heavily with every step. He did everything he could not to let on to the rest that he was in severe pain. His ability to hold his complaints inside grew more difficult as the pain in his arm and the pain in his ears and head started to combine.

After a long time suffering in silence, Gunnar heard Dr. Snow whistle a happy proclamation. "Oh goodness! I do believe I hear the hum you've all been discussing. Like a slightly buzzy sound. Like from a clothes dryer?"

Aaron came up and put his arm on the professor's shoulder. "It sounds different to everyone, but I think you got it. See, you must be magical somehow after all, aside from your brains, or you couldn't hear it."

The professor beamed with a proud smile. "Yes, I guess I must."

"I can hear it now too," said Roxanne.

"I picked it up about a minute ago," said Acadia.

"Yeah, me too," said Aaron.

"I don't hear it yet," said Calliope.

Gunnar, whose head was pulsating, reassured her. "You're lucky."

They continued on, and in about thirty seconds, Calliope joined. "Oh God, I hear it now too! If I recall, it is about another twenty minutes or so until we are there, where two rivers meet."

Gunnar could smell the crisp and refreshing spray from some far off stream. But the pleasant smell was overshadowed by the fact he now had to cover his ears with his hands to dilute the volume of the hum. There was simply no way of swallowing the misery anymore. "Oh God, please let's find this thing!" he exclaimed. Thankfully, no sooner had he griped then the group finally came to water.

"Are we there?" asked Acadia.

Calliope shook her head. "I don't think so. I don't remember it looking like this or being this close to the trail's end."

"You know," said Dr. Snow. "That little map on the brown wooden board by the entrance showed a meeting of Beaver Creek and Diablo Creek, and I believe that is where we are now. But, still west of here is a confluence of this Beaver Creek stream with another stream called Cruces Creek. Perhaps it was the meeting of those streams Calliope remembers. Maybe that is where the portal is."

"Gunnar, what do you think?" asked Calliope, calling for aid from their leader.

"I think Arthur is right. I don't think it's here. Otherwise, if we were standing right on top of it, the noise would have gone away for me, like it did in New Orleans. But I still hear it, loud and clear like a jumbo jet engine in my ears."

"Let's keep heading west then," said Roxanne, being careful not to touch Gunnar now that he had verbally expressed discomfort.

After about another 200 meters, Roxanne stopped their party with a yelp. "Gunnar, your ears are bleeding! Someone help, I can't touch him."

Calliope and Dr. Snow ran back to examine Gunnar's ears. "Sure enough," said Calliope, as she dragged her finger across Gunnar's left lobe and retracted red.

"The hum must be so loud to him, it's tearing his eardrum," said Dr. Snow.

"But it didn't do this in New Orleans," pleaded Roxanne.

"The one at the labyrinth was a false portal. Maybe the bleeding is a sign that this is truly a real portal," offered Acadia.

"Stop fussing over me," Gunnar ordered. "Just press on. It's not going to get any better until we get there."

Finally, after another 150 meters, two rivers came together. "This is it!" said Calliope, her eyes wide with recall. "See how this new river sort of loops back and around, almost making a circle again with this creek? The portal is in the middle of that half circle."

All of them practically ran to the banks of the creeks, but none faster than Gunnar. "We have to wade across the water to get there," motioned Calliope, as she sat on the ground and started to remove her shoes and roll her pants. The others followed, taking time to remove their socks and shoes and fling them over their shoulders. Gunnar though, whose intense agony willed to him to forge the stream regardless of whether his shoes became sopping wet, didn't join his friends in preparation. His socked feet were freezing in the chilled river waters and the dampness sent a rod of cold up his spine. He lost his footing and began to fall into the river. On instinct, he caught himself on a rock using his casted hand, only to feel his pinkie involuntarily shift under the splint. If any healing had started at all in a day, it was all for naught, as his pinkie was broken again and writhing. The only thing more intense than the cold and the pain from the reinjured finger was the insane loudness of the hum, and the only reason he could get through that agony was to stop that accursed howl.

Oh, what blissful joy when he reached the other side. "Yes!" he cried. "It's gone. The hum is gone. Calliope must be right, it must be right here."

With the end of his ear pain, Gunnar took stock of himself. He was shivering wildly from cold, his splint was snapped and dangling loosely to one side, blood seeped from his ears and he could hear very little, and he was disoriented from the adrenaline pumping from five different directions in his body. Despite wanting to be the confident and strong leader, Gunnar's body could not help but pass out.

Chapter Fifteen

There Only Was One Choice

Gunnar had no idea how long he'd been unconscious when he awoke to a kiss. What a blissful kiss, so warm, so tender, it took all the pain away. He could hear perfectly again, his finger felt back to normal, and he was as warm and toasty as a dinner roll. Someone had removed his wet jeans while he was out and replaced them with dry track suit pants. A jacket was also lying across his naked chest. How nice it was to be all better! In the background, he could hear a conversation between two women.

"I shouldn't have done that. Why did I let you talk me into healing him?"

"It had to be done, Roxanne. He was in no condition to even move, let alone look for a portal," said Acadia

"I know that, but now, he and I are going to have to start the bitterness all over again."

"I told you, just slap him a few times and the hate will turn to tolerability," instructed Calliope.

"Yeah, but you yourself said slaps don't last that long. If we're going to look for this portal, he needs to like me for longer than a few minutes."

"Don't worry. I'll take care of it," said a male voice.

Opening his eyes, Gunnar sat up and realized that that awful Roxanne person was there. Standing up and realizing the jacket covering him was hers, he threw it to the ground in disgust. "What did you with my shirt?" he asked scathingly.

Before he knew it, he was tackled to the ground and punched in the face a few times. Through hands he had raised to try to protect his face, he realized that Aaron was assaulting him. After three punches square to his gut and to the face for good measure, his friend retreated as though there was no quarrel.

Arising, Gunnar queried angrily. "What the hell was that for, mate?"

"How do you feel about Roxanne?" asked his rocker pal.

"She's okay. Why?"

"Okay is a good start," Calliope said.

"How much time before the pain from the punches goes away and his ambivalence turns to rage?" asked Roxanne.

"I don't know. Maybe a few hours or so? That punch to the eye was pretty hardcore," said Calliope.

Gunnar looked down at the broken splint attached to the now unnecessary cast. "Looks like this thing was a waste of money," he said, pulling out the metal splint from the top of the cast. That intrusion came off, but the plaster was going nowhere.

"So how does this whole thing work?" asked Acadia with sincere curiosity. "Is he under a spell where he doesn't even remember dating Roxanne? Does he know what's going on in the present besides what relates to her?"

Calliope answered. "I really don't know how it works."

Gunnar answered for himself. "I know why we're here. I know that I'm supposed to be in love with Roxanne, but I'm just not." He looked over his friends. Acadia still looked worried. Maybe he should just pretend to like Roxanne. After all, she wasn't repugnant. He was just indifferent to her. In a show of good faith, he walked over to his supposed girlfriend and held her hand, though the feeling was like holding on to a mannequin. "Come on. Let's look for this portal."

"What exactly are we looking for, Calliope?" asked Aaron.

"Luck," she explained. "I mean, you really can't look for it. It's just something you stumble upon."

"I thought you were supposed to be able to pinpoint it with your hearing, Gunnar," said Acadia.

"I know I got us to the general area," he said. "Let me see if I can do anything to get us to an exact spot." He dropped Roxanne's hand; he didn't want the distraction of having to pretend to take away his focus. Gunnar took a deep breath and closed his eyes. He listened to the wind, to the leaves scraping against the tree trunks, to chirps of forest bugs. Riding on the breeze and just tickling the hairs in his ears, he caught the faintest sound. It wasn't the typical harassing buzz. It was like an animal screeching.

Without even thinking, he moved toward the sound. Suddenly, in his mind's eye, he saw a burst of red come swooping down at him from the sky, stopping him in his tracks. In that second, he heard bird wings flapping frantically and the sound of the hum swallowing itself. As he opened his eyes, the sounds were gone. "I think it's right about here," he said.

Calliope approached very slowly. A few steps before Gunnar, she held out her arms like a mime and started touching the air. Then, like she had just rippled the surface of water, a blue and white light gently enveloped Calliope's hand and then expanded outward. When the lights were just the width of string and extended to about the size of a coffin, what was left was a pitch black opening. It was large enough for two people to fit in, if they huddled close together.

There was a deep gasp heard from every member of the group. This was it. Everyone waited and watched the portal open, wondering if Mama Gadreau would waltz out with stories to tell. After two minutes of nothing, everyone knew that wasn't going to happen.

Calliope was shaken. "Okay, look. She didn't come out. She's not coming out. She's probably not even there. She's probably dead."

Acadia lashed out. "We don't know that! We need to go in and look for her!"

Calliope, who was still standing perfectly still with her hand extended in the void, retorted, "I still don't know what's in there and I still don't want to find out. I'm closing the portal. We all need some time to think things through and I can't stand here perfectly still in this position for long."

"No!" Acadia begged. "If you move, we may not be able to get the portal back open. We don't know the rules of the portal."

"Even if I close it and can't reopen it, Roxanne can." Calliope didn't provide time for argument, lowering her arm and backing away. The blue and white light imploded into a tiny little dot. Calliope dragged the heel of her boot through the dirt twice, marking the spot of the portal with an X so they wouldn't lose it again.

Acadia's furrowed brow revealed she was more than a little mad. "Fine. Let's talk about it then. We all know where Calliope stands about entering the portal. I'm sure it's no surprise that Aaron and I are going in."

Gunnar turned to Aaron. "Are you really sure, mate? I mean, you heard what Delphine said. The healers can go through because they can heal themselves from pain caused by entering pure energy. Neither of you are healers. Even if there was something on the other side, you could die before you ever get there."

The rock star smiled and looked longingly at Acadia. "Not more than three weeks ago, I was willing to die for someone I didn't really love who didn't love me at all. Now I have someone who ... oh screw it ... I love, and who feels the same way about me. If I was willing to die for someone meaningless, I should be willing to die for someone that means everything."

Acadia spoke. "But you have to understand, even though we're both ready to die, we really don't believe that's going to happen. Why would the universe go to such lengths to bring us all together and get us here if we're just meant to plunge to our deaths?"

The happy elf whistled. "I'm sure you can all understand that I must go in, regardless of the consequences. To enter is a win-win situation for me. If I live and there is another universe on the other side, it would be a scientific and philosophic breakthrough that no scholar could pass up studying. And if I die, I have the very unique perspective of knowing for absolute certain that a sort of life exists beyond death. This isn't the end. At minimal, as I know from seeing Millie, I will be a sentient corporeal spirit. So, I'm not afraid to go in either way."

It was down to just Roxanne and Gunnar to express their thoughts. Gunnar knew he was supposed to say he didn't want to go, but Acadia made a good point. Why would the universe go through the trouble of presenting them this opportunity just to kill them with it?

"Everybody, can I just have a second alone with Gunnar, please?" Roxanne requested of the whole group. They all nodded as she forcefully grabbed him by the hand and dragged him about ten feet from the group.

"Gunnar, we talked about this last night," Roxanne stated in lowered tones. "And I know right now you don't really care about me or the plans we made, but I need you to remember. We said we weren't going in because we had just found each other and we wanted to live our lives together. Please don't push that decision aside because I healed you."

He looked at her as she pled. He just couldn't imagine having said that about her. There was no doubt she was objectively pretty and she had been nothing but nice to him and caring of his well-being, but there was no spark on his end, at all. In fact, it was almost as if there was an invisible wall between them that didn't exist between himself and anyone else. He had strong feelings of protection for his other friends, but when he looked at her, that feeling was buffered by something. All he could do was shrug his shoulders.

She talked in more frantic tones. "If you could just trust me and not go in, I promise that in six weeks, you'll be happy you didn't."

He still could muster no words. He didn't want to hurt her feelings, but he was edging towards a decision to go with his friends into the unknown.

She chided herself quietly. "I shouldn't have healed you back there. I should have left well enough alone. Shit!"

"Have I interrupted a lover's quarrel?" said a familiar interloper.

Gunnar's head snapped towards where the rest of the group was standing to see a light-skinned black man with piercing blue-green eyes standing behind his sister. Despite his exceptional hearing, Gunnar hadn't heard someone else wading through the water or approaching. He had been too busy analyzing his feelings for the girl who he knew he was supposed to love. Acadia wasn't moving or talking, which was uncharacteristic of her when Alphonse was around.

"Why don't you two lovebirds come join us over here? We have a lot to discuss," said Alphonse.

For some reason in Gunnar's mind, he felt he needed to put on a show for the enemy that he and Roxanne were fine. He held her hand and the pair walked toward the others. As they got closer, Gunnar saw why Acadia wasn't reacting. Alphonse had abandoned his magic pouches and pocket knife in favor of a black semi-automatic pistol. It was aimed right at Acadia's back, so Roxanne and Gunnar didn't fuss. Besides, they couldn't run. Any attempt in this wide-open space would render them easy targets if Alphonse was even a quasi-decent shot.

The non-fuzzy part of Gunnar that still possessed the strong constitution given to him by the vortex in Sedona was the first to address Alphonse. "How did you get here?"

"I've been in Taos since after our encounter in the park. I've been all over town for a week now, trying to follow the sound, trying to get the wanga doll to open up something, somewhere, to no avail."

He laughed. "I was way off. I never thought to look beyond the city limits. See, that's why I needed you," he said, pointing to Gunnar. "You were the key this whole time to finding the portal."

"Yes, but how did you know we were here, today?" questioned Gunnar.

"Why don't you answer his question, Acadia," said Alphonse.

Acadia was quiet and closed her eyes for a minute to focus. When she reopened her eyes, they lit up. "It's the twin thing. Sometimes, when Alphonse and I are close to each other in proximity, we can feel each other's presence." She turned to face her brother, the pistol now grazing her stomach. "But I didn't feel you, so how come you felt me?"

Alphonse scoffed. "Probably because you were too busy screwing that white meat of yours. You know, there are plenty of brothers in the Societe who would love to pleasure a mambo and you wouldn't have to degrade yourself with an outsider."

Despite the gun at her waist, Acadia still vituperated. "First of all, I'm not a mambo, for the fifty-millionth time. Second, we're not screwing. We are in love with each other Alphonse. Skin color and religious background are irrelevant. Deal with it."

"And for my fifty-millionth response to that, you can choose not to practice voodoo and you can choose to reject the loa, but you cannot stop being a bokor. You are a born sorceress and nothing you can do or say will make that go away."

Acadia rolled her eyes. "Whatever."

"And don't flatter yourself. Our twin connection is as dead as your faith. In fact, you owe my company today to your complete obliviousness. I'm staying at the same hotel as you, but you were all too self-centered to realize that. Last night, sleepless as usual, I was in the lobby at around midnight when I heard quite the commotion. Someone was injured and was asking the front desk clerk for directions to a hospital. Imagine my surprise when the maimed party was the blind fellow from New Orleans and the requester of directions the beige girl. I followed that fiasco and watched everything from that point on."

"Okay, you're here. I suppose you want to see if Mama's in the portal?" asked Acadia. "I can tell you for a fact, she's not. We already opened it and she didn't come out."

A giant relieved grin spread over Alphonse's face. "You found the portal and opened it? Finally, the search is over."

"And I suppose," asked Gunnar, "you'd like for one of the travelers to open it for you so you can see for yourself?"

"*One* of the travelers? There are two? Then you must be the blonde lady," he said, looking at Calliope. "It all makes sense now. That Baron," he chuckled.

"What makes sense," asked Calliope, disconcerted that the eerie stranger knew her when she didn't know him.

Alphonse replied. "If I found only one of you, I could have been shown the portal, but I couldn't have traveled through it. I would have died trying. But, because I've found both of you, you both can ensure I get in there and back."

"What are you talking about?" asked Acadia.

"Baron Samedi opened up my eyes. I learned all about your gift," Alphonse said, haphazardly pointing his gun between Calliope and Roxanne. "Each one of them can go in the portal and be fine. They can even take in someone they love and that person will heal and be fine too. But they can't take in just anybody or simply open the door and let someone try to go in themselves. They'd burst into flames. But, if you have two travelers, both of them can build a door with their bodies inside the portal to soak up the radiation and toxins that would kill the rest of us. We should be able to pass under them unharmed."

"Baron Samedi? What are you doing trusting a word he says? He's a trickster!" exclaimed Acadia.

"Who is Baron Samedi?" asked Aaron.

Alphonse scoffed. "He's only one of the great petro loa. Lord of our dead. Master of favors. You'd know that if you weren't so . . . white."

Acadia interrupted. "Don't forget, he's also a liar. All that stuff about them building a bridge with their bodies sounds hokey to me. For all you know, we could be just fine going into that portal ourselves."

Roxanne spoke up. "Look Alphonse, neither Calliope nor I had planned to go inside of the portal."

"Well, I'm afraid your plans are changing," said Alphonse, now pointing the gun at Roxanne.

He couldn't rationalize it, because he didn't really care that much about her, but something inside Gunnar compelled him to stand in front of Roxanne. He heard her whisper in his ear. "Gunnar, don't. I can take care of myself, remember?"

Still, something told him to provoke the voodoo priest. "She told you, she's not going in. I'm not either. No one knows what awaits us if we cross."

Alphonse grew a crooked smile. "You know, it just occurred to me that you aren't blind anymore, are you? You've been looking right at me this whole time. You've been observing your surroundings and the reactions on my sister's face. Under normal circumstances, I'd be pumping you for information on how you recovered. But today, when I'm so very close to an answer, I only care about my mother. So the secret of your recovery will just have to accompany you to the grave." Alphonse moved the position of the pistol to Gunnar's chest and he put his finger to the trigger.

"Stop!" screamed Roxanne. "If you kill him, I will force you to kill me too and you won't have the two travelers you need. But, if you stop and put the gun down, I'll go with you."

"Well, I won't," said Calliope defiantly. "And if it's a choice of kill me with a gun or kill me with a painful exploding ball of nuclear energy, you might as well just shoot."

"You two," Alphonse said, eerily chuckling. "You both think that because you have the healing gifts and you've healed yourselves before that you're pretty invincible. But what you don't know is that a while ago, I communed with a traveler from beyond the grave. And if I did, ask yourself this. How could I have communed with a dead traveler if people like you never die? There must exist a circumstance where you can pass on. And I promise both of you that if you don't do this for me, I'll start by killing the other four of your friends just to save space in the car and then I'll try every painful and brutal way possible to kill you, over and over, until I find the way where it becomes permanent."

No one, not even Gunnar in his mixed-up state of mind, could stop themselves from reeling at Alphonse's depravity. Even staunch Calliope didn't relish that picture of her remaining days.

Still, Acadia, who had known him longer and more intimately than anyone, challenged him. "How do we even know that this dead traveler exists?" The tension was palpable as Alphonse shifted his attention away from Gunnar and walked right up to Aaron. The mad man stuck the barrel to Aaron's temple and spoke with perfect calm. "Why must you always question me, Acadia? Don't you know that you are supposed to revere your houngan? It really makes me want to snap sometimes when I think of your insolence."

For the first time since Alphonse arrived, Dr. Snow drew attention to himself. "Might I offer a suggestion to ease the conflict here? I really don't like conflict."

"Who are you, you little insignificant old man?" questioned Alphonse. "I'm curious how you fit into all this."

Dr. Snow was uncharacteristically brash. "A professor of history tagging along for academic inquiry. But my identity is unimportant. Only my services are important."

"Services?" inquired Alphonse.

"Mind you, I do not know if this will work, as I've only ever done it once and it may in fact have been a fluke, but if it will ease my nerves, I'm willing to try. If you could perhaps tell me the name of the deceased traveler you claim to have spoken with, I might be able to confirm your assertions. You see, my friends here seem to believe I have the ability to speak to the dead. No better time to test the hypothesis than this, I suppose?"

With a look of fascination, Alphonse removed the gun from Aaron's head and moved it back perpendicular with his stomach. "You really think you could do that, old man?"

"I believe it's possible. But, there is a caveat. I am in fear of that man, there," said Dr. Snow, pointing at Gunnar. "He practically kidnapped me to be part of this little posse. He's always questioning everyone else's gifts, especially mine, and quite frankly, his lack of confidence makes it difficult for me to 'get into the zone,' as they say." Gunnar had no idea what Dr. Snow was talking about, and from the puzzled looks on everyone's faces, neither did anyone else. "He simply makes me feel inferior. And let's be honest, he towers over me in height and weight and could probably squash me with his thumb, and I just cannot stand up for myself against him. But perhaps, you could help me in this regard?"

"How," asked Alphonse with a crooked brow.

"Would you consider yourself a good shot?" queried the professor.

"I'm not a sharp shooter but I don't miss targets at close range," said Alphonse confidently.

"Well then, if you could just, graze him with a bullet on my behalf. Perhaps a flesh wound to fatty tissue in the outer thigh? I mean, you can't outright kill him because his girlfriend has expressed her unwillingness to cooperate if you do. But I can't have him go unpunished for his maltreatment of me and still be able to perform. With just a little wound, his girlfriend remains cooperative and I get the peace and satisfaction necessary to try to talk to your spirit." The crazy professor whistled a happy afterthought. "And come on, I bet you'd love to fire that thing at a voodoo nonbeliever like him."

"I like you, old man," said Alphonse with a smile. Before anyone could say anything to refute the professor's lies, a shot rang out and echoed through the expansive and empty valley. Gunnar bent over in searing pain, grabbing his thigh right about the knee. He was bleeding a lot, though it wasn't spewing. He needed to apply pressure though if he wanted the flow to stop. He fell to the ground and wrapped his arm around this thigh. When Roxanne bent over to help, he put up his finger to stop her. He loved her too much to put her through the roller coaster of healing him again.

"Now, I'm satisfied," said Dr. Snow. "Alphonse, may I have the name of the deceased?"

"Lucille Redon. She'll be French. From the 1800's."

"Alphonse, I believe I need a few minutes alone to meditate before I attempt communication. Would it be all right with you if I remove myself about 20 feet? You'll still be able to see me and I have no desire or reason to attempt escape."

"I don't know . . . " started Alphonse.

"You may accompany me if you are concerned," offered Dr. Snow. The professor saw Alphonse weigh his options. "Don't worry, they aren't going anywhere," assured Dr. Snow of everyone else. "Your sister and Mr. Rhodes want to enter the portal. Gunnar's injured, Roxanne won't leave him, and Calliope can't get far even if she starts to run."

"I can't take the chance. You're going to have to get ready with the blonde lady watching too," said Alphonse, as he motioned Calliope over with the gun.

"I'll do my best," said Dr. Snow, and the three of them walked off to a point where they could no longer be heard.

Roxanne came closer to Gunnar. "Don't touch me, darling," he muttered. "Not unless you're glad I got shot, which you bloody well should be."

"I can't believe Arthur threw you under the bus like that. What a traitor!" Roxanne exclaimed.

"No! Don't you see? He went through that charade so I could get hurt. Hurt just enough to know who I am, know what I want, and to be completely in control of my own brain and feelings. He knows me as well as I know him. When he heard your decision not to go, he had to know what mine should have been. And he had to have seen that I was wavering. He knew I needed to be in love again to remember why I wasn't going to go. So he arranged for me to get injured by the only thing out here that could injure me. And he doesn't need to meditate to talk to the dead. He's buying me time for you to bandage me and stop the bleeding. He *is* a genius!"

"So, you're back to normal?" she asked with relief.

"Yes, thank God!"

"And you love me again?"

"If I could climb that mountain in the distance and I scream out I love you, I would. And if I wasn't trying to stop myself from bleeding to death, and had a ring, and could get on one knee, I would ask you to marry me right now."

Roxanne was stunned with a mix of emotions, which resulted in tears coupled with smiles. "I'm so glad you got shot!" she said, as she held both sides of his face and brought his mouth in for a long solid kiss. She really must have been glad, as his leg was still bleeding and he was still wild about her.

Using a little pocket knife attached to her keychain, she tore off the denim of her jeans below the knees. She applied one of the strips of material to Gunnar's wound and pushed in. "This should stop the bleeding, I hope." Then, she wrapped the other pant leg just above the wound like a tourniquet.

While she tended to him, he marveled at her. "You know, I was serious. I don't have a ring and I know this is hardly the most romantic place or time, but I can't let us go into that portal without knowing if, under other circumstances, you would be my wife?"

With one hand putting pressure on his bloody leg, she took her other bloody hand and held his. "I absolutely want to be your wife. My answer is yes. But how is that ever going to happen if we go into the portal?"

Gunnar tried to appease her. "Could we die, yes? But we'll die as an engaged couple in love. Could we live? Maybe. And if so, our dream can still become a reality. Let's try to have the same faith Aaron and Acadia do. Or let's believe Alphonse and his voodoo god and accept that we'll make it. We've got to believe in something, my love, because it's very clear we no longer have a choice about whether to go in or not."

"Can't you just move the gun out of his hand with your mind?"

He considered. "No, I don't think so. I've ever only used that power twice and I'm not sure how to control it."

"Well, maybe Calliope and I can rush him together, take the gun, and shoot him. We can heal ourselves if he shoots us before we get to him."

He looked at her with sadness. "What if he doesn't aim at you? You might be able to heal yourselves, but who will heal Dr. Snow or Aaron or Acadia? I can't watch them die. And how are you going to get the message to Calliope to join in your plan?"

She nodded and removed the denim to check the bleeding. Thankfully, it had stopped. "Well, you aren't going to bleed out, but this thing could still get infected."

He tried to be optimistic. "Who knows, maybe there'll be someone who can fix me up on the other side of the portal."

"Or maybe we'll be dead and it won't matter anyway," she said sarcastically.

He tried to joke. "That's a way to think positively, I guess." They kissed again.

"How sweet!" Alphonse said bitingly. They both looked away from each other to the three that had rejoined them. "The doc is ready now to do his thing." Alphonse looked to Dr. Snow. "What should the rest of us be doing while you attempt communication?"

Dr. Snow casually shrugged his shoulders. "I've never had an audience before, so I don't exactly know. I suppose you can all just sit down and observe."

Gunnar was thankful he wouldn't have to stand and put pressure on his wound and imagined this was another bone the professor threw at him. Everyone else, except Alphonse, took seats on the ground beside him.

Dr. Snow called out to the sky in front of him like a séance medium in a bad movie. "Lucille Redon, if you are there, come to us." Nothing. Again, in a silly, spooky voice, he tried, "Spirits of the underworld, if you can hear me, show me a sign."

Alphonse cleared his throat loudly. Gunnar looked over to see Alphonse's face contorted with anger. Gunnar knew he needed to step in before their captor punished Dr. Snow as a fraud.

"Um, Arthur," began Gunnar. "I don't think it really works like it does in the movies. When you talked to Millie, how did that happen?"

"I don't know, really. She just appeared when I needed her."

"Well, perhaps you need her now," offered Gunnar.

Dr. Snow shook his head. Again, he called toward the sky, but in his own voice at a normal pitch. "Um, Millie, love. If you're there, I could really use some help here."

Suddenly, the air around them all turned extremely humid and from the pinpoint of nothing grew a slightly transparent human figure. Standing there was a woman with who looked very much like a female-version of Dr. Snow.

"Hello, Arthur," said the woman.

"Ah Millie," smiled Dr. Snow. "Thank you so much for coming."

The apparition smiled. "I did say we'd see each other again."

"Indeed," nodded the professor. "Um, darling, do you know of the predicament I am in right now?"

"Yes," she said, looking at Alphonse disapprovingly. "And I'm not thrilled about it. That said, I certainly do envy the life of adventure you've had since meeting that young man," she said, motioning to Gunnar.

Dr. Snow smiled. "Yes, it has been the most fun time I've ever had. But, since you know what is going on, you know that I need to know something. Do I have the ability to communicate with the deceased, besides you, my love?"

"Yes," confirmed Millie.

"And do you know how it works?" asked Dr. Snow.

"It's a bit different with me, because I never went to the repository, wanting to keep my eye on you. But if are wanting to reach someone not of this or any Earth, you have to work within your own mind, Arthur. What are you the very best at?"

"Science?" he thought aloud.

"Yes," she confirmed. "Don't try to summon the dead one-dimensionally, thinking that they are human shells floating in three-dimensional space around you and you are pulling them off a shelf like a jam jar. Instead, think of them as housed multi-dimensionally on a particle level. Find them on open strings. There doesn't need to be a physical model because the model is in that brilliant head of yours. See the string model in your head and think really small. "

Dr. Snow's eyes grew wide with understanding. "Of course! Human spirits must be reduced to a fraction of their size for interdimensional travel. They'd have to ... be reduced to a gigaparticle, no more. So, I'm not looking for a person, I'm looking for a particle."

"Yes, Arthur."

"Thank you so much, my love," said Arthur to his wife.

"You're welcome, my love. Now, unfortunately, where you are going, I cannot come, as I am not cross-dimensional, having chosen not to go to the repository. Just know, we will see each other again." With that, she shrank back into nothing. Dr. Snow turned to the group confidently. "Riddle solved!" he exclaimed, closing his eyes.

Gunnar watched as the professor seemed to go into a trance, with the fastest rapid eye movement behind closed eyes he'd ever seen. After about thirty seconds, a new apparition grew from nothing beside them.

Alphonse stood excitedly to attention. "That's her!"

Dr. Snow opened his eyes. "Um, hello. You should be Lucille Redon assuming I retrieved the correct gigaparticle."

"I am," said the spirit.

"Have you spoken to that gentleman previously?" he queried, pointing at Alphonse.

"Yes," she affirmed. "He belongs to Baron Samedi."

"Have you previously told him about your travels through a nearby portal?"

"I did," said the spirit.

"Is there anything you can tell the rest of us about it?"

The woman looked thoughtful. "Only that the door leads to a frightening place with evil skies and physical pain. Even if you live through the heat of the door, I don't know if you could live in that world."

"Another question, if I might," asked Dr. Snow, "for both practical and intellectual curiosity. Can soul gigaparticles communicate with each other beyond death?"

"Yes, we can," stated Lucille.

"Would you be able to tell us if someone is dead or not?"

"I believe I could," confirmed the spirit.

The doctor turned to Alphonse. "What was your mother's full name?"

Without hesitation, Alphonse responded, "Jeanette Gadreau."

To the spirit, Dr. Snow repeated, "Do you know if a woman named Jeanette Gadreau is deceased?"

Mr. Redon went silent for a moment, and then said, "There is no one among the dead in the repository with that name"

Alphonse could not contain his happiness. "I knew it! I knew she was alive! Ask her if Mama went through the door?"

"Ms. Redon, do you know if Jeanette Gadreau went through the same door you did?" asked the professor.

The apparition shook her head. "I personally do not know; let me ask someone." There was a moment of silence again, followed by, "You need to call upon a woman named Ethel Brasa."

Gunnar looked to Acadia, whose confused face revealed she had never heard that name before.

"Very well then," said Dr. Snow. "Thank you for speaking with us."

"I'm happy to do it," offered Lucille Redon. "I don't get living visitors anymore, as everyone that knew me is with me in the repository." With that cryptic goodbye, Lucille vanished back into a tiny particle.

"Go find that lady, Ethel," commanded Alphonse of Dr. Snow.

"No need to make demands," said Dr. Snow casually. "I am as curious as you are, my boy." Again, Dr. Snow quietly went to a place of rapid eye movement and, soon enough, opened his eyes as another speck of dust developed into a full-sized apparition.

The woman before them was so intensely pale, she was barely visible. She seemed confused by her surroundings and kept looking at the sky.

"Hello," said Dr. Snow in proper and extended posh English. "I'm afraid we don't know each other and I really have no idea why I was told to interrupt your eternal rest, but another deceased person informed us that you may be familiar with the whereabouts of a woman named Jeanette Gadreau. I don't suppose that name rings a bell?"

The spirit became attentive. "If we are talking about my daughter Rohesia's acquaintance, then yes, I am familiar with that woman."

Alphonse practically jumped from the terra firma. "Who's Rohesia? Is my mother with her?"

The spirit showed no ability to hear Alphonse, so Dr. Snow interpreted. "Is your daughter currently a companion to Ms. Gadreau?"

"No," said the spirit, shaking her transparent head. "They parted ways many lunar cycles ago. Almost 132 lunar cycles I would guess."

Dr. Snow's lips curled. "Lunar cycles? Is that how you measure time?"

"Of course," replied the woman. "Don't you?"

He shook his head. "No, we measure it in years. Ever heard of a year?"

Now she shook her head. "No, that's not familiar."

Dr. Snow's eyes lit up with excitement. "Oh my! You are not a deceased person from our version of Earth! You come from one of the other realms!

And yet, you are in the same gigaparticle afterlife as someone from this version of Earth. That is truly fascinating!"

"Get back to the point," barked Alphonse.

"Yes, yes," scoffed Dr. Snow. "Ms. Brasa, what do you know of Jeanette Gadreau?"

"She appeared out of nowhere one day on my daughter's doorstep, claiming to be from an undiscovered country. The Prime Receiver wanted an audience with her in Detroit-Windsor, so my daughter accompanied Jeanette to the transfer facility in Isabella-1. After leaving her with the Ferdinandans, Rohesia, my daughter, never saw or heard from her again."

Dr. Snow's speech was faster than ever, consumed with curiosity. "What's a Prime Receiver?"

"The person that collects souls upon death and transports them to the repository chamber. You know, you sort of remind me of him."

"Dr. Snow . . . " this time it was Acadia politely steering him back to relevant questioning.

"Is your daughter's doorstep in a place called Taos, New Mexico?"

The spirit squinted. "No. It's in Isabella-17."

"And do you happen to know how to get from the place where I am now to Isabella-17?"

"No, but I'm sure the Prime Receiver would know. All the dead can commune with him. Let me ask." Ethel's presence changed into what looked like water vapor floating in air, and she returned to her normal translucent form in a few moments. "He says the way to Isabella-17, and the way Jeanette Gadreau travelled from here, is through the firedoor you've already seen. I don't know what that means, but that's what he told me."

Dr. Snow smiled. "That's all right. We know what it means. Thank you so much, Ms. Brasa. You've been most helpful."

Before she shrank into particle form, Ethel looked right at Calliope. "He also wanted me to tell you three other things. The first is that the one called Alphonse is right; the two travelers should lock hands while the others proceed through the door beneath their bridged arms. The second is that the one called Acadia is a, I don't understand this word and I hope I'm saying it right, a bokor, and not to fight it. And the third thing is to tell the one called Calliope to go through despite your misgivings. Apparently, you are the mate to my daughter. I don't entirely understand that since you are both women, but I do want her not to be alone. She has more potential for both a life and longevity if she has a mate. So, please Calliope, go."

Gunnar looked at a sight he'd not yet seen—Calliope unhinged. By the time he looked back, the spirit of Ethel Brasa was gone.

"It actually worked," said the Professor. "I guess I do have a bit of a gift after all."

Calliope fluttered her eyes and spoke with excitement. "That's an understatement! A bit of a gift would be if a dead person possessed you or you were just a channel for the dead. But you made the dead visible to other people. You could make millions running séances because everyone in the room would have actual visual proof of life after death. You could answer the age old question of what happens when you die."

Alphonse, who was now casually holding the gun at his side and not directing it at anyone in particular, spoke like he was part of their group. "Acadia, I knew you were a bokor. Now, will you believe me?"

Acadia was stunned. "I, I guess I knew that. I just didn't want to be. But, if I'm going to go to the next Earth and find Mama, I suppose I'd better learn to embrace it."

Calliope continued. "I can't believe I'm going to find love in the next realm. I get to fall in love again!"

"And so," interrupted Dr. Snow, "given that Acadia will be able to expand upon her powers and given that we shall be picking up a new friend in the portal, I would state its more probable than not that we will survive going through it."

Roxanne stood up from where she had been sitting on the ground with Gunnar. "So, there is another world over there? It's not death?"

Dr. Snow whistled in his happy voice, "Apparently we can all survive going through the portal if Calliope and Roxanne do lock arms and essentially turn their bodies into a shield under which the rest of us can pass unharmed."

Gunnar was still not entirely persuaded. "But look at the sources of this information. We're taking the word of dead people. If Baron whatever-his-name-is is the evil voodoo god that Acadia says he is and he can summon the dead to his will, how do we know this isn't a trap set up by him to trick us into killing ourselves? Or, what if Alphonse is making this whole thing up as a ruse to murder his sister and kill off the witnesses and the Baron-guy told the dead what to say to make us fall for it?"

Alphonse smirked. "While there have been times when I wished Acadia dead for refusing to accept her birthright, now that I know her birthright is coming to her, like it or not, I have an incentive to keep her alive. And the rest of you have purposes too that ultimately benefit me. My sister's vanilla boyfriend will keep her happy and focused. Both

676

your girlfriend and the blond lady are my keys to the portals. You are my bloodhound to find the doors. And best of all, I have the old man, who is better than Samedi because I can still correspond with the underworld and not have to deal with Samedi's stupid jokes and senseless riddles."

Dr. Snow interrupted. "Gunnar, it is true that I cannot be positive of the motives of two dead strangers, an alleged deity, or someone who started out this conversation with a gun to our heads. But I believe Millie would not be so selfish. And I have to believe her when she tells me I have a future beyond today. Taking into account all things, if I had to put it into mathematical probabilities, I'd say we have an 80 percent chance of living and a 20 percent chance of dying. Those are statistically significant odds favoring going into the portal. I am still going in voluntarily."

"We are too," said Acadia as Aaron nodded in agreement.

Calliope exhaled. "I know I wasn't going to go, but now, I want to. If there's even a remote possibility of me finding someone in there, I want to meet her. There are more reasons now to go in than to stay out."

Gunnar looked at Alphonse and asked point blank, "Roxanne and I don't really have a choice to go in or not, do we?"

Alphonse smirked. "So far, I haven't killed any of you because I was sure you'd all make the right decision and go through the door of your own accord. But I won't hesitate to put a bullet in you if you make the wrong choice."

"Then I have one small request," said Gunnar. "Give us thirty minutes before you make us go through."

"Why wait?" asked Alphonse.

"Because of the 20 percent chance that death is on the other side of that door. If this is it, I want to say goodbye to the woman I love."

Alphonse rolled his eyes. "You two, I swear. I'll give you ten, not thirty. And not so you can say goodbye. You don't need to because we're not going to die." He motioned to Roxanne. "But I'll give you some time to clean that wound. Take him over to the stream and wash his leg."

Gunnar hobbled to the stream, bracing himself against Roxanne's small frame. Sitting so close to the water's edge he could feel the spray from the small rapids hit him in the face, Gunnar untied the tourniquet. "Help me get these jeans off," he instructed Roxanne. "We'll wash off the blood and use the denim as a bandage. I've got a pair of cargo shorts in my rucksack. I'll need you to help me get those on."

As she carefully pulled down the pant leg over the wound now caked with bloody mud, she mused, "It's funny. I was kind of hoping that the next time I helped you off with your pants, we'd be getting into bed."

He smiled as he sat back down. Gunnar used the bullet hole in his jeans to act as a fissure from which he could easily tear the cloth. He gave strips of denim to Roxanne, who soaked the material in cold water.

As she gently washed his wound, he winced a little from the pain. "I'm glad you're hurt," she reminded herself.

"Please, don't heal me again. This pain I can handle. I'd much rather walk around crippled than not be in control of my emotions."

"I won't," said Roxanne. "I think I'm getting better at controlling it."

He looked at her with the sincerest adoration in his heart. "I don't care what Alphonse said, I'm going to use this time my way. I want you to know that, despite all the strangeness of the last few months, and the vardoger, and your healing, and the whirlwind trip across America picking up stragglers along the way, that this has been the best month of my life. Meeting you has changed everything for me, for the better. If we do die in there, I know that at least I found real love before the end."

She smiled her amazing smile and laughed her incredible laugh. "I never thought I could trust somebody with my secrets or find someone who would love me enough to not worry about making love to me. But Gunnar, you are that person, and I'll always be grateful."

He looked down at the wound. The skin around it was clean and free of debris, leaving a large gaping slice that definitely needed stitches to keep infection out. Using scraps of the leftover denim, they fashioned a bandage and tied it around the cut. Then Roxanne helped him put on his cargo shorts.

Though they knew they were expected back, they lingered by the creek a moment longer. Without speaking, they both acknowledged with their eyes it was time for their last kiss on this Earth. Holding each other tightly by the neck, their lips locked and their tongues tiptoed lightly. The kiss only dwindled once Alphonse interrupted with, "Ten minutes is up!" Hand in hand, they walked back towards the others, who now looked a little nervous about the choices they had made.

Alphonse examined Gunnar's leg and nodded with approval. "Let's get this show on the road. Come here, Roxanne," their captor-turned-travelling companion commanded.

Roxanne hesitantly dropped Gunnar's hand and walked forward. Approaching the loam where X marked the spot, Roxanne put her hands out in front of her as Calliope did earlier and walked slowly forward.   Just as before, Roxanne's movements caused a ripple in the fabric of the universe and a black space emerged from nothing.

"I can't believe it! It's real! It's true!" declared Alphonse, practically in tears. "Do you know how long I've been searching for this? The anguish not finding it has caused me? A decade's worth of searching in futility is finally over," he continued to himself. Gunnar could almost feel empathy for the relief Alphonse felt at the end of his quest, if he were not such a sociopath.

"Now," commanded Alphonse to Roxanne after gathering himself. "Put one foot inside the darkness while leaving the rest of your body outside in the light."

She cautiously put one foot in the door. Gunnar searched her face for clues about what was to happen to them. He saw an unpleasant expression creep over her visage. "It feels strange inside," she commented. "It's like that point when you know you're getting a sunburn, coupled with a feeling of suction like when you put your hand over a sink drain."

Alphonse crossed over to her. "Now, blondie, come here and do the same thing directly facing Roxanne." The normally headstrong woman did exactly as she was told. "Oh yeah, I see what you mean. It hurts, but it's not unbearable."

"Okay. Grab each other's arms so that your wrists are overlapping each other. Then lift your arms as high as you can, so that people can cross underneath you."

When the two travelers touched, the discomfort intensified. "The heat is getting worse!" stated Roxanne.

"I don't know how long we can hold this," said Calliope. "The suction feels like we're about to be lifted off our feet and sucked up into a vacuum."

"Then there's no time to waste," exclaimed Alphonse. "Everyone else goes in first. I'm last."

Acadia made the mistake of being snarky. "Typical selfish Alphonse."

The malevolent man reminded everyone of his cruelty. "Or, maybe I'm not coming at all. Maybe I know that you'll all die in there. Maybe that *was* my plan all along, just like the former blind man said. See, I need to appease Baron Samedi with blood and souls in order to call on his aid again. Maybe the only way he will definitely tell me where Mama is at is if I give him human sacrifices. Maybe that's the reason for sending you all into the void and not going in first myself."

"Alphonse, you wouldn't," challenged Acadia.

"Wouldn't I?" responded Alphonse. Now, even the staunchly sure Acadia looked panicked, clearly telling everyone with her reaction that Baron

Samedi was the type of being to ask for such a sin in his name. As they eyeballed each other quickly, Gunnar could tell that everyone now felt death was a possibility greater than 20 percent. The evil brother guffawed and raised the gun from his side. Mimicking his Baron's rhymes, he stated, "My sweet sister Acadia, how I'll miss you so. The first up to gamble is you and your beau. Life or death? Heaven or hell? Lucky you to be the first to tell."

The space between Roxanne and Calliope was quite small given the short lengths of their female arm spans, so only one person at a time could fit between them. Aaron and Acadia walked hand in hand towards the darkness, but they would have to enter one at a time. Acadia paused. Aaron drew in a breath of courage and announced, "I'll go first." Gunnar watched as the musician with the mended heart gave Acadia one forceful kiss before jumping into the unknown like he was diving into a swimming pool to get the sensation of cold over with. The blackness enshrouded each of his body parts as he entered, and at the conclusion of the final emersion of all of A.J. Rhodes, the center of the blackness let out a hiss and a small blue blaze with smoke emanating from the center. Gunnar jerked back. Did Aaron just get burned alive?

Watching the bravery of her mate and having no choice to back out due to her brother's weapon, Acadia blinked her eyes hard several times and sprinted into the portal. Just as before, her body was ensconced in blackness followed by flame.

"Your turn, old man," said Alphonse, waving the gun at the professor. The ever appropriate Englishman, Dr. Snow grabbed hold of his safari vest, held his chin high, and winked at Gunnar. "With Tennyson's ode and Lord Cardigan's pluck to inspire me, I am now the human Charge of the Light Brigade." With that, he waltzed into the darkness, his essence burping out another blue fire.

The ceremony was interrupted as Alphonse turned from watching the blazes to staring at Gunnar. "Now, before we continue, I will share with the rest of you the truth of what must be done," Alphonse said as he removed his own rucksack from behind his back. In it were two very long cords of rope. "We'll need one of these to get back." Alphonse tied one of the ropes tightly around the trunk of nearby tree and then threw the other side through the black hole between the travelers' arms.

"And this one is my insurance policy," he said, as he tied one side of the rope around his own waist and then looped the other side of the rope around Roxanne's neck.

"What are you doing?" asked Roxanne.

"I can't really go last," said Alphonse. "The inner door built by you two travelers must be open for me to go through it. So obviously, I will go next and you two must be the last to enter. But, how can I trust you to come through when there is no threat against your lives?" Alphonse then looped the rope around Calliope's neck. There was very little give in the rope between the two of them. Alphonse then triple looped what was left of the rope around his chest. It was clear that once Alphonse went in, the women would have mere seconds to follow him or they would choke.

Calliope's eyes gleamed with hope. "So, if you are going in, then all those things you said about tricking us into dying to appease your god was a lie?"

Alphonse went to the portal's edge, only a step from entering. "Not entirely. Samedi did tell me that the next time I call on him, I am to have for him a human sacrifice; but, I wasn't planning on calling him right now. Of course, I didn't expect fire to shoot out of the portal either, and I don't know if that means the heat actually is too much for us, despite the travelers' protection, so who knows whether I need him now or not. I suppose it doesn't really matter to me if I do burn to my death. If I go in and I die, I will call on him and I will have fulfilled my end of the bargain by bringing him not one, but five souls. Then I'll ask for him to bring my body back to life. If I don't die and don't end up needing him, then I guess it was a lie."

He turned toward the portal, when Gunnar asked the obvious question. "Wait, five? There are six of us. What about me?"

Alphonse turned back around. "Don't you think I've noticed that the others follow you? I've seen your strength of character. There can only be one leader of this group, and that's going to be me. Don't you think I'm intimidated by the fact your blindness is somehow magically healed? I can't always be worrying about you and your powers and how or when you're going to challenge me. Assuming that there is another world through this darkness, I need all my focus to find my mother and direct the others. So, you are not coming."

Gunnar should have felt relief, but he felt only anger. "What powers? You don't have to worry about the healed sight: I didn't do it to myself. And I won't challenge you!"

"You have no idea how powerful you are, do you? You want proof? I always get what I want with magic, but all the spells I've tried on you haven't worked. In fact, you're sighted again when I cast a spell for you to go deaf. You stood up to me and defied me when I prayed for your obedience. Most telling, though, is that when the old man asked me to shoot you, I actually aimed for your heart and not your leg. I shot right at your chest and yet that bullet went nowhere near it. You somehow made that shot be just a flesh wound, regardless of my intent. That's power. And as soon as you believe that, you will no longer be controllable."

Gunnar was mortified, not just by Alphonse's confessions, but by the thought of not being with Roxanne. He would be forced to leave her alone with this sociopath. "But I thought you said you needed me to help find the other doors?"

"If we die in here or find my mother, I won't need to find anymore doors. And if we don't die and don't find her, I'll find you when we come back."

"But . . . . " Gunnar couldn't get a word in before the evil man disappeared into the portal, sucked in by flame.

Gunnar looked at the rope as it started to flow into the black hole. Within thirty seconds, the slack would be gone and Calliope would be gone with it. Within seconds of that, Roxanne too would be sucked in. Now was his only chance.

690

"Fuck that! I'm going through." He was just about to enter under the bridge of the travelers' arms when Roxanne abruptly let go of Calliope. "What are you doing? Put your hands back up so I can get through!"

Roxanne bent outward to Gunnar. "I can't let you go in if you have a chance to get out of this. It's so much easier for me to face death knowing that the man I love will for sure survive."

"No, Roxanne! I'm coming. If you end up dying in there, we're going to die together."

"If I *am* going to die, let me die knowing you'll be okay. And if I don't die, then Alphonse is right and I'll come back out and I'll find you."

Calliope understood. "Just like I made the sacrifice back in Sedona to let Lori go, you need to let Roxanne go now. Let her be at peace knowing you are safe." Just then, Gunnar watched as Calliope started to lose her balance. Her head was tugged toward the portal and blackness enveloped her.

Gunnar frantically looked at what little rope was left between Roxanne and the blackness. Any second, she'd be pulled in as well. And now, without the other traveler to make a door, it was too late for Gunnar to enter safely. Both of them instantly recognized this and both released a flood of tears. "I love you," they said simultaneously, their fingertips barely brushing against each other before Roxanne was pulled into the abyss.

Gunnar screamed and fell onto his knees as he watched a bright blue inferno jet out from the center of the darkness. As quickly as the hole had opened, it now caved in on itself with only a piece of rope protruding mid-air. Not caring that his actions reopened his leg wound and blood was now gushing into his cargo shorts, he wailed like a dog that had been run over. He felt even more lost in this second than he had when his mother died.

He didn't know what overcame him in that moment, but for a split second, his mind traveled to that Sedona hilltop. He smelled medical chemicals. He heard a woman talking about being eaten. He felt his leg healing the old-fashioned way. He saw himself moving through the sky as if flying. He knew he was not in Taos anymore. If he was, in fact, clairaudient and had clairolfaction, what he was smelling and hearing was the future. Which meant he had a future, and not on this Earth. At that moment, he knew he'd survive going through the door even without the protection of his love and friend.

The portal wasn't closed completely. All he'd have to do is whip the rope back and forth, and then in circles like a lasso, to create a hole large enough for him to duck inside of. He approached the rope to do so, when all of a sudden, he heard an all-too-familiar buzzing noise, which drew his attention to his right side. He was flabbergasted to see yet another door open out of mid-aid, and the person coming out of it was himself!

"What the . . . ?" he exclaimed.

"Hello again," he said to himself.

"My God!!" he said. "You, you're the vardoger!"

"As we discussed before, not really, but your mum would say so," confirmed his double.

"What do you mean, not really? You look exactly like me. You sound exactly like me. You appear to me before things happen to warn me. That's a vardoger according to Dr. Snow!"

"Gunnar, I am not a vardoger. I am you," said the double.

"Me?"

"Well, another you, from the Earth you are about to go to," said the vardoger.

"Wait, there's another me on another Earth?"

The other Gunnar explained. "Of the four known versions of Earth, a person may exist on some and not on others depending on whether the planetary histories of each world put their parents in the exact same situations to procreate and create them. Of course, a person isn't exactly the same in each version because environmental factors varying even slightly between worlds can change one's personality and personal path.

Let's just say that that in all versions of Earth, Agneta and Nils get together and create you. In the next Earth on the other side of that door, the version of you that exists is me and that version still has gifts. One of my gifts is the ability to see in my mind's eye any point in time in the lives of my other-world counterparts, kind of like the internal television shows Calliope describes. Of course, what I am watching can change at the drop of a hat depending on whether a certain choice changes your life's path, so I can't always be sure that what I see will actually come to pass.

My other gift is to travel at will to any other version of Earth for just a few minutes to talk with my other selves."

"So, you've been coming through a portal this whole time to visit me? That's what the buzzing noise was that I could hear but not see. And that's why your visits were time limited!" exclaimed the newly sighted Gunnar.

"Yep," his double again confirmed before continuing. "I've been watching you ever since I knew I could. I always felt such pity for you since your version of Mum died, and your version of us went blind, and your version of us couldn't find love or friendship beyond your sister."

Feeling betrayed, Gunnar asked, "If you could always see me and always come visit me, why didn't you come earlier? Where was your warning that my mum would die? Where was your warning not to drink from the stupid cup Rob gave me? Where were you when I was stranded in my loneliness?"

"Because your mum was spot on. You had to make all the exact choices you did to get to a certain point, and that was the point in time that you were ready to believe in me. Had I changed but even one thing about your life, you would not have had the courage or the understanding to be with Roxanne. Her strength and gifts are not meant for a typical man. My silence was me helping you become the best version of yourself worthy of the woman you needed to love."

Gunnar sighed. "You're right, of course. I wouldn't have met Roxanne, or for that matter any of the others, if anything in my life was different."

"What I didn't know about you, what I never expected, is for your gifts to become stronger than mine once you found your full strength in the vortex. I can travel and I can see all the Gunnars, but I can't smell or hear the future, or move things with my mind. You can do those things, and eventually, you will be able to travel and see all things too, just as I do. In the end, I anticipate that you will be the most powerful version of Gunnar across all the realms. Your gifts are just dormant, and I'm betting they will grow in each of the Earths you enter."

"So, you've been coming through a portal this whole time to visit me? That's what the buzzing noise was that I could hear but not see?" asked the newly sighted Gunnar.

"Yep," his double again confirmed.

Present Gunnar relaxed. "Well, I suppose I should thank you for watching my life and getting me and Roxanne and everyone together, even if it was almost a decade later than I would have liked."

"No thanks necessary," said the double. "Because I now have to admit an ulterior motive. You are the only gifted person in your world or mine that can actually move objects with your mind. And not just grapefruit or irons. You can move huge things; you just haven't cultivated that strength yet. And I need you and that gift in my world. My ability to momentarily travel and see other versions of me is not going to help my people, but your gifts can. You can not only move objects, and smell and hear the future, but eventually, you too will get to travel and see other versions of us, just as I do. Your gifts are dormant, but they will grow in each of the Earths you enter, starting with mine. And in the end, I anticipate that you will be the most powerful version of Gunnar across all the realms."

"Look mate, I'm happy to help if what you say is true, but I've got to get there and help Roxanne first."

"I know, but I'm not just here to tell you the whole truth about me. I'm actually here to do as I've always done. I'm here to warn you."

"Whatever you know, tell me, but tell me quick. Every minute of head start Alphonse gets is more time spent not being with Roxanne and my friends," demanded this Earth's Gunnar.

"My time is almost out anyway. I can sense the portal getting weak. Here goes. All of your friends did, indeed, just die going through the door of fire; thus, the flame, which is a fire so hot it combusts the body, even the body of someone with the gift of healing. I mean, you can't heal what is completely dead. But don't fret, Roxanne is fine. Gifted people who cross the threshold of worlds come back to life on the other side without even trying and without knowing they were dead. But, for that to occur, they unknowingly exchange reanimation for their gifts. It's that whole metaphysical balance thing, how like you have to hate Roxanne when she heals you. Aaron can no longer feel people, Dr. Snow can no longer talk to the dead, Calliope can no longer read objects, and Roxanne can no longer see the future or, more importantly, heal herself or anyone else. That's the first thing I want to warn you about. All of your friends are now vulnerable and will no longer be able to do what Alphonse will want them to do. So if he gets angry and hurts Roxanne, she's going to stay hurt.

The second thing I wanted to warn you about is that when Alphonse just died, he unwittingly allowed himself to be possessed by his god. He now has powers above his abilities as a voodoo practitioner. He will trick and lie and manipulate, but also tell the truth and make others happy if it suits his own gain. You cannot trust him at all, and yet, there will be times when you should trust him."

Gunnar was astounded and worried. "Bloody hell! All the more reason for me to get to Roxanne as fast as I can. But, if I die too, then I will be exchanging my powers for life also, won't I?" asked present Gunnar.

700

"That's why you are the most powerful of us all. Your gifts are only lost for short while and will come back once you find the seventh member of your group. In fact, some of your dormant powers will awaken when you find her. And towards the end of your journey in this second Earth, you will become so strong that you will be able to revive the lost gifts of the others. But you'll have to beat Alphonse and his Baron first."

"How do I do that?"

"You can't, not alone. Acadia will have to help you," stated the double.

"Acadia? I thought you said everyone loses their gifts?" asked Gunnar.

"She loses her ability to see the future of what is needed, but she can never lose the birthright flowing through her blood. Her sorcery is not a gift, but a condition. She shares that condition with her brother. She will have to accept and enhance that condition, if you're to defeat Alphonse and Baron Samedi."

This Earth's Gunnar nodded. "Okay. Thanks for all that, mate. I got it and know what has to be done. But I've got to get in there. Now that I know Roxanne can be killed or hurt, I won't waste another minute not trying to find her."

"I understand," said the double Gunnar. "I would say good luck, but if you can awaken and use all the gifts inside you revealed in this world, I won't have to." With that, the Gunnar of the Earth on the other side of the door disappeared back through his own portal.

Gunnar ran to the rope dangling in mid-air and circled his wrist until the rope opened up the firey door. Knowing exactly what to expect was comforting and took away all hesitation to jump in headfirst.

Hmmm. It was an interesting pain. Like baking in a Las Vegas summer while a deep sea suction seemed to pull ones brain out of their ears. Then he lost breath, like he was holding it underwater. Next came frigid cold and the awareness that this must be death.

And finally, the smell of peach shampoo filled his nose as a bright light filled his eyes.

-The End-

ABOUT THE AUTHOR

Attorney-by-day, fiction writer-by-night, A.R. Bearcluff writes what she loves—an escape from the realities of life. Her escapes include paranormal romances, urban fantasies, travel adventures, and soft science fiction tales, which she enjoys blending into cross- genre stories for all ages.

When not writing or practicing law, A.R. Bearcluff enjoys strolling the lakes and trails of the Inland Northwest border of Washington and Idaho, where she lives in lush geographical beauty with her husband and two daughters. You might also find her enjoying a night of bar trivia or karaoke, or playing tennis against her husband-tennis coach.

You can visit A.R. Bearcluff's website at www.arbearcluff.com, where you can find out more about books featuring Gunnar and friends in *The Senses Series*, as well as A.R. Bearcluff's other planned fiction series. You'll also find launch dates for future books and videos with audio snippets of the novels read by the author.